I0735155

Lightning Strikes Twice

The Trash Stealer

Two Novels by Jean Potts

Introduction by Curtis Evans

Stark House Press • Eureka California

LIGHTNING STRIKES TWICE / THE TRASH STEALER

Published by Stark House Press
1315 H Street
Eureka, CA 95501, USA
griffinskye3@sbcglobal.net
www.starkhousepress.com

LIGHTNING STRIKES TWICE
Originally published by Charles Scribner's Sons, New York, and copyright
© 1958 by Jean Potts. Reprinted in paperback by Dell Books, New York,
1962. Copyright renewed February 14, 1986 by Jean Potts.

THE TRASH STEALER
Originally published by Charles Scribner's Sons, New York,
and copyright © 1968 by Jean Potts.

Reprinted by permission of the Jean Potts estate. All rights reserved
under International and Pan-American Copyright Conventions.

"Jean Potts: A Talent to be Cherished" copyright © 2022
by Curtis Evans.

ISBN: 978-1-951473-89-1

Book design by Mark Shepard, shepgraphics.com
Proofreading by Bill Kelly
Cover Art by James Heimer

PUBLISHER'S NOTE:
This is a work of fiction. Names, characters, places and incidents are
either the products of the author's imagination or used fictionally, and
any resemblance to actual persons, living or dead, events or locales, is
entirely coincidental.
Without limiting the rights under copyright reserved above, no part of
this publication may be reproduced, stored, or introduced into a retrieval
system or transmitted in any form or by any means (electronic,
mechanical, photocopying, recording or otherwise) without the prior
written permission of both the copyright owner and the above publisher
of the book.

First Stark House Press Edition: November 2022

LIGHTNING STRIKES TWICE

When Evan returns to his Midwestern home from life in the city, he finds that nothing much has changed. Everyone's a little bit older, and they still talk about the weather. But though no one wants to be the first to bring it up, he discovers that his Uncle Win has tried to kill himself. Little Harriet, his daughter, thinks Mr. Stanley is involved. After all, he is supposedly having an affair with her mother. Then Win is found dead from what looks like a self-inflicted gunshot, and Aunt Nell, Win's overly-dramatic ex-wife, was the last person to see him. This all looks too suspicious to Evan to be suicide. So with Little Harriet crying murder, he decides to find out just what did happen to his Uncle Win.

THE TRASH STEALER

It all begins with a holdup at the bar where Joe works. A man is killed, and it's Joe's fault. The man's daughter shows up. Cynthia is spoiled, selfish and completely contrary—and Joe finds himself strangely attracted to her. He follows her back to her family in New York City, where he finds an equally contrary group of characters. They all seem to be bickering over a missing diamond necklace that is all that's left of Gran's inheritance. Cynthia's cousin Ned is convinced that she and Joe have been conspiring together to steal the necklace. Ned's parents are convinced that Cynthia is hiding it disguised as a gift for her boyfriend. And all Joe wants to do is assuage his guilt while trying to protect the infuriating Cynthia from herself.

"You'll find subtlety, sensitivity and a gentle, late-summer sadness….a well-shaped plot, an attractive young hero and the quiet authority of a first-rate craftsman."—Anthony Boucher, *New York Times*

"The terror that can invest the ordinary and the way people under stress can talk themselves into a corner are the author's special forte."—*Kirkus Reviews*

"In Potts' fictional world there are no true good or bad characters, just many shades of gray, but she writes them in a way that makes you care about them, warts and all."—B. V. Lawson, *In Reference to Murder*

Jean Potts:
A Talent to be Cherished
By Curtis Evans

Just under three months before his death from lung cancer at the untimely age of fifty-six on April 29, 1968, Anthony Boucher, dean of American mystery critics, reviewed the last crime novel that he would ever read by Jean Potts: her tenth, *The Trash Stealer*. Fourteen years earlier in 1954, Boucher had reviewed Jeans Potts' first crime novel, *Go, Lovely Rose*, and enthusiastically pronounced it "easily the best of the American crop so far in 1954." As happened so often in those days, where Boucher led, the Edgar Awards of the Mystery Writers of America followed; and the next year the Edgar for best first crime novel was presented to ... *Go, Lovely Rose*. (Raymond's Chandler's *The Long Goodbye* won the Edgar for best crime novel, meaning that Potts from the very beginning of her career found herself in the best of criminal company.)

Over the fourteen years from 1954 to 1968 Anthony Boucher had remained one of the strongest advocates of the writing of Jean Potts, a small-town Nebraska native turned New Yorker, as she produced a series of mid-century mystery crime classics like *Death of a Stray Cat* (1955), *The Diehard* (1956), *The Man with the Cane* (1957), *The Evil Wish* (1962) and *The Footsteps on the Stairs* (1966). Yet Boucher was hardly a voice in the wilderness, when it came to singing Potts' praises. Across the Atlantic, in the pages of the *London Observer*, longtime English crime fiction critic Maurice Richardson, reviewing *The Trash Stealer*, resoundingly pronounced the author "one of the most original talents in American crime fiction that should be cherished." As Stark House nears the end of its Jean Potts reprint series (only two novels remain unpublished after this current "twofer"), Potts' modern readers surely have themselves become ever more appreciative of the author's impressive legacy of crime fiction.

Lightning Strikes Twice, Jean Potts' fifth crime novel and the opening bolt in this latest tempestuous Jean Potts twofer, is another of the author's remarkable regional mysteries, drawing evocatively on her Nebraska adolescence, although the setting is prudently placed only vaguely somewhere in the Chicago hinterland. Potts herself grew up in the small town of St. Paul, Nebraska, which is a bee line of some six hundred miles from the Windy City—not exactly a stone's throw away. However, Fontenelle, the name of the habitation in *Lightning Strikes Twice*, recalls Fontanelle, Nebraska, a former boom town named after (albeit misspelled) nineteenth-century famed Franco-Omaha frontier trader Logan Fontenelle—though the burg had long since dwindled into unincorporated obscurity by the time that Jean Potts came into the world.

The setting is reminiscent of the author's slightly earlier novel *The Diehard*, with Fontenelle in *Lightning* standing in for *The Diehard*'s Turk Ridge. The town of Turk Ridge was dominated by Lew Morgan, the novel's titular diehard, while in Fontenelle the town's first family is the Hoyt-Covey clan, consisting of:

Win Covey, a prominent attorney
Harriet Covey, Win's fifteen-year-old daughter, known as Little Harriet, on account of being named for her Covey grandmother
Pearl Covey, Harriet's mother and Win's former secretary and current wife, deemed "trash" from the wrong side of the tracks by rest of Hoyt-Covey clan, whom Win married in the hope of having a son
Nell Covey, Win's discarded first wife (she never bore him children), still hanging on
Marianna Covey Hoyt, Win's matronly sister
Ralph Hoyt, Marianna's "kept" husband
Covey Hoyt, Marianna's and Ralph's dull elder son
Evan Hoyt, Marianna and Ralph's "artistic" younger son

When the novel opens, Evan Hoyt has returned to Fontenelle after several years of absence in New York, where he has been trying his hand, like the author herself, at a writing career. He knows there has been some recent unpleasantness in his family, but only upon his return to his native ground does he learn its true nature: *Uncle Win recently tried to kill himself.* The shocking story seems fishy, even when told to Evan by Win himself, and his daughter Harriet, the very definition of awkward adolescence, lets on to Win that she knows *what really happened.* Despite Win's assurance to Evan that "Lightning never strikes in the same place twice," Win soon is discovered dead indeed, from an apparently self-administered gunshot wound; and Harriet this time is loudly and unambiguously insisting that her father was murdered.

Thus commences a complicated mystery, one which implicates not only the Hoyt-Covey clan, but other individuals such as "nice girl" **Norma Schaefer**, Evan's former kinda-sorta girlfriend from high school who is still available, as Marianna loves to point out to him

Goldie Shay, another girl from the wrong side of the tracks, to whom Evan was greatly attracted in high school, though she is now married and employed as a lounge singer at the local hangout known as The Spot

Homer Nelsen, Win's law partner, who is rather smitten with Win's sexy wife Pearl

Rita, the bubbleheaded, man-crazy former maid at Win and Pearl's house, now a waitress at The Spot after having been dismissed from service by Pearl;

canny Chicago native **Ralph Wolienewski** ("he's got one of those Polish jawbreakers for a last name"), a comparatively recent arrival in Fontenelle, who owns The Spot and other businesses in the town and is rather a tough customer indeed, grimly determined to win acceptance into local society, whatever it may take.

Lightning Strikes Twice is a fine mid-century American regional mystery novel with an exceptionally effective puzzle plot with a solution that grows organically out of character, rather than being crudely imposed on stick people, so that when that when it is revealed to the reader, the motivations for people's behavior clicks credibly into place. Doubtlessly Jean Potts brought aspects of herself into the novel as well, particularly ambivalence about her native Nebraska town and an attraction to New York, which she shared with Evan Hoyt, and the social awkwardness of the precocious adolescent that is powerfully portrayed in the forever posturing "Little Harriet," whom contemporary critics, including Anthony Boucher and Avid DeVoto of the *Boston Globe*, deemed the novel's most memorable character. DeVoto pronounced *Lightning* "[r]emarkably well written and very mysterious indeed....chilling and memorable," while Boucher commended the novel's "murder-puzzle ironically suited to the social theme" and predicted: "I doubt you'll readily forget [Potts'] awkward, infuriating, tormented adolescent heroine."

Another infuriating, tormented young woman is the pivotal character in Jean Potts' tenth crime novel, *The Trash Stealer*, a teasing tale of bizarre mischances of fate which may remind some readers, as it certainly did me, of one of the late British author Ruth Rendell's psychological crime novels from the later twentieth century, warning of the dangers that one may ironically pose to oneself through one's good intentions. The protagonist of the story is Joe Florio, an amiable young bartender at The Starfish, who when the novel opens has an encounter with a likeable, middle-aged patron, Frederick "Fritz" Wall—"one of those young-old guys that look at fifty-five just about the way they did at thirty"—that unexpectedly disrupts and disorients his life. In the second chapter of the novel, Joe meets Fritz's kooky daughter Cynthia at the beach, "peering down at him through butterfly-shaped sunglasses." ("They made her look inhuman, like somebody from Mars.") Cynthia might well be Harriet from *Lightning Strikes Twice* five or so years later, had Harriet's family been even more screwed-up; and she soon embroils Joe—purposefully or not—in a boiling cauldron of calamity.

Cynthia, who in a contemporary film version of *The Trash Stealer* might have been played by Goldie Hawn, and like Harriet scored a hit with critics like Anthony Boucher, who vouched for the weird young woman as "one of the finest kook-heroines in years—a girl who is certainly a liar, possibly a thief and conceivably a killer, but whose defenseless innocence is as touching as that of Mélisande." In the book as well, Boucher avowed to his readers: "You'll find subtlety, sensitivity and a gentle, late-summer sadness….a well-shaped plot, an attractive young hero and the quiet authority of a first-rate craftsman." It was a final testament of praise from the most significant contemporary critic of twentieth-century crime fiction to one of its most notable mid-century practitioners.

—September 2022
Germantown, TN

Curtis Evans received a PhD in American history in 1998. He is the author of *Masters of the "Humdrum" Mystery: Cecil John Charles Street, Freeman Wills Crofts, Alfred Walter Stewart and British Detective Fiction, 1920-1961* (2012) and most recently the editor of the Edgar nominated *Murder in the Closet: Essays on Queer Clues in Crime Fiction Before Stonewall* (2017) and, with Douglas G. Greene, the Richard Webb and Hugh Wheeler short crime fiction collection, *The Cases of Lieutenant Timothy Trant* (2019). He blogs on vintage crime fiction at The Passing Tramp.

Lightning Strikes Twice

Jean Potts

One

Evan had forgotten about the wind. The minute he stepped off the plane it hit him, like a blast from an oven; its shriveling breath lifted his hair, flattened his light suit against his legs, whipped his tie upwards across his chin. By the time he reached the gate, where his brother was waiting for him, he felt as if his very eyeballs were drying up in their sockets. It was an outrage, that wind; an indignity to flesh and spirit.

"Fierce, isn't it?" said Covey, after they had shaken hands. Not without a certain pride, his glance swept the vast, bleached sky, empty except for the haze of dust shimmering along the horizon. "A real scorcher. This keeps up another few days, and the corn's going to burn to a crisp."

"Where's Mama?" asked Evan. "Inside?" She, not Covey, was the one he had expected to see first of all; he had been primed for the sight of her, still small and trim, waiting for him in her white ground-grippers and sheer navy-and-white print dress and pancake hat pinned securely to her Gibson girl pompadour.

So it gave him an odd little jolt when Covey said, "Mama decided not to come with me. It's kind of a long drive, and she's been feeling the heat." (And Covey could not quite repress a small, a very small, smile of brotherly triumph. Maybe you used to be the original fair-haired boy—that smile said—and maybe you still are, but the fact remains that she didn't even come to meet you, after all these years.) "So she and Dad decided to wait for you at home."

"They're all right, aren't they? Nothing wrong, is there?" For his part, Evan couldn't quite repress the anxiety in his voice, or the pang of obscure alarm that went with it. Because it wasn't like her. Heat or no heat, it wasn't like her. And there had been something about her letters lately—something different, Evan couldn't have said what. On the surface they seemed the same, from the beginning, "My dear Son," through the bits of dryly humorous gossip, to the final, familiar plea, "When are you coming home again? It's been so long. Love, Mama." He couldn't pin it down. But he sensed, or thought he sensed, an undercurrent that was different and therefore—because Mama was for him one of the few changeless figures in his shifting world—disturbing.

"They're fine," Covey assured him. "First-rate, both of them. Well, Dad's back kicks up now and then, the way it always has, and of course they're not getting any younger, none of us are. Though I must say New York must agree with you. You don't look a day older."

He had said that before, when they first shook hands. But Covey had always operated on the theory that if a thing was worth saying at all it was worth saying five times. It was a family joke, like Evan's hearty appetite and Dad's weakness for schmaltzy music. Waiting at the baggage counter, Evan felt a surge of affection for Covey, good old Covey who—what with his receding hairline and his bifocals—looked quite a few days older. Not a bad guy. A bit on the stuffy side; but Evan's opinion might be only a hangover from childhood when, as older brother, Covey had—it seemed to him—bossed the hell out of him. You could depend on him, as Evan well knew: Covey had never once refused him a loan in moments of crisis, or rubbed it in afterwards. And, if Evan had always been Mama's favorite, he knew that he was also a disappointment to her. It was Covey who had followed the pattern of life proper, in her judgment, to the Hoyt-Covey clan. A pattern beautiful in its simplicity: you settled down in Fontenelle (where else?); married a "suitable" girl; produced two or three bright, healthy children; and lived happily ever after.

During the hour-long drive to Fontenelle, Evan inquired after Covey's "suitable" wife (she was fine, first-rate), his two boys (they were fine; the little fellow was a handful), and the drug business (Covey couldn't complain). With equal politeness and lack of interest Covey inquired into Evan's activities. He understood Evan had quit his advertising job to write a play or a book or something? Well, some of those movie writers cleaned up, all right; Covey wished him luck. Meantime, when was he going to get married and settle down?

Stupefied by the heat and the dead-end conversation, Evan tried to fight down a growing conviction that this homecoming of his was all a mistake. What had he been thinking of, to abandon the dubious comfort of his New York apartment (the manuscript that wouldn't jell; the view of the chop suey joint across the street; Iris bursting in, all set for another round in their chronic battle) for the arid vacancy of Fontenelle? And in midsummer, of all the impossible seasons. Dully he watched the wide landscape wheel by. It was great, if you cared for the uncluttered look. Space, and lots of it, with only an occasional farmhouse and barns to break the monotony. Well, and the corn, miraculously green and vigorous under the blast of sun and wind, but doomed—as Covey had said, if this kept up another few days—to wither on the stalk.

How could he have done it? How could he have forgotten about the wind?

Gradually, in the course of that hot and dusty trip, Evan's inner conviction that he had been a fool to come home at all merged with a larger uneasiness, a feeling of something wrong and about to get wronger. It drove him to ask again, "You said everything's okay at home? Mama's all right?"

"Fine. First-rate. Like I said, she's been feeling the heat. And then of course she's been worried about Uncle Win." Covey paused, rather awkwardly. Embarrassed for Evan, no doubt, because he had neglected to ask about Uncle Win.

Smitten with belated concern—for Uncle Win was his favorite uncle, indeed, one of his favorite people—Evan exclaimed, "Good Lord, the heat's got me already! How is he? And what was it he had, a heart attack? I don't think Mama ever wrote me exactly what the trouble was."

"Didn't she?" Covey's glance swerved, sharply and briefly, to his brother, then back to the wide ribbon of the road. "He's coming along pretty good now. Able to be out of bed most of the day. But it was a damn narrow squeak. For a while there nobody knew whether he was going to pull through or not."

"I didn't realize it was that serious," said Evan. Trust Mama to understate whenever possible. But this explained the different tone he had detected in her letters; she must have been worried to distraction. In a family noted for its close ties, she and her brother Win were closest of all. No wonder she had urged Evan, even more strongly than usual, to come back to Fontenelle. Poor Mama, she needed him, and had been too proud to come right out and say so. And poor Uncle Win. Evan found it almost impossible to imagine him—that man of brittle elegance and charm—as a semi-invalid. "I hadn't any idea. Mama never said—"

"He's looking forward to seeing you," said Covey, and there wasn't time to pursue the subject because here they were, rattling across the bridge, with the river, low and narrow at this season, below them, and just ahead of them the straggle of Fontenelle's Main Street. "Well, there it is, the old home town. Plenty of changes since the last time you saw it. There's been lots of building in the last five years. The new school house, and all that section out beyond the greenhouse, that's all built up now. You won't know the place."

It looked the same to Evan. More sprawling than he remembered it, more—melted-down was perhaps the word. But he was tactful enough not to say so. He felt the clutch of fear. "Our house is the same, isn't it?" he asked.

And of course it was. It was as impervious to change as Mama herself, who had lived in it all her life and would no doubt die in it. ("The Covey place," it had been called in her youth, and, long after she married, "The old Covey place." Now at last, after forty-odd years, even the old-timers were beginning to call it "the Hoyt place.") Like her, it made few concessions to changes in style; though well-kept, it was forthrightly old-fashioned. A graceless and beloved big house, set far back from the tree-lined street, with its veranda banked by bridal wreath bushes, its bay window bulging out downstairs, and upstairs its screened-in sleeping porch spoiling whatever symmetry it might have had originally. The old hitching post still stood at the foot of the sidewalk. From the box elder in the front yard a bag swing still hung, with a worn spot in the grass beneath it and the step ladder propped against the tree trunk—just such a bag swing as had imperiled Evan's and Covey's necks through their boyhood, and was no doubt now imperiling those of Covey's sons.

The driveway circled around to the rear of the house; almost before Covey got the car stopped, Evan was out and running up the back porch steps. Slap went the screen door behind him; into the big kitchen; and there was Mama, hurrying to meet him.

"Well, love, you're home," she said.

He bent his head to receive the little peck of a kiss she gave him—Mama was not one for gushy demonstrations—and was astonished to see tears brimming in her eyes. Tears which she was high-handedly ignoring. Evan, too, pretended they were not there, and that there was no quaver in her voice as she called, "Ralph, they're back! Here he is!"

It was an unnecessary summons: Dad was already coming through the doorway from the library, hand outstretched, a smile lighting up his handsome face. Yes, still remarkably handsome. The years had thickened his once-athletic figure and frosted his dark hair, but they had not blurred the delicate precision of his profile or the sweetness of his expression. He was the only really good-looking member of the family. Neither Evan nor Covey—though they were both tall, like their father, and Covey had his blue eyes—was in his class.

And certainly no one had ever called Mama pretty. Even as a girl, Evan thought, she must have been homely. Her figure was neatly built, her hands and feet small and graceful; but she had irregular features, almost gargoylish in effect, and sandy, freckly coloring. She still wore her hair in the style of her youth, puffed into a pompadour, coiled into a nest on top, with tawny-colored side combs. And yet she carried this unfashionable, really rather ugly head so proudly, as if it were the head of a beauty …

Well, Uncle Win had the same air of distinction and inborn poise. That was what came of being a Covey in Fontenelle. It made you monarch of all you surveyed—so unquestionably that it never even occurred to you that you were a monarch.

He didn't get a chance to ask about Uncle Win right away. There was too much fluster, too much exclaiming and asking of inconsequential questions, with nobody bothering to listen to the answers. Covey came in, lugging Evan's bag, and left again; he and Phyllis and the kids would be over later for supper.

"Fried chicken, by any chance?" asked Evan.

"Fried chicken, naturally," Mama assured him. "*And* strawberry shortcake. I have some beer for you, too, it's in the icebox, good and cold. I'll have a glass of ginger ale, Ralph, and let's go in the living room where it's cooler …"

As indeed it was. Outside, that damned wind was still at it, and would be for another hour, till sunset. Evan could hear it lashing at the trees in the yard, turning their dusty leaves inside out. But it could not get at this high-ceilinged, dusky room. The shades at the bay window were drawn halfway down against the glare, so that the lighting effect was a pleasant greenish amber. Nothing could get at this room; it was like a room in a storybook, preserved in its own timeless atmosphere. There was the tall old clock, clicking its tongue in the corner. The portrait of Grandpa Covey, looking down at his descendants with placid confidence in their Covey-ness. The little bronze figures of a Gibson girl and her beau, poised in their eternal game of tennis across the mantel piece. The colonnades that separated living room and dining room, and beyond them the heavy, sombre dining room furniture and the twin china closets gleaming with their shelves of cut glass and silver.

"You've changed the slip covers," said Evan accusingly, and Mama laughed aloud with pleasure.

He perched on the window seat, which was his particular spot in the living room—just as Mama's little armless rocker, her "sewing chair," was hers, and the shabby Morris chair was Dad's—and for a moment it seemed as if he had never been away. There was nothing to say. Or perhaps there was too much to say.

Where to begin? "How *is* Uncle Win?" he asked. "You never told me it was so serious. In fact, you never even told me what's wrong with him."

Mama's face went suddenly haggard, as if from actual physical pain. It was Dad who answered—easily enough, though the glance he cast at Mama made it clear that he was rushing to her rescue. "He's doing fine. No cause for worry anymore, Doc says he'll be right as rain in a couple of months."

"Of course he will," echoed Mama, who had recovered by now. "He's doing fine. And so anxious to see you, Evan. Though I think you'd better wait to go over till tomorrow morning. He's always a little tired by the end of the day."

Yes. Certainly something was wrong. Evan toyed with the notion of bluntly pointing out that he still hadn't been told what was the matter with Uncle Win. Decided to wait until later this evening, when he would have a chance at Mama alone. Time enough then to get blunt and insistent.

"How's Pearl?" he asked. "And Little Harriet?" Pearl was Uncle Win's wife. His second wife. So much younger than Uncle Win—indeed, so nearly Evan's and Covey's age—that it would have seemed absurd for them to call her Aunt Pearl. And "Little" Harriet, so-called even though her Grandmother Covey, for whom she was named, had been dead long before she was born, was their daughter.

"Not exactly little anymore," said Mama, with obvious relief; she flashed a grateful look at Evan for side-stepping the subject of what was wrong with Uncle Win. She herself—as usual, if it was at all possible—chose to side-step the subject of Pearl. "She's taller than I am. Poor child."

"Poor child?" He couldn't resist teasing Mama a little. "You mean she looks like Pearl?"

"Mercy, no! I just mean— Well, you know. The awkward age. And then she's always been—a little difficult."

"Harriet's a brat," said Dad, without rancor. "Couldn't help but be, the way Win's spoiled her. All the same, I think Covey could have stretched a point and taken her with him to the airport to meet you. She'd have given her eye teeth to go."

"I know. But then why didn't she behave herself? Why did she have to pick today to explain to Covey that he and Phyllis are sheep?" Mama's eyes twinkled; even at the expense of her own family, she had a gift for detached amusement. "That's what she says. Sheep. Without television commercials to tell them, she says, they wouldn't have the faintest idea of what they like or don't like. She could have kept it to herself till tomorrow. I declare, I don't know what possesses the child! But there. I suppose you just *do* those things, when you're fifteen."

"I thought she'd be over here before now, on hand to greet a kindred spirit like Evan, a fellow sophisticate from New York ... There." Dad cocked his head as the front doorbell whirred, and got to his feet. "Anybody want to bet that's not her?"

"She worships the ground you walk on," said Mama. "So be nice to her, won't you, Evan?"

"Of course," said Evan.

It was a rash promise, as he soon found out. Surely no human creature needed to be as unprepossessing as Little Harriet. Looking at her, you were irritated: you felt she must be doing it on purpose. At least she could have stood up straight, instead of slouching like that, with her chest sunken in and her pelvis thrust forward, no doubt in imitation of some model whose picture had caught her eye. Her light-colored hair straggled across her forehead in lanky bangs, straight as straw; the rest of it was long, and frizzy at the ends. Her dress was a sort of navy-blue tube that showed off the inadequacies of her figure to perfection, and her feet—which were as large as any feminine feet Evan ever remembered seeing—were tied up in criss-crosses of what at first glance appeared to be bright-colored carpet rags. (Evan could hardly keep his eyes off them; he classified them at last as a species of rope-soled huarache.) On her hands Little Harriet wore long, rather dirty white gloves, and on her face an expression of supercilious boredom.

"Hi, Aunt Marianna," she said. Her eyes slid past Evan as if he were an uninteresting piece of furniture. "Oh, hello, Evan. Welcome to our wasteland."

He had been poised to give her a hug and kiss, along with whatever hearty inanities seemed suitable for a fifteen-year-old cousin who worshipped the ground you walked on and whom you hadn't seen for nearly seven years. He did go so far as to hold out his hand, and received a listless brush from one set of gloved fingertips. He couldn't think of a solitary thing to say, inane or otherwise.

"Sit down, Harriet," said Mama. "Won't you—uh—lay off your gloves? How about a Coke?"

Harriet's feet looked even bigger when she sat down. She did not lay off her gloves. "I don't suppose there's such a thing as a Martini in the house," she murmured, with a world-weary lift to one eyebrow.

"There certainly isn't," said Mama tartly. "Not for anybody your age."

"Never mind, Aunt Marianna. A Coke, then. By all means, a Coke. So wholesome."

"I'll get it," said Dad, and on his way to the kitchen he winked gravely at Evan.

After that a silence fell. Evan pulled himself together and said, "Well, Harriet, nice to see you again. I'd never have recognized you, you've changed so."

Harriet let that one lie on its face. Where it probably belonged. "And how are things in little old New York?" she asked, politely screening a yawn. "I suppose I'll have to go there myself someday. It's one of the things one does."

"I know. Such a crashing bore, these conventions." Evan couldn't help burlesquing her tone (Dad was right, the kid was a brat, an impossible one) but, having done so, he caught Mama's eye on him and promptly felt ashamed. All right. He'd make it up to Mama. He'd *tell* her how things were in little old New York. Mama, that is. Let Little Harriet sit there and pose in her ridiculous white gloves to her heart's content. She could leave any time she felt like it. He put himself out to be entertaining about the last seven years of his life—his apartment, the jobs he had lost or quit, the people he knew (considerable abridgement here; Iris, for instance, was better left unmentioned), the play he was trying to write.

It went over big with Mama and Dad, of course. With Evan, too. Carried away with his own eloquence, he very nearly forgot the focus of his irritation. Except for a couple of times when he happened to glance her way. She had picked up a magazine and was leafing through it.

She broke in, right in the middle of one of his better efforts. "I hear a car. Is that Covey and his little brood? Because if it is, let me out of here. I can only take so much."

Dad took a look out the dining room window and reported that yes, it was Covey. Mama jumped up, in a fluster. Was it that late already? Mercy, she hadn't realized, and here she was, with supper only half fixed … Harriet, without bothering to say goodbye, headed for the front door. Not exactly at a run; more of a shambling lope.

"Sorry to have bored you so," Evan shot after her.

She paused, just long enough to say, "Think nothing of it. I'm used to it."

"Good Lord," said Evan when the door had shut behind her. "What a monster. Somebody ought to swat her."

"I know," said Mama absently, hurrying toward the kitchen. "Poor child. Those gloves. Let's try not to let Covey get started on her. He's pretty unreasonable."

So the subject of Little Harriet was skillfully avoided throughout supper and the evening. Uncle Win wasn't mentioned either, Evan noticed. Well, he had known he would have to wait for a chance at Mama alone.

It didn't come until after Covey and brood had gone home. As if he knew what Evan had on his mind, Dad announced that it had been a long day and he was going to bed.

"Come on, Mama, let's sit out on the porch for a while," said Evan, and with a little sigh she followed him out to the porch swing.

The wind had died with the day; not a breath stirred in tree or bush. Above the thick, close darkness of the yard, of the world, the sky swarmed with stars. Even they looked hot. And how still it was! Only the rustle of Mama's palm leaf fan, and a dog barking, far off, and the whir of a June bug battering himself to death against the screen door, trying to get in to the light.

Evan wasted no time on preliminaries. "All right. What's with Uncle Win?"

It must be really bad: Mama still tried to stall. "He's been very sick, but Dr. Morrison says—"

"I know he's been very sick. What I want to know is what's wrong with him."

"Yes," said Mama. Her fan stopped rustling. "The truth is … Evan. Win tried to kill himself."

"What?" He tried to remember what he had expected or feared to hear. A stroke; a terrible, incurable disease. But something natural. Something believable. "Uncle Win tried to kill himself? I don't believe it!"

"Neither did I at first. But you have to believe it when he—when he says so himself. And he does. He says he doesn't want to get well, he wants to die—"

Uncle Win wanted to die? Uncle Win, with his quiet but deep relish for life, his dry sense of humor that was so much like Mama's, his supreme Covey confidence?

"But for God's sake, Mama! Why?"

He knew that she was on the verge of breaking down; she sat up even straighter than usual, and her voice was matter-of-fact, almost curt. "I don't know. He won't say why."

"But somebody must know, Pearl or somebody—"

"Pearl," said Mama. The way she had always said it, as if the name itself tasted bad, a bite out of a spoiled apple. "What does she know about Win? At first he tried to say it was an accident, but of course we all knew, Billy Morrison and all of us, that he couldn't have stabbed himself like that accidentally—"

"He stabbed himself?"

"With that old hunting knife of Papa's. Win always kept it in his study. He missed his heart by a fraction of an inch."

Even the June bug was silent now. Momentarily stunned, perhaps. Or just exhausted.

"How did they happen to— Who found him?"

"Little Harriet," said Mama. (Evan had been afraid of that.) "She's got a right to be—the way she is. Though to tell you the truth, I can't see that she's one bit worse, or better, than she was before. And Win's always been so absolutely dotty over her—"

Yes. Dotty. Besotted. Even though she was Little Harriet, instead of the son he had yearned for.

"Well," Mama went on in the same matter-of-fact voice, "Little Harriet went downstairs to get a chocolate bar—the candy that child eats, and at all hours, it was two thirty in the morning—and she heard a groan as she went past the study door. He was in there, slumped over his desk. All but gone, Evan. Billy Morrison says if he'd gotten there even fifteen minutes later …"

"And it couldn't have been an accident? He couldn't have had, say, a few too many, and for some reason started fooling with the knife—" For, while Uncle Win was by no means a lush, he had been known to drink quite heavily at certain periods in his life.

"He hadn't had a drink. Naturally, outside of the family we've gone on calling it an accident—" (Naturally. No Covey had ever disgraced himself by abdicating from life before his allotted term was up,) "—but Billy Morrison told me privately the next morning that he didn't see any way in the world it could have happened accidentally. And Win finally admitted that it wasn't an accident, he meant to do it."

"But there has to be some reason," said Evan. "He must have been worried about something. Depressed."

"I'm not pretending that Win's always told me what's on his mind, because of course he hasn't. But I've known him all his life, known him and—been fond of him. I can't believe he could be that worried or depressed without my having any inkling of it. And yet he must have been, and I didn't know, I didn't see. It isn't right, Evan. What's the *good* of being fond of people if you can't—if things like this can happen?" A sob overtook Mama. She turned it into a cough, and rustled her fan fiercely.

"Business worries," said Evan. "Maybe money troubles."

"That I *would* know about. The way Papa left things, if there were any money troubles to have, I'd be having them too. And as far as Win's law practice is concerned, there's not a thing wrong, according to Homer." (Who ought to know, thought Evan; he and Uncle Win had been law partners for thirty-five years.)

"Well, then, personal troubles. Let's face it, Mama, Uncle Win and Pearl can't be the happiest married couple in town."

It was a tribute to Mama's sense of justice that she answered as she did. "They're not the unhappiest, either. You've got to give Pearl credit. She does her best. If this had happened seventeen, eighteen years ago, when he divorced Nell to marry her, it wouldn't be quite so hard to understand."

Evan had been away at college at the time; even so, some of the repercussions of that scandal had penetrated to him. A choicer scandal than Fontenelle had enjoyed in decades. Winthrop Covey divorcing his eminently suitable wife (more than suitable; Aunt Nell really was a darling) to marry his secretary! His eminently unsuitable secretary: Pearl's family were trash, and she was more than twenty years younger than he.

"Well, he got what he wanted from Pearl," Mama went on, still bending over backwards to be fair. "A child. That's what he had his heart set on. That was the whole trouble between him and Nell. It's not Pearl's fault that it wasn't a son."

No argument there. Evan shifted his weight in the porch swing and pulled his shirt away from his sweaty chest. "Is Aunt Nell coming to visit this summer?"

"She's already here. Been here since June. She stayed with us a couple of weeks, and now she's visiting out at Flora Griffith's."

"Does she know the truth about Uncle Win?"

"I couldn't keep it from her," said Mama. "After all, she's one of my dearest friends, and she'd guessed, anyway, that it wasn't an accident. Like everybody else in town, I suppose. Nell blames Pearl, of course."

Yes. Of course. Aunt Nell had never gotten over the blow to her pride, any more than she had gotten over being in love with Uncle Win. Could it be that way with him, too? Could it have taken him all these years to see his blunder, irreparable now, so irreparable that he wanted to die? If so, it was the most spectacular case of delayed reaction Evan had ever heard of.

"What's the pitch when I go to see him tomorrow morning? I mean, am I supposed to know what the score is or not?"

"He'll know that I've told you. He'll tell you himself, I expect. He's quite open about it—except that he won't tell us the important thing, and I— Oh, Evan, I'm so afraid he'll do it again! If we could only find out what's *happened* to him! That's why I'm so glad you're here. He's always been fond of you, and then you've been away, maybe you'll see something that I can't, just because I'm too close to it—"

"I can try," said Evan. He restrained an impulse to pat Mama's hand; she did not take kindly to comforting gestures. Because comfort implied pity. And nobody—not even her favorite son, not even in such an extremity as this—had any business feeling sorry for Marianna Covey Hoyt.

They sat for a while in silence. The June bug had once more set up his futile buzzing against the screen when they went in.

Evan of course slept on the sleeping porch, which by some unwritten law had always been his and Covey's exclusive domain. It was supposed to be cooler than anywhere else, and though it was roomy, with three cots besides the one Evan occupied, Mama and Dad would never have thought of sleeping there instead of in their own bedroom at the back of the house. For Evan it still seemed to hold the echoes of boisterous boyhood slumber parties, midnight spreads and pillow fights. He stretched out wearily, staring at the tattered branches of the cedar that brushed against the screen and, far beyond, at the blazing stars.

But he had trouble getting to sleep. It was so damn quiet. No roar of traffic or neighbors' radios or drunken quarrels. Not a sound in the world but the busy ticking of his wristwatch. And then, just as he was dozing off, he did hear a sound, a tentative scratching on the screen. Could a breeze have sprung up, by some miracle? He opened his eyes, and saw a face peering in at him. He sat up with a jerk.

"Good Lord," he said. "What are you doing here?"

"Hello," whispered Little Harriet. "I wanted to talk to you." She relaxed her grip on the cedar—which she had no doubt shinnied up; Evan had done it many times himself—and made sure of her footing on the convenient outer ledge of the sleeping porch. "Never mind, you're decent," she added, for Evan, remembering that he had gone to bed naked, was fussing frantically with the sheet.

"More than I can say for you," he muttered. "Haven't you got any manners, sneaking around, waking people up in the dead of night?"

Little Harriet ignored the question. "I suppose she's been telling you that Daddy tried to kill himself," she said.

"Well … Yes." His tone softened. After all, it had been a tough break for the kid, finding Uncle Win like that. Maybe even a traumatic experience. Not that Little Harriet showed much indication of being thin-skinned. Still, you never knew.

"I knew she would. But it isn't so. I don't care what they say, it isn't so."

So she was holding out for the accident theory. Understandable enough. Mama would have done the same, except that she was too honest to shut her eyes to the facts.

"Maybe not. Only why would he—"

But Little Harriet's mind had apparently veered off in another direction. "When you were talking about New York this afternoon why didn't you tell about your girl?"

"My girl? What makes you think I've got one?"

"Of course you've got one. All us Coveys are sexy. Is she ravishing?"

"Not particularly."

"You mean she's a fright? So ugly you're ashamed of her? Is that why you didn't mention her?"

"Now look here, you brat. She's not a fright. If you want to get technical, she's not even my girl. She's married to somebody else."

"Oh." Little Harriet made a revolting, gulping sound. He could practically feel her face pressing in on him, against the screen. "So that's why. Married. Then it's just like Mother and Stanley."

"*What?* Mother and who?"

"Stanley," repeated Little Harriet. She seemed to be scratching a mosquito bite on the back of her neck. No gloves tonight; somebody must have pried them off of her. "Don't tell me Aunt Marianna missed a chance to spread *that* load of dirt."

"What in the hell are you talking about?"

"Maybe she didn't tell you, at that. Could be she doesn't even know it herself. There's a lot goes on around here that she doesn't hear about. She's terribly innocent, you know. Like so many women of her era."

Evan felt his temper straining. "Stop patronizing your betters. Is that what you wanted to talk to me about? Your mother and this Stanley Whoever-he-is?"

"Heavens, no. I find such things a crashing bore."

"Well, then, suppose you get to the point. If there is one. I'm sleepy." He made a move as if to lie down.

"Wait. I mean— The point is, he didn't try to kill himself."

He wished he could see the expression on her face; it was only a blur on the other side of the screen. He wished he could think of what to say. "But *he* says he did, Little Harriet," he managed at last, as gently as he could. "He admits it wasn't an accident."

"Of course it wasn't an accident!" She was still whispering, but the words came out in a scornful rush. "How dumb can you get? Accident! Somebody tried to murder him. I don't care what they say, somebody tried to murder him."

And before he could get out anything more than a gasp, she had started clambering down the cedar. He could have wrung her neck.

"Wait a minute! Harriet—"

She went right on clambering. "That's it. That's the point. You're so sleepy, go on, go to sleep."

Two

The wind, rising again with the sun, woke him. Once more the trees beyond the sleeping porch began their desolate thrashing; once more the sky took on the pale, cloudless glare that meant another scorcher. (He wondered how many times he would hear that dog-eared pleasantry during the day. And the other old standby. Hot enough for you?) He toyed, but hopelessly, with the notion of migrating indoors, to his bedroom, to see if he could get a little more sleep. He needed it. Little Harriet hath murdered sleep.

Gad, but he was teeming with fresh turns of expression this morning!

Murdered … Fantastic. Even for a fantastic pill of a kid like Little Harriet. The whole thing was as heartless an example of sensation-seeking as Evan had ever run across. Perfectly willing, not only to capitalize on Uncle Win's private tragedy, whatever it was, but on top of that, to drop her airy hints about her mother and somebody named Stanley. Anything to get attention. *Anything*. Somebody ought to shake her teeth out.

Stupid, too. Because, for God's sake, if somebody had tried to murder Uncle Win, he'd know it, wouldn't he? And he wouldn't cover up for his own mortal enemy by saying he'd tried to kill himself. Nobody on earth would be that cooperative. Except, conceivably, a defenseless, spiritless coward. But not a Covey.

And yet Little Harriet wasn't stupid clear through. That crack she had made about Mama: "She's terribly innocent, you know." No matter how much it might have irritated Evan at the time, it was true, in a way. Mama really did have a terrible kind of innocence; she had gone through life like a lucky child, never knowing what it was to struggle against unequal odds, never finding it necessary to lie or cheat or grovel, never tasting the sourness of failure. She knew, but only by hearsay, that there were such things as hunger and terror and hatred in the world. They had never touched her.

"Could be she doesn't even know it herself," Little Harriet had said. Could certainly be. "There's a lot goes on around here that she doesn't hear about." Bull's-eye, again. If Pearl was involved in some unsavory affair (and in Fontenelle all extra-marital affairs were unsavory) Mama would be the last to hear about it. And even if she should hear about it—on the wild chance that there was any busybody bold enough to tell her—Mama's innocence would stand, like a shield, between her and such gossip.

Evan had to admit it: Little Harriet was, unfortunately, not stupid clear through. Conscious of a low-grade throbbing somewhere inside his skull, he reached for the seersucker robe at the foot of his cot and padded inside to the bathroom.

When he got downstairs he found Mama in the kitchen, fussing over his breakfast. "Nonsense," she said crisply. "Of course you can eat an egg. Force yourself." (What a comfort they were, the old family jokes. And what a pleasant place the big kitchen was—geraniums blooming on the window sill, the good strong smell of coffee, the red-and-white checked tablecloth, and Evan's place set with his silver napkin ring and the fragile white china.)

"You look cute this morning, Marianna," he said as she settled down across from him with a companionable cup of coffee. She patted her pompadour demurely. "Where's Dad? Out at the farm?"

In a vague way Dad "ran" one of the Covey farms; the tenant farmer did all the real work, but Dad spent a good deal of time out there. Probably just because he loved the country. He had never done anything more strenuous since his marriage; the Coveys hadn't considered his previous occupation—that of sporting goods salesman—quite suitable. With shame, Evan remembered a smart, cheap crack he had once made at a New York cocktail party. "What does my father do?" he had said, in answer to somebody's question. "Why, my father is a kept man." True or not, it was a Little Harriet kind of crack. Anything for attention.

"He'll be back by nine," said Mama, "and you can have the car for the rest of the day. I'm afraid it's going to be too hot for golf, but I expect you can stir up somebody to go swimming with. The new pool out at the club's quite nice, Covey says. Have another muffin, dearie. While they're hot. Oh, by the way, did I tell you Norma's here, visiting her folks? Norma Schaefer?"

Evan put down his fork and gave her a look. "No, you didn't oh by the way tell me Norma Schaefer's here, visiting her folks. And get that match-making gleam out of your eye, Mama. It's no use beginning on me again. I have no intention whatever of marrying Norma Schaefer. Is that clear?"

"Mercy, who said anything about marrying her? I was just making a little sociable conversation. Don't be so touchy. I saw her at Sewing Circle the other day, with her mother. She's just as stunning as ever."

"Which is pretty damn stunning," said Evan, "if you care for horses."

"Why, Evan Hoyt, you ought to be ashamed of yourself. The idea! An attractive girl like Norma! You certainly got out of the wrong side of the bed this morning. More coffee?"

"Thanks." He watched her narrowly while she filled his cup. "Okay, Mama, let's have it. What kind of a date have you cooked up for Norma and me?"

"Why, what makes you think— Oh, all right. They've been having these dances out at the club on Saturday nights. Phyllis and Covey and all their set. I just assumed naturally you'd be going anyway, and of course so will Norma, so—"

"Uh huh. Saturday night. Well, that gives me two days to build myself up in. Like I always say, forewarned is forearmed."

"They're very nice affairs," said Mama stiffly. "The nicest we've had around Fontenelle in years, Covey says. I just assumed naturally you'd welcome any diversions we have here, of course I know it's not like New York, night clubs and all … You always used to *like* to dance."

"I did. I do. I can't wait. I'm all over palpitations." He saw what was coming, and said it with her: "'That's enough of that, young man …' You're absolutely right. Let's get back to today. What time do I go see Uncle Win?"

"This morning, I thought. As soon as Dad gets back with the car. I've already talked to Pearl, and they're expecting you. If you want me to go with you, I will, but I thought maybe if you talked to him alone—" A shadow of yesterday's haggard look crossed her face.

"Right," said Evan. He was conscious again, as he pushed back his chair, of the incipient headache rattling around back of his eyes. "That damned wind. Isn't it ever going to let up?"

It was going full tilt when, an hour or so later, he drove across town to see Uncle Win. Its feverish blast stirred up whirlpools of dust, flattened the weeds along the road, shook the car on its chassis. Evan drove slowly, trying to collect his wits for the visit ahead. But thought was impossible in the middle of this senseless commotion; it took all his nervous energy simply to endure.

Uncle Win had built a new house for his new wife. It had been spectacular seventeen years ago, and even now it was impressive: a low-slung stone job with a great deal of glass and faultlessly tailored landscaping. It had a cheerless air, possibly because—so Evan had heard—for two years after it was built not a woman in town, except Pearl and the hired girl, set foot inside it. The ladies of Fontenelle, rallying solidly behind Aunt Nell, had put the new Mrs. Winthrop Covey in her place. But good. Even Mama hadn't relented until Little Harriet was born.

Pitiless, thought Evan, as he started up the wide, shallow steps. The pitiless gentler sex. Pearl was waiting for him on the patio. For the first time in his life, Evan inspected her with more than passing curiosity. It struck him that that stretch of social ostracism (plus a good deal more, probably, that he didn't know about) had left its mark on her. A certain tightness about the set of her mouth. Something guarded, a little bit hard, in the expression of her prominent eyes. It was her light, scanty brows and lashes that made them look so prominent; Pearl was a pale strawberry blonde. Hers was not a soft-looking, nor a voluptuous, nor even a pretty face. Too much stubbornness in it for that. (Of course she was stubborn. Only a stubborn woman could have stuck it out.) And her figure, while it was passable, was not good enough to explain the effect Pearl had on you. Which was to turn your thoughts toward flesh—sweet, firm flesh with sheer nylon stretched tight over it; rounded, white flesh delicately threaded with violet veins … Even when dressed, as she was at the moment, in a modest cotton housedress, Pearl contrived to seem at least half-naked.

"Hello, Evan," she said. There was just the tiniest hesitation before she held out her hand to him. "Nice to see you again. My, isn't it hot! Another scorcher. Let's go inside, out of the wind. I was just straightening up a little out here."

She was an impeccable housekeeper, Evan remembered. Compulsively tidy. You hesitated to sully an ashtray in her living room. It was a spacious room, and no doubt tastefully decorated. Beige and turquoise, with calculated spots of tangerine. A room from which all traces of individuality—like incriminating fingerprints from a weapon—had been wiped clean. Perhaps that in itself was the mark of Pearl's individuality, Evan thought; and he remembered, with a nostalgic pang, the disorder and charm of the house Aunt Nell had kept for Uncle Win.

"Where's Little Harriet this morning?" he asked. He perched on the edge of a chair, because she seemed to expect him to sit down for a minute—or perhaps because underneath he wanted to put off seeing Uncle Win.

"Oh, that one," said Pearl. "You don't expect her to be up at this hour of the day, do you? She'd never get up before noon if she had her way."

So then he asked how Uncle Win was.

"Pretty well, thank you," she began automatically. She looked down at her hands, which were clasped into a tight knot in her lap. "I suppose your mother's told you— Yes. And I suppose she blames me. Well …

"No, she doesn't, Pearl. She can't understand what made him do such a thing." He paused, on the verge of adding, "Can you?"

She looked him squarely, defiantly, in the eye. "Neither can I. I don't care whether anybody believes it or not. Neither can I."

Did she expect him to argue the point? He wasn't going to. But he couldn't honestly assure her that he believed her, either. For one thing, it wouldn't have done any good; in whatever spot any member of Uncle Win's family chose to take his stand, in that spot Pearl would smell a rat. (Well. Could you blame her?) And for another thing, there were Little Harriet's hints about her mother and "Stanley." Plus Pearl's own attitude, which smacked to high heaven of a lady protesting too much.

Which left them in a dandy little deadlock of mutual, ingrained suspicion. And in a silence which neither of them seemed capable of breaking.

It was with acute relief that Evan heard the thud of a dog's paws on the carpeted stairway. "Buster?" He said it tentatively; but not very tentatively—he had never known Uncle Win to own a dog named anything else—and snapped his fingers.

This new Buster was one of the odder-looking ones. She was long-legged, longish-haired, black except for her stub-tailed rear end, which was white, as if she had sat in a puddle of Clorox. She smiled at Evan— she had a very sweet face—but she did not advance beyond the hallway.

The living room was obviously forbidden territory.

Pearl laughed abruptly. "Did you ever see such a ridiculous looking dog? I don't know where it came from. I wouldn't have given it house room, but you know how Win is, he'll take in any old stray that comes along."

"I know. It's too bad you don't like—"

"Of course I like dogs." She flushed slightly. "Thoroughbreds. I wouldn't mind having a boxer, something like that. But a silly looking mongrel shedding hairs all over the place, underfoot no matter where you turn …"

"She seems to have nice enough manners." As he stood up, Evan tried to suppress a thoroughly Covey thought having to do with look who's talking about mongrels. "Where is Uncle Win? I'd like to see him now, if it's all right."

"He's in his room. I'll take you right up. I'm sure it's going to do him good to see you."

And on that hollow note she led him up the stairs.

His first reaction at sight of Uncle Win was a lifting of tension so sudden and so complete that it left him giddy. Why, they've been making it all up, he thought; he's exactly the same, they've worked themselves into hysterics over nothing.

There he sat in his easy chair by the window, immaculate, as always, in his white shirt and "ice cream pants," smoking a cigar and reading the morning paper. A thin and elegant man, with straight white hair that would never stay slicked back off his high forehead the way it was supposed to, a homely, humorous face, and bushy eyebrows.

"Hey there, Evan Skavinsky Skavar," he said and, dropping his newspaper, he held out both his hands. Unlike Mama, Uncle Win was demonstrative; Evan crossed the room in a rush and was soundly kissed, hugged, and thumped on the back. "Hey, there! How's my boy?"

"Fine. What's all this they've been telling me about you being sick? Why, you look—" But then he saw Uncle Win's eyes. He had to finish. But he couldn't. "How are you, Uncle Win?"

"Oh, I'll do. Able to sit up while they change the sheets. Pull up a chair. How about a nip of brandy?" He had the bottle right there at hand, Evan noticed.

"Oh, Win, do you think— At this hour of the day? The doctor said—"

"Purely medicinal, Pearl, purely medicinal." He winked at Evan, and patted Pearl's round hip. "Give the old man a kiss, honey, and see if you can find another glass before you leave."

Obediently—mechanically, it seemed to Evan—she provided all that had been ordered. Kiss. Glass. And departure.

"Now," said Uncle Win, pouring the brandy, "let's hear what you've been up to." Easy and affectionate, so much the way he used to be— Only there had been that moment when he let Evan look directly into his eyes, and that one moment turned it all into a heart-breaking travesty.

"The hell with what I've been up to," said Evan bluntly. "It's what you've been up to …"

There was quite a long silence. Uncle Win looked out the window. "You wouldn't care to skip all this?" he said at last. "Just not discuss it, and say we had?"

"Skip it? What do you think we're made of—Mama and all the rest of us? We're not a bunch of wooden Indians, we're your family."

"My God, do you think I don't know it?" Uncle Win spoke with sudden passion. "That's why I— I know what the family means to Marianna. It means the same to me. I don't want to hurt her or any of you. I'm doing my damnedest to spare you all I can!"

"How can you say that when you won't give us any reason? You must have one. A guy like you, with apparently everything to live for—"

"All right. A reason." Uncle Win seemed to consider the matter. Carefully he tapped the ash from his cigar. His hand shook a little. It meant nothing: Uncle Win's hands always trembled slightly. "You don't think it's possible that life might simply cease to fascinate? No, I suppose not. Youth."

"Oh, stop it, Uncle Win. This is no time to start pulling rank on me. You don't think it's possible any more than I do. For a crazy mixed-up kid type, maybe. But not for somebody like you."

Uncle Win produced a wan grin. "Oh well. It was worth a try. If you got to have a reason you got to have a reason."

"Ha ha. If it's money, Uncle Win—Mama says it isn't, but I suppose she could be mistaken—"

"Not Marianna. Not about money. And I can save you time and energy by assuring you that Pearl and I haven't had a real good fight in years. Not since Little Harriet's fifth birthday party when—or so it is alleged— I came home drunk and disorderly. I'd like to be able to oblige your Aunt Nell and company, but the truth is that Pearl and I get along okay." He sipped his brandy and then went on, speaking with unusual precision. "Get this straight, Evan. Nobody is to blame for what—happened to me. It's nobody's fault but my own."

"Nobody's business, either. Is that what you're trying to tell me? Because if so, I'd like to point out a few simple home truths. Don't ask me why, but we're dopes, we're used to having you around, we don't want you to die. So it damn well is our business. You can't just walk out on us without giving us a chance to—" He got up and began pacing the floor.

He could feel the sweat trickling down his back. "Nothing can be that bad, Uncle Win. That hopeless. There's always some way out."

"You're so right, Pollyanna."

Evan swallowed hard. "You say it's not money or wife trouble. Well, I suppose there's always ill health. Some lousy long-drawn-out disease that you just found out you've got."

"Now that's a good one." Uncle Win's voice rang with admiration. "Why didn't I think of that? The only hitch would be getting Doc Morrison to back me up. Like as not he'd feel it was his bounden duty to let it be known that I'm actually as healthy as a horse. Isn't it a shame?"

"Oh, shut up." Evan sat down and put his head in his hands. Buster, who had been stretched out at Uncle Win's feet, came over and licked his nose sympathetically.

"I'm sorry," said Uncle Win wearily. "Sorry to worry you all like this. Sorry we couldn't have just called it an accident and let it go at that. It would have been easier all around. God knows I don't want it this way, any more than the rest of you. It's— Well, it's a damned embarrassing experience ..."

"Embarrassing!" Evan let out a groan. He sat, now, with his elbows propped on his knees and chin planted on his fists, staring—not at Uncle Win's face—but at his hands. Loose-knuckled, nervous hands that looked brown below the spotless white shirt cuffs. He still wore the gold signet ring that Aunt Nell had given him; he had a habit of twisting it.

"A reason," he said. "You're just like everybody else, you want a reason. Life's got to have a pattern, neat cause leading to neat effect, no loose ends that don't mean anything. It's too frightening, otherwise. But can you, personally, come up with a good sound reason for all the things you've done? Why did you go kiting off to New York? Why didn't you stay here in Fontenelle and marry the Schaefer girl and turn into a solid citizen like you were supposed to?"

"I didn't want to, that's all. That's enough reason."

"Best reason in the world. Only it doesn't end there. Why didn't you want to? I'm not saying there isn't a reason. But it wouldn't surprise me if you don't know what it is any more than I do, and even if you did know, you'd have a hell of a time trying to explain it to anybody else."

"Okay, you've thrown enough dust in my eyes. Let's get back to the point."

"We've never left it. I've got a reason too, I suppose. I just—didn't want to go on living. Good Lord, Evan, you expect me to tell you why? Call it a momentary aberration, if you've got to have a label. Temporary insanity. Say it just came over me all of a heap, how futile the whole business is, the petty pace, tomorrow and tomorrow and tomorrow, so forth and so on."

Buster had returned to Uncle Win's side, and he was fondling her silky ears. Evan kept his eyes fixed on those beloved brown hands, so full of nervous energy. What else can I do? he thought; what's the use of arguing anymore?

"So that's the way you want to leave it," he said at last.

"Don't you?"

"I— Temporary insanity." If you got to have a reason you got to have a reason. And it might, just possibly, be the truth. He made a desperate grab at the only straw in sight. "That's a nice word, that temporary. The key word, I trust? I mean—it's not chronic, by any chance? You haven't gone on, not wanting to live?"

He made himself lift his eyes. But Uncle Win was looking out the window. "Don't fret, boy," he said after a moment. "Lightning never strikes in the same place twice."

Three

"Tell me, Evan," said Aunt Nell in that marvelous, husky voice of hers. "How *is* Win?"

Here we go, he thought. He had known, when he volunteered to drive her back out to the Griffith farm after supper and an evening of bridge with Mama and Dad, that this was coming. "This" being one of the emotional conversations that were the breath of life to Aunt Nell. She could always be counted on to play her scenes big. And why not? Why waste all that natural equipment? The voice, throbbing and deep and flexible. The dramatic profile and expressive hands that, with a single gesture, could wring your heart …

"Marianna told me you saw him this morning," she went on. "Did he— No. I won't ask you that. How is he?"

"Pretty well." In his own voice Evan recognized the extra-dry tone that Mama so often adopted with Aunt Nell. She affected him the same way. He shot her a glance of mingled amusement and admiration. She was still a damn good-looking woman, even now, when she was— How old? Certainly in her late fifties. Her hair was curly, with a stagey white streak, her features large but sensitive—nose high-arched, mouth mobile and richly curving, eyes that could still flash plenty of fire.

At the moment they were flashing reproach at Evan. "Pretty well. Is that all you can say? The same old soothing syrup that everybody gives me. Even Marianna. If you only knew how cruel … They won't let me see him, you know."

They were quite right, in Evan's opinion, but he decided not to say so. "I doubt if it would do any good, Aunt Nell."

"It would. No one in the world knows Win the way I know him. Even if he wouldn't tell me in words what's wrong, I'd know. I'd sense it. It's always been like that with Win and me. He can hide it from the rest of you, but not from me. Never from me."

"Maybe not," said Evan. "He told me it was temporary insanity. A momentary aberration."

"Surely you don't believe that. He couldn't even expect you to believe it, it was simply the first thing that came into his head, and so he said it, just to—"

"Not quite the first thing. He started off with a slightly different pitch and worked his way around to insanity." There was no point, Evan thought, in trying to put a better face on Uncle Win's verbal gropings. Aunt Nell undoubtedly had her own ideas, and it would take more eloquence than he possessed to sway her from them. Were they based on anything solid? Like gossip about Pearl and somebody named Stanley? That was what interested Evan. While such tales might miss Mama's ears, they could hardly have failed to reach Aunt Nell's. He did not dare ask her outright; there was still the chance that Little Harriet had made the whole thing up.

"Ah, Win. Poor darling," murmured Aunt Nell. "When I think of what his life must have been, stuck with that impossible creature …"

"He claims he and Pearl get along okay."

"Of course he'd say that. Loyal. Loyal to the bitter end." Her hands clenched, tragically. "I blame myself, Evan. I'll blame myself to the day I die."

"Oh now, Aunt Nell. You couldn't have—"

"I could have. From the very beginning I saw what she was up to, scheming, setting her little traps for him. But I had too much false pride, I couldn't bring myself to fight her on her own terms. Oh no, I was above such things. Too proud; and so I lost him. The only man in the world for me, and I didn't lift a finger to save him. I stood by and let him be dragged down to—yes, to living death."

"Well, that's one way of looking at it," said Evan. It was time to bring Aunt Nell back to earth. "But after all, he was old enough, presumably, to know what he wanted. If you've got to blame yourself for something, seems to me it ought to be for not having the family you should have had years before. The family he wanted and you didn't."

"That was just an excuse. Her idea. She planted it in his mind. Just another of her little traps." She lifted her head for the punch line. "Do you believe for one moment that I would have refused to give Win a child if that was what he really wanted?"

"Frankly, yes," said Evan. (He'd had enough of Aunt Nell's phony streak. And her high-flown lingo: Give Win a child. She couldn't ever just plain have a baby.) "I think that's exactly what you did when you were first married. You were young and gay and pretty and you didn't want to spoil your figure, and by the time you changed your mind it was too late. I know one thing, Aunt Nell. Uncle Win wanted a son more than he wanted anything on earth."

"A son." Aunt Nell gave a malicious, and triumphant, laugh. "Well, she didn't do any better for him than I did. Look what he got. Little Harriet."

Evan was startled, even a little shocked, at her bitterness. But he was also ashamed of himself for having provoked it. He needn't have been so rough on her. "Yep," he said, with an attempt at lightness. "Little Harriet. All the same, he dotes on her. And who knows? Maybe she'll outgrow it—whatever it is."

"No, she won't. She'll break his heart for him before she's through. A piece of riffraff. Just like her mother. The morals of an alley cat."

"Who's an alley cat? Little Harriet? Pearl? I never heard—"

"Of course you never heard. You've been away for seven years. And Marianna hasn't heard because she's—because she's Marianna. But you can take my word for it, she's the only creature with ears that hasn't heard it. I mean the only creature. You can't tell me Win doesn't know that every pool hall loafer in Fontenelle is snickering over the way his wife's carrying on with a—" Having gone so far, Aunt Nell clamped her mouth tight shut.

"With a what? You can't leave me hanging over the cliff like this."

"Oh yes, I can. And I will. You think it's all spite with me, anyway. Let somebody else tell you the truth about your precious Pearl. Maybe then you'll believe it." She folded her arms and stuck out her chin. No doubt about it, Aunt Nell could be the most exasperating woman in the world.

"Have it your way," said Evan. If tongues were wagging as freely as Aunt Nell claimed, it would be no trick to find out the who and what of Stanley. And if Uncle Win did indeed know about it … He finished the thought aloud. "I suppose that might give him a reason. The blow to his pride. And yet, Aunt Nell, it doesn't sound quite right to me. I can see him raising hell with Pearl, maybe even throwing her out. Or I can see him shrugging his shoulders and waiting for her to come to her senses. But it doesn't seem like the kind of blow that would—crush him. Besides, there's Little Harriet. Wouldn't he make some other arrangement for her, instead of just walking out on her and leaving her in Pearl's hands?"

"We don't know what arrangements he made," Aunt Nell pointed out. "Because his plan misfired. And if he left any kind of a suicide note involving Pearl, it's long gone now. She'd see to that, all right."

"Little Harriet got there first. She's the one that found him."

"Makes no difference. They're two of a kind. I'm sure he knows about Pearl, because when I saw him—"

"I thought you said you haven't seen him."

"I haven't. Not since the day he—not since it happened. I had an appointment with him at his office that afternoon. He's always taken care of my business affairs for me, you know."

In other words, he had continued to support Aunt Nell since their divorce. It occurred to Evan that her "business affairs"—a series of ill-fated gift shops in Chicago, real estate ventures in Florida and tea rooms in Arizona—must have cost Uncle Win a pretty penny.

"Did he seem depressed to you?" he asked. "Despondent? Upset about anything?"

"Not in the least. It was the other way round. He knew I was feeling blue—the troubles I've had with this last tea room, you wouldn't believe it—and he went out of his way to cheer me up. You know how he can turn everything into a joke. Well, that's what he did with The Kettle on the Hob. We laughed ourselves sick. Homer kept poking his head in the door—I'm sure he thought we were drunk, he never did approve of me, you know—and of course that would set us off all over again."

All very jolly. And yet at some point they must have stopped laughing themselves sick over The Kettle on the Hob and mentioned Pearl. "Did he tell you he knew about Pearl?" asked Evan.

There was a tiny hesitation—just long enough for him to add, in his low suspicious mind, Did you tell him about Pearl yourself? Is that why you're so sure he knows?

"He didn't tell me in so many words. I don't remember how the subject came up." (She carefully looked out the car window as she said this.) "I don't even remember exactly what he said. Something about how much gossip there is in a little town, and how he figured he ought to get a medal for keeping Fontenelle supplied with juicy morsels ..."

"And he was still in good spirits when you left?" asked Evan.

"Yes. There wasn't the slightest indication that he was seriously worried about anything. I couldn't believe—" The throaty voice vibrated like a fiddle string. "I'd have sensed it, Evan. You can't tell me I wouldn't have! Something terrible happened later on that night. And if only they'd let me see him— She's afraid to. She's afraid of what I'll find out."

"But look, Aunt Nell, you're not making sense. If he already knew about Pearl—as you say—and if it didn't worry him seriously, then how can you say Pearl's to blame?"

"Of course she's to blame." So much for the little matter of logic. "I don't care whether it makes sense to you or not. You mark my word, she's at the bottom of it."

Evan gave up. He should have known better than to argue with Aunt Nell, he thought as he turned into the Griffith driveway and brought the car to a stop. Well, at least he knew better than to take every word she said as gospel truth. She wasn't exactly a liar. But for her the borderline between fact and fiction was often conveniently hazy. Then, as he glanced at her and saw that she was crying, his heart smote him. The crying itself meant nothing; she had long ago mastered the technique of using tears for dramatic effect. But there was nothing artful about these tears. Indeed, she was trying to hide them—bending her head, pretending to hunt for something in her purse. He could see the cords standing out in her throat, and the ugly twist to her mouth.

"There, Aunt Nell. I'm sorry. I didn't have any business saying some of the things I said to you. Don't mind me. I'm just a lousy—"

"No," she gulped out. "Like they say—the truth that hurts ..." She pulled her hands away from his and covered her eyes. "What does it matter about me, anyway? It's Win, Win's the only one that matters ..."

That at least was the truth, thought Evan as he started the drive back to town. (She had pulled herself together, had even managed a ghost of her luminous smile when he kissed her goodnight at the Griffiths' door.) For all Aunt Nell's selfishness and willfulness, and for all her phony streak, she had never wavered in her genuine devotion to Uncle Win. Very likely it worked the other way too: Uncle Win had married Pearl, all right, but not exactly for love. That was why Evan found it hard to believe that Pearl's "carrying on"—no matter how flagrant—would constitute a really crushing blow. He mustn't close his mind to the possibility, though. Aunt Nell might be off base on a good many points, but she had convinced him that Stanley was no figment of Little Harriet's imagination. He would bear looking into; the only question was, where to start looking.

The sign caught his eye as he made the turn back onto the highway. "Dine and Dance," in pulsing red and blue neon. "Hamburgers—Hot Dogs—Beer." The name of the place—"The Spot"—was illustrated by a target-like, frantically spinning circle. Evan slowed down to get a better look. Something new in night life for Fontenelle. New and thriving, if the number of cars parked in front of the two-story stucco building was any indication. The door opened to admit a batch of new arrivals, and jukebox music beat out into the hot night. Evan turned in and parked. After all, the place was air-conditioned. He noticed, as he stepped out onto the gravel driveway, there were half a dozen tourist cabins scattered farther back, under the scrawny cottonwoods. Evidently The Spot had everything.

They weren't kidding about the air conditioning. A blast of chilly, stale air set him to shuddering as he walked in, and he was further confused by the extraordinarily feeble lighting system. He could make out a good-sized dance floor, lit principally by the garish jukebox, and lined on two sides by booths, in each of which burned a flashlight-sized lamp. The effect was at once shrill—for there was a great deal of racket—and furtive. If he had been hoping to see somebody he knew (and maybe he had been, in a subterranean way) he was disappointed. Most of the patrons looked like high school kids. Oh well, he might as well have a beer, as long as he was here. He groped his way toward the back. There didn't seem to be any bar; only a counter behind which a large, bedraggled woman was grilling hamburgers and hot dogs with one hand and opening beer bottles with the other. The cash register was presided over by a surly-looking specimen in a loud sports jacket; as he passed, Evan heard him snapping at the waitress over some mistake she had made. Now that his eyes were growing accustomed to the twilight gloom, he spotted an empty booth, slid into it, and settled down for a little first-hand observation of the younger generation.

It didn't turn out that way. Just as he was taking his first sip of beer (not quite cold enough) Goldie came along and jolted him back into his own younger-generation days. He didn't recognize her at first; he took her for some possibly befuddled soul who had momentarily lost her bearings. She had a glass in one hand. With the other she steadied herself against his table. She peered down at him for a moment before she spoke.

"Well, blow me down if it isn't Evan Hoyt! What you doing? Slumming?"

"Goldie!" he cried, and struggled to his feet, hand outstretched. It was her crack about slumming that tipped him off. In their high school days they had had a frustrated sort of crush on each other: Goldie wasn't considered quite "nice," and—snob that he was—Evan had only once gotten up the nerve to take her to a party openly. Even at that early age, Goldie knew very well what the score was. She didn't blame him for being a social coward, but she couldn't resist needling him now and then, just so he wouldn't forget that that's what he was.

"Sit down, Goldie. Lord, am I glad to see you!"

It was the truth. There wasn't a single one of his regular crowd that he cared two cents for, but Goldie ... You could *talk* to Goldie, and she would know if not with her head, then with her heart—what you were talking about. And he had always gotten a warm pleasure out of just looking at her. So much so that he was almost afraid to look at her closely now, in case the years had been too damaging. No. As she sat down across from him, so that what little light there was fell on her, he felt a surge of relief. She was heavier, she just missed being blowzy, but the old charm was still there. Even as a kid, she had had a full-blown quality—like a rose at the peak of its bloom, destined to fade soon—the pathos of beauty that cannot last. A pink, golden-hearted rose. No girl had ever been more aptly named than Goldie.

"Well?" She was smiling tremulously. "Don't tell me I'm the same sweet kid. Believe me, I'm not. You're the one that hasn't changed. As skinny as ever—and I bet you still eat like a horse, too. It isn't fair. How's the world been treating you, anyway?"

"It's a short, dull story. The boy who didn't make good. How about you? I suppose you're married?"

Of course she was. To Bob Shay. (He discovered that he had never liked Bob Shay. Big loud-mouthed Irish roughneck.) Three children—and if he thought he was going to get out of looking at pictures of them, he had another think coming. She fumbled in her handbag and drew out snapshots of three tow-headed little girls. They were dolls, if she did say so as shouldn't. Living dolls. Bob was in the construction line. (That sounded pretty glib and vague to Evan. Like as not the big lug didn't even support her.)

"Stick around a while tonight and you'll probably see him," she said. "He usually picks me up after work."

"You mean he works till this hour of the night?" It was nearly midnight.

"Not him," said Goldie, and something both sad and defiant flickered across her face. "Me. I work here. The Songbird of The Spot. That's me."

"No kidding!" That explained the over-dressy black lace job she was wearing, and all the rhinestone bracelets—though, to tell the truth, Goldie's clothes had always been a bit on the flashy side. "So you've turned into a full-fledged night club singer. Shades of 'Gay Madrid!'"

"Gay, mad, sad Madrid," sang Goldie, and at the memory of that scintillating vehicle—the Junior Class operetta in which she and Evan had played the leading roles—she threw back her head and laughed. Whatever else time might do to her, it could not keep her from laughing in the old rich, free way. The laughter of a woman who knew how to enjoy life, and could make you enjoy it too, thought Evan. Those long-ago spring evenings when he had walked Goldie home after operetta practice; the Spanish dance they had performed, complete with tambourines; and the kisses ("Ricardo kisses Inez lightly," the stage directions had read.) Oh, they had practiced that, all right …

"Well, why not?" said Goldie, sobering. "I always did like to sing. I get a kick out of it, beating a few chords out of that old wreck of a piano and going to town on a good song. I'm not temperamental, I don't care if the customers drown me out. They get a kick out of it too. And just between you and I and the lamp post, we can use the money. Not that there's any danger of me getting rich on what Stanley pays me."

"Stanley?" said Evan. "Who's he? The guy that runs the place?"

"That's right. Mr. Stanley, I should have said. That's what most people call him, he's got one of those Polish jawbreakers for a last name. You wouldn't know him. He's only been here a couple of years. Came here from Chicago and opened this joint and from all I can gather he's making money hand over fist—one way and another."

A provocative expression: one way and another. There were the tourist cabins, in addition to the hamburgers, hot dogs, beer business, which seemed fairly brisk. And then there was the second floor of The Spot; Evan began to wonder about the characters he had seen going up and down the stairway. They didn't look like high school kids. Any more than Stanley did—if Evan was correct in assuming that the keeper of the cash register was Stanley in the flesh.

"Well, good for him," he said. "Is he the thug type in charge of the cash register?"

"That's our Mr. Stanley." Goldie cast a cautious glance over her shoulder. "Wears his money out counting it. Though I'll say this for him. When he takes a notion to spend it, brother, he spends it. He's thrown two of the fanciest parties Fontenelle ever saw. Not that it's done him any good."

There she went again. Another provocative expression. "What do you mean, done him any good? Did he expect it to?"

"You bet he did. He thought he could buy his way into the sacred inner circle of Fontenelle society. Just like that. I could have told him that all the champagne and caviar this side of the Mississippi wouldn't get him an inch of the way in. But he didn't ask me. He didn't ask me to the parties, either. Only the elite. They stayed away in droves. All except—" She took a hasty gulp of her drink. Her eyes got big. Gray eyes, with just a shade too much mascara.

"All except one certain member by marriage of the elite Covey clan," said Evan. "Is that what you started to say? Don't mind me. I've already heard several dark hints, and I fully intend to pump you for all you're worth. Is Stanley the guy that Pearl's supposed to be carrying on with?"

"There may not be a word of truth in it. You know how those things are, once they get started. And the gossips around here have been gunning for Pearl for years, ever since your uncle married her. They're going to talk, anyway. She might just as well go ahead and have herself a fling." For a moment Goldie seemed to brood. "Don't get me wrong. I'm not saying that's what she's doing. And if she is, I'm not standing up for her. I just think she's had a raw deal, that's all."

"These two parties that she went to and nobody else did—is that the whole story?"

The expression on Goldie's face told him it wasn't. "They say it started a long time ago, before he ever came to Fontenelle. She used to go to Chicago for weekends quite often. She doesn't anymore. So of course that proves it. They say. Why would a guy like Stanley pick a town like Fontenelle—they say—if there wasn't something fishy going on? He's got a hunting lodge up in the hills, and she's supposed to meet him out there, somebody saw her car, somebody else saw him picking her up in his car ... They say. They say. Who the hell cares?"

"I wouldn't ordinarily," said Evan. "I suppose Uncle Win might. That is, if he knows about it."

She flashed him a glance of instant perception and sympathy. "All I can do is guess, Evan. I'd guess that he does know. He's no dope, your Uncle Win. Besides, several people in town would just dearly love to tell him. His ex-wife, for one. And that spoiled brat daughter of his, for another."

"Little Harriet?" Well, why not? It fit in very well with his own conviction that Little Harriet would do anything to get attention. Anything at all.

"I shouldn't have said that, I guess. After all, she's nothing but a kid. Come to think about it, she's probably had kind of a raw deal, too."

"Does she ever come in here? It seems to be kind of a hangout for high school kids."

"Not the real nice ones. Let's face it, The Spot's a dump. When kids like Harriet turn up here—I guess I've seen her here once or twice—you can bet their folks don't know about it. In the better circles, Mr. Stanley's name is M-U-D." Again she glanced back over her shoulder. "Lord, would they love to find some excuse for closing him up! They never will, but let 'em dream. He knows more about staying just inside the law than everybody in Fontenelle put together. A very sharp operator."

"He looks it," said Evan bitterly. "Damn it, if she's going to pull a stunt like this, why does it have to be with a Chicago gangster, or whatever he is? Why couldn't she have picked somebody respectable?"

"Yeah," said Goldie, and the way she said it made him flush. "Frightfully common of her, wasn't it? She should have called a family conference and gotten the Covey okay before she decided who she was going to jump into bed with. Honest and true, Evan, sometimes you make me—"

"All right. All *right*."

"And another thing. He may not be what you call respectable, but you can bet your bottom dollar Mr. Stanley's never had much trouble getting any woman he happened to want. Plenty of these oh-so-respectable ladies that are tearing Pearl to pieces wouldn't mind one little bit being in her shoes. Let's change the subject. How come you're not married by now? Or maybe you are …"

"Not me." He grinned at her. "We can't all be like Mr. Stanley. The answer to every maiden's prayer."

"Never say die." She was smiling too, her flash of temper gone as quickly as it had come. "How about Norma Schaefer? They tell me she's still laying around loose … My, my. What am I saying? A nice girl like Norma. Look, it's time for me to earn my so-called salary. If I can get the customers to turn off the jukebox long enough to listen to me." She stood up and held out her hand. "You're going to be around for a while, aren't you? I'll be seeing you again, then. And listen, try not to worry about— you know. I mean, what's the use?"

"Sure. Sing pretty, now."

He ordered another beer and listened to her first couple of songs. She wasn't much good on the piano, but her voice was pleasant— unpretentious and forthright. She was obviously popular with the customers; they crowded around her, calling out requests, joining in when the spirit moved them. It gave him an agreeably melancholy feeling to watch her; if he squinted his eyes she looked practically unchanged, the schoolgirl Goldie he had been in love with. Yes. In love. Only not enough to forget that she wasn't quite the kind of girl he ought to be in love with.

Bob Shay came in while she was still singing, and Evan's melancholy abruptly lost its agreeable quality. He left as soon as he could do so unobtrusively. (The red-faced lug. And even more of a beer belly on him than Evan would have predicted.)

On his way out he stopped at the vending machine for a package of cigarettes; from this spot he had a good view of the cash register and Stanley behind it. He still looked surly to Evan. Not only a sharp operator, but a dangerous one. Well, maybe that was what made him such a surefire hit with the ladies. The brute appeal: too much jaw, coarse dark hair, something vicious about the set of the neat, small ears. Only his high forehead did not match the rest of his face. He was not particularly tall, but his shoulders were hulking—even allowing for the excessive padding in that sports jacket. His fingernails were highly polished, and he wore a flashy ring. He must have sensed that someone was watching him; for a disconcerting moment Evan found himself looking straight into Stanley's deepset eyes. There was a gleam of recognition in them, at once knowing and curious—and of course it was entirely possible that he had learned Evan's identity from one of the other customers. In fact, he had no doubt made a point of doing so. A sharp operator like Stanley would always keep an eye out for strangers. But what made it really disconcerting was that Evan was aware of something vaguely familiar, reminiscent, about Stanley's face. As if he might have seen the fellow somewhere before …

At last, in embarrassment, he smiled and made a gesture of goodnight. Stanley's hard, measuring stare did not change, though his mouth lifted in what might have been a smile. Then again it might have been a sneer.

As he went out the door (and, after the air conditioning, the heat hit him like a blow between the eyes) Evan decided that it was almost certainly a sneer.

Four

It was loathsome, going to the movies alone—and on Saturday night, when everybody who wasn't an utter dog had a date—so loathsome that Little Harriet always made a point of arriving late and leaving early. That way there was less chance of seeing or being seen by her contemporaries. Those lucky, loathsome girls who seldom bothered with Little Harriet unless they wanted to cadge something. Those even more loathsome boys who never gave her a second glance. She couldn't bear watching them, and for their benefit—just in case any of them should happen to notice her—she assumed her most supercilious air.

For Daddy's benefit she lied. Well, pretended. Pretended that she was meeting "some of the kids" downtown; that she wasn't the slightest bit interested in boys or dates or any of that stuff; that she was the popular, attractive daughter he so wanted her to be. And maybe he lied to her. Maybe he only pretended to believe. That was all right too, if it made Daddy happier …

Of course, once she was inside the movie, slumped on her backbone with her legs comfortably wound around each other and her candy bar unwrapped, it wasn't loathsome at all. In the impersonal darkness she could feel the familiar, unsatisfactory Harriet dissolving, and another self-emerging like a flawless butterfly to appear on the screen before her own eyes and everyone else's. She was what she watched. For a couple of hours her own life did not exist; all its ragged uncertainties (Mother and Stanley, the terror of what might happen to Daddy, her own miserable inadequacy) were transformed into neat, solvable problems.

Sometimes—and this particular Saturday night was one of the times—the spell lasted all the way home. She slipped out the side exit and floated along the quiet street, still bemused and free. There had been some lovely sad parts tonight; the rich flavor of chocolate and caramel and peanuts in her throat mingled pleasantly with the taste of tears.

But the minute she walked into the living room, the spell was gone and there she was, thumped back into the same old self, the same old life. Mother was sitting on the couch. Knitting. She was an expert at it: her needles flashed at breakneck speed and with fascinating precision; she could have done it blindfolded. She sat with her legs crossed, her foot in its high-heeled red sandal swinging in nervous rhythm. Little Harriet knew what those scarlet slippers meant, and the sleek cat expression on Mother's face. Stanley.

"For heaven's sake," said Mother. "What have you got all over your face? It's a sight."

And sure enough it was. Against her will Little Harriet looked in the mirror and saw the smear of chocolate at one corner of her mouth, the lipstick smudge at the other, the traces of tears. It was a loathsome face, anyway, all bones and sharp lines and straw hair.

"So what?" she said.

"Well, wash it. That's so what. And another thing, if you don't clear some of the junk out of that room of yours I'm going to go in there and do it myself. I mean it, Harriet, I'll give you till noon tomorrow. If it isn't done by then—"

"Don't you dare. It's my room, you've got no business snooping around in my things. You stay out of there."

"Keep your shirt on," said Mother calmly. "I haven't been in there. You left the door open, that's how I know what a mess it is. But I'm warning you, I'm not going to stay out of there if you haven't cleaned it out by noon tomorrow—"

"Oh, all *right!* I heard you the first time. You don't have to keep *nagging* me." Little Harriet flounced out to the kitchen, yanked open the refrigerator door, and took out a Coke. A piece of chocolate cake left from supper also caught her eye; thus laden, she passed majestically along the hall again, heading for the stairs.

"How was the movie?" called Mother in a conciliatory voice.

"Loathsome. Is Daddy still awake?"

"I don't think so. He went to bed an hour ago. Try not to wake him, won't you?"

The knitting needles were still flashing, the frivolous red slipper still swung, the secret, cat expression deepened almost to a smile. So sure of herself, thought Little Harriet, with her shapely legs and her chignon. She thinks that's smart, I suppose. Well, *I* think it's common, she was trash to begin with, and a chignon isn't going to change her.

"You going to sit up and knit all night?" she asked.

"It's too hot to sleep. I'll be up after a while." Yeah. After a good long while, after she's had a chance to sneak out and back in again. "Good night, dear. Sleep tight."

Little Harriet did not answer. She plodded upstairs, staring at her own graceless feet, hating them, from the bottom of her heart hating the part of her that envied Mother, commonness and Stanley and all.

She tiptoed past the door to Daddy's room. But he was not asleep, after all. "That you, Little Harriet?" he called, and her heart lifted. "Come on in and say goodnight."

He snapped on the bedside lamp as she went in, and she saw that he was in bed, propped up on several pillows. Not sleeping. Not reading. Just lying there with his thoughts—and what sorrowful thoughts they must be; his face was drawn, and she had never noticed before how his temples caved in. She would not notice now. It was only a trick of the light.

"Hi, Dirty Face," he said, and he kissed off the chocolate and lipstick. "Aren't you home early for a Saturday night?"

She had one of her impulses to stop pretending and pour out the humiliating truth—that she had gone to the movies alone because nobody had asked her for a date and what was more nobody ever would, not if she lived to be forty-seven. But there was something so wistful in his eyes …

"Oh, it was all pretty blah. Nobody interesting around tonight." She deposited her bottle and cake on the nightstand and curled up beside him. "Nobody but kids. I prefer older men."

"Like Evan, I suppose?"

"Don't be silly, Daddy. He's my cousin." (She was mad for him. The way his eyebrow quirked, just the left one, and that lean, distinguished look. And his voice. It made her knees melt just to remember his voice.) "He took Norma Schaefer to the club dance tonight."

"So I hear. Your Aunt Marianna's still in there pitching. She's a determined woman."

Still, thought Little Harriet, he could have gotten out of taking Norma if he'd really wanted to. No matter how determined Aunt Marianna was. So he must sort of like Norma. She sighed. "Daddy, did you tell Evan?

About—you know—how you were stabbed?"

She felt his arm stiffen, but he kept his voice easy. "I told him just what I've told everybody else. Except you. We said it was going to be our secret, and it is."

It was all very well for Daddy to keep calling it their secret. But the secret was not even half hers; she knew only that there was one. He had admitted so much to her (and to no one else; she had that to cling to) but no more. So how could it be called her secret? And she remembered, guiltily, that she couldn't be trusted even that far; the other night on the sleeping porch she had blurted out to Evan what she had promised to tell nobody. For the lowest of all reasons—simply because she wanted to show off. Well, at least partly to show off. But partly, too, because …

"I'm scared," she whispered. "Oh Daddy, I'm so scared."

"Now, Skeeter, we've been through all this before." He took her chin in his loving, slightly trembling hand and turned her face up to his. "There's nothing to be scared of. I've never lied to you, have I?"

"No. But they might come back …"

"They won't. You have to take my word for it. I know it isn't fair. But there isn't any other way. I can't tell you anymore. You just have to believe me when I say they won't come back. Can't you do that for me? Can't you trust me?"

Ah, if only she could tell him how she loved him, how glad she would be to die in his place … It was going to happen, he was going to die. His eyes, so mortally sad. And the caved-in place at his temple. She reached up and touched it. It was really there. But there was the gun, she thought, Uncle Ralph's gun. At least she had been able to do that for him. The pain in her chest was strangling her.

"That's my girl," said Daddy. "That's my good, brave Little Harriet."

She flung her arms around him, gulped out an approximation of "Good night," and rushed blindly toward the door.

"Hey," he said, "don't forget your lunch. We can't have you starving to death before morning." And for a minute the spark of merriment was back in his eyes, he looked like himself again. She managed to make a face at him as she picked up her "lunch." She even managed a quavering laugh.

But in her own room the storm of tears broke. She threw herself on her bed and buried her face in the pillow. Afterwards she felt lightheaded, rather exhilarated. And ravenous: without turning on the light, she wolfed her provisions. It was hot, and so still that, even with the door shut, she could hear the electric fan whirring in Daddy's room. Presently there was another sound. Or rather, a series of sounds that Little Harriet had heard many times before—the back door opening and closing stealthily, the barest whisper of footsteps in the driveway, the purr of a car starting up. She got to her window just in time to see the tail light disappearing down the street. Mother, off for her rendezvous. It was as if the sultry night had swallowed her up. Not a breath of air stirred; not a star showed in the blackness overhead. There was a far-off, ominous rumble of thunder.

Had Daddy heard that secret departure? And if he had, did he care? Mother would be ready with an explanation, anyway: it was too hot to sleep, she had gone for a ride …

Little Harriet gave one last hiccoughing sob and put her head down on the window sill. Sleep engulfed her.

She was struggling to say something. It was terribly important for her to tell Daddy, or Evan, or whoever it was. But when she opened her mouth nothing came out but a high, worried whine. "Shut up, Buster," said Daddy-or-Evan. "Stop making like a watchdog." And she was struggling to stop them. It wasn't noon tomorrow, but that didn't make any difference to them; there they were—Mother and Stanley—barging right into her room as if they owned it, pawing through all her treasures. "Junk," they said. "Clear out the junk." Outrage choked her. They wouldn't pay any attention to her. They just went on smiling their cat-smiles, and her terrible message remained pent up in her aching throat: Daddy! Don't die! *Daddy!*

She came awake violently. She was sticky all over with sweat, and her right arm prickled with pins and needles. Daddy's voice reached her distinctly, "Don't be silly. Why should I hate you?" Downstairs a door closed.

She scrambled to her feet. The nightmare had not quite loosed its grip on her; she still had a feeling of panic and urgency. But around her loomed the furniture of her room, ghostly but familiar—flounced dressing table, the armchair with its load of clothes and magazines, her record player on the desk, the faintly glimmering mirror, the rumpled bed. Her little luminous-dialed clock on the bedside table showed twenty past one. The electric fan in Daddy's room continued its comforting whir.

He was downstairs, though. And so were they. Mother had dared to bring Stanley here, to Daddy's house, and Daddy had heard them … Little Harriet began to shake. Her hands, her knees, her head—all jerking away as if she were one of those windup toys that, once started, must run through their paces no matter what. She clamped her arms around her body, trying to stop it. She set her teeth and screwed her eyes shut. But the shuddering went on.

Well, then, she would ignore it. She would walk across the room—one foot in front of the other, very simple—and open the door and go downstairs. Or maybe not go downstairs. Maybe call Daddy first. "Daddy, who is it? Who's there?" And he would call back, "What do you mean, who's here? Nobody's here but me. You've been having a bad dream."

But surely she had not dreamed his voice before: "Don't be silly. Why should I hate you?" Or the sound of the door closing. It might have been the front door; they might have been leaving. If it was the study door, they were still there. That was what she must find out.

She discovered that she was still standing in the middle of her room, abjectly shaking. One foot in front of the other, very simple; and somehow she had not managed it. This won't do, she thought; supposing Daddy needs help and here you are, jittering. It will be your fault. He has the gun, but supposing, supposing … She made herself take the first convulsive step toward the door. The second. Another. She stopped with her hand frozen on the door knob and her voice frozen in her throat. It was impossible, after all, to call out.

Did she hear a murmur of voices from the study? It might be only the fan buzzing in Daddy's room. It might be only her imagination. Open the door. Go downstairs. *Find out.* The necessity of knowing; and, at the other end of the seesaw, a strange, dragging reluctance. Don't open the door. Don't go downstairs. Don't find out. There may be something worse than uncertainty.

All the same, she turned the door knob at last and peered out into the quiet, dimly lit hall. She was no surer now than before; the door to Daddy's room stood open, and the hum of the fan was louder. She was still shaking. Sweat trickled down the backs of her legs.

If she turned off the fan, then she could tell whether the voices were really downstairs or only in her head. She made herself creep along the hall to Daddy's room. She had to go all the way in; the fan stood on the chest of drawers. Thunder rumbled again, quite close now, and for an instant lightning licked through the dark, empty room. It must be going to storm. That was why she had this feeling of waiting for something to happen. When she was halfway across the room a sudden gust of wind sprang up, sucking the blind flat against the window and slamming the door shut. Her heart thudded in her chest. Then stillness again, and the waiting feeling.

It came just as she clicked off the fan. The report of a gun. Muffled but unmistakable. She recognized it instantly; she had been waiting for it all this time. She felt that she was screaming, but as she tore out of Daddy's room and down the stairs she heard only two sounds—her own pounding footsteps and Buster, barking frantically in the basement.

Five

The telephone did not awaken Marianna. Always a light sleeper, she had already heard the wind rising, and she was prowling through the house, closing the windows against the storm that threatened to break at any moment. Upstairs all was in order; Ralph asleep, undisturbed by the slap and rattle of the window shades which had aroused her; Evan not home yet. And it was late, she thought hopefully, all of two thirty. Her mind conjured up a highly satisfactory scene in which Evan and Norma were saying a lingering goodnight on the Schaefer front porch. Such a lovely girl, Norma. So suitable. Who knew? Why shouldn't he— now that he had had his little fling away from Fontenelle, on his own— why shouldn't he decide that it was time to settle down, why shouldn't he come to his senses about Norma? Leave him alone, Ralph was always saying, let him live his own life; and of course Marianna had no intention of doing anything else. But all the same …

She padded downstairs in her slippers and nightgown and methodically made the rounds. Kitchen, dining room, library, living room. In the hall the candelabra-like lighting fixture on the newel post was turned on, as always on nights when one of the family was out. It had been so when she and Win were young, and all through Covey's and Evan's adolescence. A long time, now, since she and Ralph had had any reason to leave the light on when they went upstairs to bed. The sight of it filled her with a contented glow.

Everything was going to be all right, now that Evan was home where he belonged. Somehow, by his mere presence, he had brought her world back into balance. And Win's world, too? She paused in the hallway, twisting her plaited hair, trying to hope. And maybe Win's world too. In her heart she had always linked the two of them together, Win and Evan. Not that they were so very much alike. Oh, there was the family resemblance. But Covey had as much of that as Evan, and she did not love him in the same special, anxious way. Poor dear Covey, he had never given her a moment's worry.

As far back as she could remember, she had fussed over Win, one way or another. Covered up for him at home when he was kept in after school. Pulled him through his homework; and, in high school, suffered with him when he didn't make the baseball team, wept with pride when he won the prize for debating. Not that he expected it of her, or—like as not—even wanted it. But she couldn't help feeling responsible. And then there were the girls. Even in his teens, Win had now and then shown the most distressing taste when it came to girls. (Well, and look at Evan and Goldie. Goldie! At least that particular disaster had been avoided, even though he had remained impervious to a nice suitable girl like Norma.) She could remember several similar near-disasters in Win's youth. One or two college scrapes—nothing really serious; just what you might expect from a high-spirited young law student kicking up his heels in Chicago, away from home for the first time in his life. But then of course there had been Nell. A marriage that had seemed so lucky to Marianna, so exactly right; and that had, in the end, gone so tragically wrong.

Don't think about it, she told herself; what good does it do, to stir up the old bitterness and shock? (Pearl Jacobs. Maybe she should have been prepared, after Win's early lapses in taste. But she hadn't been. She had never dreamed that Win would actually … Pearl Jacobs Covey. The name still stuck in her throat.) Above all, don't think about the heartbreaking riddle of Win's stabbing himself. Evan is home where he belongs; everything is going to be all right, now that Evan's home again.

What a desolate sound the wind made, whimpering around the bay window! It always did that; she could remember it from her childhood, it meant nothing, nothing except that a storm was brewing. There. Another flash of lightning. Quite sharp this time; the telephone on the hall piece let out a short, apprehensive jangle.

But then it rang again. Instantly she thought of Evan. An accident; he and Norma had gone to the dance in the Schaefers' car, and he wasn't used to driving it. Or maybe he drank too much nowadays, Win used to, sometimes …

"Hello," she said into the phone. Her voice was so matter-of-fact that it startled her.

"Marianna?" It was Pearl. She sounded as if she had been running. "Marianna, can you come over? It's Win. He's—" She did not catch the rest. Her ear denied what it had heard; and she said calmly, Of course, they would be right over.

The telephone (there was an extension in their bedroom) had awakened Ralph. He met her on the stair landing, and she was aware, in a numb way, of his steadfast arm around her shoulders. He must have listened in. But she told him, anyway. "It's Win. Something's happened to Win."

Win's house was ablaze with lights, and there were cars in the driveway. Pearl's. And the Schaefers'—Marianna saw Evan and Norma and Little Harriet running up the walk. Inside, Pearl was standing at the hall telephone. In a white sleeveless dress and frivolous, scarlet slippers. With her hair pulled back in the chignon that gave her face such a peculiarly exposed look. As she put down the phone she turned on Little Harriet, and her voice was hard.

"Well, it's about time you showed up! Haven't I told you, over and over again, not to leave him alone? And now look what's happened! I might have known—"

"She found him first, Pearl," said Evan. "Don't waste time blaming anybody. Get Dr. Morrison over here before it's too late."

"I've already called him." Pearl closed her eyes for a moment, and caught her lower lip between her teeth. "But it's too late. Nobody can help. It's too late, I know it."

Again Marianna's ears denied what they heard. With no effort; after all, what did Pearl know about Win and whether or not he could be helped? Of course it was not too late. She lifted her head resolutely and put her arm through Evan's. Together they walked into the study.

Win was sitting at his desk, his head thrown back in stiff finality, his arms hanging straight down on either side. He had on his pajamas and a light cotton robe. The gun lay on the floor beside him, and there was a small, dark hole in his right temple. And Marianna's eyes—crueler, more honest than her ears—would not deny what they saw: Win had gone away. Beyond any help; forever out of reach of her love and worry and anxious pride. It was all worthless. It had not saved him.

"There, Mama," whispered Evan. "Don't—"

"I won't. I'm all right." What steadied her (though of course she had no intention of collapsing in public anyway) was the expression in Evan's eyes—grief, mixed with a bewildered, childish look of betrayal. As if something had caved in for him too. She remembered what he had told her about his talk with Win. Don't fret, Win had said to him, lightning never strikes in the same place twice …

There was Little Harriet, too. Poor child. Dazed. And sticking close to Evan. Not touching him, just standing close to him. No, of course Marianna was not going to collapse.

They got back to the living room just in time to see the doctor coming in the front door. Billy Morrison, who had grown up with her and Win, and who looked now—as he had looked when he was a boy—like a walking skeleton. They waited in the living room while he made his examination. Covey came, too— Had Pearl called him? Or maybe Ralph—anyway, there he was, subdued and rumpled, helplessly hovering near the sofa where Marianna sat between Ralph and Evan. Little Harriet perched on the sofa arm.

Pearl was across the room from them, by herself. After a moment Norma, who had been standing by the window, at a discreet distance from everybody, went over and patted her shoulder.

It didn't take the doctor long. He closed the study door very quietly behind him. "Can't tell you how bad I feel about this, Marianna," he said. His bony face looked sad and old. "Plain enough what happened, I guess. I've called the sheriff. He'll be right over. He'll have to ask a few routine questions, and I'll have to make out my report as coroner." (It jolted Marianna. But of course Billy was right. No getting out of it this time. No glossing it over as an "accident." This too must be endured.) Billy was going on, asking if Win had left a note, and almost before he got the question out of his mouth Little Harriet spoke up.

"No. There wasn't any note. I found him. I heard this bang, like a shot, and then I came downstairs and if there had been any note I'd have seen it. So—"

"You found him, honey?" The doctor inclined his cadaverous length toward her. "I see. You got downstairs to the study ahead of your mother and—"

"First I looked in Daddy's bedroom." Little Harriet's eyes flicked toward her mother, and away again. "He wasn't there. But then I saw there was a light downstairs. I came down, and—and I didn't know what to do. Finally I thought of Evan, and I took Daddy's car and went to find him. I went to the club first, only the dance was over, so I went to The Spot, and he was there."

"But didn't she call you, Mrs. Covey?" asked the doctor. "Didn't you hear the shot, too?"

"No," said Pearl. "I wasn't here." She faced them without turning a hair. Well, she had been doing it for years, ever since the day Win married her. "It was so hot I couldn't sleep. Win was asleep, or I thought he was, and Harriet was here, upstairs in her room. I took my car and went for a long ride, trying to cool off."

She didn't expect them to believe it. All the same, there it was. (*Where was she?* thought Marianna. And in the same instant, *No. I don't want to know*.) After a moment of dead silence, Pearl went on. "I must have gotten back just a few minutes after Harriet left to find Evan. When I saw Win's car wasn't in the garage I thought she'd taken it and sneaked off somewhere. The front door was open, and all the lights on, so I knew something was wrong—"

There was another silence, broken only by a high whining from the basement, where Buster must be shut up, worrying her heart out.

Then the doorbell rang, and in came Sheriff Novak, a beefy, moonfaced young man who had obviously been awakened out of a sound sleep. With an apologetic air, as if he were intruding (and indeed he was, in Marianna's opinion) he followed the doctor into the study; their voices reached the living room in a discreet murmur.

When they came back, the sheriff cleared his throat and said, "There's one other thing. Uh. The gun."

It had not registered in her mind before. Now it did, with a vengeance. "I can't understand why you'd have such a thing in the house, Pearl," she said bluntly. "After what happened before. If I'd had any idea—"

"I didn't have any such thing in the house," snapped Pearl. "I've got that much sense. I don't know any more about it than you do."

"Well, he didn't just pluck it out of the blue. Win never owned a gun in his life, and he hasn't been out of the house for a month. It's beyond me how he could get hold of a gun without somebody knowing it."

Ralph cleared his throat. "Now, Marianna," he said mildly. "Take it easy. I wouldn't want to swear to anything yet, but that gun looked real familiar to me. Wouldn't surprise me a bit if it turns out to be my target pistol. My .22."

"Your gun! Why, Ralph, how could—" But at that moment her eye chanced to fall on Little Harriet, roosting there beside Evan like some outlandish bird, rigid with tension. Evan was looking up at her, too. Very thoughtfully.

"What about you, Harriet?" he asked. "Do you know where he got the gun?"

"Who, me?" But her face turned red; suddenly she jumped up. "All right, so I got it! It was me. I stole it from Uncle Ralph a week ago!"

"You!" Pearl streaked across the room; her hand smacked against Little Harriet's cheek. "My God, how dumb can you get! You knew what he'd do with it. Oh, I could—"

"You keep your hands off me! Don't you dare touch me! You didn't care what happened to him!" For a ghastly moment their voices snarled together, mother and daughter screeching recriminations at each other. Two alley cats fighting. In Win's house. With Win lying dead in the next room.

Evan stopped them. Marianna didn't know just how. But he did it. Those unbridled voices ceased. All at once Pearl was back in her chair, breathing hard but otherwise composed, and Little Harriet was huddled in the corner of the sofa with her face in her hands. Everybody else was standing up. Which was rather odd: Marianna had no recollection of getting to her feet.

"Now, honey," murmured the doctor. "Let's calm down. Don't cry, honey."

But Little Harriet was not crying. When she lifted her head Marianna saw that her eyes, tearless and smoldering, were fixed on Evan in fierce appeal. "I did it to protect him," she said. "I was the only one that knew somebody was trying to kill him—"

"*What?*" gasped Marianna. It was as if someone had hit her in the stomach.

"They were. I don't care what you all say. He didn't try to kill himself. He didn't. My Daddy wouldn't." Her voice grew shrill; she made her hands into fists and beat them on her knobby knees. "You all kept saying— The other time, and this time too. But it's not true! I don't believe it! I won't, I won't, I *won't* believe it!"

Her eyes were still fastened on Evan. He said gently, "But Harriet, you can't just say that, without any reason. Besides, if it had been somebody else, that other time, he'd have said so. Don't you see that? He wouldn't have told us he did it himself if it wasn't true."

"Of course he wouldn't," said Pearl scornfully. "I never heard anything so crazy in my life. She's just making this up because she knows she's to blame for stealing that gun and letting him have it. I can't help it, I should think even a five-year-old would have better sense—"

"Pearl," said Marianna. Not loudly. All the same, Pearl withered into silence. "I should think even you would have better sense than to talk to the child like that. Maybe she did the wrong thing, but at least she did it for the right reason, because she loved Win."

"And I didn't. Is that what you mean? I'd like to know why the hell you think I've put up with what I have for the last seventeen years." Pearl gave an ugly laugh. "Oh, I knew we'd get around to this. I knew you'd wind up putting the blame on me."

There was only one way to deal with trash. Turn your back on it. Marianna did so. "I hope you'll excuse us, Billy," she said. "You too, Mr. Novak. None of this has anything to do with the gun."

"I stole it to protect him!" cried Little Harriet. "I know how to shoot— you showed me, Uncle Ralph—and I thought if they tried again I'd have the gun, I could kill them first. Daddy knew that was why. I wasn't going to tell him, only he caught me hiding it, so then I had to tell him. And he said it might not be a bad idea, at that, only let's keep it downstairs in his desk instead of in my room, I was going to hide it in my record player, under the turntable … He was *glad* I'd thought of it. He knew that was why, because I didn't want them to kill him!"

Marianna felt her heart sink. Oh Win, she thought, how could you? To take advantage of the poor child, just because she had this crazy idea …

"He'd have left me a note!" Little Harriet was shrilling once more. She looked around at the circle of faces turned toward her, mostly pitying, all incredulous. It came out in a desperate rush: "And—and there was someone here tonight! I heard them, before the shot. Voices. Talking. Somebody was here, talking to Daddy."

A crude, wild bid for attention? If so, it succeeded—at least with Sheriff Novak. His round eyes grew rounder. "What's that? Somebody was here? Who?"

"I don't know." Again that flick of a glance toward her mother. "But I know there was somebody. I heard them talking—"

"Quarreling?"

"Oh, for heaven's sake!" cried Pearl. "Can't you see she's just showing off? Of course nobody was here!"

But somebody had been. The realization brought Marianna bolt upright. She had clean forgotten, until this instant. One of those queer tricks your mind sometimes played on you. Little Harriet wasn't lying; who should know better than Marianna? Well, no harm done. She could straighten it out in no time.

"Excuse me, Pearl," she said, "but Little Harriet isn't just showing off. I happen to know that Nell—"

It was the strangest thing, the way Ralph and Evan and Covey were looking at her. Billy Morrison, too. What had she said that was so appalling? The plain truth: Nell had been here, no reason on earth to keep it a secret any longer. If Pearl didn't like it she could lump it.

As a matter of fact, Pearl was looking remarkably pleased. "Nell was here? Well! Isn't that interesting!"

Sheriff Novak seemed to think so. Only he wasn't quite sure who Nell was. The doctor told him, rather irritably. Win's wife. Former wife. The first Mrs. Covey.

"Oh," said Sheriff Novak. "His ex-wife. What was she doing here?"

A simple-minded question, if Marianna ever heard one. "What was she doing here? Why, she was visiting Win, of course. They've always been good friends, and she hadn't seen him since his—his accident. Personally, I didn't see any reason why she shouldn't, but—"

"Well, I did," Pearl put in. "After all, it's my house. I ought to have some say about who comes here and who doesn't."

Marianna did not argue the point. She ignored it. "Nell asked me to help her and Win arrange it, and I did. He called me tonight, while Nell was at our house, and she came right over. In Griffiths' car. She'd borrowed it to drive into town." They must call Nell, she was thinking. Should have done it before now. She dreaded it; Nell was sure to make a scene …

"What time was this?" the sheriff was asking.

"Why, let me see. Quite late. Nell was getting ready to leave, anyway. It must have been after midnight."

"So she was the last one to see Mr. Covey alive."

"I guess so. What of it?"

To her astonishment, Sheriff Novak blushed like a schoolboy. "Well, uh, Mrs. Hoyt, what I mean is, you see how it is. Here's the kid, claims somebody was trying to kill her father, he didn't commit suicide, and you've got to admit he didn't leave a note, and—uh—"

"You're not for a minute suggesting that Nell *shot* him!" He ducked his head miserably. "Nonsense! She was devoted to him. Everybody knows that. Really, Mr. Novak, I'm surprised at you. I'd never have mentioned that Nell was here if I'd had any idea you were going to take this attitude."

Evan cleared his throat. "We live and learn, Mama. The sheriff's only trying to do his duty. He doesn't know Aunt Nell the way we do, or he'd see how absurd—"

"Of course it's absurd," said the doctor. "Aside from everything else, it was obviously suicide. You saw that yourself. No signs of a struggle. Win had the gun in his desk. He wouldn't just sit there and let somebody shoot him without a murmur. So he didn't leave Little Harriet a note— what of it? He didn't leave a note the first time, either. Don't you know a hysterical child when you see one?"

"I am not!" shrieked Little Harriet. "You don't want to believe it, so you won't even *listen* to me. I was the only one that knew they were trying to kill him—"

"Who? Did he tell you who?" asked the sheriff, and the question rocked Little Harriet into momentary silence. Then she turned on him sullenly.

"Why should I tell you? You don't believe anything I say, anyway."

It was typical of her. Born contrary. And for once Marianna was glad of it. Surely, now, the sheriff would see what was so distressingly clear to the rest of them: Little Harriet had nothing whatever to tell; she was making a last, fanatic stand for a cause that could never have had any basis except in her own mind. She *had* to believe in murder, instead of suicide. Not to believe in it would make her, in her own eyes, guilty of Win's death. Marianna's throat ached with pity.

It was impossible to tell, from the sheriff's face, what he saw or didn't see. His expression was one of blank helplessness. But he seemed to be a very stubborn young man. "I never said I didn't believe you. I just asked— Well, now look. Let's leave that part of it lay for now. I know you folks are all upset, only natural, but like Mr. Hoyt said, I've got to do my duty, and— Well, seems to me I ought to have a talk with Nell, the other Mrs. Covey, being's she was the last one to see him. That way we'll have the record straight. You see how it is." He glanced apologetically around the room.

Billy Morrison was the first one to speak. "Far be it from me to try to stop a man that's hell-bent on doing his duty. If you want to get Nell over here and ask her whether she shot Win, go right ahead. I'll tell you one thing, though, you're letting yourself in for more than you realize. If you think these folks are upset, wait till you see Nell." He began fussing in his little black bag. "In the meantime, I'm going to give Little Harriet here something to quiet her down …"

Not, apparently, if Little Harriet had anything to say about it. She screamed that she didn't *want* to be quieted down. She knocked the doctor's outstretched hand aside. She blazed out, even at Evan: "You're just like the rest of them. You're against me too. I thought you were different, I thought you'd see. But you don't believe me either …" When he went after her—she had headed for the stairs at her awkward shambling lope—and put his arms around her, she tried frantically to wriggle free.

And somehow, in the course of that ludicrous hassle, the note slipped out from inside her blouse, where she must have tucked it, next to her heart. She made one futile grab, as Evan bent to retrieve it. Then she clamped her hands on to the newel post and waited, wordless and motionless as a stone.

"What's this?" he said …

It was Win's suicide note. The creamy, engraved stationery with tonight's date at the top; the bold black strokes of Win's handwriting; the characteristic phrases—all unmistakably his, and all proof beyond any doubt of Little Harriet's piteous lie. It seemed to Marianna, as she held the sheet of paper in her hand, that the ache in her throat was past bearing, in another minute she must cry out ignominiously. Because Win's note held no message, no word of explanation except what they already knew: he loved Little Harriet, and he had made up his mind to die. "No use trying to explain why. It's complicated, and not very interesting, and nothing to do with you. Anyway you look at it, it's all my own doing. Don't let them blame you about the gun—I'd have found another way. You be good now, Skeeter, and be happy, and remember I love you …"

Through a haze of pain she heard the sheriff's voice—hushed, and also very relieved—saying, Well, he guessed this settled it, he'd be pushing off unless Doc wanted him to … Sorry he'd had to put them through all this. Real sorry about Mr. Covey. Anything he could do, don't hesitate …

Then there was Ralph saying, "I'm taking you home, Marianna." For a minute she hid her face against his shoulder, and after that she could bear it again.

One other thing registered with her. Little Harriet, still stony-faced and wordless, held out her hand, and Evan gave her Win's note and clasped his hand over hers. As if he were sealing a compact. What was he saying to her? Marianna thought she caught the words "Tomorrow morning."

Somebody opened the front door. Ralph let her out, into a gust of wind and rain.

Six

At ten o'clock in the morning Evan gave up trying to sleep and crept down to the kitchen for coffee. The hot spell had broken with last night's thunderstorm; a gentle, soaking rain was falling like a benediction. Dad, who had beaten Evan to it and already had the coffee going, said it was just what they needed. It would save the corn. He was always afraid of hail, with these long stretches of hot wind, but this was great, couldn't be better.

"I didn't think you were up yet," said Evan. "Is Mama awake too?"

"Awake, but I talked her into staying in bed and trying to rest." He was fussing with a tray; Evan saw that he had made cinnamon toast, very crisp, the way Mama liked it, and had laid out her favorite teaspoon and the miniature crystal cream pitcher that had been a traditional feature of invalid trays ever since Evan could remember. "She's not going to get over this in a hurry," Dad said quietly, before he picked up his little offering of comfort and went out through the swinging door. His own handsome face was lined with fatigue, his shoulders a shade less straight, it seemed to Evan.

He poured himself a cup of coffee and sat down at the table beside the window. Outside the lilac bush trembled slightly under the steady drip of rain; a cheerful-looking robin splashed in a puddle beside the driveway.

Oh lord, thought Evan, there would be Aunt Nell to cope with today, and all the dreary business of funeral arrangements, and the flood of condolences from shocked friends. But first of all there was Little Harriet.

She haunted him. The way she had looked when he first caught sight of her at The Spot last night, so scrawny and lonesome, craning her neck toward the dance floor, trying to find him. But when he started toward her she took a step backward and held her hands out in front of her, more as if to fend him off than to greet him. "Daddy's dead," she said, when he and Norma got her outside. She glared at him. "I don't know what to do. He's dead." (How could she be so sure? He had fumed at her for not having called the doctor first, had clung to the notion that Uncle Win might be lying there wounded while she kited around the countryside looking for Evan instead of … Not until he walked into the study with Mama and saw for himself had he understood how she could be so sure.)

There were other, even more haunting bits. Hysterical or not, she had seemed to him oddly convincing. Or was it only that he *wanted* to side with her? Not because he particularly liked the kid, but because she sparked in him the old, youthful impulse to rebel against—well, against the self-assurance of the Hoyt-Covey clan. (He had felt stung, almost outraged, when she turned on him and accused him of being "just like the rest of them.") The impulse to rebel. It had possessed him all through his own stormy adolescence. He knew how it felt to scream his head off and still not convince anybody; he recognized Little Harriet's rage as his own.

Of course she had been lying all the time. There was Uncle Win's suicide note to prove it.

Even he could not take her murder story seriously after that. But he could show her that he was not "just like the rest of them;" he could stick with her in spite of the lie—such a forlorn, understandable sort of a lie— if only because she had no one else, now that Uncle Win was gone. There was one other reason why he was going to keep his promise to her and see her this morning. Last night he would have sworn she was not telling *all* of her story. The ghost of that impression still flitted through his mind.

It turned out that Dad, in his unassuming way, had already begun dealing with some of the tiresome details that today was sure to hold. "I've talked to Nell," he told Evan, when he came back to the kitchen. He sat down at the table with a cup of coffee, too. "I'm going out to Griffiths' after her. She insists on coming in, and Marianna seems to want her, so I guess it's all right. Of course she went all to pieces—you know Nell—but maybe the worst will be over by the time I get her in here. Thank God Win's note turned up when it did last night. Otherwise she'd have blown the roof off." He paused, smiling a little. "I love your mother dearly, but there are times when I have considered buying her a muzzle, and last night was one of them. There was no earthly reason why the sheriff had to know anything about Nell's visit to Win."

None whatever. Except that Mama was—as Little Harriet had said— terribly innocent. Supremely unaware of anybody else's point of view. "Oh well," said Evan, "it turned out all right. Did you tell Aunt Nell about Little Harriet and the gun?"

"Couldn't get out of it. She said what else could you expect from riffraff like Harriet and Pearl … Of course Pearl's the one she blames most. She's at the bottom of everything, in Nell's opinion." There was a speculative look in Dad's eye, as if he were wondering just how much gossip Evan had heard.

"I know," Evan assured him. "She doesn't make any more sense than Little Harriet, you know. Claims Uncle Win knew the gossip about Pearl and wasn't seriously worried about it. But that doesn't keep her from blaming Pearl. She's going to have it both ways, no matter what."

Dad nodded. "If you want to get technical, I'm the one that's to blame for that gun business. I shouldn't have left it there in the cabinet—you know where I always keep it—where anybody could get at it. If only I'd noticed in time that it was missing, but it never occurred to me—"

"What's the difference? He'd have found some other way. He said so, in his note. Don't you start a guilt complex. We've already got Little Harriet's. That's enough for any family."

"She's such a prickly kid. Hard to get next to. Win was the only one that could ever do anything with her." Dad sighed. Then he glanced at the clock and stood up. "Well, it's time I got going. Lots of things to see to. Tell you what, Evan. Win's car is still out there at The Spot, where Little Harriet left it when she went looking for you. I've got the keys. Why don't I drop you off there on my way out to Griffiths' and you can drive it back for Pearl?"

Evan jumped at it. Here was what he wanted—a chance to keep his promise to Little Harriet. Somehow or other they could get away from Pearl long enough for a private talk. For whatever it was worth. At least he would have discharged his duty, made his sentimental, comradely gesture toward the spirit of youthful rebellion. Quite likely a farewell gesture; it was time he turned into an adult.

Though, on the way out to The Spot, he did not feel at all like an adult. Some chance combination of circumstances revived in him a feeling he had often had in his boyhood, a feeling that Dad—this soft-spoken, affectionate, apparently understanding father of his—was a stranger to him, someone he could never really know. Perhaps it had its roots in jealousy; perhaps in a certain delicate reticence that was part of Dad's personality. But there it was: an insurmountable barrier between Evan the boy and Dad the man. He made an effort to break through it. "Dad," he said, "have you any idea why Uncle Win did it? I suppose it shouldn't make any difference—he's gone, anyway—but somehow it wouldn't seem quite so bad if I could understand why."

"I know how you feel." (But Evan doubted it. Why should Dad know any more about him than he knew about Dad?) "But I'm blessed if I can understand it, any more than you or anybody else." He did not look at

Evan; his finely cut profile remained silhouetted, inscrutable and remote, against the rain-washed car window. "It's just one of those things. We'll never know now."

The windshield wiper switched and sighed, switched and sighed. Then they were at The Spot; Evan turned up his coat collar and opened the door. "See you later," they said, and they smiled at each other hopelessly, across the barrier.

There was one other car parked in front of The Spot. A flashy, cream-colored convertible. Three guesses whose, thought Evan, settling himself behind the wheel of Uncle Win's conservative gray model. And sure enough, before he could pull out, the door of The Spot opened and here came Stanley, cinching up the belt of his trench coat on his way to the convertible. What surprised Evan was that the fellow came over and spoke to him.

"You're Evan Hoyt, I think? Stanley Wolinewski." (Or something like that.) "Pleased to meet you." He spoke with a faint accent, a barely perceptible thickening of consonants. Raindrops glistened on his vigorous black hair. Familiar? Reminiscent? Of course not; where would Evan ever have met him before? He puckered his forehead in an expression that Evan took at first for a scowl and then realized might be intended to convey sympathy. "Very sorry to hear about your uncle, Mr. Covey. A terrible thing." And Stanley showed his teeth. A smile or a sneer; take your choice. Evan showed his, too. He stepped on the starter.

But he was no match for Stanley and his effrontery. "Give Mrs. Covey my sympathy, will you?" Still showing his teeth, he lifted one thick-fingered hand in a gesture of goodbye or—it was entirely possible—of dismissal.

Evan saw Pearl just long enough, and he was feeling just sore enough, to deliver that message from Stanley. She was ready to leave—for the undertakers, she said—when she opened the door to him. She looked as naked in her shiny plastic raincoat as in any other garment she put on; her face, too, looked naked, Evan thought. Pale, smooth, and antiseptic, like a face sculptured out of soap.

She blinked a little at his mention of Stanley. And her hand, with its long red nails and diamond-studded wedding band, made a quick outward thrust, involuntary and instantly suppressed. But that was all.

"Thanks for bringing the car back," she said. No, there was nothing else he could do this morning. "Thanks, anyway. My folks are driving over this afternoon. They'll take care of things."

Evan didn't argue with her. But, he thought, Mama would have something to say about how much care the Jacobs tribe took of things.

Pearl's father and brothers, when they could spare the time from drinking, ran a shiftless kind of dray business in a little town forty miles away. Her mother took in roomers. Disreputable roomers, it was reported. One of the brothers had carved out quite a career for himself as a chicken thief. If Pearl thought she was going to turn Uncle Win's funeral over to that bunch of dirty, sticky-fingered, no-account …

"Hi," said a strangled-sounding voice from the doorway, and there stood Little Harriet, with half a candy bar in her hand and the other half in her mouth. She had on a bedraggled pink negligee with marabou trimming. She swallowed—graphically, like an ostrich—said, "Come on in," and stuffed the rest of the candy bar into her mouth. It was a chocolate candy bar.

"Don't let me interrupt your breakfast," said Evan.

"Come on. Have a cup of coffee." Licking her fingers, she led him into the kitchen. It was even more immaculate than the rest of Pearl's house. A sterilized surgery of a kitchen.

Little Harriet waited until she heard the front door close behind Pearl. Then she said, "I didn't think you'd come." She turned quickly toward the stove. But not quickly enough; Evan saw that her eyes had filled, suddenly, with tears.

"I don't know why not. And if you ask me, I timed things perfectly. Very shrewd of me to get here just as your mother was taking off. Or maybe I've got it figured wrong. Maybe you wanted her in on this private conference."

"Jesus Christ, no," said Little Harriet. She slopped some coffee into a cup from the electric percolator and shoved it across the table to him. "The rest of them are bad enough, but she's— You know what she's going to do? She said she's going to get rid of Buster!"

It seemed rather an anti-climax to Evan, but he tried to look suitably shocked.

"Well, she'll have to get rid of me too," Little Harriet went on passionately. "I'll hide Buster some place, I'll run away with her, I'll even give her to you to keep Mother from—"

"Okay. I'll take her home with me if you want me to. Look, Little Harriet, we haven't got all day. I didn't come over here to discuss Buster's future with you."

"So that's the way you feel about it. Nobody asked you to come. Why did you?"

"Because I'm not sure you told everything you know last night," snapped Evan. "I don't know what you're holding back, and I don't know why. It's also possible that all I'll get out of you is another pack of lies, like the one about the note, and if that's what you've got in mind, damn it—"

"You don't have to swear at me," said Little Harriet mildly. She sat down across from him and propped her chin in her hands. Her eyes shifted away from his. "Certainly I held something back last night. You don't think I'd tell them, do you? With her standing right there, and all of them waiting for a chance to jump on her and tear her to pieces, just because they think they're so superior, so much better than she is—"

"Make up your mind, will you? If you mean your mother, are you for her or against her? Or scared of her? Or what?"

Little Harriet wailed out what he recognized as the truth: "I don't know! She's just as good as they are, I don't care if she isn't a Covey! Only she didn't have to slap me, and—and Buster—" She unpropped her chin, put her head down on the kitchen table, and went through the motions of weeping. Evan suspected that part of it was sham.

Not all of it, though. He gave her shoulder blade a little pat. "Don't cry. They're not here now. You don't need to be afraid to tell me. Just what did you hear last night, before the shot?"

"Voices. Talking. I hadn't heard Daddy go downstairs, I thought he was still in his bedroom. But he wasn't. I heard him say, 'Don't be silly. Why should I hate you?'"

Evan repeated it to himself, testing its flavor. "He said that to Aunt Nell? He must have. Go on. What else?"

"I didn't know about Aunt Nell. I thought—" She gulped. "I'd already heard Mother leave, before I went to sleep, and I thought it was her coming back. I thought she'd brought *him* back with her."

After a minute Evan said, "You mean Stanley. You think she went out to meet Stanley last night?"

"Sure. So does everybody else. Even Aunt Marianna didn't believe that dopey story she told about going out for a ride to get cooled off. She sneaks out to see Stanley all the time. They go up to his lodge in the hills. I followed her once."

"My God," said Evan. "Does— Did Uncle Win know about Stanley?"

Little Harriet's eyes hardened. "I never told him. She was scared I would. I could tell the way she'd look at me, and at first I was going to. But then I changed my mind because I—" Something flared in her angular, unprepossessing face. "It isn't fair, the way Daddy treats her! Used to treat her, I mean. Like she wasn't really a person. Like she was just something kind of handy to have around— Why did he marry her, if that's the way he felt about her?"

Evan shifted uneasily in his chair. "To get back to last night. Do you know what time it was when you heard these noises downstairs?"

Yes, she did know; she had looked at her little clock, and it was twenty minutes past one. "I listened at my door for a while." (He had a sharp picture of her, listening, sweating with anxiety, shaking with the violent half-loves and half-hates that rent her.) "I didn't know what to do. All I heard was Daddy saying that about Don't be silly, and a door closing. I couldn't tell whether they were still there or not. Finally I went into Daddy's bedroom to turn off the fan, and that's when I heard the shot—"

And this was all she had to tell? Evan felt at once relieved and let down. "It's plain enough now. You just jumped to the wrong conclusions. It wasn't your mother and Stanley you heard downstairs. It was Aunt Nell. Let's see, twenty past one … She must have been leaving, you heard the door closing after her. Uncle Win went back to the study and wrote his note to you—"

"You don't need to rub it in. I knew if I showed the note to everybody it would be just like the first time, they'd say it was suicide."

"But that's what it was," Evan pointed out patiently.

"It was not! Maybe this time, but not the first time. Daddy didn't stab himself! He'd have told me, he never lied to me, he'd have left me a note …"

Well, maybe he had. What was to prevent her from hiding a first note, as she had tried to do with last night's? Evan did not have the heart to say it, but he could not help thinking it.

She was going on passionately: "He lied to everybody else, but not to me. I was the only one that knew. It was our secret. He said I mustn't worry, they wouldn't come back, and so I promised not to tell anybody."

"You did tell me, though. The other night on the sleeping porch."

She flushed with shame. "I was so scared. I couldn't help it, I was so scared they'd come back. He said they wouldn't, and I had stolen Uncle Ralph's gun for him, but all the same—"

"Did he ever tell you who 'they' were?"

"He didn't tell me anything except what I knew from the start—that he didn't stab himself." Her voice quavered. "He kept calling it 'our' secret, but I guess—I guess it wasn't very much mine."

"Who do you think it was?" But she would not answer him; she kept her eyes lowered and gave an incongruously casual shrug. "Little Harriet, we're not going to get any place if you hold out on me. If you think it was your mother, you must—"

"Of course I don't think it was my mother. She wasn't here that night. She wasn't even in town. My grandmother Jacobs was sick, and Mother drove over there to stay all night and look after her."

"Well, who was here? Who *could* it have been?"

"They played bridge. Like they did lots of Saturday nights. Daddy and Uncle Ralph and Doc Morrison and Homer Nelsen. Of course they weren't here when it happened. They'd gone home a couple of hours before. So had Rita—"

"Rita?"

"She was working for us then. She stayed late to fix lunch for them, and then she had to wash everything up afterwards. Mother would have had a fit otherwise. She can't stand it if you leave one little old *glass* in the sink overnight. They were all still here when I got home from the movies. I watched them play a couple of hands, and then I— No, wait. The phone rang, and Daddy went into the study to answer it."

"Somebody called him up? Who?"

"He said it was a wrong number. But it took quite a while, for just a wrong number. And when he came back again he looked kind of—I don't know, kind of surprised. After that I went upstairs to bed."

"But you woke up later. Did you hear something that woke you up?"

She hesitated—sorely tempted, Evan suspected, toward fabrication. He gave her a forbidding look, and she shook her head reluctantly. "I was hungry. That's why I woke up. I was starving to death. So I went downstairs for a candy bar. The light was still on in the study, and I heard this funny noise, like a moan, and—" She put her knuckles up to her mouth. "Everybody kept asking him what happened, and at first he said it was an accident. That didn't shut them up, so then he said he did it himself. They were dopey enough to believe him, but I knew it was somebody else. I told him so, and he said—"

"Go on. Tell me exactly."

"He said, 'What makes you think that? Did Rita— Or no. It must be the knife. You must have seen it. Is that it?'"

Something prickled along the back of Evan's neck. He said, "Well, of course you saw the knife. It was right there. Wasn't it?"

"Sure. That's what I told him. And he said, 'It doesn't mean anything, you know. I lost it—I thought I lost it years ago. I hadn't lost it at all. It must have been there all the time. I'd simply overlooked it.' I said, what do you mean you thought you lost it? It's always been right there in your desk, Grandpa's old hunting knife." She was aware that she had caught Evan's attention; she paused for effect. "And he said, 'Oh. That knife.'"

"But there wasn't any other knife! That was the only one. What was he talking about?" She shook her head mutely. "Rita. You said he mentioned Rita?"

"I asked her—in a roundabout way, you know, because I'd already promised Daddy to keep it a secret—but she doesn't know anything about it, either. Get right down to it, Rita doesn't know much of anything about anything. You can't help liking her, but she's dumb as they come. She finished washing up about one thirty and said goodnight to

Daddy—everybody else was gone, and he was in the study reading—and that's all she knows."

There was a longish silence. "So the only real thing we've got to go on," Evan said at last, "is the business about the knife."

"What do you mean that's the only real thing? He admitted to me that it wasn't an accident or suicide."

She had brought the subject up first, though. There was always the possibility that Uncle Win had seen his chance and capitalized on her unshakable conviction that he would not, could not, have attempted suicide.

As if she had read his mind, Little Harriet said, with quiet despair, "You don't believe me either. You think I'm just making it up."

"No. No, I don't think that." Surely, if she had set out to spin a tale from whole cloth, she would have concocted something more lurid and glib. As it was, he couldn't quite disregard what she had told him. What in the hell *could* he do with it? There was no refuting Uncle Win's note: he had, in the end, killed himself. You couldn't start a murder investigation without a murder. "If somebody stabbed Uncle Win, I want to know who and why. It's just that—"

"So do I. And when I find out I'm going to kill them," said Little Harriet matter-of-factly. But there was something forlorn and childish about the way she caught hold of Evan's arm when he started to leave. "Evan. Can I go home with you? Please?" He must have looked surprised, because she went on hurriedly. "It's all those Jacobs relatives. They're coming this afternoon and—and I can't stand my grandfather Jacobs. Daddy couldn't stand any of them, either. I don't see why Mother has to have them here."

Spoken like a true Covey. Evan had a feeling, though, that her disdainful air was a front for—what? Fear? Was she scared to be alone with Pearl?

"Okay," he said. "I'll take you and Buster both home with me. Only you've got to get out of that damn pink feather rig first. It's—"

"It's a stunning negligee. Daddy gave it to me for my birthday. It's got real lure."

"Sure. That's what I mean." He gave her a little push toward the stairs. "I don't trust myself. It brings out the beast in me. Hurry up, let's get going."

Seven

Uncle Win's funeral, which took place on Monday afternoon, was an extremely quiet affair. There was no pretending, this time, that what had happened to him was an accident, though the Fontenelle *Gazette* chose to report, without further elaboration, that he had been "found dead" in his study. But everybody knew what the sheriff's findings and the coroner's report had said. Suicide. Ah! What opportunities for dark, rich conjecture, for the chewing over of old and present gossip!

Mama could not protect Uncle Win from the wagging tongues, but she could, and did, close the doors against prying eyes and avid faces. He had never been a church-goer, so it was natural enough that the brief funeral services should be held at home—not in his own house, but in the one where he and Mama had grown up, which, though now officially "the Hoyt place," still symbolized the heart of the Covey family. Aunt Nell, who seemed part of the family, was there, and so were the Jacobs tribe, who did not. And there were a few, hand-picked friends of Uncle Win's—Dr. Morrison, Norma Schaefer's father, Homer Nelsen, who had been his law partner for so many years.

The only open display of emotion was provided by Pearl's mother, Old Lady Jacobs, who wept voluptuously throughout the proceedings. (This circumstance, thought Evan, would have tickled Uncle Win.) The Jacobs menfolk—besides Pearl's father, there were three brothers, not counting the chicken thief, who was unavoidably detained in the county jail—had been awed, either by Mama or by Pearl, into a state resembling sobriety. Pearl herself looked very chic in her black dress and hat. As chic, and as expressionless, as a mannequin in a store window. Beside her Little Harriet fidgeted and chewed her fingernails. Mama, who could not abide public demonstrations, sat erect, her homely, proud face drained by misery. And Aunt Nell, having already spent herself in storms of tears, was now playing the role of a woman whom grief has turned to stone. Perhaps it really had.

There was a rather curious splitting up when they drove back to town from the cemetery. Mama had given the Jacobses house room while the funeral was in progress—she could hardly do anything else—but they were not invited back afterwards. Nor would they ever be again, thought Evan, as long as Mama had breath in her body. She turned her back on them and rode home without so much as a word of farewell. And Little Harriet went with her. Evan had been wondering what she would do; she had stayed at the Hoyts' since yesterday morning, when she asked to go home with him. He watched, now, while she hesitated for a moment before she followed Mama to the car. Pearl was watching too; she did not reply when Little Harriet, with an embarrassed, over-casual flap of her hand, said, "'Bye, Mother. See you later." Nor did Pearl speak to Evan, who had driven her and her parents to the cemetery and now drove them home. Mrs. Jacobs turned off the tears, now that she no longer had an audience worth mentioning, and addressed genteel pleasantries about the weather to the back of Evan's head. When a person was "a little fleshy, like myself," she said—the understatement of the year—they felt the heat something terrible. Old Man Jacobs, not to be outdone, launched into an exhaustive comparison of this summer with last summer and the summer before that, and had worked his way back to "Now you take five years ago," by the time Evan pulled up in Uncle Win's driveway.

At this point Pearl surprised him by asking him in. He couldn't very well refuse. Besides, the invitation whetted his curiosity. Pearl wasn't inviting him out of sociability; he would bet on that. Maybe she was planning to light into him for luring Little Harriet away from home. The three Jacobs brothers had already reached the house, and were ensconced on the patio. Straight out of Tobacco Road. Pearl's parents followed her and Evan inside, where they sat down, expectantly, in the living room.

He found her attitude toward her family a bit puzzling. She seemed to get no particular comfort, or pleasure, from their presence; indeed, she paid very little attention to them, treating them with a kind of bored tolerance. And yet she had turned to them in her hour of trouble. Instinct? A gesture of defiance or malice toward the Coveys? It crossed his mind, too, that she might enjoy showing off her possessions—her expensive clothes, her fine house, her whole impressive way of life— might, in effect, be saying to the Jacobses, Look how far I've come up in the world; in spite of you, look where I am now.

"How about a drink, Pop?" she asked, and the old man's face lit up, under his scraggly moustache he licked his lips secretly. This was what he had been waiting for. So, apparently, had Mrs. Jacobs, though she achieved a touch of ladylike restraint. Well, she wouldn't say no, just a drop of something to settle her nerves …

"Come and help me tend bar, Evan," said Pearl, and as soon as the kitchen door swung shut behind them she turned to him with an accusing air. "All right, what did she tell you? I know Harriet. I know why she went home with you the other day and hasn't been back since. She isn't fooling me any. All of a sudden she's devoted to Buster. Ha! She doesn't care about Buster any more than I do. She's scared to come near me. She's been lying her head off about me, and she's scared I'll find it out."

"She's scared, all right," said Evan. "I'm not so sure she's lying."

"Oh, of course you'd believe her. She's Win's darling daughter. She can do no wrong." While she talked, her hands were busy setting out liquor and glasses. Now she took a tray of ice from the refrigerator and emptied it, expertly, into the ice bucket. There was something extraordinarily venomous in that combination of mechanical efficiency and unbridled speech. "Just don't forget. She's my daughter too, whether you and Marianna like it or not. You've got no right to turn her against me."

"Oh, stop it, Pearl. If she's turned against you it's not my doing, or Mama's, or anybody's but your own."

"So now we're getting it. The official Covey line, straight from headquarters. I never was a fit wife for Win. It has now been decreed that I'm not a fit mother for Harriet."

"Well," said Evan. "Are you? Here, I'll take that in." He marched out with the tray of drinks, feeling that for once he had scored.

The three Jacobs brothers could probably scent liquor a mile away on a windless day. They were still on the patio, but clustered at the door, like a bunch of hound dogs with their tongues hanging out. Without a word—he did not trust himself to speak—Evan offered the drinks, and without a word the Jacobses, one and all, accepted.

Pearl was ready for him when he got back to the kitchen. She was leaning against the sink, sipping her drink, with an air of controlled fury. "I'd like an explanation of that last crack of yours, if you don't mind," she said. "If it's not asking too much."

"I think you know very well that Little Harriet told me about your friend Stanley. Not that I hadn't already heard it, of course." He could not have explained what made him, in the next breath, change his tone so abruptly. He thought of Iris. He felt an acute distaste for the holier-than-thou role he was adopting. "Look, Pearl, I wish you'd get it out of your head that I'm blaming you. I'm not against you, even if I am part Covey. I don't give a damn about you and Stanley, really."

She did not believe it. Not a word of it. "'My friend Stanley,'" she burst out bitterly. "That's Fontenelle for you. Pass the time of day with somebody you're not married to, and the whole town's buzzing, they've got you sleeping together right on Main Street! I'm sick and tired of it. Just because I was the only one with the common decency to go to those parties he gave … Well, why shouldn't I? Do you think I don't know how it feels to have every two-bit snob in town snooting me? Do you think I'm ever going to forget—" She broke off as the door swung open, to reveal one of the Jacobs brothers, looking thirsty. "Here," she said. "Take the bottle."

He did so, with alacrity. When he was gone, she swept on fiercely. "And how do you think it feels to be married to somebody that treats you like you were nothing but a damn incubator? That's all I ever meant to Win. Three miscarriages before Little Harriet, and he wanted a son, so I wasn't even a success as an incubator! Because I couldn't have any more after her. It's a wonder to me he didn't divorce me and try somebody else. I wish he had! Oh God, I wish he had!" She gave a tearing sob. Evan had the feeling that she had forgotten he was there; he would have given a good deal not to be. Physical nakedness was one thing—Pearl always gave that effect, he was used to it—but he was too much Mama's son not to be repelled by such emotional nakedness. And yet a little too honest to deny that Uncle Win had indeed used Pearl—arrogantly and ruthlessly used her, as if she were not a human being but (Little Harriet's phrase came back to him) "just something kind of handy to have around."

"Little Harriet's more loyal to you than you think. It's true she told me about you and Stanley, but give her credit, she didn't blurt it out last night in front of everybody. She was trying to protect you—"

"*Protect* me!"

"She thought it was you she heard downstairs. You and Stanley. She had a pretty good idea you'd gone out to meet him, and when she heard voices downstairs she thought you'd brought him back here for some reason—"

"For *what* reason? Why on earth would we come back here?"

"She didn't stop to figure anything out. That's just what came into her head, and it scared her. I suppose she expected some kind of a row."

"A row. And then she heard the shot." Pearl's cold, light-colored eyes glittered. "Oh. I get it now. Don't try to tell me what a sweet loyal kid she is. All that business about hiding Win's note, trying to make out somebody killed him— She just wants to get me and Stanley arrested for murder, that's all. Protecting me! Ha!"

"Pearl! Listen to me—" But he might as well give up. No matter what he said, she would twist it to fit the pattern of her ingrained resentments. To her he was the enemy, and whatever he defended—even her own child—she automatically rejected. "Okay. You happen to be wrong, but have it your way. She didn't pull off her murder story, so what's the difference?"

"None. I just want to get the record straight on one point. Stanley wasn't anywhere near this house the other night." She added quickly, "Or any other night. It was your precious Nell, sneaking in here behind my back, and she'd have been in the soup but good if Win's note hadn't turned up when it did. I almost wish it hadn't."

"You'd have been in the soup, too, right along with Aunt Nell. Everything would have come out about you and Stanley."

"It's no secret, anyway. I know that. Marianna's probably the only person in town that hasn't heard it. Even Win—"

"So he knew it. Is that why he killed himself?"

"You think he'd kill himself over me? Don't be silly. I wasn't that important to him."

There was so much bitterness in her voice that Evan's mind took a startled leap back beyond last night to that other night a month ago, when, according to Little Harriet, "somebody" had stabbed Uncle Win. Supposing Pearl had not been looking after her sick mother, after all; but here at home, involved in a quarrel with Uncle Win. A strange, wrong-side-out quarrel in which she, the faithless wife, was goaded into fury because her husband did not care whether she was faithless or not, she was not that important to him … It might have seemed the final humiliation to her. She might have snatched up the knife and stabbed him out of sheer frustration. Would Uncle Win have covered up for her afterwards with his tale about an accident and a suicide attempt? It was conceivable, Evan supposed. But that he would lose his will to live and end by actually shooting himself— Never. A contradiction in terms.

"He mentioned another knife to Little Harriet. Not the one he was stabbed with. Another one. Do you know anything about that?"

Pearl finished her drink and turned to rinse out her glass at the sink. Over her shoulder she said, "Another knife? What are you talking about?"

He told her. She was drying the glass now, polishing it within an inch of its life. "It's the first I ever heard about another knife," she said when he was through. "Just something else Harriet made up. But go ahead, believe her if you want to. And you obviously do. You'd love to blame me, all of you. If I didn't murder Win outright, then I drove him to suicide."

"I told you before, I'm not blaming you. But something happened that made him decide he wanted to die. Didn't he ever even *mention* Stanley to you?"

She hesitated. "He mentioned him, yes. As if, in a roundabout way, he was trying to pump me about Stanley. But he never brought anything out in the open. It got to the point where I wished he would, just to get it over with. Once or twice I tried to do it myself—after all, I'm human, strange as it may seem to you, Win mattered to me too—but it wasn't any use. He shied off and played dumb, as if he hadn't the slightest idea what I was talking about."

A snide sort of cat-and-mouse game? It was not the reaction Evan would have expected from Uncle Win. But there it was. Unless Pearl was lying …

She seemed to brood for a moment. Then she gave Evan a singularly straight look. "Finally I decided the hell with it. I don't *care* anymore why he killed himself. I don't care about any of it anymore. I just want to get as far away from here as I can and never, never as long as I live, come back. No more Fontenelle. No more Coveys. I've had it."

Evan suddenly lost his temper. "Great," he said. "I suppose Stanley goes with you, and you live happily ever after on Uncle Win's money."

"All set with a cute little motive, aren't you? Well, for your information, there isn't anybody in Fontenelle that Stanley couldn't buy and sell several times over. One thing he doesn't need is Win's money."

Which was very likely true, he thought as he slammed out of the back door. (No more Jacobses for him. He'd had it.) But Uncle Win's position in what Goldie had called "the sacred inner circle of Fontenelle society"—ah, there was something different, something that Stanley might thirst after with all his soul.

The trouble with this particular cute little motive being that you couldn't steal a man's social standing by killing him, any more than you could buy your way in with champagne and caviar. You couldn't inherit it, either, the way you might inherit a man's widow. Particularly when the widow happened to be née Pearl Jacobs. And Stanley was too sharp an operator not to know it.

"Hey, Evan! Want a ride?"

He had been too lost in his own thoughts to notice what went on around him; now he looked up, startled, to see Homer Nelsen's neat coupe pulling up at the curb, and Homer himself leaning sidewise to open the car door for him.

"Hot again, isn't it?" said Homer. "Good corn weather. Just so long as we don't get any more of that damned wind." He had shed his jacket and pushed back his straw hat; a moist red welt showed on his forehead. Homer always looked hotter than anybody else. He was shaped like a small barrel, a solid-fleshed, countrified man with squinty eyes and the characteristic Scandinavian space between his two front teeth. But though he might look like a farmer in town for the day, Homer was a shrewd and sound lawyer—without Uncle Win's flashes of brilliance, but also without his tendency toward impetuous snap judgments and love of the long chance. They had worked very well together; Homer left what he called the fireworks to Uncle Win and concentrated on the hair-splitting details that were his own bread and meat.

Today he had the air of a lost dog. "I thought it went off pretty well this afternoon, didn't you?" he offered diffidently, as Evan slid in beside him. "Short and sweet, the way Win would have wanted it. How's Pearl bearing up?"

"All right," said Evan. "I didn't stay long. She's got the whole Jacobs outfit there."

There was something reproving about the way Homer kept his eyes straight ahead. "Must have been a little hard for her to take, Nell being there. And then Little Harriet going home with your mother, afterwards. Doesn't seem right, somehow."

"Seems righter to me than for her to be watching the Jacobses guzzle whiskey. As for Aunt Nell, I don't see why she shouldn't be there. She's one of Mama's best friends, and say what you like about her, she's always been devoted to Uncle Win."

"Sure," said Homer. "Why not? Win's been staking her to any harebrained scheme that caught her eye for years. I know. He figured he owed it to her. Well, maybe. All I can say is, Nell's been just as expensive a proposition as an ex-wife as she was as a wife, and that's saying plenty."

It was a familiar story; Homer had always complained about Aunt Nell's extravagance. But Evan was not prepared for what came next. "It was high time he came to his senses. That's what I told him the last time she was up at the office, screaming her head off because he cut her down to size on this new deal she was set on. Let her scream, I told him. She's picked some dillies in the past, but this one. This is one for the books. A dude ranch, so help me. Even Win wouldn't stand for it.... You want to go straight home? If you're not in any hurry, come on up to the office with me. Chew the fat for a while. I haven't seen anything of you since you got back."

Evan, who had intended to go straight home, promptly changed his mind. Uncle Win's office—Homer's now, of course—was up above the bank, a suite of three rooms that had seemed luxurious to Evan when he was a child. It looked much more modest now. The oriental rugs were worn in spots; the leather chairs were a bit scuffed; the bookcases, once so impressive, were just sectional book cases crammed with dry-as-dust law books. It also looked very empty.

"I let Elaine go for the day," said Homer. "I knew there wouldn't be anything doing, and she was no earthly use anyway, boo-hooing all over the place." His glance followed Evan's, toward the big mahogany desk where Uncle Win used to sit, in a cloud of cigar smoke, teetering in his swivel chair, and he added, "I'm sort of used to seeing him not there. He hasn't been in since—since he got sick, you know. So I'm sort of used to it."

He stood still for a minute. Then he closed the door between the two adjoining office rooms and sat down at his own desk.

Evan settled down in the armchair. As soon as the necessary pleasantries were out of the way— How did it seem to be back in the old home town? How were Homer's wife, children and grandchildren?— he steered the conversation back where he wanted it.

"So that's Aunt Nell's latest scheme," he said. "A dude ranch. She didn't mention it to me. But then I suppose she dropped it when Uncle Win turned her down."

"She had to," said Homer with satisfaction. "That last tea room cleaned her out. But let me tell you she didn't give up easy. I never heard a woman raise more hell in my life."

"When was this?" asked Evan. "Recently?"

"A month ago. It was the day he—you know, when he tried it the first time. She hasn't turned up here since. For once Win stood pat. He gave her as good as he got."

It jolted Evan. He remembered the jolly scene Aunt Nell had described, when she and Uncle Win had laughed themselves sick over The Kettle on the Hob. A lie. Possibly an innocent lie, the kind Aunt Nell so often told.

"Of course now that he's gone," Homer went on, "she can have her damn fool dude ranch. She gets not only his car and the fishing cabin by the river, but plenty besides. Oh, he left her well provided for, all right, and I'll bet you anything you like she blows it all in, every last cent, inside of a year. I told him so. If you feel you've got to take care of her, I told him, then do it right. Set up a trust. Dole it out to her. Don't hand it to her in a chunk. 'You mean, spoil all her fun?' he said to me. 'I haven't got the heart to do that to her, Homer. Not to Nell. She'd rather not have it at all than be rationed.' She would, too. She never did have a lick of sense about money."

"I know," said Evan absently. He knew, too, how willful she was, like a spoiled child bent on having her own way at any cost. Would she have given up the dude ranch, without one more try? Mightn't she have gone to see Uncle Win that same evening, after he and his cronies finished their card game? The argument could have started all over again, she could have grabbed the knife and … He wouldn't have turned Aunt Nell over to the police. He loved her. Did he love her so much that her attack on him would rob him of the will to live? It was impossible, Evan found, to put such a question to Homer, who was already prejudiced against Aunt Nell. He said tentatively, "I can't see him stabbing himself just because they'd had a quarrel about a dude ranch …"

"Neither can I. And when I mentioned it to Win he hit the ceiling. Said just because I'd always had it in for Nell I was trying to put the blame on her, she had nothing whatever to do with it, and neither had anybody else, it was his business, and he wasn't going to stand for me spreading any such a story about Nell— Well, of course I had no intention of doing that. Ordinarily I wouldn't ever have mentioned it, even to Win, I never meddled in his affairs. But my God, when somebody you've known all your life takes a notion to kill himself—" Homer mopped his brow. "—it *eats* on you. Why? Why? Why? I saw him that night, you know. Played cards with him, and he was in fine fettle. There wasn't the slightest indication of anything worrying him. I just can't understand it. If it had happened years ago, back there when he divorced Nell to marry Pearl—"

"You like Pearl, don't you?"

Homer seemed startled, possibly even a little shocked, by the question. "I certainly haven't anything against her," he said primly. "I know you folks don't think much of her. But I never could see but what she made Win a pretty good wife. I'll say this for her, she was one crackerjack of a secretary. The best we ever had."

She would be, thought Evan. "From what she told me this afternoon, I gather she's planning to leave Fontenelle."

"Yes," said Homer. "She talked it over with me, and I advised her to. She ought to get a pretty good price for the house. Then she'll have her share of Win's estate. He didn't leave her any more than he had to, but with her head for business she'll make out all right. So will Little Harriet. There's a trust fund for her."

"I wonder if she's as anxious to get out of town as Pearl is. Well, if she isn't, she can always stay with Mama and Dad. Like as not Pearl will marry again eventually ..."

He paused, and Homer said, again with that air of primness, "I wouldn't be surprised. Why shouldn't she?"

"No reason whatever. From all I hear, she's already got one candidate lined up. This Stanley Whats-his-name, the fellow that runs The Spot—"

"From all you hear!" Homer's ruddy face darkened. "By God, I don't blame her for wanting to get out of this dirty gossiping town! It's all a pack of lies! Pearl wouldn't marry that guy if he was the last man on earth. She wouldn't wipe her feet on him!" He stopped, as if puzzled with his own vehemence. And, with a speed that left Evan dizzy, he switched the subject to the fishing trip he and Doc Morrison were planning for next weekend.

There was no mistaking his relief when, a few minutes later, Evan stood up and said it was time he headed for home.

Eight

It was okay, staying at Aunt Marianna's. Any place would have been okay with Little Harriet if Evan was there. But it wasn't just that. It was something about the house itself: Daddy had grown up here. He must have run up and down these stairs thousands of times; must, summer after summer, have heard the mourning doves sobbing in the box elders and the wind rattling the bay window. His face—how strange to think of it: Daddy with a boy's face, minus his white hair, his glasses, the lines like parentheses from nose to mouth—had glimmered back from the mirror in the hall piece. There was still a black stain on the library floor where, Aunt Marianna said, he had conducted a memorable experiment with his chemical set. And his initials were carved on one of the legs of the dining room table.

At moments he seemed so close to her, as if he were only waiting for her to speak the magic word, turn the magic key that would bring him back …

He's dead, she would tell herself in a harsh whisper. There was his note, pinned inside her blouse, to prove it. Magic word. Magic key. How dumb could you get? Nothing could bring him back. He was dead. They had killed him. No matter what the note said. No matter what everybody else—Evan too, part of the time—believed. They had killed him.

In her mind "they" had no name or face. Not yet. But she could wait. She would never give up until she knew who it was that she hated.

She saw the difficulties, even without Evan to point them out to her. You couldn't expect the police to start a murder investigation when they were convinced there had been no murder. And after the business about Daddy's note who was going to believe anything she said? No one. Except possibly Evan. No more rash outbursts, he told her. They must take it easy. They must concentrate on the stabbing. For some reason he was very anxious to talk to Aunt Nell—and that, at the moment, was impossible. Aunt Nell had collapsed two days ago, right after the funeral. Aunt Marianna was taking care of her. Alcohol rubs. Cool sponge baths. Trays of clear soup and delicate custards. Quite often it was Little Harriet who carried the trays upstairs to Aunt Nell's bedroom; there she would be lying, with one beautiful hand dangling over the edge of the bed, a damp towel on her forehead, and her mouth set in a suffering expression. Usually she did not open her eyes. Little Harriet would tiptoe into the darkened room, set down her tray, and tiptoe out again without a word. Once, though, Aunt Nell spoke. Little Harriet stopped at the door, startled and thrilled by that throbbing voice: "You loved him too, didn't you?"

"Yes," said Little Harriet and she waited, but that was all.

("She'll get tired of playing Elizabeth Barrett Browning," Evan said. "Any day now. Meanwhile, it's doing Mama a world of good, having somebody to take care of." He did not explain what he wanted to talk to Aunt Nell about. "All in good time," he said. "Don't rush things.")

So they were both waiting, and it was okay, because Evan was there, and she had a feeling of belonging …

Just as Daddy seemed illogically close to her these days, Mother seemed remote. At rare moments she rose to the surface of Little Harriet's mind; most of the time she stayed deep underground. They had had a couple of stiff little telephone conversations. How are you? Fine. How are you? No mention of when Little Harriet was coming home. If she wanted me she'd ask me, Little Harriet told herself. She doesn't want me. She's glad to be rid of me. Well, she needn't think I care. Aunt Marianna wants me, if she doesn't.

And then, while Evan was having his morning coffee, Aunt Marianna said to him briskly, "I think you ought to take Little Harriet home today." The kitchen floor gave a sickening lurch under Little Harriet's feet; her ears rang with shame (Aunt Marianna wants you. Ha!); her face felt as if it were on fire.

"What the hell for?" said Evan. "She's all right here. Aren't you, kid?"

She achieved a shrug. "I don't care. I was going home, anyway. Any time's okay with me, if you're tired of—tired of—" Her voice went high and thin; it all but broke.

"What?" The coffee pot tilted in Aunt Marianna's hand. She looked startled and cross. "Why, what's the matter with you, child? Who said anything about—"

"You did, Mama," said Evan. "You said I ought to take her home."

"Well, of course. But I didn't mean it that way. She shouldn't be so touchy. Mercy, Harriet, if I was tired of having you here, don't you think I'd say so?" When Evan burst out laughing, she added, "*Now* what's funny?" and went on peering anxiously at Little Harriet.

It was all right again; the floor stopped lurching.

"It's the principle of the thing," Aunt Marianna explained. "I'm not going to have Pearl thinking we've turned Little Harriet against her. That's what it looks like, even if it doesn't happen to be true. She's got a right to see her own daughter and straighten out whatever it is that's come between them. Or try to."

"Supposing she doesn't want to?"

"Of course she wants to. They're still mother and daughter, no matter what. They can't just split up without a word to each other. It just isn't *right*."

She made it sound so simple. Right and wrong. Mother and daughter. In Little Harriet's inner ear the words echoed wistfully. She remembered the time, several years ago, when Mother had taken her along on a trip to Chicago, just the two of them; they bought new hats and went to the ice show and Mother was so different and nice … It was only that once, though. All the other good times were with Daddy.

They were looking at her questioningly. Waiting for her answer. Leaving it up to her. If she said no, they wouldn't make her go. She could go on staying here, and maybe after a while she would forget about the half of her that was not Covey but Jacobs.

She bent down and tousled Buster's ears. (Buster had the run of Aunt Marianna's house. Day and night.) "Okay," she said, as if it didn't matter at all. "Might as well get it over, I guess. If you'll go with me, Evan."

But during the drive across town she became aware of a queer, trembly feeling. Mother had said when they phoned her that it was okay to come over. But what if she started in all over again about the gun and Daddy? And Stanley? She knew, now, that Little Harriet had told Evan about her and Stanley. In Mother's eyes that must be the blackest mark of all.

On the other hand, if they didn't quarrel, what were they going to say to each other? Little Harriet's mind went blank. And, as if that weren't enough, there was the prickly problem of whether or not she was expected to kiss Mother when they met …

She had a moment of pure panic when they drew up in front of Daddy's house, because Evan acted as if he might be intending to wait for her in the car. "You're coming in with me, aren't you?" she croaked, and right away he said sure, if she wanted him to.

Mother flicked a cold glance at him. She put her hand out toward Little Harriet, and they still might have kissed—out of nervousness if nothing else—only Mother smiled slightly, and after that it was hopeless. Mother's smile reduced Little Harriet to the status of a naughty child. She might as well have said it out loud: Well, it's about time you stopped this nonsense. I wondered how long you could keep it up. You've been pretty silly, haven't you?

So all they said was "Hi," and "Hello, there." Then Mother sat down and lit a cigarette. And then, in a cool, conversational tone, she dropped her bombshell.

Little Harriet, who was sprawling in one of the big chairs, did not move a muscle. But Evan was still standing. He took a backward step and let himself down, gently, onto the beige sofa. "You what?" he said.

"I'm selling the house to Stanley," said Mother. "Why not? He's made me a very good offer. Homer Nelsen says I'd be a fool not to take it. Well. I'm taking it."

"For Pete's sake." Evan's eyes met Little Harriet's. She kept hers blank. It wasn't hard; she was absorbed in a series of vivid mental pictures—Stanley making himself at home in Daddy's study, in his bedroom, lolling in Daddy's favorite chair on the patio. "For Pete's sake, what does Stanley want with it? Is he going to *live* in it?"

"That's something you'd better ask Stanley," said Mother. "I don't know why he shouldn't live in it if he wants to. It's not a national shrine."

"But— But I thought you were leaving Fontenelle!"

"I am," said Mother. Period.

Then her eyes, too, slid toward Little Harriet. "I'm going to Chicago. I've always wanted to live there. You'd like it too. Wouldn't you, Harriet?"

The sound of her own name jarred Little Harriet into operation. Her elbows and knees jerked in and unfolded. She hoisted herself up onto her feet. She could feel her midriff pumping in and out like a bellows. "Not if you're there," she said hoarsely. "I wouldn't go to heaven if I had to go with you. It's perfectly *foul* of you to sell Daddy's house to Stanley, and if you think I'm going to have anything to do with you after this …"

"You're not of age yet, you know. And I'm your mother. The law has something to say about such cases." There was a cold glitter in her eye; Little Harriet realized that she was furious.

But so was Evan. "The law also has something to say about mothers that aren't fit to have custody of their children. If you want to make that kind of a mess out of it, go ahead."

"You keep out of this!"

"Try and keep me out of it. Harriet's right, it is foul of you. It's an outrageous thing to do, and if I had the money I'd outbid Stanley just to keep you from doing it."

"But you haven't got the money," said Mother, and she smiled. "Isn't it too bad. Because I don't care who I sell to. The highest bidder gets it. As for you—" She turned toward Little Harriet. The words themselves were harsh, but with them went a gesture so groping and unguarded that it flashed through Little Harriet like an electric shock: She wants me. She *does* want me, after all. For a sweet, perilous moment she felt her own hand tingling with the impulse to reach for Mother's, find it and melt into it …

The chime of the doorbell saved her. (For she could never have forgiven herself for betraying Daddy. That's what it would have been; Mother was selling his house to *Stanley*.)

Furthermore, it was Stanley who was ringing the doorbell. Mother's flustered air made it clear. She jumped up. "That may be Stanley now. He wanted to take another look at the basement, but I didn't expect him until later—" She hesitated, glancing from Evan to Little Harriet in acute annoyance. Because neither of them budged. With Little Harriet it was a physical impossibility. With Evan it was stubbornness; an angry flush showed in his forehead, and he had the Covey set to his jaw.

"Let him in," he told Mother. "Why not? Let's have a real old home week."

Stanley was wearing slacks and a sports shirt, very sharp. Monogrammed. Little Harriet had never seen him before at such close quarters, in broad daylight. There was nothing, now, to soften the impact. That sneering smile. That flat, chilling stare. He followed Mother into the living room confidently. Her color was a little higher than usual, but otherwise she had regained her composure. "You've met Harriet, I'm sure," she said. "Do you and Evan know each other?"

"We've met," said Evan. He ignored Stanley's half-outstretched hand. "Pearl tells me you're buying the house from her."

"Yes," said Stanley with satisfaction. The uncompleted handshake had not dislodged his smile. Nor had Little Harriet's stony silence. "It's the best house in town. Your uncle knew what he was doing when he built it."

"I'm sure he'd be pleased to hear you say so."

"Quality," said Stanley, and thumped the wall with his thick, proprietary hand. "And style. That's what I like. Real class."

"You're going to stay in Fontenelle, I take it?"

"Why not? It's a good, live town. Good business. A good house. Why not?"

"Sounds like you've got it made, all right," said Evan.

Mother cut in nervously. "You wanted to see the basement, Mr. Stanley?"

"Yes, Mrs. Covey. If you please, Mrs. Covey." He laid the mockery on with a trowel. He all but winked at Evan. And he let his hand rest casually on Mother's arm as she led him toward the hall.

Evan followed doggedly. After a minute so did Little Harriet.

Stanley stopped at the study door. It stood open; sunlight sifted in through the blinds and lay in trembling, mote-filled bars on the familiar furniture. Unlike the rest of the house, this room was distinctively Daddy's. For Little Harriet it had the same atmosphere as Aunt Marianna's home—mellow, so steeped in Daddy's personality that again she could almost believe there was a magic word to bring him back. She held her breath against the pain of imagining him here, where she had so often seen him, surrounded by his favorite pictures and books, sitting at his old-fashioned desk. It was still cluttered with the little belongings he had accumulated, for one reason or another, through the years—the miniature of Grandmother Covey as a young woman, fringed and brooched; the little beaded deerskin tobacco pouch (though Daddy never smoked a pipe); the pear-shaped stone that he used as a paperweight; the ivory letter opener with a tiger carved on its handle. This room seemed to her to hold the very heart of his life. And of his death; he had died here, last Saturday night.

It must seem so to Evan and Mother, too. Possibly even Stanley got a glimmer. Nothing changed in his broad, impassive face as he stood looking in at another man's room, another man's life. But his bulky shoulders stiffened, and his hands slowly clenched. Little Harriet heard him draw in a long breath. Then he walked into the study and sat down at Daddy's desk. (She had known he was going to. He had to.)

The chair creaked as he settled himself in it, getting comfortable. The raw colors of his sports shirt clashed against the muted richness of leather and tapestry. For an instant Little Harriet had a strange double image—Stanley's coarse hulk superimposed on the thin, elegant figure of Daddy. A smoldering feeling grew in the pit of her stomach.

"I like this room. You know?" said Stanley abruptly. For once his face had lost its customary sneering smile. "You know how it is when you're a kid, and you want something so bad it makes your guts ache … No, you don't know. You didn't grow up in a Chicago slum like me."

"I know, though," said Mother.

"Well. I wanted a room of my own. I'd never seen a room like this, but it's funny, you can want something you've never seen. A room of my own. A room just like this." Back came that loathsome smile of his. "And now by God I've got it," he said softly. He pressed his thick, manicured hands on the desk in front of him. The ivory letter opener caught his eye. He picked it up, and as he did so Little Harriet felt her inner smoldering burst into fire. Here it was: the focus for her hate.

"You haven't, either!" she shrieked. She rushed at him. "You put that down! I don't care if you do buy the house, that isn't yours! That's Daddy's!" She snatched it from him. "Don't you dare—"

"Okay, okay." He looked both surprised and irritated. "Pipe down, kid. I'm not trying to steal your old man's junk."

"You are too! You want to grab everything he ever owned. Every single, last, solitary thing he owned."

"Oh now, I wouldn't go that far." Amused now; and that was good, that made her hate him even more. "There's one of Daddy's belongings I guess I can do without, and that's a spitfire kid by the name of Harriet. She's going to get into trouble someday, calling people thieves."

"You're worse than a thief! You're a—"

"Harriet," said Mother sharply. "Stop it. Right now." She moved forward, and Little Harriet whirled on her.

"Don't you touch me. You're as bad as he is. You think I don't know what you did to Daddy. You and Stanley—" She stopped, just short of the precipice. "And now you're letting him take over everything, and you think I'll go off to Chicago with you, just as if none of it ever happened. Well, I won't! It's all right with me if I never see you again as long as I live. Yes, and I'll get even with you too, *Mr*. Stanley, you wait and see if I don't. You're going to wish you'd never heard of Daddy."

"Now listen, kid," began Stanley. She saw, with exultation, the mean glint in his eye. She had no intention of listening to him.

"I'll wait for you in the car," she said to Evan as she brushed past him.

But at the front door she paused, unable to leave, after all, without listening. At first it was profoundly quiet. Until Mother gave a sudden, artificial laugh. "I don't know what gets *into* Harriet sometimes," she said. "She says the craziest things. Of course she doesn't mean them, nobody takes her seriously."

And Evan said, "Of course not. Especially now, when she's so overwrought. It's been a terrific blow to her, Uncle Win's suicide."

Scared, thought Little Harriet. Both of them. Scared of Stanley. Chicken. Well, *I'm* not …

"Sure," Stanley was saying. "But somebody ought to tell her to watch it. She could get into trouble someday, a kid like that, if she don't learn to keep her mouth shut."

She curled her lip. But she also shivered slightly (from hate, she told herself; of course not from fear) as she went out the door.

Nine

That was the day Aunt Nell called off her state of collapse. With a flourish, naturally; she chose supper time to make her entrance, thus assuring herself of an audience. They were properly impressed. Evan and Dad sprang up to get a chair for her and help her into it. Mama and Little Harriet scurried to lay a place for her.

She acknowledged all this attention with a frail smile. They mustn't fuss, she said; she was all right, only a little shaky. She did look rather ethereal, Evan thought, possibly because she hadn't had much solid food, and no sociability, for the last couple of days. There was also her costume, a filmy, bluish-gray dressing gown which lent just the right touch of charming melancholy. She certainly did not look or act like a woman with a guilty conscience. Yet she had lied to Evan—or at least misled him—about her interview with Uncle Win in his office. And she was the last person to see him alive. Would she ever have mentioned that final visit at all, if Mama in her innocence had not done it for her? It was an interesting point; Evan pondered it all through supper.

It turned out to be quite a project, getting Aunt Nell alone for his little talk with her. Before he had a chance to suggest taking her for a ride in the cool of the evening, Dad said he was going to drive out to the farm, and did anybody want to come along? Little Harriet was the only one who voted yes; at least that got her out of the way. But for only a limited length of time, and it wasn't going to take Mama forever to do the dishes, either. As she pointed out, when Aunt Nell offered to help: "Now, Nell, I won't hear of it. It won't take me fifteen minutes. You and Evan sit down in the living room, and I'll be right with you."

He perched on the window seat and jittered. Aunt Nell disposed herself gracefully on the couch. In the end it was she who unwittingly started the ball rolling.

"Somebody ought to do something about Little Harriet's clothes," she announced. "Heaven knows she's no beauty, but there's no need for her to look all that bad. I was noticing her at supper. She's got perfectly good bones."

"Plenty of them, anyway," said Evan. He had been too preoccupied to see it before, but there it was—the familiar, crusading gleam in Aunt Nell's eye. "What is this, Operation Ugly Duckling?"

"Well, why not? Poor child. You can work wonders, you know, with a little imagination." She gave him a sharp glance. "Would you mind explaining to me what you're grinning about?"

"Nothing. Except that only the other day Little Harriet was a brat, a piece of riffraff, just like her mother. Now all at once she's a deserving character with perfectly good bones. It couldn't be just because she's shucked Pearl off and come over to the side of the angels. Or could it?"

Aunt Nell's frank, infectious laugh rang out. "Of course that's it. Partly. It made me realize I've been misjudging the child. What chance has she ever had, with a mother like that, and all of us taking it for granted she was a chip off the old block? Well, it's going to be different from now on. I for one am going to see to it that she gets some decent clothes."

"Good for you," said Evan. And the opening he saw was such a natural he couldn't resist it. "It's not only less expensive than a dude ranch, it ought to be a lot more satisfying."

Instantly she stiffened. "Who said anything about a dude ranch?"

"Not you. That's for sure. If it weren't for Homer Nelsen, I'd still be under the impression that you and Uncle Win had a jolly good time that day, instead of a bang-up quarrel."

"Homer Nelsen. He never could keep his nose out of other people's business. What if Win and I did have a little business disagreement? What of it?"

"It just strikes me funny you didn't mention it yourself. All was sweetness and light, you told me. Why did you say that when it wasn't true?"

"Because it wasn't important! What is this, anyway? If you're trying to suggest that Win went home and stabbed himself simply because we had an argument about a dude ranch—" She paused. Mama was standing in the doorway, her head tilted inquiringly. "Come on in, Marianna. Your son may want to put you through the third degree too."

Mama blinked. "You didn't tell me you'd had a quarrel with Win, Nell. I didn't realize that was why you were so anxious to see him again."

"Oh, for heaven's sake!" cried Aunt Nell. "A quarrel! I thought the dude ranch deal sounded good, and Win didn't think so. That was all."

"You mean he wouldn't fork out the money for it," said Mama, who seldom saw any reason for avoiding flat-footed statements. "It must have been a bad bet for sure, if he turned you down. He never did before. Goodness knows he should have, but he never did."

"Thanks," snapped Aunt Nell. "I'm getting pretty sick of being told what a poor head I have for business. Just because I've had bad luck once or twice."

"It's been more than once or twice," Mama pointed out calmly. "And really, Nell, a dude ranch—"

"Never mind that," said Evan. "You say—and I believe you—that Uncle Win wouldn't stab himself just because he'd had a business argument with you. Was that all it was? Just a business argument?"

Aunt Nell's face grew whiter, her eyes more luminous. "It started with the dude ranch. I never meant to— But I can't seem to help it, I lose my temper and say these awful things ..."

"So you told him about Pearl and Stanley?" (Out of the corner of his eye Evan saw Mama open her mouth and close it again. Even she could not stay unsuspecting forever.)

"Why are you badgering me like this?" cried Aunt Nell. Our Heroine at Bay. Hands fluttering at her throat; head lifted, brave but defenseless. "Haven't I suffered enough? When I found out what Win had tried to do, later that night, it was as if I had stabbed him with my own hands. Yes. I felt like a murderer." Having said the word, she looked appalled.

And she hurried on: "At first, I mean. When I calmed down, of course, I saw how crazy it was. Because he already knew about Pearl and Stanley before I told him. I meant to hurt him, and he wasn't hurt. He already knew and didn't much care. All the same, I felt I had to see him. And Pearl wouldn't let me in the house. She wouldn't even let me talk to him on the phone."

"So you didn't see him at all until the other night, just before he shot himself," said Evan. He watched her, helplessly aware of his own inability to tell whether or not she was lying.

"That's right. We had a wonderful hour together. I'll be grateful for it till the day I die." Her voice shook with the pathos of it.

"Had he changed his mind about the dude ranch?"

"We didn't discuss it." (Of course not. Too crass.) "I said, 'I'm sorry, Win,' and he said, 'I know, darling,' and it was just as if we'd never quarreled. We sat there in his study, quietly talking." She smiled tremulously, sadly. "About the old days, when we were first married, how happy we were, how much in love …"

"Oh, stop it!" Suddenly angry, Evan got up and began to pace the floor. "Stop dramatizing yourself and face a few facts. Don't tell me you just sat there and reminisced. Not with a man who'd already tried to kill himself once—right after a quarrel with you—and who, a couple of hours later, was going to do it again, this time for keeps. You claim he was the love of your life, you could sense without his telling you when something was wrong. Well, it didn't take any extra-sensory perception to figure out that something was wrong with Uncle Win. I saw it. One look in his eyes, and I knew he didn't want to live anymore. I tried to find out why, and you must have too. You must have at least asked him if it was on account of the quarrel he'd had with you."

She didn't answer right away, and when she did her voice had lost its vibrancy; her hands, ordinarily so expressive, lay like a bundle of limp flowers in her lap. "Of course I asked him. Of course I tried. It was no use. He said I mustn't blame myself, it wasn't anybody's fault. I had the feeling he was—already gone. I couldn't help him, I couldn't even get near him—" She put her face in her hands and sobbed.

"There," said Mama. "I declare, Evan, you ought to be ashamed of yourself. What's the good of putting us through this all over again? It's not going to bring Win back. Why can't you leave it alone?"

He was stung into blurting it out: "Because Little Harriet still insists he didn't stab himself. She says he admitted to her that somebody tried to kill him. Oh, I know you can't believe everything Little Harriet says. She lied about the suicide note. But supposing she isn't lying about this?"

Aunt Nell, though she had stopped sobbing, kept her face hidden in her hands. But Mama's eyes—shocked, distressed, and yet undaunted—did not waver from his. "All right. Supposing Win lied to her. If he was determined to kill himself he might have seen his chance—because she already had this notion that somebody else had stabbed him—and used her to get the gun for him. A cruel, cowardly thing to do. But he might have done it."

"I know it, Mama. There's no doubt in my mind that he was determined to kill himself. After the stabbing. All of us saw how terribly changed he was. We were all scared of the same thing, and sure enough he did it, he shot himself. But from all I hear, the stabbing was completely different. It never occurred to anybody that he might be planning suicide. Not to you. Not to Aunt Nell. Not to his three cronies—and they saw him just a couple of hours before it happened. Everybody was dumfounded. You've got to admit it's an argument in Little Harriet's favor."

"But if somebody tried to kill him, why didn't he say so?"

"Maybe because it was somebody he loved—"

"Nonsense. He couldn't possibly love somebody that tried to kill him." There it was, Mama's credo in simple black and white. No bothersome subtle shadings. She gave a sigh of relief. Suicide in the family, inexplicable and harrowing though it was, was still preferable to murder.

But Evan went on doggedly, "There's one other thing. Was there ever any question about what knife Uncle Win was stabbed with?"

Aunt Nell lifted her head; her chin was trembling uncontrollably.

"Of course not," said Mama. "It was there in his chest when he was found. Your Grandpa Covey's old hunting knife. Of course there wasn't any question. Why?"

"Because he said something to Little Harriet about another knife. When she told him she knew he hadn't stabbed himself, he said, 'What makes you think that? Oh. It must be the knife. You must have seen it. It doesn't mean anything, you know. I thought I lost it years ago—'"

"Oh!" said Mama. "*That* knife. His old pocketknife. Why didn't you say so? No great mystery about that. Though I must say I was surprised to see it again after all these years. Billy Morrison and I found it that night, after he stabbed himself. Next morning when he asked me about it—he seemed to have it on his mind—I said, yes, we'd found it, and he gave it to me for a keepsake. I have it right here, in my sewing chair." She pulled open the drawer under the seat of the little armless rocker, where she kept her sewing things—spools of thread, strawberry pin cushion, scissors, darning egg. From the jumble she drew a pocketknife. An old-fashioned one, of a kind not often seen anymore, with "Winthrop E. Covey" engraved on it and a place in the handle for photographs.

"My picture," murmured Aunt Nell. "And yours, Marianna. He had it when he went away to law school. I remember how upset he was when he lost it."

"Only he never really lost it," said Mama. "I said to him, 'Win, where in the world did that come from, after all this time?' And he said he'd run across it when he was going through a box of old stuff a couple of days before. Not lost at all. Just mislaid." She studied the two girlish, fading faces pictured in the knife and added candidly, "Mercy, I was homely. And that hat of yours, Nell. I thought it was absolutely stunning at the time."

After a minute Evan said, "But why would he mention it to Little Harriet? She hadn't seen it, but he thought she had, and he assumed that was what convinced her that he hadn't stabbed himself. Why would he …"

Mama searched for, and found, an explanation. "He was fuzzy in the head, from all the dope Billy Morrison gave him. That's all. His mind was wandering a little. And I must say, Evan, I think it's a mistake for any of us to encourage Little Harriet in these ideas of hers. You're only making it harder for her, and goodness knows it's hard already, with Pearl acting like she is."

"I know, but if the kid's right—"

"If she's right, then don't you think you're going out of your way to complicate things?" Aunt Nell's voice was back to normal, strong and rich and pulsing with a variety of emotions. Among them bitterness. "Why pick me for your grilling? Pearl's at the bottom of this. With a wife like Pearl, why would Win want to live? If anybody killed him, she did. She drove him to his death, and even that's not enough for her, she has to flout his memory by selling his house to that scum Stanley … She did it, she killed him! It wasn't me! It wasn't me!"

"Now, Nell," said Mama mildly. She had been exposed to Aunt Nell's outbursts most of her life; they didn't ruffle her in the least. What an oddly assorted pair they were, Evan thought—the one so nearly beautiful, the other so nearly ugly; and worlds apart in temperament. Yet they were as close as if they had been blood sisters. "Of course you didn't kill him. Nobody said you did. Nobody even thought it for a minute." Mama reanchored her side combs and looked up at Evan with indomitable assurance.

"Okay, Mama," he said, and retreated to the front porch.

Little Harriet was sprawling in the porch swing, more or less on her back, with her knees jutting out like the parts of some complex machine.

"What are you doing here? I thought you went out to the farm with Dad."

"I changed my mind." She slapped at a mosquito. "I wanted to hear what you said to Aunt Nell. You didn't get very far. Did you?"

"You could have done better, I suppose."

"I wouldn't have tried. A waste of time. She didn't stab Daddy. She loved him. I can tell."

"Sure she did. And he loved her. My point exactly. Don't you see, Little Harriet? If anybody stabbed him, it must have been someone he loved. Otherwise he wouldn't have protected them, he'd have called in the police. He not only didn't call in the police, he lost his will to live. Well. He couldn't have loved many people that much …" His pet theory. It still made sense to him, even though Mama had disposed of it with so little ceremony. In the silence—for Little Harriet made no comment—he checked off the people Uncle Win had loved. Mama. (But Mama as a would-be killer was inconceivable.) Little Harriet. (Also inconceivable. Besides, she and she alone had cried murder.) Pearl? (He could see her as a killer, all right. The question was whether Uncle Win had loved her enough to protect her.) And Aunt Nell …

Still no comment from Little Harriet. He wished it wasn't so dark; her face was just an inscrutable blur. The feeling grew in him that her mind was off on an entirely separate track, and with it came a chilling memory of the scene in Uncle Win's study this morning. To hate Stanley was one thing—and of course she hated him; so did Evan—but to threaten him was something else again. Something so dangerous and ridiculous that it made his hair stand on end. He said sharply, "It certainly lets Stanley out. Uncle Win wouldn't have covered up for him."

"Guess not," said Little Harriet. She added, with a kindly air, as if she were patting him on the head, "Well, anyway, you did find out about the other knife."

"For what it's worth. That leaves Whats-her-name. Rita, the maid that was there that night. What happened to her, anyway? She doesn't work for your mother anymore, does she?"

"Nobody works for my mother any longer than they have to. If they don't get mad and quit she gets mad and fires them. I don't know which it was with Rita. She used to be one of Aunt Nell's lame ducks. That's what Daddy called them. Nell's lame ducks. She gave Rita a job, when she had that gift shop in Chicago. Then she worked for us for a while, and now she's waiting tables out at The Spot."

"At The Spot? She is?" Well, there was no other lead. He could tackle Rita himself and see where it got him. He felt hopeless and frustrated and annoyed with Little Harriet—who, having gotten him involved, now seemed to have lost interest in the whole affair. From the way she was acting, you'd think it was all settled.

She stood up, stretched, and looked down at herself thoughtfully. "Perfectly good bones," she said. "That's better than being just pretty. Isn't it?"

Ten

Friday night at The Spot, and Goldie, having finished her first stint at the piano, settled down in the back booth and lit a cigarette. Lord, she was tired. And it was only a little past eleven. At least two more hours before she could hope to get out of here and home to her sick baby. Not bad sick, just fussy sick with a summer cold; but Bob was out of town on a job, and that left nobody but Goldie's kid sister to take over. A good, sensible kid. There was nothing to worry about. All the same, Goldie decided, if she got a chance she was going to nip over home—it wouldn't take more than ten minutes, she could go the back way—just to make sure everything was okay.

Not too busy, for a Friday night. The usual gang of high school kids, a couple of truck drivers … Well! To what did they owe this honor? It was Evan Hoyt and Norma Schaefer coming in the door; automatically Goldie's hand lifted to smooth her hair. Norma looked nice (if you cared for the type) in pale pink linen, one of those jobs that looked so simple and cost you your eyeteeth; and Evan looked homely and distinguished and—well, like Evan. They didn't see Goldie, and for a few minutes she lost track of them, because here came Rita, switching everything she had to switch, as usual.

"Do me a favor, Goldie?" She had that gleam in her eye; Goldie knew what was coming. "Pinch-hit for me for a little while? I just got a phone call, something I gotta tend to …"

"Don't give me that stuff. I saw you and Stanley with your heads together. I know what you've got to tend to. Another real important business engagement with Stanley in one of the tourist cabins."

Rita giggled and tossed her Italian haircut. "Shh. Nobody's supposed to know. Just for a little while, Goldie. Please?"

After a minute Goldie said, "Okay. If I could stop you by saying no, believe me, I'd say it. I'm not kidding, Rita. You're asking for trouble, getting mixed up with a guy like Stanley."

She was wasting her breath. Rita had heard nothing beyond that first word, "Okay." Her bright, mindless gaze skittered away from Goldie to Stanley, and even farther, to the scene (in Technicolor, no doubt) that would be enacted later in the tourist cabin: Herself in Stanley's arms … "Gee, thanks. You're a doll, Goldie. Thanks a million."

Bound and determined to make a fool of herself, thought Goldie. If not with Stanley—and you had to admit it, Rita had been waving it in his face ever since the day she started working here—then with somebody else. Only why couldn't it be somebody else? Anybody but Stanley.

It wasn't any skin off of Goldie's nose. She didn't know why she was worrying about a nitwit like Rita. But the fact remained. She stubbed out her cigarette, and felt inside her the solid knot of anxiety, like a clenched fist.

Evan had never been able to figure out what it was about Norma Schaefer that made him think of one of those big Belgian horses. If you got right down to actual measurements (God forbid) you would probably find that she wasn't out-size at all. Matter of fact—the jukebox started up again, and Norma said yes, she'd like to dance—she wasn't quite as tall as Iris. But Iris dancing was like a willow swaying in the wind, whereas … Norma never missed a step. Her sense of rhythm was accurate. How, then, did she manage to reduce dancing to the level of a brisk, healthful gymnasium work-out?

Healthful. Maybe that was the key word. Norma exuded health and vigor. Perfect teeth, fresh complexion, shining brown hair that always looked as if she had just given it a thorough brushing, eyes as clear and blue as a child's. Wholesome and unexciting. Like a girl in a toothpaste ad.

But she would make somebody—somebody else—a wonderful wife. Evan could see that. If they (her family as much as his) hadn't tried so hard to ram her down his throat, he might really have appreciated her. There was plenty to appreciate: comradeship, good humor, sympathy and understanding. All admirable qualities, and all they inspired in him was a blind, reflexive kind of resistance. Did Norma sense that? Might she even feel the same toward him?

He drew back a little to see her face better; and surprised there an expression so secret and dreamy that it made him feel like a peeping Tom. Her eyes were half-closed, her lips parted in a faint smile. To make it worse, she caught him watching her, and flushed to the roots of her hair.

He gave a nervous laugh. "These old songs. They take you back, don't they?" No, that was no good, the wrong thing to say. "I'm all out of practice, dancing. Don't get around much anymore."

"No? From what Marge Lane said—I saw her in Chicago last winter, she stopped off on her way back to New York—I gathered you get around plenty."

So she knew about Iris. Or at least she knew Marge Lane's version of Iris. Not that it mattered to him, one way or the other.

She went on, in a voice as quiet and unsmiling as her eyes. "With you it's always got to be somebody—unattainable. Funny, isn't it? Like Goldie, in high school. Like whoever it is now. Unattainable, for some reason or other."

It was so unexpected, coming from Norma. Unexpected and revealing; for an instant he saw her habitual air of casual friendliness as a screen, one she had devised long ago to hide—what? The self-conscious agonies of a girl who knows she is being thrown at someone who doesn't want her? Someone, furthermore, that she herself wants? He hunched his shoulder in alarm. She just might be right, too, about that unattainable business …

"Norma," he began, just as the music stopped, so that the word jumped out into a sudden vacuum.

"Everything okay, Mr. Hoyt?" Stanley, making like the suave host. Right at their elbows; Evan was conscious of relief and resentment, in equal parts. "Nice to see you again. You too, Miss Schaefer." Stanley's voice lingered over her name. His eyes lingered even longer, and it was a peculiar thing, the power of that leisurely and presumptuous stare. Norma did not shrink from it. She bloomed under it; the wholesome, unexciting toothpaste ad girl Evan had always seen when he looked at her was transformed into what Stanley saw. Which was, very obviously, a desirable woman.

It was as astonishing—and as short-lived—as that other, peeping Tom moment. They were back in their booth, sipping their beer; Norma was her easy, companionable self again (if it was a screen, what a comfortable one!) and they were chatting, as they had done off and on all evening, about Little Harriet.

"I think she was just blowing off steam, with that talk about 'getting' Stanley," said Norma. "She knows better than to try to tangle with him." Evan had given her the high points of the scene in Uncle Win's study. He had withheld from her two angles: his qualms about Aunt Nell (it made him ashamed, even to think of them); and his reason for suggesting that they drop in at The Spot tonight. Which was that he hoped to lay the foundation for a little talk with Rita.

So far he had not made much progress. When she brought their first round of beers he had struck up a little conversation with her: She was Rita, wasn't she? He had often heard Aunt Nell speak of her … That sort of thing. Rita had responded with radiant smiles and flighty giggles. But it was clear that her mind was elsewhere. (A chronic condition with

Rita? Evan had strong suspicions.) Her eyes kept darting toward the front counter, toward the other booths, toward Norma, back to Evan and away again. She had a big, squashy mouth, a disheveled brunette hairdo, and an interesting, remarkably bouncy figure.

At the moment she was sashaying around up front. On the pretext of needing another package of cigarettes, Evan excused himself and caught up with Rita beside the vending machine. He came right to the point. "There's something I'd like to ask you about, Rita, when you've got a little time to spare."

"Really?" She fluttered her eyelashes. "Well. I couldn't make it tonight, Mr. Hoyt. I'm already dated up tonight." She glanced toward the booth where Norma was sitting, and giggled. "Well. I guess you are too."

"I didn't mean— Maybe tomorrow, then? Tomorrow afternoon," he added cautiously.

"But tomorrow's Saturday! I couldn't possibly make it on Saturday." She patted her carefully disarranged locks. Inspected her bright pink fingernails. "Tell you what, Mr. Hoyt. You give me a ring sometime—I stay at Shoemakers', you know—sometime when you're free, and if it should so happen that I'm free too, why, fine and dandy." And away she switched. That figure of hers really was animated.

She certainly didn't act as if she were in possession of sinister or explosive information. She might be, though, without realizing it herself. Any way you looked at it, it was going to be like grappling with a bushel of loose feathers. But with Rita the only possibility in sight, what else could he do? He sighed at the prospect.

Back in his seat across from Norma, he said, "The thing that beats me—I mean one of the things—is Pearl. If she and Stanley are so mad for each other, how come she's leaving town and he's staying?"

"I can't believe he really intends to live in your Uncle Win's house," said Norma. "He must be buying it as an investment. And Pearl probably sold it to him out of spite as much as anything else, just because she knew it would make the rest of you sore."

"Maybe." But Norma hadn't seen Stanley walking into Uncle Win's study. She hadn't heard him say, "A room of my own. A room just like this." Whether he intended to live there or not, Stanley wanted that house.

"Maybe I can find out for you," said Norma. "From Stanley. He's called me a couple of times this week."

"What?" He stared at her. "Stanley's been making a play for you?"

"Incredible as it may seem to you. Nothing cheap about his invitations, either. A drive out to the lake for dinner. All like that. Maybe I ought to take him up on it next time, just to pump him."

"I wouldn't advise it," he said stiffly. "You've got no more business messing around with Stanley than Little Harriet has."

"I expect not," said Norma. "Here comes Goldie. Shall we ask her to join us for a beer?"

After she had hung up the phone, Pearl went back into the living room and picked up her knitting. As a tranquilizer, she had found, there was nothing to beat it; while her quick, skillful hands busied themselves with the familiar pattern of movements, her mind worked too, finding a pattern of its own.

So. He couldn't make it tonight, Stanley had said. There was this deal cooking. He couldn't get away. Damn it, he had added. And then the line about how they would make up for it tomorrow night.

A good line. Only Pearl had heard it before. In fact—her knitting needles came to an abrupt halt—she had now heard it just once too often. She wasn't having any more, thank you. It was time for a showdown. She had thought none would be necessary. A passing fancy of Stanley's; let it pass without comment. She could afford to. Because Stanley was hers. She knew it, as surely as she knew that Win had never been hers. You could call it love if you wanted to; Pearl herself had stopped thinking in such romantic, high-flown terms long ago. Marriage had knocked a lot of nonsense out of her, including any illusions she might once have had about marriage itself as the happy, happy ending. It was not her ambition to be Stanley's wife. (Strange as it might seem to the Ladies Sewing Circle of Fontenelle. And luckily for her; since it was not Stanley's ambition to be her husband, either. He would marry— if he married at all—for practical, social reasons, and that was all right with Pearl. Who should understand better than she the social climber's itch?)

Let him marry some dandy little well-connected prize package if he wanted to. Let him stay here in Fontenelle; Chicago was, after all, only a couple of hours away. Her hold on him was too fundamental to be loosened by trivialities. He would still be hers in the only way that mattered to either of them; she would still be his.

Lovers, she thought. We are what people call lovers. It was not a word either she or Stanley was in the habit of using. They dispensed with words. There was no language for the violent, primeval chemistry between them. None was needed.

This Rita business, though ... It had gone far enough. Pearl's mind was made up. Not that she thought of Rita as a serious rival. Or as a menace, either. But for a moment she sat very still, remembering how Evan had asked her about the knife. The other knife. She was almost sure, quite sure, she had sidestepped that little pitfall without a hitch. No. Certainly Rita was not a menace. By chance Pearl had fired her at a time when The Spot was short a waitress, and by chance Stanley had hired her. It was as simple as that. And Stanley was no man to resist an easy lay; Pearl knew him, and Rita, too well to have any doubts about what must have happened at once, if not sooner. But it was not going to go on happening.

Thoughtfully she tapped a cigarette. They must have some kind of a date tonight. Was Stanley likely to invest a great amount of time or money when he didn't have to? Not on your life. He would certainly not take a cheap little waitress—who, incidentally, was supposed to be on duty, earning her salary at The Spot—any place where he would be seen with her. At the very most he might drive her up to his lodge in the hills.

So all Pearl had to do was drive out to The Spot (she had never been inside the place, and she had no intention of going inside tonight; why frighten off her birds?) and check on Stanley's car. If it was gone, she would take a chance on the lodge. (How well she knew that back road!) If his car was still there, she could park in the lane across the highway from The Spot and—being careful only to keep out of sight—reconnoiter. She might even decide to wait in his car instead of hers. A reception committee of one. Surprise, surprise. The idea rather appealed to her.

She slipped off her wedding ring and her diamond. It was an automatic gesture. She never wore them when she was going to see Stanley; they belonged to another part of her life, another Pearl. That is, they used to … What difference did it make now? There was no other Pearl anymore. Only Stanley's.

Win, she thought, oh Win. It too was automatic and pointless. A cry out of her past, the same sort of mute, futile appeal that used to well up in her often when she was first married. Win, help me, look what they're doing to me, look what they're making out of me.

Futile. But no more so now than it had been then. She should know better than to cry out to Win. Alive or dead, he did not hear or care. Whatever "they" had made out of her—a hard, calculating, spying woman, capable of anything—it was Win who had first taught her how little a word like love could mean.

In the upstairs hall, Nell paused at the door of Little Harriet's room. Over her arm she held the dress she was making for Little Harriet. Basted. Ready for a fitting. Of course if the child was already asleep …

It came on without warning, the way her premonitions always did; first a feeling of blank stillness, then the flash of mental lightning. They seldom failed to reveal the truth. (Or if they did, Nell promptly forgot them. That was what Win used to say. Nell's premonitions and Nell's lame ducks. He always made fun of them both.)

Well, it was nothing to joke about. If this premonition turned out to be right, if Little Harriet really was off on some hare-brained excursion to get even with Stanley ... The consequences might even be fatal, thought Nell. She felt that she was probably blanching. Certainly she shuddered. Her hand tightened on the door knob; she turned it—not quite noiselessly—and peered in.

Darkness; for the first moment she could not even make out the shapes of the familiar furniture. Silence. A smell of fingernail polish hanging in the warm, still air. And now she could see—with relief, of course; only she did so hate an anti-climax—the hump of Little Harriet under the quilt on the bed. All right. So her premonitions weren't infallible. She had never claimed they were.

But just as she was on the point of withdrawing, here it came again. Blankness, flash. Blankness, flash.

Would anybody huddle under a quilt on a night like this? And the complete silence; not the slightest breath of sound.

So convinced, this time, that she did not bother to be cautious, she went over to the bed and touched the hump that was not Little Harriet at all. Pillows. The old routine, tried and true; and the sleeping porch, with the cedar beside it, made to order for the kind of escape Little Harriet had pulled off tonight. With no one the wiser, except for Nell and her premonition. Thank God she had heeded it! The consequences ...

They stared her in the face, no longer a matter for pleasurable shivers, but solid and immediate. Little Harriet was really gone, and it was no good telling herself that this might be only some harmless, childish junket. It might be. But supposing it wasn't?

She switched on the light and looked at her watch. A quarter past eleven. Half an hour or so since Little Harriet had announced that she was going upstairs to bed. With a great show of yawning; that was perhaps what had triggered Nell's premonition mechanism. Evan might have been suspicious. But he wasn't there. Only Marianna and Ralph, contentedly believing what they wanted to believe—that the child had forgotten all that nonsense about Win's death, about "getting" Stanley.

Nell found, rather to her surprise, that her mind was working with clarity and precision, providing her not only with the what to do, but the how. It was going to be easy, now that she had Win's car at her disposal. Hers now, according to the will, and Pearl said *she* didn't want it; she had already turned it over to Nell, along with the keys to the fishing cabin that was also Nell's now, according to the will. She snapped off the light and went down the hall, into her own room; there on the dresser were a couple of letters she had written in the afternoon. She picked them up, and her purse.

Downstairs, all was as she had left it—Marianna in her little armless rocker, hemming curtains, with Buster dozing at her feet; Ralph stretched out in his Morris chair; syrupy music purling out of the radio. Nell's voice rose crisply above it, and Ralph, startled out of his pleasant bemusement, said, "Yes, Nell? What did you say?"

"I'm going to run down to the post office with these letters." She held them up. "I just remembered them, and I want to make sure they go out. If there's anything you want me to pick up while I'm downtown, Marianna—" She waited, hanging on to her patience, while Marianna decided no, there was nothing. Then she gave them a bright smile, poor innocents, and headed for the door.

Into the car (she did love driving it, having it for her own), out of the drive, and she was on her way. A feeling of well-being grew in her as she sailed down Main Street. She was handling a tricky situation with quiet competence; even Win—if he were here to see—would have to admit that for once she was resisting the impulse to dramatize.

Of course there was always the chance of miscalculation. Little Harriet might not be at The Spot at all. In which case … She put the thought firmly out of her mind. She would cross that bridge—and with quiet competence, too—if and when she came to it.

Gravel kept getting in Little Harriet's sandals. Sometimes she could shake it out by way of the open toes. Other times she had to stop and undo those damn buckles and brush it off the bottoms of her feet. They were sticky, and they hurt. So did the skinned place (a souvenir of her trip down the cedar tree) on the inside of her knee. She didn't want to be seen, so whenever she heard a car coming she ducked off the side of the road—more often than not into a patch of sandburs.

It was farther than she thought. Of course she had never walked it before. What a temptation Daddy's car had been, sitting right there in the driveway, and she could so easily have snitched the keys from Aunt Nell's purse … But she didn't dare run the risk of being heard. This way was safe. That was about all you could say for it.

It wasn't just a matter of gravel and sore feet, either. She was finding it harder and harder to ignore an inner hollowness, a stirring of uneasiness and doubt. How brilliant and bold her idea had seemed at first! And so simple: if she couldn't get Stanley for stabbing Daddy, she would get him for something else. Ever since The Spot opened, people had been buzzing about the things that went on out there. Nobody was ever really specific about what things. Illicit crap games in the room upstairs? Liquor sold to minors? Dope pushing? Gangsters holding their sinister confabs? There were dark hints, too, about who rented the tourist cabins, and why.

Personally, Little Harriet favored dope pushing. It would make such stunning headlines: "Fifteen-year-old Girl Exposes Narcotics Ring." And there would be a photograph of her, an angle shot highlighting the strange fascination of her face, with its perfectly good bones …

But just how had that fascinating fifteen-year-old girl gone about her exposing? Not by simply marching upstairs and flinging open the door. That was for sure.

Well, how? Once more Little Harriet paused to grapple with the gravel situation. By now she could see The Spot. Its neon sign stared at her like an enormous, derisive eye, and she felt her heart sink. No use kidding herself. She had no idea whatever of what to do when she got there.

In another moment—for she plodded doggedly on—she spotted the Hoyt car, parked among several others in the driveway. And of course that settled it; she couldn't possibly go inside now. Evan was sure to see her (he *would* have to pick tonight, of all nights, to bring Norma out here) and he was also sure to figure out what she was up to and start yakking at her about how tough Stanley was, she mustn't try to buck him, et cetera, et cetera.

What a bust! To come all the way out here for nothing …

The sound of an approaching car sent her scuttling around the corner of the building. From the shadows she watched Stanley's roly-poly pal—the one they called Joe—park beside Stanley's convertible, get out of his car, and hitch up his pants. Had he seen her? If so, it didn't seem to worry him. Before he went inside he paused briefly to relight his cigar.

All the same, it had very likely been a narrow escape. Little Harriet felt a flurry of excitement. This was more like it. And another thing: those tourist cabins, squatting back there in the black, sultry night. Why not? As long as she was here anyway, why not? She began to creep along the side of the rough, stucco building, and in her mind the stunning headline underwent a slight revision: "Fifteen-year-old Girl Exposes Call Girl Racket."

At first—coming from the neon dazzle in front to the darkness behind—she could see nothing at all. But nothing. It was as if she had been struck blind. She kept stepping into holes and getting a foot full of warm, sandy dirt. It beat gravel. Then, gradually, the cabins began to take vague shape, and the scraggly cottonwoods above them. There was a dim light showing in the farthest cabin.

Hey, thought Little Harriet, this really is something. She began groping her way forward again. Away from the stucco security of The Spot itself, the starless, soundless night closed down on her. Like being in a cave. There were still unexpected holes under her feet, and now and then patches of coarse grass or weeds. Once she bumped smack into a tree. She giggled nervously.

All at once, half way toward that glimmer of light in the farthest cabin, she got scared. Why? Had she heard a rustle behind her? Caught a glimpse of movement out of the corner of her eye? She stopped and looked back over her shoulder. (It took a lot of doing, what with her neck gone suddenly rigid, and the pounding of her heart.) Nothing. Nothing at all. But someone could be there, all the same. Someone unheard and unseen, watching her, stopping when she stopped, waiting to take another step until she took one. That was the ghastly thing about it— not to be sure of the difference between reality and imagination. To feel herself slipping out of control, and not to be able to stop …

She did not intend to run. But her witless legs took charge of her. They jerked into a crazy stumble, even though one fragment of her mind remained calm and sensible and still not sure. No power on earth could have made her look back of her now. The unheard, unseen someone must be gaining on her, his merciless hands stretched out for her throat: "Fifteen-year-old Girl Found Strangled …

She gathered her breath to scream. But she never did. Down she plunged, and something splintered in the side of her head, and after that it was all blackness.

Eleven

Well, why not? thought Goldie when Evan asked her to join him and Norma for a beer. She could still keep an eye on things for Rita, with business as slow as it was tonight; and she wasn't going to get a chance to nip over home until Rita came back. The Lord only knew when that would be. Stanley certainly wasn't rushing out to keep his date with her. Still up there at the cash register, having one of his private conferences with his pal Joe.

So why not have a beer with Evan and Norma? After all, the good old high school days ought to be water over the dam by now. But in spite of their concerted efforts, the conversation was pretty stiff in the joints. Evan was jumpy; Norma had to work just a little too hard at her good-sport role; Goldie herself found that some of those high school snubs still rankled, even in her easy-going heart. She couldn't very well leave yet, though. Unless one of the other customers should signal for service. None of them did. And that so-and-so Stanley … No doubt it was his idea of fun, to keep Rita waiting like this. It was at least fifteen minutes since she had slipped out the back door, and he still hadn't turned the cash register over to Joe and gone out to meet her. Joe wasn't even in sight anymore.

Maybe this was Stanley's way of giving Rita the brushoff. Let's hope so, thought Goldie, and wondered how long it would take Rita to catch on.

Not as long as she might have expected. The next time she glanced toward the back door, there was Rita coming in again, looking anything but happy. Goldie finished her beer and stood up. Here was her chance to make her excuses, say her little thank-you piece, and brighten everybody's life by shoving off.

Rita waited for her at the door. Spilling over with indignation and hurt feelings. "He called it off. Left me sitting out there a good half hour, and then sent Joe to say he couldn't make it. Business. He can't get away with this. I'm going to tell him off!"

"Go ahead," said Goldie. "Tell him off. Only look, I want to duck over home and check on the baby. So don't get yourself fired till I come back, will you?"

She paused at the door, waiting for a moment when Stanley didn't happen to be looking her way (after all, what he didn't know wouldn't hurt him) and it was the funniest thing, what she thought she saw, just as she slipped out. A woman that looked enough like Mrs. Nell Covey to be her. Coming in the front door. Well, of course she must be mistaken. Her imagination, or the poor lighting, had played a trick on her. What on earth would Mrs. Nell Covey be doing in a joint like The Spot?

Lord, but it was a dark night! Black as the inside of a pocket. But Goldie knew the way by heart. Cut off the path here, just this side of the third cabin; angle through, between the two cottonwoods …

She thought at first that it was a bundle of clothes there under the tree. It wasn't, though. When she knelt down her groping hands touched a skinny arm, some longish frizzy hair. She fumbled in her bag for her cigarette lighter; its tiny flame showed her enough to send her running, awkward in her high heels, back to The Spot.

Luckily, she caught Evan's eye right away. She didn't have the breath to make a sound. (Which was just as well; no sense getting the whole place in an uproar.) He was beside her in a flash, and when the back door had closed behind them, she panted it out: "Your Uncle Win's kid. Little Harriet. Out there under the tree. An accident or something, call the doctor …"

Neither of them had noticed Norma until then, but there she was. Must have been right on Evan's heels; and Goldie had to say this for her, she kept calm and didn't waste time asking fool questions. "Go ahead, Evan. I'll get the doctor," she said, and ducked back inside.

Goldie led the way, and held her lighter while Evan dropped to his knees beside that pathetic huddle. "She's breathing," he whispered. "I can feel her pulse." But Little Harriet did not stir while he felt her arms and legs, her neck, her head. He found a lump there, above her ear. The size of an egg. Her face was so white and still that Goldie felt her heart sink.

"What was she doing out here?" she asked. "I can't figure it out." Apparently Evan couldn't either; he didn't answer. Goldie heard herself going on, in a low, nervous voice. "What I think is, I think she must have stumbled over this root. Look. See how it kind of hunches up out of the ground?" Anyone might trip over it in the darkness. A sinewy, tough tree root thrusting its way to the surface of the sandy soil. "She must have stumbled over it. And hit her head against the tree on the way down. Knocked herself out."

Again Evan didn't answer. The rest of the time they waited in silence. Norma, sensible right down the line, had waited in front of The Spot for Dr. Morrison, so she could bring him around to the back without going inside. All the same, the word seemed to have spread, because it wasn't long before people started turning up. Among them Mrs. Nell Covey. So it hadn't been Goldie's imagination or the poor lighting. And—you could have knocked her over with a feather—Mrs. Pearl Covey. The kid's mother, with some very snappish remarks to Evan about how, if Little Harriet had been staying at home where she belonged, Mrs. Pearl would have seen to it that she didn't get a chance to sneak out and go snooping around … Mrs. Nell put on quite a show, wringing her hands and giving out with throaty gasps.

Dr. Morrison paid no attention to either of them. After he had looked Little Harriet over by his flashlight, he straightened his long, lanky frame and said, "Nasty bump on her head. I want a better look at her. Give me a hand, Evan, and we'll move her into one of these cabins where I can see what I'm doing." She was beginning to come round; she gave a faint moan when they lifted her, and Goldie caught a glimpse of her face in the flashlight beam—dull and swollen-looking, twitching a little.

"The farthest cabin," said Goldie. "I think it's unlocked." She went ahead, because she knew where the light switch was, and the water and towels from the lavatory. That was how she happened to be there and hear what Little Harriet said when she first came to. "Evan," she mumbled, and he grabbed her hand quick and said, "Sure. I'm right here." Little Harriet's eyelids kept fluttering, not quite opening, not quite closing. Then all at once they did open, wide, and before they went out of focus again she said in the same thick mumble, "They hit me."

Out of her head, Goldie told herself firmly. Or maybe she had heard wrong. No, Evan's face told her that much. The others weren't inside the cabin; they huddled anxiously at the door. "What did she say?" somebody whispered.

Of course Dr. Morrison must have heard. But his mind was on calling the ambulance. Getting his patient to the hospital. Norma went to phone.

And then who should turn up but Stanley. All bland concern. "What seems to be the trouble? They tell me there was some kind of an accident …" His flat stare took in the doctor and Little Harriet, brushed casually past Evan and Goldie, and at last rested on Mrs. Pearl. There was no interpreting either of their expressions. "What happened?"

They all started to talk at once, as if they had a great deal to tell instead of precious little. But in the confusion of voices, Mrs. Nell's was the one that stood out. Deep and important-sounding, like a pipe organ. "I had this feeling about the child. Something warned me … And you heard what she said, didn't you? She said somebody hit her."

Stanley looked properly startled. "Somebody … Who? Why would anybody hit her?"

"Why, indeed?" Mrs. Nell pulled out another stop or two. "I should think you might be able to throw some light on that, Mr. Stanley. In view of what went on at Win's house yesterday. As I understand it, Little Harriet told you what she thought of you. And you made it just as clear that she was going to get into trouble if she—"

"Oh, for heaven's sake!" Mrs. Pearl broke in shrilly. "How ridiculous can you get?"

"What is this, anyway?" Stanley didn't sound in the least upset. Just plain curious. "You folks think I lured the kid out here, bopped her over the head just because she got a little sore and talked out of turn?"

"I think it's entirely in character," said Mrs. Nell. Spunky enough, thought Goldie; but still no match for Stanley.

He thought it over. "Well, then, nothing to do but call the sheriff and get him to investigate the whole thing. Hell, if somebody did clobber her, I want it cleared up. Right now. After all, I'm responsible for what goes on at my place. I'll get Novak out here right away."

Goldie had a picture of what the sheriff's investigation—with Stanley supervising—was going to amount to. Just exactly nothing. He would say (and Goldie herself would have to back him up) that he had never left his post at the cash register. Oh Lord, would she also have to say that Rita had sneaked out?

She was still worrying about that particular angle when the ambulance arrived and departed, with Little Harriet aboard and all the Covey connections following in their separate cars. Stanley didn't let them get away until he had put the finishing touches on his performance as cooperative and open-faced citizen. "No need to tell you folks how sorry I am about this. Anything I can do, don't hesitate to call me. I'll get the sheriff right on it."

He did, too. And Goldie needn't have worried about the Rita angle; it never came up. As soon as the sheriff heard Little Harriet's name, he got a deliver-me look in his eye. "That one," he said. "I've met up with her before. I know how much you can believe of what *she* says. Hid her father's suicide note on me. Tried to make out he was murdered … Well. Let's give a look around. Where did it happen?"

Right away he spotted the tree root. Nobody could miss it. Goldie told her story, and Stanley told his—all about how Little Harriet had it in for him and had no doubt come out here with the idea of stirring up some kind of trouble. Who, Stanley? Of course he hadn't known she was anywhere on the premises. He'd been inside all evening. Even if he had known the kid was snooping around, he wouldn't have cared. He had nothing to hide. As for trailing her and clipping her over the head—well, you didn't go after mosquitoes with a cannon.

Sheriff Novak laughed obligingly. There were a few more questions before he left for the hospital. He was going to talk to the Coveys, he said, and to Little Harriet—or rather, listen to her, if she was in any shape to talk.

But he wasn't going to believe her, thought Goldie. No wonder Stanley was pleased.

He was practically spilling over with the milk of human kindness. "Why didn't you tell me your baby was sick, Goldie?" he said. "I'd have given you the night off. You know that. Matter of fact, there's no reason why you shouldn't go on home right now. Go ahead."

Real big of him. Sure. It was almost quitting time, anyway; and if she knew Stanley he'd chisel a couple of extra hours out of her, sooner or later. She decided to beat it before he changed his mind.

It wasn't more than a five-minute walk to her home, which was one of a row of shabby, wrong-side-of-the-tracks houses on the edge of town. There was a round flower bed of salvia and zinnias in the front yard, a battered tricycle beside the porch, and a tire swing sagging from the one tree. Be nice when we can move, thought Goldie as she went up the walk. It was an automatic thought with her, and it no longer had any particular urgency. They kept talking about moving, but something always came up—doctor bills, or truck repairs, or a job Bob had counted on that didn't pan out. Always something.

She tiptoed through the living room, where her kid sister sprawled on the couch. Dead to the world. Not a peep out of the three little girls in the bedroom, either. Even the baby was sleeping peacefully. There was no reason why Goldie shouldn't turn in herself. But somehow she didn't feel sleepy. Too tired, she guessed; all wound up over finding Little Harriet. She went back to the kitchen, sat down in the breakfast nook, and eased off her high-heeled pumps.

"They hit me." Of course it would seem that way to Little Harriet. Wandering around out there in the dark, looking for trouble. Naturally she'd decide that the tree root was a personal enemy who had leaped up and tripped her. Besides, according to Sheriff Novak, she was a born liar. Trying to make murder out of what everybody knew was suicide. Everybody knew it was suicide the first time, too, in spite of the fancy coverup job the family and Doc Morrison had done. Poor guy. Poor Win Covey. Bound and determined to die.

Evan looked enough like him to be his son. The same proud, homely face. The same air of elegance. But Win Covey had no son. No son, and too many wives.

Either one of those wives, in Goldie's opinion, spelled trouble. She had always had a sneaking sympathy for Mrs. Pearl; it dated back to the time—after high school, after Evan was long gone—when Goldie was still eating her heart out. She used to tell herself, back then, that it wouldn't have worked, look at Evan's Uncle Win and his new wife, it would have been like that for her and Evan, only worse ... Because Goldie didn't have Mrs. Pearl's endurance. She would have been crushed.

Not Mrs. Pearl. Hard as nails. Stanley had met his match there, all right. It darted through Goldie's head, quick as a snake's tongue: Had Mrs. Pearl gotten wind of what went on with him and Rita? Was that how she happened to be at The Spot tonight? If so, Rita was just about the luckiest girl in town. Let Mrs. Pearl catch her out in that cabin with Stanley, and she'd have more than hurt feelings to worry about.

As for the other Mrs. Covey, Mrs. Nell—well, there was more than one way of spelling trouble. Goldie would be the last to deny that Mrs. Nell was a real charmer, a real lady. All the same, there was something about her, something a little bit phoney ...

A movement outside the back door caught her eye. There stood Evan, peering in hopefully. "I was afraid you'd already gone to bed. I know it's late, but I just thought I'd like to see you. Unless you're too tired."

"Of course not." She padded across the kitchen in her stocking feet and unhooked the screen door. "How's Little Harriet?"

"Doing okay. Doc's going to keep her at the hospital for a day's observation, but he says there's no cause for worry."

"Thank God. Come on in and sit down. I'll make a cup of coffee."

She saw at once that he was strung up. But his eyes brightened a little as he looked around him, and Goldie felt a flush of pleasure and pride in her kitchen—the pleasantest room in the house; she was glad he was seeing it instead of the living room. The linoleum, except for that worn spot in front of the stove, was clean and bright; the curtains had a design of jolly-looking strawberries; and on the window sill above the sink there stood in a sparkling row six glasses of freshly made currant jelly with paraffin on top.

"This is nice," Evan said as he slid his long legs under the table in the breakfast nook. And all the time Goldie was putting the coffee on, she could feel him, contentedly watching her.

"Well?" she said, when she settled down across from him. "Does she still claim somebody hit her?"

"Sure. Insists on it. They hit her. They meant to kill her."

"Who are 'they'?"

"Stanley, of course. He was on the lookout for her, she says, because she'd told him she was going to 'get something' on him. She didn't much care what. She just wanted to get even with him for buying Uncle Win's house, and—well, and a few other things. At first she intended to go inside The Spot. But she saw our car outside, and she knew I'd send her on her way in nothing flat. So she slithered around to the back. Her story is that she saw a light in the farthest cabin, and she was heading out there, planning to investigate, when she felt somebody following her … Was there a light on in that cabin when you found her?"

Goldie shook her head.

"I suppose she could have made it up. Or— Hey, you know who it might have been? Pearl! She was cagey as hell about how she happened to be at The Spot tonight. Maybe she and Stanley had a rendezvous out in that cabin. I bet they did. I bet—"

"I wouldn't if I were you," said Goldie. This had gone far enough. "It was Rita out in that cabin. Not Pearl. And all I hope is that Rita realizes what a close call she had tonight. Because if Pearl had caught her and Stanley out there together … Don't look so stunned, dearie. That's the way Stanley is. He plays the field."

"He certainly does. My God. Pearl, and Rita, and— And he's even been making a play for Norma. Did you know that?"

"Doesn't surprise me in the least. Just like it didn't surprise me to hear he was buying your Uncle Win's house. It's got class, the kind of class your Uncle Win had and that Stanley wants. Even more than money. Even more than Pearl. And that's saying a lot, because I've got a feeling that with him and Pearl it's for keeps. The real thing."

"The real thing! How you can say that, when here he is—"

"You can love somebody without wanting to marry them," said Goldie quietly. "Didn't you ever notice?"

There was quite a little silence. Then Evan cleared his throat. "The sheriff came up to the hospital and talked to Little Harriet and the rest of us. Just routine. He didn't believe a word Little Harriet said. I suppose you can't blame him."

"How about the rest of your folks? Do they believe her?"

"Of course not," said Evan with sudden bitterness. "I'm the only one that ever believes Little Harriet. It's too, too unpleasant—that's their attitude. Let's pretend it isn't happening."

"I thought your Aunt Nell believed it, from the way she lit into Stanley."

"Oh well, Aunt Nell. She managed to sound just as wrought up and crazy as Little Harriet. She always overdoes things." He chewed his lip and stared into his coffee cup. "Goldie, how do you figure Rita?"

It was an unexpected switch. "How does anybody figure Rita? A dumb little cluck. A pushover for any man that looks at her twice. What of it?"

"She keeps popping up all over the place. One of Aunt Nell's lame ducks. One of Stanley's little side dishes. One of Pearl's ex-maids. She was at Uncle Win's, you know, the night he—stabbed himself. Earlier in the evening, of course. Before it happened. Did she ever mention anything about that night to you? Or about Uncle Win?"

Goldie tried to think. Certainly she and Rita had talked about Win Covey's death. Like everybody else in town. Rita had said what a nice man he was, how much she liked him. (Name a man Rita didn't like. Try and do it.) But Evan wasn't talking about the night Win Covey died …

"She had plenty to say about Pearl," said Goldie. "What a bitch on wheels she was to work for. She was going to quit, anyway, when Pearl fired her. Or so she says. She doesn't see herself as one of Stanley's side dishes. She thinks she's beating Pearl's time … Hey, I do remember one thing she said about that night. She heard your Uncle Win laughing. She was just leaving, and he was in his study, and she heard him laughing."

"*Laughing!*"

"That's why it stuck in her mind, I guess. To think he'd be laughing like that just a few minutes before he stabbed himself."

"But he was alone in the study! Or *was* he? Did somebody come to see him—"

"He could have been talking on the phone. He must have been. Because if somebody came to see him, Rita'd know it. She was there." Evan was looking at her so queerly; it gave her the shivers. "And she never said a word about anybody being there. She wouldn't keep a thing like that to herself!"

Evan just went on staring at her. Finally he said, "How about you, Goldie? Do *you* believe somebody bopped Little Harriet tonight?"

There he went, switching again. "I don't see how it could have been Stanley. He was inside, in plain sight, all evening." But Joe hadn't been in plain sight all evening. He had been sent out to the cabin to tell Rita she didn't have a date with Stanley … That hadn't been Evan's question, anyway. Do you believe somebody bopped Little Harriet? Not Stanley. Somebody. Several other people had been mousing around The Spot tonight. The kid's mother, Mrs. Nell, Rita— Goldie took a firmer grip on herself. "Besides, why should he bother? What damage could a kid like that do him? It's like he told the sheriff, you don't go after mosquitoes with a cannon. No, I don't think Stanley would take such a chance. And why would anybody else bop her, for Lord's sake? Might as well skip it."

"Sure," said Evan irritably. "Skip it. Pretend it isn't happening. You're exactly like my mother!"

Which struck Goldie so funny that she threw back her head and laughed. At once the baby set up a fretful cry from the bedroom and had to be brought out and comforted. "How pretty she is," Evan said, and he patted her plump, pink feet. Then he put his hand under Goldie's chin and tilted her face up so he could look into her eyes.

She gazed back steadily, caught up in one of her moments of perception. It's all over, she thought, with a surge of sad relief. For both of us. All really and truly over. We've never quite accepted it till now. We missed the boat back there in high school, and like as not a good thing, too, and I've got my babies and Bob, they're what I want, and Evan's got—whatever it is he's got … And we both know it. At last. It's all over.

"Poor Goldie, you're tired," Evan said gently. "I've kept you up long enough as it is." He bent down as if to kiss her, and wound up brushing his hand along her hair.

After he was gone, while she was still sitting there in the kitchen with the whimpering, half-sleeping baby in her arms, several things clicked into place in Goldie's mind. The disjointed way he had switched around, from Rita to his Uncle Win to Little Harriet. "I'm the only one that ever believes Little Harriet," he had said, and there was the sheriff's crack earlier in the evening: "Hid her father's suicide note on me. Tried to make out he was murdered." And Rita had heard Win Covey laughing …

Crazy. Little Harriet was a crazy kid. But Evan, who wasn't crazy, who was doing his best *not* to believe her, couldn't quite manage it. Murder.

"Shh," whispered Goldie. The baby had dropped off to sleep and no longer needed comforting. All the same Goldie whispered it again: "Shh. Shh."

Twelve

Stanley said, "I don't know what you mean by that crack." Not batting an eyelash. But Rita sensed the wariness in him. Who did he think he was kidding?

"You don't know what I mean." A laugh, shaky with excitement, swelled in her throat. It was all working out even better than she had planned. She had turned up for work an hour early this afternoon, looking for a chance to tell Stanley off, and he had played right into her hands. Here they were, out in the cabin (his idea) and don't think she wasn't telling him off. She looked him right straight in the eye and said, "I mean just what I said. You can't do this to me. I don't have to take it, and I'm not going to. You think you can push me around any old way. Like last night, keeping me waiting all that time, and then sending Joe out to say you couldn't make it. Like I was just some floozy. Like I was nobody."

"Now, Rita. Honey." He took a step toward her, and she backed away, nearer the wall. They had left the door open; even so, the little box of a building was stifling in the heat of afternoon. "You know better than that. Honey. Of course you're not a floozy. My God, I hate it as much as you do, the way we have to sneak around. But it's not always going to be like this—"

"You keep away from me," she said tensely. This was where she had to watch herself. Because if she let him kiss her, if she let him so much as touch her … "I'm sick and tired of playing second fiddle to Pearl Covey. You think I'm dumb or something? You think I don't know why you stood me up last night? Pearl, that's why. All of a sudden you've got important business. Who do you think you're kidding?"

"I'm not kidding anybody. I had no idea she was out here. I've told you how it is with Pearl and me, Baby."

"Sure. I'm sick and tired of that, too. You got mixed up with her without ever meaning to. I'm the one you're nuts about. How come I'm the one that gets stood up, then? Well, from now on it's going to be different. Or else."

"Or else what?" He was giving her the flat, hot stare that turned her bones to water; when she shrank back again (only she was already up against the wall) he smiled lazily. She closed her eyes, waiting, aware of what was going to happen—his urgent hands, the slow, knowing kiss—aware that she was as good as gone, and so was her plan, and who cared? Who could keep track of a plan, or worry about last night or tomorrow, when now was all that mattered? She shivered, feeling the first leisurely brush of his fingers; then he pulled her up against him roughly

From the open doorway behind them a cool voice said, "I'm so sorry. I'm afraid I'm interrupting."

Pearl looked even cooler than her voice. Immaculate in a pale green sheath. Not a hair out of place. She was smiling. Her glance flicked past Rita (but that flick was enough; it turned Rita into a tousled, rather sweaty floozy) and settled on Stanley. There was a moment of total silence.

Then he said, "Hi, Pearl. Where did you come from?"

"You mean, how long have I been here? Long enough. It's been too, too interesting. Only Rita never did answer your last question. Or else what? I don't know about you, but I can't wait to hear or else what."

"What? Oh, that. You're right, come to think of it, she never did answer. How about it, Rita? Or else what?"

They both turned toward her; the impact of their combined stares—Pearl's cold and contemptuous, Stanley's challenging—threw her into panicky confusion. Had she really said that? Had she really had a plan?

Yes. Yes, she had. It came back to her now. Only with a different focus: tell Stanley off had become tell Pearl off. The nerve of her, walking in like this, trying to push Rita around, looking at her like she was nobody. I can fix her, Rita thought; I've got the both of them right where I want them.

"Never mind or else." She was stammering a little, from excitement. "It's not going to come to that. Because I'm not taking any more off of either one of you, from now on it's going to be different—"

"It certainly is," said Pearl. "Get this straight, Stanley. Fun is fun, and all that. Up to a point. You can go on playing your little game with Rita, if that's what you want. Only, if you do, there's no more you and me. It couldn't be simpler. All you have to do is take your choice."

It was as if Rita wasn't even there anymore. Robbed of the lines that should have been hers (and so quietly, so neatly!), her presence not so much ignored as forgotten, she could only stand on the sidelines and watch the strange look that passed between the other two.

"And it's nothing to you, one way or the other?" Stanley asked at last. His voice sounded thick.

"I didn't say that. You can have either one of us. But you can't have it both ways. Not anymore, Stanley. Not anymore." Oh, cool as a cucumber. So damn sure of herself and of what his choice would be …

"I'll say he can't!" Rita burst out. "Let him choose. I'm not worried. You'll find out who he'll choose, you'll see—"

Pearl's light-colored, glittering eyes never swerved from Stanley. "Either you get rid of this cheap little tramp right now, fire her and get rid of her, once and for all, or you and I are through. Is that clear?"

"Why, you—" began Rita, on a long-drawn breath of outrage, but Stanley's hand closed over her wrist warningly, and his voice cut in, no longer thick and unsure.

"Listen, Pearl. You've got it all wrong. You're making a mistake."

"All right, then, I'm making a mistake. That's how it is. Take it or leave it, and let's get it over with."

"Then there's only one thing I can do, of course." Of course. Rita's mind, simmering though it was—cheap little tramp, am I!—snatched at the phrase. Of course. He'll choose me, she'll find out who rates around here, only one thing he can do. Of course …

She could not believe what she was hearing; her ears buzzed as if an angry fly were trapped there. But Pearl's face, pinched with triumph, convinced her.

Stanley was firing her. He was choosing Pearl.

"Here." With his free hand he fumbled in his pocket and drew out a tight roll of bills. "This will help square things. I'm sorry it's turned out this way, Rita …"

"You're sorry!" She tried to yank her wrist free, but he was too strong for her. "Just because she tells you to, you think you can pay me off and … Oh no, you don't! You don't get rid of me that way! I can fix you—"

"Now, Rita, wait a minute, I know you're sore and all that, but let's be reasonable, let's not talk crazy." As he spoke, Stanley moved without seeming to, so that it was his face she saw, instead of Pearl's, and his voice blurred (she no longer had any clear idea of what he was saying) into a throbbing sound, like the purr of a tiger. Maybe she could have resisted that, but there was his hand, too, the subtly changing pressure of his fingers on her wrist; still powerful, but different, insinuating a secret, wordless message. The same message that was in his eyes. She could not look away from them, any more than she could pull free of his hand. Her mouth opened a little. She felt her arm melting, all of her melting under the pressure and beat of that unmistakable promise: Take it easy, Baby, let's kid Pearl along, keep her happy, of course we're not through, you and I, we've only just started …

Stanley knew, the instant she got it. His head tilted backward toward

Pearl, ever so slightly, in a tiny, derisive signal. He half-smiled. Just before he turned, he winked at Rita.

Oh, she could have laughed out loud at Pearl, standing there with that smirk on her face, thinking she had won. It was all Rita could do to keep a straight face while she put on her act of flouncing out. She saved the best for her parting shot: "Okay, take him. He's all yours. Who wants him, anyway?" She tossed her head and left, on a wave of pure and secret elation.

It carried her along, all the way home—even though the truck driver who picked her up and gave her a ride into town was a real sourpuss. Hardly passed the time of day with her, let alone trying to date her up. Not that it would have gotten him any place, of course, not with Stanley sure to call her tonight, as soon as he could shake Pearl.

Once in her room at Shoemakers', she kicked off her red wedge sandals and flopped on the bed. The heat—even now, so late in the afternoon—was stifling. Mrs. Shoemaker's hens clucked drowsily in the backyard; otherwise it was deathly quiet. Outside her window she could see, below the dark green blind, the leaves of the elm tree hanging limp and wilted-looking. The blind was crooked and cracked; the sun shining through its worn spots made a pattern of dazzling pin pricks. Like a face, thought Rita, a face that she knew and yet could not quite place. Pearl's? Stanley's? It was funny how, when she was away from him, she could never recall in detail what he looked like. Just a general effect of darkness, powerfulness, with no clear picture of brow or chin or nose. Pearl's face, now, was indelibly stamped in her memory: smooth and pale as an egg, with those light-colored, prominent eyes, the sharpish nose, and, in contrast, the full, red mouth …

Ah, but Stanley's voice—that she could remember. Not what he said, but the throbbing sound itself that, like even the casual brush of his hand, set up a trembling in her. Powerful and dark and at the same time shot through with spangles, as dazzling as the sun-pricked blind she was staring at. Staring and staring, until it all melted together into one vague shimmer—the feeling of elation, Stanley's voice, his hand on her wrist, that look he had given her at the end. Like a shower of gold, transforming defeat into victory. She gave herself up to its spell; for a moment what had been said in the tourist cabin became what might have been said. Stanley rose magnificently to her defense at that phrase of Pearl's: cheap little tramp. Stop it, he thundered; you are speaking of the woman I love …

Abruptly the spell was broken. Love. It was a word Stanley never used. Not once; though it had gushed out of Rita time after time, though she had begged him for it. Love me, Stanley, love me.

He had not said it, nor anything like it, this afternoon. He had stood by without a word while Pearl called her a cheap little tramp. He had tried to pay her off with money. Had fired her, because that was what Pearl told him to do. What was one little look when you balanced it against those heavy facts?

Rita swung her bare feet to the floor and sat up on the edge of the bed. Her off-the-shoulder blouse was sticky with sweat against her ribs. But inside she felt the chilly weight of reality, the shudder of misgivings.

He had not called her, either. Surely by this time he could have gotten away from Pearl. If he wanted to.

Supposing he didn't want to. Supposing she, not Pearl, was the dope, tricked all the way down the line, and too dumb to know it until now, when it was too late.

Oh, but it wasn't too late. She still had in reserve what she had not used this afternoon. She could use it any time. Any time at all. Like now? Sure, like now. It was as strong as ever. Rita herself was not sure just how strong. But then neither was Stanley. She was one up on him there. At least she knew what she knew. And Stanley didn't! The realization sent her spirits soaring. From the beginning he had circled around it cautiously, never quite daring to bring it out in the open, no doubt praying to God that she would. Well, she hadn't. Not even this afternoon, when they both started in on her. "Or else what?" So Pearl was just as much in the dark as he was.

She couldn't help it; the laugh simply swelled up in her throat and burst out. They thought they could push her around, did they? Why, she had them exactly where she wanted them! The only question was how to use what she had so it would do the most good. There were several possibilities; she could pick and choose. Nell Covey? That screwy kid, Little Harriet? One of the Hoyts?

It hit her like a flash of lightning. Evan Hoyt. Of course! Hadn't he come right out—the other night at The Spot—and asked her for a date? She had it made. She really had it made.

She could hardly wait to get to the telephone, downstairs in the front hall. And yet, once there, she hesitated, struck not so much by conscience as by a stab of hope. Stanley might still call her, it wasn't even six yet, at this very instant the phone under her hand might ring and there his voice would be, his dark, spangly voice showering her once more with gold.

The instant passed. The phone did not ring. But the stab of hope had left its mark; she would keep tonight open, she decided, just in case. Besides, what kind of an impression would Evan have of her, if she let it be known she was at loose ends on a Saturday night? He didn't seem like her type, but you never knew about these skinny, quiet guys. Sometimes they surprised you.

She hoped, as she dialed the number, that Evan's mother wouldn't answer; there was something about Mrs. Hoyt that always threw Rita into a dither. Luck was with her. She recognized, with a rush of relief, Nell Covey's voice. "Hello? … Oh, hello there, Rita! How are you, dear?"

Mrs. Covey had such a special way of saying the most ordinary things. Like when she was running the gift shop in Chicago, where Rita had worked for a while, she'd say to a customer, "Can I help you?" with that big, warm smile, as if she couldn't think of anything in the whole wide world she'd rather do than help you. Like now. "How are you?" As if she really truly cared how you were. Oh, she could give you what-for, too, as Rita had found out, more than once. She laid down the law, but good, over that fellow—what was his name?—kind of squinty-eyed, and it was true he kept forgetting to pay back the money he borrowed, but how he could dance. And the elevator operator, his name was Tony … Only she wasn't hateful about it, like the other Mrs. Covey. And she never held it against you afterwards. Once she had blown off steam, that was the end of it.

She sounded real surprised when Rita asked for Evan. "Who? Evan?" she asked, as if she couldn't have heard right. But then she hurried on. "Why, yes. Yes, of course, dear. Here he is right now."

For a second after he said hello Rita's mind went blank. She heard herself giggle tensely. "I suppose you think I've got a nerve, calling you like this," she began. "It's not like I was in the habit of calling up guys, especially guys I don't hardly know. And I don't want you to get any *ideas*, you know, or anything like that."

"Not at all. I'm very glad you called." He sounded glad, but a little nervous, too, and it wasn't any trick to figure out why. If Rita knew anything about Mrs. Covey, she was right there at his elbow, listening. She made no bones about being curious; it never seemed to occur to her that some things were none of her business.

"Well, you know what you were mentioning last night, about let's get together some time—"

"Of course. How about tonight?"

Wow, thought Rita, did he ever snap me up on that one. He must really have a thing for me … With an effort, she remembered her resolution. "Oh, I couldn't possibly make it tonight. Tonight's Saturday. But I was thinking, it just so happens that I'm free tomorrow—"

"Fine. How about if I pick you up at Shoemakers' tomorrow afternoon at four?"

"At four?" She had been counting on an evening date. But maybe he'd take her to the club for a drink; that's what his crowd did on Sundays. She would wear her new eyelet … "Okay. Four o'clock. Toodle-oo, then, Evan, till tomorrow—"

She broke off with a gasp. Out of the corner of her eye she had caught a flicker of pale green at the front screen door. She turned jerkily; the receiver slipped in her clammy hand and clattered against the table before she got it hung up. The late afternoon sun struck the screen at a slant, turning all the tiny squares into bright fuzz, with the blob of pale green beyond. Then the door clicked open and shut again, without haste.

"I think we'd better have a little talk," said Pearl quietly. "Shall we go upstairs to your room?"

Somehow Rita found the breath to say, "I haven't got anything to talk to you about. I don't see why—"

"I've got something to talk to you about, though. For your own good." And she started up the stairs. Inside Rita's room, she sat down on the dressing table bench and took a package of cigarettes from the big pouch purse she was carrying. It matched her high-heeled sandals. The color of butterscotch. "Here's the point, Rita. I'm not sure you really got it, while we were having our little session with Stanley."

"Oh, is that so!" Rita stayed on her feet, with her back to the door, and her hands clenched in the pockets of her full cotton skirt. "Maybe it's you that didn't get the point. Did you ever think of that? It just so happens—"

"It just so happens that I saw the look Stanley gave you, there at the end. You fell for it, didn't you? You still don't believe he's really through with you. That's why I'm here. To set you straight, once and for all. You never had a chance with Stanley to begin with, and you never will have. If you've got any ideas along those lines, get rid of them right now. Believe me, I'm doing you a favor."

"I don't need any favors from you, thank you. I can look out for myself. If you've got to worry about somebody, start worrying about Stanley. You may think he's through with me, and he may think so, but I've got something to say about it too. You're going to look pretty sick when you find out what I've got up my sleeve."

"You've got exactly nothing up your sleeve," said Pearl. "Let's not waste any more time, Rita. Stanley's mine. You keep away from him. Don't you ever try to see him again. Don't even call him up. I'll find it out if you do, and I won't stand for it. Is that clear? I will not stand for it. As for what you're planning to spill to Evan tomorrow, you can forget about that, too. You're not going to tell him anything. Because if you do …" The corners of her mouth lifted a little, in the cruel semblance of a smile. Her eyes were like glass, almost as transparent, and unblinking.

"Yeah," whispered Rita, with a last desperate clutch at her assurance.

"If I do?"

"If you do I'll kill you," said Pearl matter-of-factly. Without looking away from Rita, still without blinking, she reached into her purse. "Do you understand?"

Incredulously, Rita stared at the gun in her hand. It was real, and steady as a rock, and it was aimed at Rita's heart. She put out her hands as if to fend it off; they wobbled in front of her, and her knees wobbled too, only her throat tightened up agonizingly, so that her voice came out in a croak. "No. No. I—"

"You don't understand? You don't believe me?"

And now the words came tumbling out, fast and frantic. "Yes, I believe you. Oh God, yes. Please. I believe you. I never meant— Look, it was a joke. Honest. I'll do like you say. I'll go away. Anything. Only don't— Please, because I don't want to die, I don't want to die …"

"Then stay away from Stanley," said Pearl. She dropped the gun back in her purse and stood up.

Thirteen

The Shoemaker house was across the street from the high school building. Which was one reason it was a rooming house: in the wintertime the out-of-town teachers stayed there because it was convenient and because the only alternative was the Fontenelle Hotel on Main Street, where nobody ever stayed except some poor benighted travelling salesman unlucky enough to be stranded in town overnight. Summer provided slimmer pickings for the Shoemakers; most Fontenelle residents had homes of their own. But there were a few perennials, like old Mr. Chester, who had nowhere else to live, now that his wife was dead. And Rita, who, at the age of thirteen, had been left behind when her mother ran off with a carnival man. This qualified Rita as one of Aunt Nell's lame ducks. Perhaps it also accounted for her romantic cast of mind.

It was a chunky house, brown trimmed in white, with an air of determined respectability. Lace curtains at the windows. A row of tiger lilies along the porch. A modest sign—"Rooms"—on a post in the front yard.

Evan arrived on the dot of four. The afternoon was hot, heavy with that special Sunday torpor. Old Mr. Chester sat on the front porch in one of the white wicker chairs, with the Sunday paper in his lap and the fly swatter handy. His bald head was sunk far down on his chest. He was snoring lightly.

There was no answer when Evan rang the doorbell. Or when he knocked. He peered in through the screen door at the hall and the tidy, empty living room, where the shades had been drawn against the sun. A dim vista of potted plants, overstuffed furniture, crocheted doilies.

"Ain't nobody home. They've all gone off somewheres."

Old Mr. Chester, roused out of his nap, was peering, beady-eyed, at Evan. He stretched his wrinkled neck, and his toothless jaws worked in and out. He looked remarkably like a turtle.

"Rita?" said Evan. "I was looking for Rita."

"Ain't nobody home," repeated the old man. A fly caught his attention. Stealthily he reached for the swatter, held it poised for a tense moment, brought it down with a sudden whack. "Got him. Looks like we're going to get some rain, the way them pesky flies are biting."

"Do you know where she went?"

Mr. Chester blinked at him. "Who?"

"Rita. I'm looking for Rita."

"Ain't seen hide nor hair of her all day. Mrs. Shoemaker could most likely tell you where she's at."

Evan drew a long breath. "Well, where's Mrs. Shoemaker?"

"Drove off somewheres in the car. Her and the Mister both. Ain't nobody home." Once more Mr. Chester went through his fly-stalking routine. "Missed him. Looks like we're going to get some rain, the way them pesky—"

"But she *must* be here." Evan opened the screen door and called her name. His own voice bounced back to him, urgent and forlorn. If she had wanted to change the date, or break it, surely she would have let him know. That is, any other girl would have. Maybe Rita considered it chic to be late.

He sat down on the porch steps and waited for fifteen crawling minutes, during which old Mr. Chester stacked up a score of seven hits and five misses. Rita did not come rushing up the street, breathless with apologies. Mrs. Shoemaker did not return from somewheres with a simple, comfortable explanation of Rita's absence. Evan himself was kept busy fighting off the alarm that threatened to replace his annoyance.

"Which is her room?" he asked abruptly. "Rita's room. Where is it?"

"Head of the stairs." Then old Mr. Chester stretched his turtle neck and blinked in belated reproof. "She ain't allowed to have gentleman callers in her room. It's against the rules. Mrs. Shoemaker—"

Evan was already halfway up the stairs. There was no answer when he knocked on Rita's door. He had expected none; the whole house had a lifeless feel. He realized that he was scared, and when he tried the door and found it unlocked he realized what he was scared of …

But the room was empty. Quite tidy, except for the clutter of cosmetics on the bureau. The bed was made up, with a shrunken, crinkle-striped spread covering its lumpiness. The curtains stirred in the breeze.

Back on the porch, old Mr. Chester said, "I told you there wasn't nobody home."

"I know. Do you know when Mrs. Shoemaker will be back?"

"They went off somewheres in the car. No, I couldn't say when they'll be back. Some time along in the evening, most likely."

"I see. Well. Thanks, anyway."

"Don't mention it," said old Mr. Chester, and reached, stealthily, for the fly swatter.

Evan sat in the car for several minutes, trying to sort out his thoughts. No use looking for Rita at The Spot; it was closed on Sundays. So was everything else in Fontenelle, except the drugstore and the De Luxe Quick Eats. He could try those two places, and he could call Goldie to see if she had any ideas, and he could check with Mrs. Shoemaker when she got back from wherever she was …

There were half a dozen kids in the drugstore, whooping it up over Cokes and ice cream sodas. There was one customer at the De Luxe— the fellow from the filling station was polishing off a wedge of apple pie and a cup of coffee. There was no answer when Evan tried Goldie's telephone number.

Now let's not get hysterical, he told himself, and in his mind he went back over his telephone conversation with Rita. Her giggles, her coy backing and filling—they indicated (didn't they?) that to her Evan was just another guy who had asked her for a date. Well, there was that odd little gasp at the end; he had said his "Goodbye" into a vacuum. But Rita was the type that gasped easy. It was reassuring, too, to remember Aunt Nell's reaction. "Was that silly girl asking you for a *date?*" she said, when he hung up. (Trust her to stick around, shamelessly eavesdropping on other people's phone calls.) "Honestly, if she isn't the limit! The things I went through with her, when she was working for me! All the same, young man, you're not to take advantage of her. Because Rita's not a bad girl. Just brainless when it comes to men."

Little Harriet would have taken no such light-hearted view. If she had known about it, which she did not. She had been released from the hospital yesterday afternoon, apparently none the worse for wear; and Evan saw no point in getting her stirred up all over again. He could just imagine what deep-dyed skullduggery she would read into his date with Rita. Rita knows something, she would have insisted; she's got something to tell you.

There was no getting away from it: Rita *had* been at Uncle Win's house the night of the stabbing. She *had* reported to Goldie that puzzling bit about hearing him laugh. And she *hadn't* kept her date with Evan.

He got back in the car and cruised aimlessly for ten minutes or so. The Shoemakers' garage was still open and empty; old Mr. Chester interrupted his fly swatting long enough to report that no, Rita hadn't come back, he hadn't seen hide nor hair of her all day …

At the club—there wasn't a chance in a million that Rita would be there, but he could think of nowhere else to go—he found Norma in the group milling around the bar. "Let's have a drink outside," he said, and already he felt better. Norma would restore his perspective. He could count on her for a calm, sane view of the Rita affair.

But the tête-à-tête he had anticipated was not to be. The first person they ran into on the terrace was Stanley. He was not a club member— that took votes as well as money—and he was not there as the guest of a member. Not, that is, until he spotted Evan and Norma.

"Hello, there! Nice to see you, Miss Schaefer." He ought to know, thought Evan; he was certainly giving her the once-over. He went on to explain that he had stopped at the club because he was looking for someone (Pearl?) who turned out not to be here, after all.

"How's this table?" asked Evan, and before he could lift a hand Stanley, that flower of chivalry, had pulled out a chair for Norma and was seating her. After which he seated himself and indicated, with an affable wave of his hand, that Evan was welcome to join them if he wanted to.

It was Stanley who took charge of ordering the drinks. Stanley who pointed out that the view from here was good. Exactly as if he owned the place. And his manner toward Norma—a slick mixture of bold admiration and respect—made it clear that, having moved in on them, he had no intention whatever of moving out.

Well, then, supposing Evan simply blurted it out: Do you know where Rita is? One look into Stanley's flat, hard eyes, and he realized how far that would get him. If Stanley did know, he was certainly not going to admit it. And if he didn't know, Evan would be tipping him off. Throwing Rita to the wolves, so to speak. No, it was too risky. The silly girl might already have gotten herself into enough trouble, without outside help.

But the longer he sat here listening to Stanley trying to ingratiate himself with Norma, the more aware he became of his own inner uneasiness. He had to find out where Rita was.

"Excuse me a minute," he said suddenly. At the phone booth inside, he tried Goldie first. Still no answer. That left Mrs. Shoemaker. He hoped to God old Mr. Chester didn't consider it his duty to answer the phone in the Shoemakers' absence.

A feminine voice said Hello, and at once relief flooded him. "Rita?" he asked. He had probably just missed her, he must have misunderstood the time …

"Rita isn't here." The voice sounded final, as if its owner were on the point of hanging up.

"Wait a minute. Is this Mrs. Shoemaker? … Mrs. Shoemaker, this is Evan Hoyt, and I wonder—"

"Why, hello there, Evan." The voice was cordial now; and when Evan explained that he was "sort of anxious" to get hold of Rita, Mrs. Shoemaker said of course she could help him.

"Rita's out of town. Left last night for Chicago."

"What? She did?" It could be, of course. She could have been scared into leaving town, scared so badly that she hadn't even called Evan to let him know. "Are you sure?"

"Well, now, all I know is what it said in the note she left me. Said she was aiming to catch the nine o'clock bus. I'm holding the room for her. She asked me to. Said she didn't know just how long she'd be away. I thought at the time, what about her job, has she lost it or quit it or what? But the room's just standing there vacant, anyway, and apt to stay that way, summertime, so no harm holding it for her."

"She didn't mention where she was planning to stay in Chicago?"

"Why, no. No, she didn't. I hope—" Mrs. Shoemaker paused, doubtfully. "There isn't anything wrong, is there?"

"Probably not. It just surprised me to hear she'd left town. Well. Well, thanks a lot, Mrs. Shoemaker."

Back at the table, Stanley was apparently being quite amusing about some experience of his in Chicago; Norma tried—but not too hard—to include Evan in her smile. He did not smile back. Mrs. Shoemaker's story had not dissolved his uneasiness. And all at once he remembered that bureau in Rita's room, with its clutter of cosmetics. Would she go off to Chicago for an indeterminate length of time without her mascara and lipstick and all the other fixings? Unless she had two of everything … He could not help it: dread swept over him, as it had in the moment before he opened the door of Rita's room.

"Excuse me," he said, and he stood up. "I've got to get back to town. I didn't realize it was so late. You ready, Norma?"

She looked up, startled. He supposed he had sounded pretty abrupt. "Hey, I just ordered us another drink," said Stanley. "Stick around."

"Sorry, but I can't. Something I've got to do. Don't worry, I'll tell them to put it on my tab." For once he had gotten under that thick hide of Stanley's; his swarthy face flushed. Very gratifying.

But then he saw that he had also nettled Norma. The puzzlement in her eyes was giving way to annoyance. "I think I'll stay a while," she said coolly. "You obviously have another date, anyway."

He couldn't explain, with Stanley there. And it was far too complicated a message—even if she had been in a receptive mood—to transmit without words. There was nothing to do but depart; and hope, as he did so, that he didn't look too much like a dog slinking off with its tail between its legs. He didn't permit himself a backward glance. He didn't need one; he already had a sufficiently vivid mental picture of Stanley sitting there gloating his damn head off.

The lobby of the Fontenelle Hotel, which doubled as the bus station, was his first stop. He was not really surprised at what he learned there: Rita had not caught the bus to Chicago last night. There was only the morning train on Saturday, and none at all on Sunday, so that was out. The one other possibility was that she had hitched a ride in a car or truck.

No one was in sight at the Shoemakers'. But the slam of the car door behind Evan brought Mrs. Shoemaker trotting around from the backyard, where she had been working in her garden. She was a wiry little thing with a habitually anxious air, and when she saw Evan the lines in her forehead puckered even more. "Oh my," she said at once, "is it something about Rita?"

"She didn't take the bus last night. Do you think she might have hitched a ride with somebody?"

"Why, I guess she could of." Mrs. Shoemaker wiped her hands abstractedly on her apron. "I wasn't here when she left. It was Lodge night, chicken supper and initiation afterwards, so we left a little after six and didn't get home till way late. Wasn't anybody here but old Mr. Chester, and he goes to bed with the chickens. She said in her note she was going on the bus … Was it something important you wanted to see her about?"

"I don't know," said Evan truthfully. "I was supposed to pick her up at four this afternoon. She called me about five thirty yesterday, so it must have been after that that she decided to go to Chicago."

"Why, forevermore," said Mrs. Shoemaker helplessly. "She called you, you say? And then for her to pick up and leave for Chicago …"

"If she really went. You'd know—wouldn't you?—what luggage and clothes she'd take with her. I've got a feeling we ought to check, just to make sure."

"Of course I'd know. I could tell in a minute. She hasn't got but the one suitcase. Oh my. I thought at the time, Evan, what's she doing home at this hour of the day, is she sick or what? Only I was busy getting ready for Lodge, and then Mrs. Covey came to see her …"

They were inside, headed for the stairway. Evan stopped in the middle of a step. "Mrs. Covey? Pearl was here to see her?"

"Must of been about five thirty," said Mrs. Shoemaker. "Rita was downstairs in the hall, using the phone—" Calling me, thought Evan; no wonder that conversation had broken off suddenly, with a gasp. "—so she let her in, and they went up to Rita's room. Didn't stay more than fifteen minutes or so."

"Rita didn't leave with her, did she?"

"Oh no. I saw Mrs. Covey leave. By herself. Besides, I heard Rita moving around in her room afterwards. Then when we got home from Lodge, here was her note saying she was going to Chicago."

Except that Rita had not gone to Chicago. Or, if she had, she had set off without her suitcase. It was on the shelf in her closet, which also contained—according to Mrs. Shoemaker—all Rita's clothes except those she had been wearing in the afternoon. A full, striped skirt; a white cotton blouse, off-the-shoulder; and a pair of red wedge sandals.

"She'd of worn her new hat!" cried Mrs. Shoemaker. "Rita loves to dress up, she wouldn't go off on a trip in her tacky old everyday clothes. And look, there's all her make-up stuff on the bureau!" She turned to Evan, her little anxious face screwed up as if she were getting ready to cry. "Her bed wasn't slept in last night. But if she didn't go to Chicago, where did she go? What's happened to her?"

"Now don't worry, we'll find out," Evan assured her. He steered her down the stairs, producing on the way quite a little stock of soothing remarks. She listened trustfully and respectfully, nodding now and then in anxious agreement. Of course Rita hadn't disappeared; nobody could do that in a town the size of Fontenelle. And yes, Evan should get right over and talk to Pearl, like as not Rita had told her all about her plans.

Pearl's first words, when she answered the doorbell, were, "Is it Harriet? Is she—"

"She's fine," Evan said, disarmed in spite of himself. "Doing okay. There's something else I wanted to ask you about."

Her face hardened, but she unlatched the screen door and ushered him into the living room. "Just so it doesn't take too long," she said. "I'm expecting Homer Nelsen. Some business matters I want to go over with him."

She was wearing a black, sleeveless dress. It was just tight enough, that dress, so that when she sat down the firm flesh of her thighs swelled and strained beneath it. Evan shifted his gaze resolutely upward and said, "It's about Rita. She seems to have disappeared."

"That's all right with me," said Pearl.

"I don't doubt it. When you saw her yesterday afternoon at Shoemakers', did she say anything to you about leaving town?"

"No. It's a great idea, though. Is that what she's done?"

"She left a note for Mrs. Shoemaker saying she was going to Chicago on the bus. But she didn't catch the bus. And if she went some other way, she didn't take her suitcase or any of her clothes. The only thing that's missing is Rita herself."

That seemed to make an impression on her. She sat perfectly still, her head up, like an animal scenting danger. Then she took a cigarette from the box beside her and tapped it. "I don't want to pry, but where do you come in on this?"

"I think you know as well as I do. You overheard her talking to me on the phone yesterday. Didn't you? We made a date for this afternoon. Only Rita didn't keep it. It occurred to me that you might have had something to do with the way she changed her mind about seeing me."

"Now, really, Evan!" She gave a brittle laugh. "You know I wouldn't dream of interfering in your private affairs. I must say I'm sorry to hear you have such low tastes, but, after all, you're of age."

He took a firmer grip on his temper and said, "Maybe my interest in Rita wasn't strictly social. I know damn well yours wasn't. As for Stanley's interest in her—"

"For your information, Stanley fired her yesterday afternoon. That's how interested he is in her. One word from me, and he sent her packing. I was there when he did it." It flashed out of her in unguarded triumph. She bit her lip.

"Then why did you go to see her?" asked Evan.

"Because Rita's not very bright. You may have noticed. I wanted to make good and sure she'd gotten the idea." There it was. Take it or leave it. She was looking him in the eye; Evan felt the same grudging admiration he had felt for her on the night of Uncle Win's death, when she had faced the Coveys alone. "I don't believe you!" Desperation made him blurt it out. "An extra, private session just to say Hands Off Stanley all over again? No. I think you were—well, scared of Rita. Scared of something she knows—about you or Stanley, I don't know which. Scared of what she might tell me—"

"Such as what? You already know all about me and Stanley. All you'll ever get out of Rita is the same dear old gossip."

"I won't even get that out of her, now that she's disappeared. Look, Pearl, this is for your own good, whether you realize it or not. Unless Rita turns up, and damn quick, you're going to have a lot of embarrassing questions to answer. The sheriff's going to be very much interested in your visit to Rita, and the dustup you and Stanley had with her."

"I realize that." She said it with a kind of weary candor. "I can't help it. I don't embarrass very easy anymore, anyway. Nowhere near as easy as—well, as your mother, for instance. Does she know you're going to gallop off to the sheriff and the general public with the news that Mrs. Win Covey and a hussy of a waitress have been fighting over—"

"No, she doesn't know it."

"I just wondered." Pearl smiled, coolly and maliciously. "There's the door-bell. I think I told you I was expecting Homer. So if you'll excuse me ..."

Fourteen

The last thing Evan intended or wanted was a family conference on the subject of Rita's disappearance. But there was the slim chance that she had called him, belatedly, at home; he decided to stop in and check. That was where he made his mistake.

Rita had not called him. But Mrs. Shoemaker had—not with any news, but out of worry and good intentions and curiosity—and, naturally enough, had imparted all she knew of the situation to Mama.

"For mercy's sake, Evan," said Mama, "what in the world were you thinking of, making a date with a girl like Rita? Not that I have anything against her, but really. And what's all this about Pearl going to see her yesterday? I declare, I just don't understand—"

He told her. He also told Dad and Aunt Nell, since they were milling around in the kitchen, too, fixing the individual snack that constituted Sunday night supper. Only Little Harriet was missing, no doubt making like a convalescent on the living room couch.

When he was through, Mama said, in a voice that quavered slightly, "But if you report her missing ... Evan, you don't mean you intend to tell the sheriff about Pearl and Stanley and—and all?"

"If I don't, somebody else will, Mama. Mrs. Shoemaker knows Pearl was there. Goldie knows Stanley was fooling around with Rita. Like as not somebody else overheard the three of them quarreling yesterday afternoon. It's bound to come out, one way or another. And I for one can't help thinking it's the reason Rita's disappeared. Why else would she—"

"Nonsense," Aunt Nell broke in crisply. She popped a sliver of ham into her mouth and licked her fingers. "It's a good thing I'm around to keep you from making a fool of yourself, Evan. The idea of running to the sheriff with this tale about Rita disappearing! Ridiculous!"

"What's ridiculous about it? She's disappeared, hasn't she?"

"Well, let's put it this way. She didn't sleep where she was supposed to last night. If I know anything about Rita—and believe me, I do—she's simply off having herself a whee, and she'll turn up sooner or later, hungover but happy, ready to settle down till romance strikes again."

It jolted Evan. Aunt Nell passing up a chance to jump on Pearl and Stanley with all four feet? Aunt Nell turning conservative when she could have reveled in such sensational drama? It was true, she did know Rita better than he did … "But she didn't even dress up," he began slowly.

"All that means is that somebody came along unexpectedly," said Aunt Nell. "A truck driver. A travelling salesman. It could be anybody."

"Sure. Rita's always picking up guys." At the sound of Little Harriet's voice, Evan turned. She was standing in the doorway behind him. Wearing the pink job with the marabou trim; otherwise she looked all right. Friday night's accident or attack, whichever it was, had done no lasting damage. It seemed to him that she was avoiding his eyes. "Don't be a dope, Evan. She hasn't disappeared. She's just been mislaid. Hey, that's a pretty good line. Just been mislaid."

The brat. She had started the whole thing, with her talk about murder, and now she was weaseling out on him. He would settle with her later.

Dad was looking thoughtfully from Aunt Nell to Little Harriet and back again; when he caught Evan's questioning eye on him he smiled, rather apologetically. "I don't see the harm in giving her a little more time. Before we call in the police, I think we ought to check a few more angles. Plenty of people may have seen her downtown last night after Pearl paid her that visit."

"Of course they must have," said Mama happily. "No need to drag the family into it at all. Now make out your supper, Evan. There's plenty of salad, and … You say you just walked off and left Norma with that man, that Stanley? That wasn't any way to do, dearie. What's Norma going to think of you?"

"Nothing good," said Evan. "That makes it unanimous." He probably did owe Norma an apology. But when he tried to call her there was no answer. After a moment's hesitation, he called Mrs. Shoemaker.

"Did Rita ever do this before?" he asked, cutting in on her worried twitterings. "I mean, stay away overnight?"

Well, now that Mrs. Shoemaker thought of it, there had been several times … "Only she always let me know. Of course, this time she left me a note, too. I suppose she *could* have just gone off with a—a friend …"

"That's what Aunt Nell seems to think. She's known Rita for years, you know, and she says there's no cause for alarm."

As before, Mrs. Shoemaker snatched at whatever crumbs of comfort were offered her. And she ticked off for Evan quite an impressive list of Rita's friends—mostly male, from out of town, and without last names. There were a couple of Fontenelle natives, though; as Dad had said, it wouldn't do any harm to check a few more angles.

It didn't do any good, either. The three possibilities he located on his quick trip around town had nothing to offer in answer to his discreetly casual questions. One of them had seen Rita Thursday night. Not since. The second one had just gotten back today, after a week on an out-of-town job. Didn't know from nothing. The third, the fellow at the gas station, announced despondently that he hadn't had a Saturday night off all summer, how the hell would he know where anybody was …

Back home again, Evan "made out" his supper and fidgeted and tried at intervals—always unsuccessfully—to get Norma on the phone. That was what he was doing when Homer Nelsen rang the doorbell. There was an air of excitement about him; Evan's first thought, as he opened the screen door, was that Rita had been located and that Homer had done the locating. It was only when they reached the living room that he caught the true state of affairs. Homer was hopping mad.

"I don't know what you thought you were doing," he began, breaking in on the greetings and invitations to sit down. He faced Evan rigidly, his squinty eyes blinking, his solid belly heaving with indignation. "But there's such a thing as criminal slander, and I'm going to see to it that Pearl doesn't have to put up with any more of this nonsense from you or anybody else. You've gone just a little bit too far, threatening her with the sheriff, accusing her—"

"I didn't accuse her of anything. I was simply trying to find out what she knew about Rita."

"I know exactly what you said to her," said Homer. "She told me all about it, down to the last dirty insinuation. I only wish I'd gotten to her place sooner. If I'd been there, believe me, I'd have told you where to get off at."

Evan felt his own temper wearing thin. "What about Stanley? I suppose she told you all about Stanley too?"

"Why shouldn't she? She has a perfect right to sell Win's house to him or anybody else that offers her a good price, whether you folks like it or not. A simple business transaction, and just because it doesn't suit you, just because you've always had it in for Pearl, you're willing to believe all the malicious gossip you can dig up."

"Listen, Homer, Pearl herself admitted to me that when she went out to The Spot yesterday, she and Stanley and Rita had a bang-up fight. Are you trying to tell me they were fighting about a simple business transaction?"

"Certainly not," said Homer with dignity. "Pearl had no way of knowing, when she went out there to talk business with Stanley, that she was going to walk into that kind of a mess. But Rita—Well, frankly, the girl's not only short on brains, but a tramp to boot."

"That's not true," said Aunt Nell suddenly. Her eyes flashed. "She's no more of a tramp than your precious Pearl. And you're the one that's short on brains, if you ask me."

"I'm not asking you," snapped Homer. "I'm very well aware of your opinion of me. I'm not blaming Rita for believing the gossip about Pearl and Stanley. It's all you could expect of a girl in her position, with her mentality. Naturally, when she accused Pearl of coming between her and Stanley, Pearl had to defend herself."

"I see," said Evan. His voice was tinged with respect—not only for Pearl and her ingenious twisting of facts, but for Homer and his capacity for unswerving loyalty. He was not short on brains, no matter what Aunt Nell might say. He was a shrewd man blinded by devotion. (For it still seemed too incongruous to use the word love in connection with a barrel-shaped, balding country lawyer who himself would probably be the first to deny any such feeling.) "But then why did she go to see Rita afterwards?"

"She wanted to reason with the girl. She hadn't realized, till Rita kicked up that scene at The Spot, how vicious the gossip was. She was too shocked to say much at first. Afterwards she decided to talk to Rita alone and try to convince her it was a pack of lies."

There was a moment of silence. Then Aunt Nell burst into derisive laughter. "Homer," she said, "you slay me. Of all the cock and bull stories I ever heard … And the man believes it. Look at him. He actually expects us to believe it too!"

Homer's face turned an even angrier red. "I don't expect you to believe anything that doesn't suit your own selfish purposes, Nell. I know you too well for that. But I must say, Marianna, I'm surprised at you. I thought Win's good name meant enough to you so that you wouldn't stand by and let it be smeared out of pure spite."

"Mama had nothing to do with it," said Evan quickly. "If you've got to blame somebody, blame me. I'm the only one that takes Rita's disappearance seriously."

"Why, yes," said Dad, with his disarming smile. "We've all been telling Evan not to be hasty about calling in the sheriff. Even Nell. None of us want to smear Win's name any more then you do, Homer. We just—"

"You're just out for Pearl's blood, and you have been ever since the day Win married her." Homer was not to be mollified, not even by an old friend like Dad. "Oh, I've watched you from the beginning. I know injustice when I see it, and it's gone far enough. You've let Nell lead you by the nose all these years. You think she's 'your kind.' Well. She's nothing but a selfish, jealous, grasping—"

"Oh now, Homer," said Mama reasonably. "You know Nell's not grasping."

"No? Look at the way she's grabbed the car and the fishing cabin. Couldn't even wait for Win's will to be probated. She's got no right—"

"I have too!" cried Aunt Nell. "Win left them to me! Pearl turned the keys over to me herself. I've got every right!"

"Not legally," said Homer. This was home ground to him, and he had clearly hit a live nerve with Aunt Nell; he looked very nearly cheerful. "Legally you have no right whatever to take possession of either one, until after probation of the will. If I wanted to, or if Pearl changed her mind, I could demand and obtain the car and the keys, and you could be restrained from using it or the cabin until such time as—"

"You mean somebody else can go out there any time they want to?" In her agitation Aunt Nell sprang to her feet. Her eloquent hands went into action. "But I've already moved some of my *things* out there! Little Harriet went with me this morning and helped me. I'm going to make it into a little studio. It's mine! Pearl gave me the keys, and nobody else has any business out there!"

"As you say," said Homer smugly, "we all know Nell's not grasping. Oh no. Not in the least." With a sense of timing unexpected in him, he let his case rest. "Goodnight, all. Just remember, any more funny business with Pearl and you'll have me to deal with." He marched out. Galahad in a wrinkled seersucker suit.

Aunt Nell flew out of the room after him, her voice still raised in passionate dissent. "It isn't true! It's my property, you just try taking it away from me, and you'll find out what's legal ..." The slam of the screen door behind Homer put an end to her outburst. Then came the rush of her feet as she ran upstairs.

After a moment Little Harriet sauntered out too, with an elaborate air of boredom. But once in the hall, Evan noticed, her feet sounded just as fast as Aunt Nell's.

"Well, for mercy's sake," said Mama. As if for reassurance, she patted her pompadour. "What was Nell making such a fuss about? I can see how she might want the car, but that little old cabin— Why, it's nothing but a shack. What did she say, a studio?"

"Seems to me Nell's been acting funny all evening," said Dad. As soft-spoken and easy-going as ever. But there was a spark in his eyes as he leaned forward. "Apparently what set her off was the idea that somebody else might go out to that cabin. It's peculiar, you know, when you think about it."

They thought about it, the three of them. And as they thought they drew closer together, like conspirators. Mama shifted her little sewing rocker nearer Dad's chair; Evan perched farther out on the window seat.

He said, "It didn't occur to me before, but Rita might turn to her if she was scared. And I think she *was* scared, I think Pearl threw the fear of the Lord in her. Where was Aunt Nell last night, Mama?"

"Why, she was home all evening. You remember, Ralph, I was of two minds about going over to the Morrisons' to play bridge, with Little Harriet just home from the hospital and all, but Nell offered to stay with her. Urged us to go …"

"She had a phone call while we were eating supper," said Dad. "Seven thirty or so. It was after that she got so insistent. We just *had* to go to the Morrisons', she wouldn't have it any other way."

They thought that over. "It would be just like Nell," Mama decided. "She's always been a great hand for excitement and secrets and dramatics. Ever since she was a girl. That was what made her such fun."

"No wonder she didn't want me calling in the sheriff," said Evan. "She hadn't expected me to get that worked up over Rita … It all fits together, slick as a whistle. She's got Rita out there in the cabin, hiding out because she's scared of Pearl, and of course Little Harriet knows about it, it was probably as much her idea as Aunt Nell's."

"For mercy's sake," Mama murmured. She stood up, obviously prepared for the blunt, head-on approach that was all life had ever required of her in the way of diplomacy. "I'm going right upstairs and tell the both of them— Why not, Ralph?"

Because Dad was shaking his head. "Wait a minute, Marianna. Why don't we make sure we're right before we say anything to anybody? It won't take us twenty minutes to drive out there and check. That way we'll know what we're talking about."

"But supposing Nell hears us leave and wants to know where we're going?"

"In that case," said Dad, and his eyes twinkled, "you keep your mouth shut, Marianna. Let Evan and me do the lying. It's not your long suit."

As it turned out, nobody had to do any lying. They got away without interference. Dad, who was more familiar with the back river roads than Evan, did the driving, with Mama tucked in cozily between them in the front seat. Indeed, there was a cozy, light-hearted air about the whole expedition, the feeling of setting off on a lark.

"Poor Rita," said Mama. "I feel sorry for her, stuck in that cabin all by herself. There's not even any electricity. Isn't Nell going to be surprised, when we bring her back home with us—if she'll come, that is."

Whether they brought her back home or not, Evan had made up his mind about one thing: he was going to extract from Rita whatever she knew. Their little talk had been postponed long enough.

The road was narrow and unmercifully rough. Weeds crowded in rankly on either side; here and there the low-hanging branches of willows brushed against the car with a slippery, swishing sound. There was no breeze. The air was heavy with the smell of the river. By the time their headlights picked out the shadowy shape of the cabin, the road was even narrower, and all but choked by the undergrowth.

Evan led the way with the flashlight. There was no light in the cabin, and not a whisper of sound. Rita, if she was inside, must be asleep, or—more likely; she would have heard the car—crouching there in terror.

"Rita!" he called. "Don't be scared. Rita!" And he lifted his hand to knock on the door. Then he saw that it was not locked, or even shut tight. For the third time that day, dread swamped him, a conviction that something terrible was about to happen. He turned toward Mama and Dad, groping along a few yards behind him.

"You folks stay where you are." His voice sounded unfamiliar and breathy. "I'll take a look inside."

The door creaked as he pushed it open. He heard a fly buzzing; smelled kerosene, whiskey, something else, sweetish. The flashlight beam wobbled its way around the cabin's one room, with its few pieces of rickety furniture. Chairs, smoke-blackened fireplace, kitchen cabinet and oil stove, some fishing tackle in a corner …

And the cot. Rita was lying on it; he recognized the striped skirt and red sandals Mrs. Shoemaker had described. She was not asleep, nor was she crouching in terror. The knife—he caught its gleam on the floor beside her—had put an end to sleep and fear and everything else for Rita. Her arm, which hung down over the edge of the couch, was laced with blood, and her off-the-shoulder blouse was no longer white. Brainless when it came to men, Aunt Nell had said. A big squashy mouth and a bouncy build. No more of that for Rita, either. Nothing but the buzzing fly and the sweetish smell.

Behind him he heard a sharp intake of breath. Dad was standing there. His handsome face, illuminated for an instant by the shaft of light in Evan's hand, looked haggard. He turned and called, "Go back to the car, Marianna. I'll be out in a minute." With the same air of quiet authority he took the flashlight from Evan and crossed the room to the cot.

Evan lit the oil lamp on the table. Its yellow glow set off the pathetic, homely details of the room—the bread and cheese and plate of fruit on the cabinet, the coffee pot on the stove, a scattering of movie magazines and funny papers on the floor. A bottle of whiskey and one glass with an inch of drink in it stood on the battered table beside the cot; another glass lay broken on the floor, beside a tipped-over ash tray. Knocked from the table in a scuffle, perhaps? The knife looked like a common butcher knife, old, its blade worn thin in the middle.

"There's nothing we can do for her," Dad said, straightening up. "We'll have to call the sheriff. Might be just as quick to drive into town and get him."

"You and Mama go ahead. I'll wait here."

Neither of them mentioned Aunt Nell. But Evan could think of nothing else. He stood still, listening to the sound of the car as it started up, backed with a faint splintering into the undergrowth, and sped away. Afterwards the silence closed in unbearably. He went outside and leaned against the rusty pump. The thought of Aunt Nell went right along with him. She had overheard his phone conversation with Rita, might very well have realized that their date was more than mere sociability …

Then Rita's dangerous knowledge must have concerned, not Pearl or Stanley, but Aunt Nell. And it must have been very dangerous knowledge, because Rita was lying inside the cabin stabbed. Much as Uncle Win had been stabbed—with whatever weapon happened to be handy at the moment. The old souvenir hunting knife for Uncle Win; the butcher knife for Rita. Both of them struck down in a flash of fury. It was the only way Aunt Nell was capable of striking anyone down.

More than that, it was the only way to explain Uncle Win's protection of his would-be murderer. Evan's own theory came back to haunt him: it had to be someone Uncle Win loved. So much that he had been driven, in the end, to actual suicide. (So he was not lying when he said to Evan, "Don't fret, boy. Lightning never strikes in the same place twice." He was making a private, macabre joke.)

Well, he had loved Aunt Nell. Not even divorce and remarriage had cut the bond; he had gone on supporting her, indulging her in her impractical ventures … Except for the dude ranch. There was the dude ranch quarrel, on the very afternoon before the stabbing. There were Aunt Nell's evasions and distortions of the truth, so characteristic of her, so apparently harmless.

Even the fact that Rita had let herself be spirited away to a lonely fishing cabin by the very person she had reason to fear —even that did not get Aunt Nell off the hook. It was entirely possible that Rita did not know how dangerous her knowledge was, or to whom it was dangerous. Besides, Pearl had scared her out of the few wits she possessed. To her, Pearl was the person she had reason to fear. Aunt Nell—her old friend, her lady bountiful—was the one to turn to for help. That was how it must have seemed to Rita; and when (like as not all unwitting) she had let slip to Aunt Nell her damaging information ... Evan tried to shut out of his mind's eye the picture of that charming face convulsed with rage and panic, that slender, graceful hand reaching for the knife.

Through the heavy air came the sound of a car bucketing down the rough road. Headlights made a reckless sweep across underbrush and cabin; the roar of the engine shuddered into silence; the car door slammed. Evan found that he could not move.

It was Aunt Nell, headed for the cabin at a stumbling run. In the headlights her shadow fled beside her, a black, wild witch. She was unaware of him, and the knowledge gave him a feeling of shame and guilt. He must call to her—a warning, a threat? Anything to let her know she was observed. But no sound came out of his aching throat.

She had reached the cabin door before he broke out of his paralysis and started toward her. She took two steps inside the cabin, and then he must have made some sound that alerted her, because her head jerked around toward him. Her face was the face of a stranger, blank-eyed. She screamed his name, lurched away from him, and then suddenly pitched forward into his arms.

Fifteen

It was really all Evan's doing. Those who so desired could blame the liquor. (That delicious, pernicious last drink, bless its heart.) As for Norma, she preferred to place the responsibility where it belonged, squarely on Evan's shoulders. Except for Evan, she would be home where she belonged instead of where she was. Which was at the lake. Having dinner with Stanley. And enjoying it.

She was grateful to Evan. Deeply grateful. It had been—at last, at last—too much, his calm assumption that she would go trotting back to town with him the minute he felt like leaving the club. And after he had made it so clear that he had a date with somebody else! (With Goldie? She must strike him as absolutely irresistible, now that she was married. Just that much more unattainable.)

Norma was also grateful to Stanley. He might not be a "nice" man—as a matter of fact, he wasn't; he was a crass, tough show-off, full of big-money talk, frankly bent on seduction—but at least when Stanley looked at her he saw a woman, not a duty. Too much of a woman, maybe. Though there was no cause for alarm. She wasn't exactly a child; she knew how to deal with men who made unwelcome advances and had to be put in their place. Which was, of course, what she would do with Stanley. If and when. So far, he had been meticulous about not touching her, except when he helped her in and out of the car. So very meticulous; so determined to show her that he knew how to treat a lady. It was all part of the softening-up process, like his suggestion, now, that they have another brandy.

She couldn't help smiling. "No, thanks. You've plied me with enough liquor. It's time we started home."

He did not persist, and, naturally, she was grateful to him for that too. She had about decided there were not going to be any unwelcome advances, after all, when, a couple of miles outside of Fontenelle, he slowed down and said, "We could turn off up here. Want to see my lodge? It's going to be real class, when I get it fixed up."

"Thanks, but I don't think so. Not tonight."

"Why not? Scared I'll make a pass at you?"

"Certainly not. Of course I'm not scared."

"You don't need to be. I won't make any passes. Not unless you want me to. How's that for a deal?"

Well, really! She discovered that she had said the ridiculous phrase out loud, and in the most ridiculous, high-dudgeon tone.

"Yeah. Really." Here they were at the turn-off. The motor was idling. "On the level. So what have you got to lose? What's wrong with taking a quick look at the joint?"

"There's nothing wrong with it. I just—"

"Okay, then. We're on our way." He made the turn swiftly; she slid halfway toward him and felt his hand on her arm, steadying her. "Excuse me," he said decorously.

She could still insist on being taken home. If she wanted to bother. If she didn't mind his thinking that she was scared, or (what an idea!) that she didn't trust herself …

Meanwhile, the convertible sailed along, until at the top of quite a steep hill there rose the solid mass of Stanley's lodge.

"Looks pretty good from here, don't it?" he said. "Of course there's still a lot of work to be done on it. Landscaping, all this scrub's got to be cleared away, terraces, a patio—I've already started that. Come on, I'll show you."

The patio at this stage was only a space cluttered with bags of cement and workmen's tools. But just wait, Stanley said, it was going to be terrific, a view of the river, everything.

Norma realized that he was showing her a dream. His voice thickened with eagerness as he told her where the swimming pool would be (when he got the dough for it), how there would be gardens on this side, with a fountain (marble, the real thing, none of this cheap junk for him); his eyes shone as he led her inside to the living room. It was a fantastic mixture of fake rusticity—shaggy beams, bearskin rugs—and such ultra-modern touches as air conditioning and a hi-fi set that had cost Stanley a real piece of change, in case anybody asked.

Buried under all the talk about money, which was the only measuring rod Stanley knew, was the core of the dream: he would have a real show place; Fontenelle was going to sit up and take notice before he was through. A vulgar, rather sad dream, Norma thought; why should Fontenelle matter that much?

"It's wonderful," she said. Well, it was. Weird and wonderful. "I had no idea it was anything like this. I expected a sort of shack, like the cabins down by the river. Just a place you came to when you felt like roughing it."

"Oh no. I come up here lots of nights, even during the week. There's this farm girl—Helga somebody—she comes in Sundays to clean it up for me. You really like the place?" He was so openly anxious for her approval; his usually impassive face looked, for a moment, so vulnerable, that Norma was touched.

She sat on the sofa—a monster of a sofa, heaped with cushions and covered with an Indian blanket—while he mixed them a nightcap. For, now that she was here, where was the harm in one last, mild drink? None. No harm in Stanley, either, in spite of what Evan might think. "You've got no more business messing around with Stanley than Little Harriet has," he had said. Dog in the manger. And of course what put Stanley beyond the pale for Evan and the rest of Fontenelle was his affair with Pearl ...

At the thought of how often and often Pearl must have been here, just here, on the sofa, Norma found herself sitting up very straight, practically rigid. And a voice that might have been her mother's, might have been Evan's, might have been her own, echoed incredulously in her mind: *You mean you went out with* Stanley? *You went up to that* lodge *of his with him?*

Well, she was tired of always doing what was expected of her. She was tired of "nice" men who took her for granted. Stanley was different and exciting and—

And still very much on his best behavior. He brought her her drink and then sat down on the sofa, but at a discreet distance from her. There was room for one and all on that sofa. To be sure, he was giving her another one of those looks. "You know," he said, "I had you figured wrong. I mean, you and Evan. When you stayed at the club instead of leaving with him—Jesus, I couldn't believe my luck. I still can't. The way I figured, nobody but Evan had a chance with you."

"Evan and I?" she said, and it was wonderful, how detached she felt. I really *am* cured, she thought; Evan and Stanley between them have cured me. "Oh, with Evan and me it was just one of those school day things. You know. Family stuff. My mother kept telling me what a nice boy he was, and his mother kept telling him what a nice girl I was, and the only reason he takes me out now is just—just force of habit—" For a perilous moment her detachment threatened to crack. She stared at her feet in their black linen pumps. Grayish now, covered with fine cement dust from the unfinished patio. Then her eyes lifted, imploringly, to Stanley.

And he did not fail her. "Force of habit," he repeated. "How dopey can a guy—even a guy like Evan Hoyt—get?"

"Not dopey. Just sick to death of the whole subject. So am I. Now. It took me quite a while longer, that's all. I don't know why I'm telling you this. I guess because I'm grateful to you—"

"Grateful to me! For what?"

And still—oh, meticulously!—he did not touch her. How would it be when he did? She was aware of an astonishing, consuming curiosity. More than that. She was acutely aware of Stanley's physical presence. It had nothing to do with liking or not liking him as a person, or even with liking or not liking his looks. It was a direct, animal, mindless perception. Fascinated, she watched the unhurried movements of his hands as he took out a cigarette, and, on the first drag, the tremor of his mouth. His jaw was slightly undershot, so that his lower lip was unusually full; there was a cleft in his chin. How would it be when those sure, unhurried hands moved upward along her arms, when that full mouth pressed down on hers?

She had no intention of doing it. But she was doing it. She was leaning toward him (unable to look away from him), she was saying in a breathless whisper, "Yes. Grateful. For treating me like a woman ..." she was trembling, waiting for the hands to touch and the mouth to kiss. Now. So slow and expert and compelling. She let herself sink back, clasping and clasped, and she felt—with what jubilant release!—her own identity dissolve. No longer a person. Only a mouth opening to his, a body melting under his, and against her breast the stroke of his powerful, secret heart ...

He was saying a name. "Norma. Norma." A meaningless name. And then abruptly not meaningless. *Her* name; it yanked her back to herself, clapped her once more into the inflexible mold of her own identity. Not a person? Of course she was a person. Norma. Norma Schaefer. Old Judge Schaefer's granddaughter, grappling like an animal with this impossible other person who also had a name (Stanley. Stanley what?) and an identity as inescapable as her own. In a convulsion of shame, she wrenched away from him.

"No," she said. "No. Stop it."

At once he sat up. Straightened his tie. Smoothed his hair; it was straight and coarse and vigorous, and his face had a kind of peasant immobility. There was a smear of lipstick beside his mouth. How could she? Oh, how could she? After a moment he said, "I'm sorry. I thought—"

"Go on. All right. Say it. You weren't going to make a pass at me unless I wanted you to. You thought I wanted you to. Don't you dare say it!" She scrambled to her feet and stood with her back to him, her hands clenched, her face burning.

"Take it easy." His calmness infuriated her even more. All along he had kept calm, coolly experimenting with her, coolly noting her responses. Hadn't he? Of course he had. And here she was with her heart still ignominiously pounding. "Take it easy and listen for a minute—"

"I'm not interested in anything you have to say. Don't apologize. Don't explain. Don't say a word. I know exactly what you're thinking, and I couldn't possibly care less. It's nothing to me if you spread it all over town—and you undoubtedly will—how Norma Schaefer's not so much, after all, you got her up here, you could have made her if you'd wanted to, even if she is supposed to be mad for Evan Hoyt— That's why you did it. Isn't it? Just to get back at Evan."

"What kind of crazy talk is that?" She saw, with elation, that she had made at least a dent in his calmness. He was standing now, too; there was a glint in his eye. "I don't give a damn for Evan Hoyt, one way or the other. And I'm not going to go shooting off my mouth about you, either. You've got me all wrong, Norma. Norma—"

"Oh, of course. Sure. You just brought me up here to take a quick look at your lodge. I'm not a complete idiot. I knew all along what was coming, that's what makes it so— Oh, I could die, I could die!"

"But you've got me all wrong. Okay, so I could have made you if I'd wanted to. If that's all I wanted, do you think I'd have stopped just because you changed your mind? Don't kid yourself. You're no one-night stand for me. That's not the way I want it. The way I want it, I want to marry you."

"You what?" she whispered. "You want to what?"

"You heard me." And she had heard him; her ears rang with the incredible words. The defiant, absolutely sincere, absolutely incredible words. "I want to marry you."

She burst out laughing. It was like a chain of firecrackers, one peal of laughter igniting the next, and each time it seemed about to sputter out the realization—he means it, he's serious, his intentions are *honorable!*—would spark it all over again. She put her hands up to her mouth. She rocked back and forth.

"You think it's funny," said Stanley softly. "It's a big joke, huh?"

"I'm sorry. I just—"

Through a haze of hilarious tears she saw his face. The laugh froze in her throat; her very bones turned cold. There was an ugly, dusky flush along his high cheekbones, and his deep-set eyes gleamed white. Yet he seemed to be smiling.

"I'm sorry," she repeated unsteadily. "I shouldn't have—"

"Only it's so goddamn funny, isn't it? Me thinking I could get anybody like you to marry me. Funniest goddamn thing you ever heard in your life. You just couldn't help laughing your snooty, upper-crust head off. I don't know my place, do I? I'm supposed to try to lay you. Sure. Because I'm a slob, that's all I got on my mind, that's all I'm good for. And anyway, slumming's such fun, isn't it? Let's tease the guy up a little, find out how the other half lives."

He still had that fixed, chilling smile. And she could not make a sound. Not even when he took hold of her. "You want to know something, Miss Norma Bitch Schaefer? I got as much right to ask you to marry me as anybody in town. I'm as good as you or Evan Hoyt or any of the rest of your good better best families ..."

The ringing of the telephone saved her. Stanley let go of her so suddenly that she tottered back onto the sofa. She cowered there, trying to stop shivering and make a dash for the door while he was at the phone. He might have left the keys in the car. Or she could get home on foot, or hide somewhere ...

It must be Pearl who had called him. Who else could it be, at this time of night? He was saying very little beyond a tense "Yeah?" now and then. And though his eyes were fixed on Norma during most of the conversation, she had the disconcerting feeling that he might not be seeing her at all. Toward the end he turned his back to her and asked a question, very low, that she did not catch. "Where?" he said, and the rest was just an unintelligible murmur.

After he had hung up he stood absolutely still for a minute. Then he said, "Come on. I'll take you home." His voice was preoccupied and impersonal. So were his eyes. It was as if the telephone call had wiped Norma and the whole scene with her clean out of his mind. "Hurry up," he said, and she followed him obediently out to the car.

He drove fast, and he did not say a word, not one word, all the way into town. And to Norma, benumbed by the rush of air against her face and the abrupt change in Stanley's manner, speech was an impossibility.

Until they stopped in front of her house and Stanley reached across to open the door for her. (No more of the elaborately chivalrous gestures he had made earlier in the evening; he was not even going to see her to the door.) Then she found that there was something she wanted to say, after all.

"You were right, you know," she faltered as she got out of the car. "I don't blame you. Only I really meant it, what I said about being grateful—"

He seemed puzzled at first, too abstracted to grasp what she was talking about. "Oh, that," he said, and he gave her a sardonic smile. "You're welcome."

The convertible zoomed off up the street.

Sixteen

"Holy Mother," said Sheriff Novak in a hushed voice. He stared at Rita on the cot, and as he stared the sweat broke out visibly on his round, beefy face. Then he swallowed, also visibly, and backed out of the cabin door.

He had arrived with Mama and Dad, a couple of minutes after Aunt Nell fainted. She was still stretched out in the weeds and sand; beginning to stir, though, and Evan dreaded what her first, unguarded words might be. (Even now, the impulse to protect her against outsiders was automatic with him.) Mama was on her knees beside her, sprinkling her with water from the rusty tin cup Evan had found beside the pump.

"What's Mrs. Covey doing here?" said the sheriff. "You folks didn't tell me she was here."

"We didn't know it," Mama told him crisply. "She got here after Ralph and I left. She's fainted, that's all. You tend to your part of it, and we'll take care of Nell."

But it was no use. Aunt Nell's eyelids were fluttering open. She looked up into Mama's face and said, with appalling distinctness, "Marianna. I killed her. Oh, Marianna ..." She gave a wrenching sob.

"What was that? What did she say?" The sheriff squatted beside her. His eyes were round as marbles. "What did you say, Ma'am?"

Still sobbing, heedless of Mama's attempts to shush her, Aunt Nell struggled up into a sitting position. "It was me. I brought her out here, and now she's dead ... I saw her, on the cot, the blood, she's dead ..."

"We know she is, Mrs. Covey. You say it was you that killed her? Here, let me help you up, Ma'am. You stabbed her?"

"Of course she didn't," snapped Mama. "I'm surprised at you, Mr. Novak. You've got no business asking her questions when she doesn't even know what she's saying."

Mr. Novak blushed. But he did not let go of Aunt Nell's arm. She was on her feet now, her disheveled figure and dazed face dramatized by the car headlights. Aware, as she would be on her death bed, of her audience: Mama still on her knees, rigid with anxiety; Dad and Evan side by side; the sheriff sweating in his orange and green sports shirt.

"I want to talk," she said. "I have to talk. I must. Ask me anything you like, Mr. Novak." (Oh God, thought Evan, she's beginning to enjoy it, she's Marie Antoinette being gracious on the guillotine steps.)

"Well." Overcome by the magnitude of his opportunity, Mr. Novak seemed for a moment unable to think of anything to ask. Then he got a grip on himself. "Well, Mrs. Covey, why did you stab her?"

"Oh, I didn't," said Aunt Nell, quickly, earnestly. "But whoever did it, I'm guilty. Yes. I'm guilty of murder."

Mama cried out in desperation, "Stop it, Nell! Stop talking like that! Can't you see he *believes* you?"

"You mean he believes I stabbed her?" Aunt Nell's voice rose incredulously. She looked down at Mr. Novak's thick hand on her arm; then up at his face. It was an open face. There was no mistaking what went on in the mind behind it. There was no mistaking, either, that what she saw there scared Aunt Nell. Guilty or innocent, she could no longer afford to wallow in histrionic self-blame. "But he can't possibly— Look, Mr. Novak, I brought her out here because I was trying to help her. She called me up last night—terrified, poor girl, she didn't know what to do or where to go—and right away I thought of the cabin, I thought she'd be safe here. Look, Mr. Novak, you don't have to take my word for it. Little Harriet came out here with me this morning. She knows I didn't kill Rita."

"Little Harriet? The kid again, huh?" A suffering expression crossed Mr. Novak's face.

"She'll tell you. Rita was alive, she was fine, when we left. About eleven thirty this morning. Little Harriet can tell you. I was *fond* of Rita. Devoted to her. Why on earth should I stab her?"

"Why should anybody? Only somebody sure as hell did … You claim she was scared. She happen to mention what she was scared of?"

For just a second Aunt Nell hesitated, as if in a frantic, last-minute search for some other solution, some way of keeping the family dirty linen decently out of sight. But the sheriff's hand was still heavy on her arm; even Mama must see that there was no other way … "She was scared of Pearl. Pearl went to Shoemakers' yesterday afternoon and threatened her, actually threatened to kill her if she didn't stay away from Stanley. That's why she turned to me for help. She was scared of Pearl. I can't help it, Marianna. I'm sorry, but I just can't—"

"I know it," said Mama miserably. "Oh my, that poor girl—"

Mr. Novak cleared his throat. But whatever he was about to say was lost in a commotion of newly arriving cars. Dr. Morrison in the ambulance, and right behind him the deputy sheriff and the town constable. They piled out purposefully and headed for the cabin.

It was the deputy sheriff who noticed the rug at the foot of the cot. A shabby, dingy rag rug on which several grayish footprints showed clearly. "Hey," he said. "Somebody's tracked it up. What is that stuff?"

It was too fine and powdery for sand. Too light in color. "We'll check it," said the sheriff. "Same way with the glasses—the busted one, too—and the knife. Hi, Doc. Give me all the dope as quick as you can, huh? What time it happened and all."

"Oh sure," said Dr. Morrison glumly. "Right down to the minute."

The sheriff turned back to Aunt Nell. "Now I'm going to ask all you folks to come back to town with me. We'll be more comfortable in my office. What we've got to do, we've got to begin at the beginning and get it all straightened out. I want to talk to Little Harriet too, and the other Mrs. Covey. Mrs. Pearl." He was still not letting Aunt Nell out of his sight. In his face, as plainly as on the dial of a compass, the needle of suspicion quivered and swung, back and forth, between the two Mrs. Coveys.

Or so it seemed to Evan. "She was scared of Pearl," Aunt Nell had said. "Pearl threatened her, actually threatened to kill her ..." Was Aunt Nell counting on Little Harriet to back her up on this point, too? Daughter against mother, thought Evan, and he felt his heart sink like a stone.

As soon as she heard Homer Nelsen's voice over the telephone, Pearl knew that there was trouble. The very fact that he was calling her, when he had left her house only a couple of hours before, meant that something was wrong. Besides, he was stuttering, as he always did under stress. Stuttering badly.

"Pearl? Is that you, Pearl? Listen. It's all over town. Listen."

"Yes, Homer." (The Hoyts, she thought, they've filled him up with all the garbage about me and Stanley. That's all it is. Well, and I knew they would. Not that they can really turn him against me. Not my faithful Homer.)

"That girl. Rita. She's been murdered. Out at Win's cabin—it was Nell that took her out there, God knows why—and they found her there dead."

Pearl sat down. She had not thought her knees would bend, but they must have, because here she was, no longer standing up.

"You there, Pearl? … Listen, might as well face it, we know damn well that Nell's not going to miss a chance like this to do you dirt. They all know you went to see Rita yesterday afternoon, and they're going to twist it around to suit themselves. They can't make it stick, of course, don't worry about that, but there it is, that's what we're in for. Might as well face it. Pearl?"

"Yes. I'm all right. You mean the sheriff's going to call me in and—"

"Don't worry. I'll go with you. I'm coming over to your place right now, just wanted to make sure you were there. Remember, it's going to be okay. All you have to do is tell the truth, what you told me tonight. It's going to be okay. You can count on me."

Her faithful Homer. She could count on him. She had to count on him, and on what she had told him. Never mind what she had admitted to Evan. She must simply deny it. Brazen it out. And never mind what Rita might have told Nell before she was murdered. Might have? Must have.

The gun, thought Pearl, get rid of the gun … No, no. Don't get rid of it. The Hoyts knew she still had it, the gun Win had shot himself with; its absence would be more incriminating than its presence. Leave it in the desk drawer, where she had put it when she took it out of her purse last night. No one could prove that it had ever been in her purse. No one could prove anything, now that Rita was dead. All she had to do was—

"Stanley." She must have said it out loud; it bounced back at her from the walls. Stanley. Stanley. Stanley. And her hand—which felt, like the rest of her, brittle as glass—reached for the phone, and the next instant drew back. Did she dare call him? Did she dare *not* call him?

Last night, when she told him, "We don't have to worry about Rita anymore. I've settled her hash," his face had closed up in the cagey look she knew so well. "Oh?" he had said. "So who was worried? What kind of a line did she try to hand you?" She had snapped back at him: "I couldn't be bothered listening to anything that tramp had to say. I simply told her to stay away from you or I'd kill her …"

And she remembered, with a thrill of terror, that Evan had asked about the knife, the other knife.

She had no choice. Risky as it might be, she had to talk to Stanley. Now. These few minutes before Homer got here might well be their last, their only chance. As she dialed the number of the lodge she discovered that she was praying. Please, God. Make him be there. Please, God. Please. Help me. Help me.

The sheriff's office was in the courthouse. Up two flights of wide marble staircase, and there the grandeur ended. The office itself had a splintery wooden floor, streaked tan walls, and a naked, glaring light bulb dangling from the middle of the ceiling. It reeked of stale tobacco smoke, and it was full of people.

As she walked in with Evan and the deputy sheriff, Little Harriet felt embarrassingly calm. It worried her. What was wrong with her that she wasn't crying or something? Rita is dead, she repeated to herself; she has been murdered. Just think of it. Murdered! Her heart, which ought to be pounding wildly, did not even skip a beat. She looked back at the roomful of drawn faces, all turned her way, and into her head there popped another of those loathsome, rag-tag comments: Hail, hail, the gang's all here. Like when they came and told her the sheriff wanted to ask her a few questions because Rita had been found stabbed. In the cabin. That's invariably fatal, her disgusting mind had quipped, nobody ever survives being stabbed in the cabin …

They had broken the news to her gently (well, of course; they naturally expected her to throw some kind of a scene) and now Evan was guiding her to a chair as if she were an invalid, too frail to manage by herself, and everybody, including the sheriff, was looking very sorry for her. Poor Little Harriet. Poor kid. Maybe they would decide she was in a socially acceptable daze. She hoped so.

She didn't get it right away, what the sheriff was driving at with his questions. He began with Rita's telephone call to Evan. Yes, Little Harriet knew about that; they had let her out of the hospital by then, and she had been in the living room, on the couch, where she could hear Aunt Nell and Evan talking about it. "Aunt Nell kidded him about it. Said he wasn't to take advantage of Rita, even if she did have a crush on him. She thought it was funny, Rita asking him for a date."

"What about you? Did you think it was funny?"

"No, I didn't. I thought the reason Rita called him was because she had something to tell him about—" She could feel it in the air; what they expected from her was another outburst about Daddy. What kind of a dope did they think she was? They'd had their chance—not just the sheriff, but all of them—and Evan was the only single, solitary one of them that had paid any attention to her. A bunch of ostriches, sticking their heads in the sand, pretending Daddy had stabbed himself because it was more *comfortable* that way. Oh no. She wasn't going to give them another crack at brushing her off as a screwball. "—about the other night," she finished. "I thought Rita knew who it was that bopped me over the head, out at The Spot. Turned out she didn't. But that's what I thought."

The sheriff gave a grateful sigh. "All right. What happened next? After Rita called Evan and made this date with him, then what?"

"Well, then Rita called Aunt Nell. I heard that, too, because I was still in the living room, having my supper off a tray. Everybody else was in the dining room. You can't hear telephone conversations from there. So Aunt Nell said let's keep it a secret—" And what fun it had been, having a secret with Aunt Nell! How exciting she made everything seem! "—and she waited till after they'd all gone out, and then she went to see Rita. She wouldn't take me along, because the doctor said I was supposed to keep quiet. I was dying to know what was up, so when she got back she told me all about it." An even more thrilling secret: Rita scared, turning to Aunt Nell for help, and Aunt Nell's absolutely inspired idea about the fishing cabin, hiding her out there.

"She told you all about it," said the sheriff. He seemed to be waiting.

"Well, sure. Rita had had this fight with Stanley, that's why she was scared. So Aunt Nell thought of the cabin, and leaving the note for Mrs. Shoemaker. That was to throw everybody off the track, see, they'd all think Rita was in Chicago, and we'd have a chance to figure out the next move."

"I've already told you all this, Mr. Novak," put in Aunt Nell. She looked funny, Little Harriet thought. Not a bit like herself. She didn't even sound like herself. "Naturally I wanted to spare the child as much as I could. It's just as I explained to you. I said—"

"You've said a lot of things tonight," said the sheriff. "Like the one you started off with, that it was you killed Rita."

Little Harriet's mouth dropped open. She got it now—what the sheriff was driving at with his questions, why Aunt Nell didn't look like herself. He thought, cripes, he thought Aunt Nell had done it! Her heart gave a great lurch, and that was the end of her worries about feeling too calm. From now on the problem was going to be to *act* calm, no matter how much she might want to scream and holler. Because screaming and hollering, to the sheriff, meant a screwball kid, which in turn meant Little Harriet, which in turn meant …

So she waited quietly and answered quietly when he asked about her visit to the cabin with Aunt Nell. Only this morning? Yes. Only this morning. "We took Rita some stuff to eat, and some magazines. And we planned how we'd get her off to Chicago tomorrow. Aunt Nell didn't have enough cash to lend her, but she was going to the bank tomorrow morning. Because Rita wanted to get out of town."

"You talked to her yourself? She told you who she was scared of?"

"Sure, I talked to her. I wanted to find out who bopped me." Who, if anybody. Because, though naturally she wouldn't admit it, she still wasn't sure. Imagination or reality? She had gone on insisting that she couldn't have tripped, hoping against hope that she might convince herself, if no one else. And Rita had been no help; all the way down the line Rita had frozen up on her. It had exasperated her—yes, but it had hurt her feelings a little, too, because Rita always used to be so friendly, in that dumb, breezy way of hers. Not this morning. She just kept shaking her head, and at last she had turned on Little Harriet, so cold and sullen: You asked me before, kid. I already told you, I don't know from nothing about your Daddy stabbing himself. I don't know from nothing about you conking out, either. So stop asking me. I got troubles of my own.

She hadn't even talked about her fight with Stanley. (She who used to regale Little Harriet by the hour with confidential reports on her dates and boyfriends. In the old days, when she was working for Mother.) Just that she was scared and wanted to get out of town. Come to think about it, Aunt Nell hadn't gone into much detail, either. On account of Mother, Mother and Stanley. Of course that was why. They thought it was too shocking for her innocent little ears, the tale of what a two-timing bastard her mother had gotten mixed up with. Quaint of them. She had known from the beginning that Stanley was capable of anything.

"And when you left, Rita was—she was alive? She was okay?"

"Sure she was. She waved us goodbye from the door." Calm. Calm. Don't scream. Don't holler. Because if you do Mr. Novak won't believe a word you say; he may not believe you anyway. She could not help going on: "And if you think Aunt Nell could have gone back again afterwards and— Well, she couldn't have! She was at Aunt Marianna's all afternoon."

"Of course she was," Aunt Marianna put in. "Ralph and I both told you that. Nell was with me all day long, from eleven thirty on. It's simply ridiculous, your attitude that we're all lying—"

"Now wait, Mrs. Hoyt. I know you and Mr. Hoyt ain't lying. But I got to check things, on account of what Mrs. Covey said when she first came to. Besides, who knew Rita was out there in that cabin? Mrs. Covey and the kid. As far as we know, that's all."

"My point exactly." That was Homer Nelsen, sitting beside Mother and looking quite a bit like a boiled tomato. Maybe not so red. But just as moist. "There hasn't been one shred of evidence that Pearl had any idea of Rita's whereabouts. Not one shred. There's just been a lot of loose, spiteful talk about Pearl threatening the girl—and that's Nell's story, you'll notice, not Little Harriet's, nobody else's—"

He went on talking (and other people too; all at once the room seethed with voices) but nothing more got through to Little Harriet. It all melted into a hot, meaningless blur. Ears, and she heard not. Eyes, and she saw not—except for Mother's face. She saw it with terrible clarity. A face white and stiff as cardboard, with eyes that met Little Harriet's and (it couldn't be happening! But it was, it was) slowly filled with tears. She neither blinked them back nor brushed them away; Mother never cried, she didn't know *how* to cry …

It was those incredible tears that made Little Harriet understand. Aunt Nell off the hook meant Mother on. A lot of loose, spiteful talk. Nell's story, not Little Harriet's. Oh, thank God, not Little Harriet's. (Even if it were true? Even if Rita really had been scared of Mother, not Stanley? Yes, even if it were true.)

It could be true. In her heart Little Harriet knew that it probably was. So what? It was still Stanley who had stabbed Daddy, Stanley who had killed Rita—and nobody connected the one with the other, Stanley wasn't even *here!* Old Novak had made up his one-cell mind to hang Rita's murder (even he couldn't call this one suicide!) on either Aunt Nell or Mother. If not one, then the other. And eager-beaver Little Harriet, busily clearing Aunt Nell, had been too dumb to see what she was doing to Mother.

Calm. Calm. Don't scream. Don't holler. You know what they'll say if you get off on Daddy, if you so much as whisper that there's a link between what happened to him and what happened to Rita. Yes, and Mother will be the first to cut you off if you start talking about Stanley. No matter how much she knows about him, she'll never give him away, not even to get herself off the hook. Which is where she is, but good, unless the sheriff decides you've been lying, as usual.

"Now wait," he was saying. "Now wait. Don't everybody talk at once—"

At that moment the door opened, and in came the constable with a big, flustered, red-armed girl. Helga Jorgensen. Her father's farm was on the river bottom, just south of the Covey cabin; a couple of winters ago, while she was going to high school, she had worked for Aunt Marianna. The reason she was here was that she had heard (like everybody else in the countryside) about Rita, and the talk that was going around, how it was maybe Mrs. Nell Covey that did it, and so Pop said she better tell the authorities, being's she had seen Rita out there at the cabin …

"You saw Rita, you say?" asked Mr. Novak. "What time?"

This morning, Helga said. Well, not really morning. It was about twelve thirty, because she was late getting over to Mr. Stanley's lodge today—she went over every Sunday to clean for him—and usually Pop took her in the car, only today the car broke down, so she had to walk. That was how come she saw Rita, because she took the short cut, back of the cabin, and there was Rita, pumping water.

"She didn't see me. But I got a good look at her. I've seen her in town lots of times. Hadn't been I was in a hurry, I'da stopped, because it struck me kind of funny, a girl being out there by herself. But it wasn't any of my business, and I was already way late, so I just went on." Helga glanced around her and grinned, self-consciously and anxiously, at Aunt Marianna. "I don't know if it makes any difference or not, but Pop said I'd ought to tell the authorities, and so—"

"It makes all the difference, to me." Aunt Nell sounded like herself again, and her face was radiant with relief. "Twelve thirty. A good hour after we got back to town from the cabin, and Rita was alive. It's not just my word for it anymore, or just Little Harriet's. It's Helga's word, too. Oh, thank you, Helga, thank you!"

Even the sheriff had to respond to that big, warm smile of hers. It made things so nice and simple, too; now he was free to focus his single brain cell on Mother. Mother, who didn't have the devoted Hoyts to back her up, or even a screwball eager beaver like Little Harriet to help get her off the hook. Nobody but Homer Nelsen. Mother, who was going to keep Stanley out of it, no matter what it cost her.

So it wouldn't do any good for Little Harriet to mention Stanley, even if she could manage to do it calmly. (And she couldn't. Right now the screams were roiling up inside her; it took all her will power to hold them back.)

So nothing would do any good? No way out of the trap? She clenched her hands in her lap, clenched her eyes shut, held her breath in a rage of concentration.

And she saw the way out. The dazzling, daring, only way out. *Because I saw Rita*, she thought; *we talked to each other, and who can prove what she said to me or didn't say?*

The sheriff was dismissing Helga, thanking her for coming forward with her information. She had done just right, she was the original civic-minded kid, and he for one appreciated …

Little Harriet stood up and said in a cracked voice, "Can I go now? I've told all I know, and I have to—I want to get out of here. Please. Can I?"

"I don't see any reason why not," said the sheriff. (Poor Little Harriet. It showed in his face: rough on the poor kid, her own mother and all, and the worst still to come, at least she won't have to listen to that.) He wasn't a bad guy. Just dumb. "Don't see any reason to keep you folks either, Mr. and Mrs. Hoyt. Much obliged for your cooperation." He turned to Aunt Nell. Very polite. "I'd appreciate it, Mrs. Covey, if you'd stay a while. There's one or two points I want to go over again, about what Rita told you—"

Little Harriet didn't stay for any more. She shot out into the corridor; even so, Evan had beaten her to it. (And without waiting to be dismissed by the sheriff; he had nipped out, right after Helga.) There were people milling around, and Dr. Morrison was coming up the stairs. Maybe Aunt Marianna and Uncle Ralph would stop for a word or two with him. That would give her extra time. Their car? No, too risky. Daddy's; Aunt Nell had almost surely left the keys in it. If not, she would find another way.

She paused for a second, suddenly trembling at the thought of what she was about to try. All alone. Evan was the only one who might … But his back was turned toward her. He had caught up with Helga at the foot of the stairs, and he was intent on her. Asking her something. Putting his hand on her big red arm while he talked to her. So intent. So much in earnest. Little Harriet scuttled past unnoticed.

All right, then. All alone. It was the only way out of the trap, and if it didn't work—well, that was all right too. Who cared? Who would want to live in a world furnished with traps that had no way out? Not Little Harriet.

She ran down the last flight of stairs and out into the hot, still night.

Seventeen

"Where's Little Harriet?" asked Mama.

Startled, Evan let go of Helga's arm and turned around. "Isn't she with you? You were all still there when I came down."

"Yes, but she was a little ahead of us, and then we stopped to speak to Billy Morrison—I thought she was catching up with you."

"Well, she wasn't. Maybe she's still up there."

"Dearie, I *saw* her start down the stairs. She must have come right past you. How on earth could you have missed her?" Mama's voice sharpened a little with anxiety. "She must have seen you, too. I don't understand why she didn't—"

"Now, now," said Dad. "She's probably waiting for us in the car. Can't blame her for wanting to get out of here. I feel the same way."

"Yes, of course. Only the look on her face, poor child. I thought of course she was heading for you, Evan."

Maybe she was, thought Evan, and I was too busy talking to Helga to notice. He hesitated, torn between the two urgencies—Helga (he *thought* he had gotten his point across, but could he count on her to carry through if he left her on her own?) and Little Harriet, desperately in need of somebody—him—to head for. He might be overestimating his own importance to her. But he still could not run the risk of failing her.

"Helga," he said hurriedly, for Mama and Dad were halfway down the stairs, waiting for him. "Listen, Helga, I can't stay, but you go back up there. Tell them what you told me. That's all you have to do. It could be terribly important. You'll do it, won't you, Helga?"

"Well, I guess so, if you say so." She didn't look enthusiastic about it, but she began plodding up the stairs again. Slowly; and casting dubious glances back at him. He would simply have to trust to God that she didn't change her mind.

Little Harriet was not waiting for them in the car. She was nowhere in sight, though surely, if she had started walking, she hadn't had time to get very far.

"Wait a minute," said Dad. "Where's Win's car? I mean Nell's. It was parked right next to us—remember?—and now it's gone. Little Harriet must have decided to drive it home instead of waiting for us."

"That's it, of course," Mama agreed nervously. "That's what she's done. Win used to let her drive it. But not by herself. Oh dear, she really shouldn't have, and without even asking."

Home? "I don't think so. I don't think she's gone home." Evan realized that he had blurted it out in something like panic. Which would not do at all; he needed to keep his head if he was going to figure out anything as complicated and unpredictable as the workings of Little Harriet's mind. Having backed the car out into the street, he let the motor idle for a couple of minutes and made himself concentrate.

She had been so unexpectedly quiet up there in the sheriff's office. (And he had been too absorbed in his own train of thought to see that her docility might be a danger signal.) Not a single hysterical outburst. Not a single word about Uncle Win. Or about Stanley. She was a fanatic on the subject of "getting" Stanley. A fanatic, but no dope. Unfortunately. Perfectly capable of realizing that hysterical outbursts were a waste of time and breath; perfectly capable of dreaming up who knew what other crazy tactics …

Drive home first and check? No. Because if she was there she was safe; and if she was not there they would only be losing precious time. He must play his hunch. He did not dare do anything else. The Spot? Or Stanley's lodge? They were at opposite ends of town. The Spot was closer, so they tried it first. It was deserted, closed up tight. Neither Aunt Nell's car nor Stanley's convertible in the driveway. No cars at all.

"That takes care of that," said Evan as he headed back through town. "Next stop Stanley's lodge. Watch for the turnoff, Dad. I'm not sure I know where it is."

The trip seemed endless to him. He kept trying to calculate how much of a head start Little Harriet had had. Fifteen minutes, perhaps.

Another ten wasted on The Spot. And Aunt Nell's car was faster than this old boat. Too much time, any way you looked at it.

"There's somebody there, all right," said Dad. "That's it, at the top of the next hill. See the light?"

The light, yes. But they labored up the last hill to find no sign of either Aunt Nell's car or that flashy job of Stanley's.

Evan had been so sure his hunch was right that he could only stare stupidly at the empty driveway, the empty garage. But they *must* be here. Someone must be. He and Dad got out and circled the heavy stone building, dark except for the one light in the living room. There was a faint rustle of wind in the brush. Their own breathing. No other sound. No other out-of-the-way spot where a car—two cars, both of them light-colored—might conceivably be parked.

"He's got quite a place here, hasn't he?" said Dad. He paused beside the half-finished patio, looking thoughtfully at the tools and bags of cement. So did Evan.

They knocked at the doors; peered in the picture window at the spacious, vacant living room. (Straight out of Hollywood, thought Evan. That couch. And bearskin rugs yet.)

"There's nobody here," he said at last. "We might as well go back to town. I'd still like to know where the hell Stanley is."

"Maybe the sheriff's called him in," said Dad. "He's bound to, sooner or later."

True enough. If for no other reason than that Rita had worked for Stanley. But Stanley's car was still nowhere to be seen, either on Main Street or beside the courthouse. And if they didn't find Little Harriet safely at home when they got there … Evan's mind stopped in its tracks. He had played his hunch to the end of the line. He had no more ideas.

He needed none. Thank God. There was Aunt Nell's car, parked, not in the driveway, but in front of the house, at the foot of the long sidewalk that bisected the front yard. "There!" Mama let out her breath in sharp relief. "The child just drove home, after all. All this fuss over nothing. I didn't believe for a minute she'd done anything else—"

She broke off, at the sound that came from the house. Not a loud sound. But a distinctive one. Evan wrenched open the car door and headed for the back porch at a run.

"Don't move," said Little Harriet. "I know how to use this, and I'd just as soon plug you as not." The gun in her hand wobbled some, but there it was, a gun. And there was Stanley, bent over Aunt Marianna's little sewing chair. Not moving. Just staring. He had dropped his flashlight when she first walked in on him. Thank God for the flashlight; otherwise she wouldn't have caught on that there was somebody in the house. (Wherever Stanley had left his car, it wasn't anywhere in sight.) And thank God she had parked in front instead of in the side driveway; otherwise he would have heard the car and beat it.

"What have you got in your hand? What are you doing here?" Her heart was hammering so hard that it made a ringing in her ears and her own voice sounded funny and far-away.

He did not answer. Cautiously, his eyes still fixed on the gun, he straightened up. If only she could keep him from guessing how rattled she was, so rattled that for the moment she couldn't remember the first thing Uncle Ralph had taught her about how to shoot …

She might have managed if she hadn't heard the car in the driveway. It distracted her; automatically, she half-turned. For no more than a split second. But that was all Stanley needed. He was across the room and on her in a flash of movement that was like lightning. She was not conscious of pulling the trigger, but the gun went off anyway, and when she threw it into the dining room Stanley knocked her aside and went after it, and somehow she hung on like a cat, clawing at him, until he gave her that last vicious swipe. No matter that she had already heard the slam of the screen door on the back porch and footsteps pounding through the kitchen. Too late. He had killed her. She was dead.

She opened her eyes to discover that she was stretched out on the floor with her head under the dining room table. Stanley was also stretched out, near the sideboard, and Evan was sitting astride him. Little Harriet had an impulse to giggle. She sat up carefully. She did not seem to be dead, after all.

Aunt Marianna was there, too. "Get the gun, dearie," she said to Evan in her ordinary, matter-of-fact voice. Then she began fussing over Little Harriet.

"Never mind," said Uncle Ralph. "I've got it." It didn't wobble in his hand the way it had in Little Harriet's. When Evan and Stanley were on their feet again, he added, "What's been going on here, anyway?"

Little Harriet took a long breath. "He tried to kill me. Just like he killed Daddy and Rita. He knocked me down and— At least this time I know for sure. Nobody can call me a liar, like you all did about the other night, out at The Spot."

"I didn't call you a liar," said Evan. "I believed you."

"Well, you shouldn't!" She bit her lip. "I mean, I don't know whether I was lying or not. Maybe I *wanted* Stanley or Joe or somebody to clip me—"

Stanley snorted. "Well, I didn't. Neither did Joe. I didn't know you were out there, and even if I had I wouldn't have bothered. Why should I?

Tonight, sure." He turned to the others. "The kid's crazy. She pulled a gun on me. I had to sock her to get it away from her."

"She pulled a gun on you? Nonsense. Where would she …" But Aunt Marianna's voice trailed off. Even she recognized the gun as Uncle Ralph's, and she knew well enough where Little Harriet had gotten it.

"It was still there in Daddy's desk. I picked it up tonight, before I went up to Stanley's lodge, because I was going to—" She felt a pang of sorrow for her dazzling, daring plan to bluff Stanley into believing that Rita had told her "everything." No chance, now, to use her lovely phrases: The game is up; I know all; you are undone. Aunt Marianna, who had never grasped the rudiments of bluffing, would be sure to give her away. But, child, if you knew all this—Little Harriet could hear her asking it— why in the world didn't you tell the sheriff?

It didn't matter, anyway; she no longer *needed* to bluff. "Ask him what he was doing here in the first place! He was ransacking the house, that's what he was doing! Look at the library, look at the living room. Ask him what he was hunting for, ask him what he had in his hand when I walked in on him!"

He still had it; she could tell from the way his hand jerked toward his pocket. He hesitated, no doubt weighing his chances of resistance. They weren't good. Not with Uncle Ralph holding the gun and Evan ready to jump him again, if necessary. They were non-existent.

Whatever Little Harriet had expected, it was something more sensational than what he drew from his pocket. She did not even identify it until Aunt Marianna gasped out, "Why, that's Win's! His old pocketknife! Why would anybody want to steal that? It's not worth a thing!"

"That's right," said Stanley. His eyes gleamed. "Not worth a thing."

"Then why did you steal it?" asked Evan.

Stanley eyed him coolly. "I'm nuts about antiques. Any more questions, bright boy?"

"I'll tell you why!" It was like something exploding inside Little Harriet. "Daddy's knife, he asked me about it, he thought that was how I knew he hadn't stabbed himself. Stanley was there that night, and the knife proves it, that's why he had to get it back. Yes, and that's why he killed Rita, too, because she knew too much—"

"Somebody killed Rita?" said Stanley. "On the level? I thought that was just some more of the kid's crazy talk."

Evan gave a short laugh. "You did, did you? I suppose you didn't even know where Rita was."

"Sure I knew. She went to Chicago. I tried to call her this morning because I wanted to pay her what I owed her, and Mrs. Shoemaker told me."

"Don't try to give me that stuff. You knew damn well Rita was in that cabin down by the river. Helga told you. You drove her home after she finished cleaning your lodge today, and she told you she'd seen Rita at the cabin earlier, on her way to your place. What's more, Helga's up in the sheriff's office right now, telling him what she already told me."

"She *is?*" whispered Little Harriet. So that was why he had been so intent on Helga, up there at the courthouse. He hadn't deserted her, after all; he didn't believe Mother was guilty. She swallowed, and tasted tears.

"Listen," Stanley was saying. "Helga could have told everybody in the county where Rita was. That makes 'em all murderers?"

"Not everybody in the county had a quarrel with Rita yesterday. Just you. And Pearl."

"Leave Pearl out of this!" That had gotten through to Stanley, all right. And Evan must realize it, because he pressed harder.

"Leave her out of it? After all, she threatened Rita. She admits it. She's not saying one word about you, though. She's apparently willing to take the rap for you, and you're obviously willing to let her, but even so—"

"Shut up! Who says I'm letting her take the rap for me?"

"Well," said Evan reasonably, "she's the one that's up in the sheriff's office, getting a working over. Not you. But even so, she can't cover up for you forever. The sheriff's bound to get around to you before long. On account of Helga. Other things, too. Footprints, for instance. There were some very interesting footprints on the rug in the cabin where Rita was killed. Looked like cement tracks, didn't they, Dad?" He paused, and Stanley licked his lips. "That's quite a patio you're building up at your lodge. I noticed it when we were up there tonight."

His eyes shifted to Stanley's shoes. They were streaked with whitish dust, and they had left prints in several places on the dining room rug, especially where Evan and Stanley had scuffled. Quite a lot of prints in that spot.

"So go ahead," said Stanley. He was looking at the knife in his hand now, and there was a curious, gloating smile on his face. "Call the sheriff. Tell him you've cracked his case for him. What are you waiting for?"

No one moved, and his smile deepened. "I'll be very glad to talk to the sheriff. If you're so sure I killed Rita—"

"It has to be you," said Evan. "You or Pearl."

"You leave Pearl out of this! She's got nothing to do with it. Any of it." Furious and contemptuous, he faced them. Each of them in turn. He hates us, thought Little Harriet. Oh, how he hates us, and he must have hated Daddy too. Just on account of Mother? I don't see why he … "You think you're something. Don't you? All of you with that goddam superior look on your face. You'll find out. I may be in a spot, but take my word for it, you and your precious superior family are never going to be the same again, either. You're going to have to crawl in the mud right along with me."

Aunt Marianna was the first to rally. "I suppose you mean the scandal about you and Pearl …"

"No, Mrs. Marianna Covey Hoyt. I don't mean the scandal about me and Pearl. You're not going to get off that easy."

That challenging stare of his. As if the gun were in his hand, instead of Uncle Ralph's. "He means Daddy!" cried Little Harriet. "He killed my Daddy, just like he did Rita!"

"But Win shot himself," quavered Aunt Marianna. "You know that, Little Harriet. He left you a note—"

"He didn't leave me a note when he was stabbed! Because he didn't stab himself. Stanley did it. And Rita saw him at our house that night, that's why he had to kill her too. He *was* there. The knife proves it. Only why did Daddy—"

"Yes," said Aunt Marianna. "Why didn't Win say so? When he gave me the knife, he just said it had turned up after all these years, not lost at all. If the knife proved that you were there—and it must prove something; otherwise you wouldn't have come here looking for it—" She gave a short, arrogant laugh. "It's simply preposterous. Why should Win cover up for you?"

"Don't laugh at me," said Stanley. "I'm warning you. Don't laugh."

Laughing, thought Little Harriet, Rita had heard Daddy laughing that night. And in her mind she saw the picture so sharply: Daddy in his study, facing Stanley with his unshakable Covey assurance, laughing …

"You're right about one thing," Stanley was going on. His face was still fixed in that smile of rage and derision. "The knife proves something. It proved plenty to him, all right. But he'd sooner die than give me my rights. That's all I wanted from him, what I've been cheated out of all my life. My name. And he wouldn't do it, damn him, damn him, he'd sooner die—he did die because he couldn't stand to admit it even to himself. I had the knife, I proved it to him, and it didn't make any difference, to him I was still the dirt under his feet, he laughed in my face." He drew in his breath violently.

"You had the knife?" echoed Aunt Marianna. "He lost it years ago, when he was in college …"

"That's right. When he was in college. Just a fun-loving college boy out for a night of good clean slumming. Where's the harm in laying some dumb Polack girl? What if he does knock her up? He's never going to see her again, she's too dumb to even think of trying to trace him, too scared of her old man to let him know the fix she's in. Too scared to do anything but run away from home and raise her brat the best way she can."

"Your mother," said Aunt Marianna.

"My mother's dead," said Stanley. "The kind of life she led, you don't last long. You wouldn't know about such things. Neither would your wonderful brother Win. Too busy being the big-shot lawyer to bother about dirt like me. Well, I caught up with him. I swore I would when I was a kid, and I did."

That's why he hates us, thought Little Harriet. She had a queer, remote, floating feeling. That's why he had to have Daddy's house. And the knife. That's why everything. His forehead's like Daddy's, high and proud, Daddy always wanted a son, only when he found out he had one …

"I didn't kill him," Stanley said loudly. "He did it himself. I never meant to kill him. The only thing I wanted from him was his name. My name. Covey. I've got a right. All he had to do was own up to who I am. I had the dough. I was willing to pay him. He laughed in my face. And then he got sore and pulled that hunting knife on me, and when I tried to grab it away from him— God knows I never meant to kill him, I still don't know how it happened. I got out of there so fast I even forgot this." He hefted the pocketknife in his hand. "I had to get it back. Only Pearl didn't know where it was—"

"My mother's got nothing to do with this!" Little Harriet gave a great gulp. "You said so!"

"That's what I'm saying now. She knows I saw Win that night, and she knows I left a pocketknife there. Period. I told her Win and I had a discussion about her. Not a row. A discussion. And she called me tonight and told me about Rita. That's how much Pearl's got to do with any of it."

Little Harriet remembered Mother's face, up there in the sheriff's office, her face stiff with suffering, and the tears brimming in her eyes. No, she hadn't known about Daddy. She still didn't know who Stanley really was. But what terrible dark suspicions Rita's death must have wakened in her mind; how alone—more alone than Little Harriet, even in her worst moments—she must have felt.

"If you think she told me what Win had done with the knife—well, she didn't. He never mentioned it to her. Nobody told me. I guessed it, and I figured now was my chance, with all of you up at the sheriff's office hashing over Rita."

"Yes," said Evan. "Rita. She was at Uncle Win's that night, she saw you—"

"She wouldn't tell me how much she knew!" It came out in a flash of bitter exasperation. "I thought if I gave her a job and made a play for her— But even then she kept on stalling, and she wouldn't let *go* of me, she still thought I'd give up Pearl for her. Don't get me wrong. I'm not confessing anything. I'm just telling you where we all stand. All of us Coveys." His eyes met Evan's scornfully. "Well. What are we waiting for? I'm ready to talk to the sheriff any time. Only not just about Rita. How you going to like it, having it all come out?"

No, thought Little Harriet, no. But Aunt Marianna lifted her head proudly. "Call the sheriff, Evan." She turned back to Stanley. "You claim you're a Covey. You ought to know how we're going to like it," she said, and Stanley flushed as if she had slapped him.

"I claim I'm a Covey. You know damn well I'm a Covey. So did he, even if he wouldn't admit it." (But Daddy had admitted it. By refusing to tell the truth about the stabbing. By killing himself.) "Well, you can't get out of it any longer. It's been eating on me all my life. The name that belongs to me. I'll have it if it kills me, and if it does, by God, I'll die under my own name."

No one spoke. Until Evan, back from the telephone in the hall, came over to Little Harriet and put his arms around her, and she couldn't stand it any longer, she burst into tears. Because it was all her fault; if only she had kept still the way Daddy had told her to … But, being herself, she *couldn't* have done anything else; and (it came to her in the middle of a sob: a glimpse of the human condition) Mother couldn't have done much different, either. Nor Aunt Marianna, nor Daddy himself. Stanley too? Yes, Stanley too.

The waiting seemed to be making him uneasy. He kept shifting the pocketknife from one hand to the other. His identity. And his weapon. As potent as the gun Uncle Ralph was holding. They could force it away from him … No. It would still not keep him from talking, his story would still be there for them to deny. Try to deny.

At last he said defensively, "I know. Sure. I could take the rap for Rita and leave it at that. Keep my mouth shut about the rest of it. But why should I? What's it to me if the Coveys get smeared from here to hell and back? What have the Coveys ever done for me?"

"Nothing," said Aunt Marianna. "No reason why you should protect us."

"That's right. A whole lot of nothing. Worse than nothing. He wouldn't give it to me, the one thing I ever asked him for or ever would, and still he wouldn't …" And now it was as if he were arguing with himself. "Why should I care if it killed him? Why should I care what it does to me or any of the rest of you? I got a right. It's my name too."

"Yes," said Aunt Marianna. "Your name too. You can do whatever you like with it."

Into the silence came the sound of a car. The sheriff. Turning into the side driveway. There. The motor stopped. The car door slammed. Only a minute or two now. As long as it would take the sheriff to come in through the back porch.

"All right. I can't do it," Stanley said abruptly. He thrust the knife toward Aunt Marianna. "Here. Take it. Keep your mouth shut about it. That's what I'm going to do. Don't ask me why. God damn it, I don't know why."

But Little Harriet knew why. Aunt Marianna knew, too. And, being Aunt Marianna, she said so. She held out her small, square, freckly hand. It was steady as a rock. "Thank you, Mr. Covey," she said. "Thank you very much."

THE END

The Trash Stealer

Jean Potts

One

"Hey, there. How's it going?"

"Can't complain," said Joe truthfully. He reached for the Scotch. "On the rocks, dash of soda?"

"How about that. The second time I've been in here, and already you've got me tagged. You even remembered the brand. What's your system? Or is it a trade secret?"

"I'm a genius," Joe confided. Maybe he was, at that. A minor, all-purpose genius who seemed to take naturally to whatever job came along, just so it wasn't permanent. Like this summer of tending bar at The Starfish: the boss had been dubious about hiring a young fellow with no experience; yet after two months here was Joe making like a professional with trade secrets, and the boss propositioning him to come along when he headed for his Florida joint in the fall.

He might even go, depending on what else turned up in the meantime. Might carve out a career for himself, Joe Florio the perfect bartender. Ha! Not that he wasn't enjoying this summer. The pay suited him. So did the hours, which gave him a good part of the day to spend as he pleased, swimming or lazing on the beach with his little playmate Ellie. So did the work; even on nights when the pace got a little hectic, he stayed relaxed, good-humored, and quietly in control of the situation. In a way, it reminded him of summers he had spent as a counselor at a boys' camp. He had liked that, too.

"Quiet this evening," the guy said, swishing his Scotch around over the rocks. He was one of those young-old guys that look at fifty-five just about the way they did at thirty. His hair was pewter gray, but maybe prematurely; the lines between his eyes could have been put there by the strain of a high-pressure job as easily as by time. He was wiry and quick-moving. "Where is everybody? Church?"

"It's early yet," said Joe. "There's always a lot of beach parties on Sunday. It'll liven up later on. Coming," he added; the only other customers, the three old girls from the Inn, were due for refills. They were regulars who showed up every evening on the dot of six-thirty; at eight, mildly loaded on Tom Collinses, they tottered back to the Inn for dinner. The Starfish concentrated on drink rather than food, though sandwiches were available for the non-discriminating.

"I'm not complaining, you understand," the guy said when Joe drifted back to him. "I'm all for peace and quiet, myself. I like it better now than the way it was the other night. If you remember, it livened up a bit too much."

"Those kids, you mean. Yeah. A few beers, and they're apt to get noisy."

"Noisy and nasty. For a few minutes there I didn't like the looks of things at all. I must say, you did an expert job of handling them."

"Mostly bluff. I look tougher than I am." It was one of his talents as a bartender, and Joe knew it. To begin with, there was his good old crooked nose; who was to know that he had broken it tripping over his kid sister's doll carriage, instead of in a fight? The slightly battered effect was what counted. Then there was his hair, which stood up stiff and fierce-looking above his basically amiable face. And, though he was of only average height, he was broad and heavily muscled in the shoulders. He grinned. "Don't tell them I said so."

"A bluff. You mean you don't really have a gun? I heard one of them say you had."

"Oh, I've got a gun all right. It's the boss's. His idea. He was held up a couple of years ago, and he got it then. But there's a difference between having a gun and using it." To tell the truth, Joe didn't like to think of the damn thing lying there in its hiding place beside the safe in the rear. He couldn't see himself shooting anybody, not even if it was his own safe that was being rifled, his own joint that was being wrecked. "Though I will admit, if anybody could ever get me sore enough to use a gun, it would be those young punks. They really make me see red sometimes."

"I know what you mean," said the guy. "But I was held up a while back, right on Park Avenue it was, and I found out then and there how much of a hero I am. Handed over my wallet meek as Jesus. Couldn't do it fast enough. No sir, I'd never put up a fight. After all, it's only money. Buy you a drink? Or don't you drink on the job?"

Joe didn't usually; he preferred to save his few modest drinks for after work with Ellie. But he could tell from the guy's expression—a hopeful, lonesome little smile—how much he wanted company. "I could use a beer," he said. "Thanks." They clicked glasses and sipped. Outside, the sun was still strong but slanting. Occasionally a car flashed by, a bunch of kids pedaled past on their bikes, or dawdled along on foot, slurping ice cream cones. Inside, all was dim and cool and tranquil. The hour for reminiscing and philosophizing.

"Before the Depression really hit, when we still had the place at Rockport ..." one of the old girls was explaining dreamily.

And at the other end of the bar Joe said, "All the same, it's handy stuff to have around. Money. If you've ever been broke—"

"I have been. I didn't like it. But it's like a college education, a hell of a lot more important if you haven't got it than if you have."

"You could be right," said Joe, who sometimes wondered where he would be now if he had stuck it out and finished college. Tending bar in a classier spot than The Starfish, maybe? "I guess the mistake is to figure any one thing is going to solve all your problems. That's expecting too much, even of money."

"Right. You get different problems, that's all. Take it from me." Again there was the flickering, lonesome smile. He looked as if he might know, at that. About both kinds of problems. Broke he may have been in his time, but if Joe was any judge, he had also had his share of high living. There was an easy-come, easy-go air about him that suggested— not the professional gambler, nothing that calculated—but the taker of chances, the rainbow chaser, the rolling stone who could stand anything but monotony. Not unlike Joe himself. He was going on with quiet intensity, staring way past Joe, into his own secret life. "There's only one reason I wish I had money. Only one person I'd like to do something for. All the money I've spent on myself, and on other people, people that didn't mean a thing to me, any more than I did to them, but not a penny for the one person in the world I give a damn about. That's no way to operate."

"Doesn't make much sense," Joe agreed.

"None whatever," said the guy briskly. "Next time I make a wad it's going to be different. All I have to do is make it. And I've done it before. Why not again? That's one of the things about money, see, it's habit-forming. Once you've had a taste of it, like as not you're hooked. Can't do without it. So you keep on making it and spending it, and the more you make the more you spend, and … well. There ought to be something more to life than that."

"You don't look like a money grubber to me," said Joe.

"No? What do I look like?"

"I don't know exactly. Something more in the line of—well, you could be some kind of an artist."

"For the love of God!" The guy laughed abruptly. Under the sunburn his face flushed—in anger, embarrassment, pleasure? Impossible to tell. "What put that into your head?"

It had rather surprised Joe himself. "I get these flashes of intuition. They're usually wrong."

"This one sure was." He fumbled in his pocket and drew out a business card: Shangri-La Travel Service. Cruises and Tours a Specialty. Frederick Wall. "Fritz for short. But the crazy part of it is, I've always had a yen to paint. If it hadn't been for my mother, I would never have done anything else. No great loss to the world, I guess. But I like it. It makes me happy."

"So I was right, after all. Some kind of an artist."

"A frustrated one. But maybe it's better to be a might-have-been than an outright flop. When I get fed up with the travel racket or whatever, I can always sneak off and paint myself back into sanity. This week, for instance. I'm holed up at the Stewarts' shack—you know it? Down by the cove, they're off in their sailboat—having myself a ball. You ought to see the collage I'm working on. I can't believe it myself." His face had lit up as he talked; this time his smile was infectious.

"I'm a square," Joe confessed. "Van Gogh's as far out as I go. Stewart. Isn't his place the one with the iron deer in front? He's a big, baldheaded fellow?"

"That's him. He's in the insurance business. I've known him for years."

"Joe!" one of the old girls warbled. "Check, please, Joe. Happy hour's over!"

They had no sooner departed, giggling, than in swarmed a thirsty crowd from the golf course. After them came the city people bent on winding up the weekend with a bang; the lower-keyed locals; and finally the stragglers from the beach parties, bemused by sea and sand, not to mention more drinks than they needed before they ever hit The Starfish.

All in all, the boss's favorite kind of evening: brisk. Add tonight's take to what was already stashed away in the safe, and he would have a nice healthy roll for the bank first thing in the morning. One of the world's money grubbers, the boss, and contented to be just that. No vague dissatisfactions for him; no yearnings for "something more" out of life. On Sunday nights he usually dropped in at closing time for the simple pleasure of counting the proceeds. Tonight, though, his game leg was kicking up again, and Joe would be left to do the job at his own stepped-up and considerably less reverent pace.

He could meet Ellie that much earlier; she was one of the college kid waitresses at the Inn, which closed at ten. His nice little brown-haired, soft-voiced Ellie, enthusiastically doing her bit to make life worth living. She cast a pleasant glow, even on nights like this one, when he was too rushed to think of her consciously. For though his hands went about their business almost automatically by now—he got a mild charge out of being able to measure, mix, shake, with so much accuracy and speed—there was more to tending bar than pouring drinks and making change. Joe had also developed a sharp eye and ear for spotting trouble in advance, and an unobtrusively glib tongue for averting it. Trouble in all its manifestations: the drunks who must be eased out but not antagonized; the arguments that must not be allowed to boil up into quarrels; the freeloaders and floozies and jealous husbands or wives or sweethearts. And of course the young punks. There were only a couple of them tonight, and they didn't stay long.

Neither did Joe's fellow philosopher, the travel agent and frustrated artist, whatever his name was, Fritz for short. Once the place started filling up, he slid off his stool and left. Not without a friendly wave. "So long, Joe. Be seeing you."

Joe hoped so. He rather liked the guy.

Theoretically, The Starfish closed at twelve-thirty, but it was after one when the last of the city crowd cleared out and left Joe to lock the door and switch off the neon sign. Half an hour more to tidy up a bit, check the money in the cash register and transfer it to the safe, and Joe would be on his way too. Another weekend wound up. He worked fast, spurred on by the thought of Ellie waiting for him. It was quiet, almost eerily so after the hubbub of the evening; the air was smoky, with the faintly fruity, faintly stale smell peculiar to bars. And with only two lights on— one up front, one in the rear—it was even murkier than usual. Not that Joe paid much attention to his surroundings; he was too busy counting the cash.

A nice bundle all right, he thought as he headed for the safe, which was enshrined behind a decorative arrangement of driftwood next to the Gents. Too bad the boss wasn't here to gloat over it.

The whisper came just as the safe door swung open, obedient to his knob twirling. "Okay, hand it over. Don't make it tough for yourself. Just do what I say, and you've got nothing to worry about."

He froze, more in astonishment than fear. Though why he should have considered himself and The Starfish immune, when holdups happened all the time …

Could he have imagined that whisper behind him? He straightened up warily, and it came again. "I've got you covered. Keep your hands off the safe and turn around."

Out of the gloom a figure was moving toward him in stealthy, menacing steps. A shadow-dark figure, except for the extended left hand (the right one he kept buried in the pocket of his black trench coat; even in the dim light Joe could see the bulge there) and the head, which must be covered with a nylon stocking. It loomed up there like a balloon, light-colored and faceless, in its weird way the crowning touch of reality for Joe. A young punk's trick: one of them must have sneaked into the Gents to hide until closing time. He could have gotten in through the back door; it had been unlocked until eleven or so.

He shuffled closer, close enough so that Joe could hear him breathing. One last step, and he was shoving up against Joe, grabbing for the wad of bills, his left shoulder jamming Joe's to show how tough he was. His right hand was no longer buried in his pocket. There was a gun in it, all right; but Joe was beyond caring. The sudden, mindless outrage that boiled up in him left no room for fear or logic. He did not even think of the boss's gun in its hiding place beside the safe. All that mattered was the intolerable fact of this punk trying to push him around.

Beside himself with fury, Joe shoved and jammed back. "Get away from me. Who the hell do you think you are? Take your hands off me." He struck out wildly. There was a surprised grunt from the punk; the gun seemed to leap out of his hand and go off on its own—the sound in that low-ceilinged room was shattering—before it clattered to the floor. The punk bent as if to scramble for it, and Joe's next blow spun him around so that now his back was to the safe. He managed to keep his balance, though, and landed one good punch. Pain exploded in Joe's nose; he stepped back a couple of paces and hit for the last time, a soul-satisfying smack that connected and set the punk crashing backward. Out like a light. Joe waited a minute to make sure, and to catch his own breath. Then he went up front and called the police station and the boss. There was still not a sound, not a stir, from the punk. He decided to call the doctor, too.

He sat down on one of the bar stools and waited for them to come. His knees seemed to have turned to water. Blood dripped in a slow, cold trickle from his nose. Every now and then a fit of shaking seized him, like a gust of high wind. Nerves. Reaction. Or premonition?

"Nothing for me to do," said the doctor. "He's dead. Cracked his skull against the safe door when he went down."

"My God, Joe," said the boss. "To think of you tackling him like that, and him with a gun. That took nerve, boy, real guts. More than I've got, I'll tell you right now."

"I thought you said a young punk," said the cop. The doctor had pulled off the nylon stocking first thing, of course, exposing the pewter-gray hair, the young-old face, ageless in death as it had been in life. "Anybody know who he is?"

"I do," croaked Joe. "He was in here earlier tonight. Left me his card." He went back to the bar and got it. Shangri-La Travel Service. Cruises and Tours a Specialty. Frederick Wall. "Fritz for short," said Joe, and the shakes hit him again, gale force.

Two

He chose the spot for its isolation: it was near the cove, a stretch of coarse sand and pebbles, with clumps of tough, scrubby little bushes sprouting here and there. Too far from the water to attract bathers; too far from the paths that wound past the scattered cottages to appeal to strollers. He propped himself, not very comfortably, against a hillock, and tried to keep from staring at his hands, which fascinated him.

Killer's hands, he thought. I killed a man last night.

Yet they were outwardly the same loose-jointed, nimble-looking hands that could do so many different things. Too many different things; they could strike out in senseless, lethal rage without any instructions from Joe himself. They might still look like the trusty servants he had always assumed them to be—he watched as they innocently, submissively flexed and unflexed at his command—but he knew better now. They had a will of their own; at any moment they might leap again into independent action and leave him to face the consequences. For of course he was stuck with them and their doings.

And so incidentally was Frederick Fritz-for-short Wall, poor devil, what was the difference to him whether Joe had intended to kill him or not? Either way he was just as dead.

Okay, as the boss said, he started it. And he had a gun; that made it self-defense. But Joe knew that he would have been in no danger if he had behaved rationally and handed over the money without argument or fuss. That was the unpardonable thing—that he had taken another man's life for the meanest of all possible reasons. Money. A lousy wad of bills that didn't even belong to Joe.

The boss hadn't helped any, calling him a hero, trying to give him a reward. A reward! Blood money. When Joe told him what he could do with it, and the job too, he had looked hurt, bewildered, but still respectful. "You want a vacation, Joe? Sure, sure, anything you say. Write your own ticket. I don't get it, Joe, why you should be upset. After all, a guy tries to rob you, you've got a right to stop him. He had it coming, didn't he?"

Joe drew his knees up and rested his aching head against them. No use trying to explain to the boss that money was not that important. It was to him. But not to Fritz, not to Joe; and yet it was for money that the one had been killed, and the other had killed. How could that be? Fritz Wall was not a brainless young punk. He had no criminal record. Why should he have risked his life, and lost it, in a miserable holdup attempt?

Only one reason I wish I had money, he had said; only one person in the world I give a damn about. Looking off into space as he said it, as if he had forgotten Joe and were talking to himself. Even at the time, Joe had sensed how serious he was about this person, whoever it was, that he wanted to do something for. What he hadn't sensed was the urgency, the desperation in Fritz.

Well, he saw it now. Saw, too, his own unwitting role in edging Fritz along the way to taking his final, fatal chance. For Joe had minimized the risk; had led Fritz to believe—had himself believed—that he would put up no resistance. It's only money. Mostly bluff, he had said; I look tougher than I am. Possibly that was what decided Fritz, the final little nudge across the line separating I-might from I-will.

There was a scrabbling of pebbles behind him. Just a dog, he hoped. But when he lifted his head, here was this girl peering down at him through butterfly-shaped sunglasses. They made her look inhuman, like somebody from Mars. She was pretty weird otherwise, too. Hair like last year's bird's nest (a very large, careless bird); spooky-pale lipstick; a sleeveless garment, phosphorescent-pink and black checks, that ended long before it reached her knees and had portholes in the sides.

"Hello," she said. "What are you doing here?"

"Nothing. Do you mind?" He put his head back on his knees and waited for her to go away. When she did not do so, he added pointedly, "The idea was to get away from people."

"Me too," she said, and sat down beside him. "If I'd brought my bathing suit, I could go for a swim."

"Don't let me keep you," said Joe.

"What's your trouble? A hangover?" She removed the butterflies for a closer inspection of him. The effect was still Martian: hers was a loose wrist with the eye makeup. The eyes themselves were okay. Clear, greenish-gray.

"Hangover's as good a word for it as any," he said.

"I didn't think bartenders drank. That's who you are, isn't it? The bartender at The Starfish?"

Oh God. His public. "Not anymore. I resigned."

"Really? On account of what happened last night?" She continued to regard him with bold curiosity. "How peculiar. You don't look like the type. To resign, I mean. I'd expect you to stick around and enjoy the applause. Why not? You deserve it. After all, most people don't have the nerve to do what you did."

He was not sure whether she was needling him or not. She might be, through some nutty sense of social consciousness. She looked young enough; twenty at the most, Joe thought. But also young enough for the straight hero-worshipping business, ready to flip over any kind of a celebrity. Even a killer. Joe stared at his hands. Either way, there was nothing for him to say.

"I said, most people don't have the nerve to—"

"I heard you the first time. Lay off, will you?"

"Aren't we touchy! I was just trying to be friendly. You're not the only one with headaches, you know. How about me? What kind of a day do you think I've had, having to come all the way out here by myself? Answering questions, all the rest of it." She sniffed and trembled her lip. If she kept working at it, she might actually squeeze out a couple of tears.

"I have no idea what kind of a day you've had, or what you're doing here, or—" He felt a sudden chill of suspicion. "Who are you, anyway?"

"I thought you were never going to ask," she said. She pushed the bird's nest even more askew. "I'm Cynthia Wall. Only daughter of the late Frederick Wall. My friends call me Cyn."

He was profoundly shocked. Frederick Wall's daughter! And here she sat, dry-eyed, flippant, callously chatting with his murderer! Not to mention the gaudy impropriety of that thing she was wearing. Even if she had no family feeling (Joe's own was strong and deep) she ought to show more respect for the dead.

She was staring back at him brazenly, as if she were reading his mind and sneering at the script. He would not have noticed what was happening to her throat except that she put her hand up to hide its convulsive, painful working. The hand itself was a childish, grubby little paw that did not match the rest of her.

That was when the idea first started working in Joe: if it should turn out that the one person Fritz cared about was his daughter—and it could be—then maybe he could somehow or other make it up to her. In a small way, of course; nothing could bring Fritz back. But his death wouldn't be as completely pointless as it was now. And Joe's conscience would be eased a little.

He cleared his throat. "Did you say you came out here by yourself? Alone?"

"Sure. You might know it would be my address and telephone number they found among his what-do-you-call-them, effects. Just mine, none of the others'. So I was the one they called."

"The others? You do have family, then. And you mean to say they let you—"

"Do I have family! Oh, brother!" She cast her eyes heavenward. "The only one I'm on speaking terms with at the moment is Gran, Daddy's mother, and she's a million years old and has a heart condition—that's one of those expressions that always break me up. Heart condition. Doesn't everybody have one? Well, anyway, there was nothing to do but dump it in poor old Duffy's lap and get out here and claim the body or whatever it was I was supposed to do."

"Who's Duffy?"

"She looks after Gran. Her underpaid companion. You know. Dedicated."

"But surely somebody could have come with you. I mean, it's a hell of a thing for a kid like you to have to handle by herself."

"Gets you right here, doesn't it? Boo boo hoo." The crisis in her throat—which might have been all his imagination, anyway—had long since passed; her eyes were as tearless and derisive as ever. "Listen. I didn't want anybody. Is that clear? I didn't even call Duffy until after I got out here, and then I didn't go into all the sordid details. Just that Daddy was dead."

"I didn't mean to kill him, you know," Joe burst out. "God help me, I'd give anything if it hadn't happened."

"Now, now, calm down. I didn't track you down to wreak vengeance or anything like that. I did it because …" She let her voice trail away. Her expression became rather dreamy. "I don't really know why. I recognized you right away. They told me what you looked like. What are you going to do, now that you've quit at The Starfish?"

"Nothing, till this business gets settled. They released me on bail." Provided by the boss, of course. Jumped at the chance. Joe supposed he ought to be grateful. All right, he was. "After that, I don't know. Get another job, I guess. Somewhere else. Not around here."

"It looks like kind of a blah place, anyway. I mean, what is there, besides the beach?"

What more should there be? It had been enough for Joe and Ellie: the lazy hours of sand and sun and sea; and at night the sky thick with stars, the endless swell and sigh of the waves, the sweetness of unhurried lovemaking. But to Cynthia Wall it would be just so much blah. Joe could feel the restlessness that radiated from her. It was as if she were running a fever. For a moment he permitted himself to wonder what it would take to satisfy her craving for excitement.

"Some people like it," he said stiffly. "Your father seemed to. He said he was having a ball. Painting himself back into sanity. Of course he could have just been handing me a line." Probably was, in view of what happened later.

"So he gave you the frustrated artist bit? I've been hearing it all my life. I guess it was for real, though, because there are these pictures over at the Stewart place. And a collage. It's wild. I never saw any of his stuff before. He always tore it up or burned it or something. And besides, he wasn't around very much."

"No?" Anyway, it hadn't been just a line.

"I'm a product of a broken home," said Cynthia. "You have to make allowances for me. I was only a baby when they got divorced, but it was still a traumatic experience. And then my mother married this character named J. Randolph Muggins, of all things. And had these three little Muggins monsters. So naturally I've always been a problem. They sent me away to school, camp in the summer, and palmed me off on Gran whenever she'd let them. You can't blame them. A simple matter of self-preservation. Those were the days. If J. Randolph got one of his attacks of acute economy I could always put the bite on Daddy."

"I see." She couldn't be the one Fritz had meant, then; the only one he cared about but had never spent a penny on. Unless she was lying. And she might be. "Did your father marry again too?"

"No, he never legalized the proceedings with any of them. Not even Marian. She's the perennial. His business partner, among other things. A real dog. He had terrible taste in women. Look at my mother. She cured him, I guess. Once was enough." She was silent a moment, inspecting him. "Go ahead, disapprove of me. I'm used to it."

Used to it? She insisted on it. "That's beside the point. What I want to know is, why did he do it? Why? He wasn't that kind of a guy. I liked him. Or would have, I think, if I hadn't killed him before we had a chance to get acquainted. He came in earlier for a drink, see, and we got to talking. Not for very long, but when you're a bartender you get a lot of practice sizing people up. I guessed he was some kind of an artist."

"Congratulations. With your clairvoyant powers, you shouldn't have any trouble figuring out why he did it. What's so mysterious? He did it for the money, of course. Very simple."

"But if he was that desperate—"

"No 'if' about it, is there? He did it. So he must have been that desperate." She shoved a couple of hanks of hair out of her eyes and added complacently, "I expect maybe he needed it to buy me a present."

"To buy you a present!"

"Sure. He was always buying me presents. To appease his guilt complex. Because he walked out when I was a baby. He kept trying to make it up to me."

"That's not enough to make him turn thief, for God's sake!"

"Oh, I don't know. There might have been a little more to it this time." She looked at her watch and stood up. "I hate to rush off, but I've got to make the 6:07 train back to town. Isn't it a pity. Just when things were getting interesting."

"Wait." Joe scrambled to his feet, in sudden, sweating agitation. "Tell me what you mean, 'a little more to it.' I've got a right to know. I'm going to have to live with this for the rest of my life. Don't you understand how I feel?"

"But the train, sweetie. There's not another one till some ungodly hour in the morning. And I've got all Daddy's works of art to grapple with."

"I'll help you," said Joe. "Come on, there isn't too much time."

The Stewarts' cottage, where Fritz Wall had spent the last days of his life, looked cheerful on the outside, with its blue shutters and flagstones and tiger lilies. But the inside seemed to Joe dismal and clammy. The big living room was cluttered with shabby furniture; the tiny bedroom held only a lumpy iron bed. The place was deserted. The police had made their search and found nothing startling; the Stewarts, off in their sailboat, had been reached by telephone but would not be back for another day. There were a few dirty dishes in the kitchenette sink. But Fritz's paints had been tidily stowed away in their case, presumably by Fritz himself. His "works of art" were stacked beside the fireplace wall, three splashy abstractions, mostly mustard yellow.

"Here's the collage," said Cynthia. "I told you it was wild. Of course it's not finished."

Joe peered at it, bemused. Finished or unfinished, who could tell? It was a complicated mess of bent nails, shellacked magazine clippings and Army blanket scraps, torn wire and other objects not easily identifiable at first glance. Could that be half of a pair of false eyelashes? He remembered his manners and said cautiously, "It's very interesting."

"You don't have to be polite," Cynthia told him. "Find some twine or something, will you, and tie the paintings together. Otherwise I'll never get them on or off the train. There's another bag besides the paint case. I do think it's inconsiderate of you not to have a car. You could at least drive me to the station."

Joe, who had already called the taxi service, did not reply. Brat, he thought, and started hunting for twine. She obviously had no intention of lifting a hand. Sprawled on the couch, with her feet stretched out in Joe's way, she smoked a cigarette and told him what to do and how to do it. Her slippers more or less matched the phosphorescent-pink part of her dress, and her feet looked dirty.

Actually, it wasn't much of a job aside from the pictures. Fritz Wall had traveled light. And most of his belongings were already in the one suitcase, either because he had been living out of it or because he had planned to leave soon and had packed in advance.

Cynthia wriggled her toes and said, "They're shipping the body tomorrow. Duffy can cope, from here on in. I figure I've discharged my daughterly duties. Besides, she'll enjoy it. She dotes on funerals."

"When was the last time you saw your father?"

"Before this morning, you mean? They met me at the train, you know, and took me to this place, and his eyes weren't quite closed, and his mouth—" Again her hand jumped to her throat in that telltale gesture. Then she caught Joe's eyes on her and said, "It was quite interesting. I'd never seen a stiff before. However. The last time I saw him alive was, I don't know, two or three weeks ago. He dropped in at my apartment one evening to ask me what I wanted for my birthday. I'll be twenty-one the end of this month. So I said either a Jaguar or a mink coat. Or of course just the money, if he'd rather."

"Wow," said Joe. "How come you didn't mention a diamond necklace while you were at it?"

"Diamond necklace? What made you say that?" The sharpness of her voice rather took him aback; he shrugged and spread his hands in a why-not gesture, and after a second she returned his grin. "Oh, you mean as long as I was thinking big … Yeah, I guess I should have. Not that it matters. I won't get anything now, will I?"

"Not even a mink coat," said Joe cheerfully. "Poor underprivileged Cynthia."

"My friends call me Cyn." Joe didn't doubt it. Spell it either way, it was still appropriate. "And I wasn't kidding about the mink or the Jaguar. Daddy knew it. He would have come through, too, if only—"

"If only I'd handed over the money the way I should have," Joe finished for her. "If that's why he did it, I should think your conscience would be giving you a little trouble, too."

"Don't be silly! How was I to know he'd try a stunt like that? He never had before. All right, maybe I never asked him for that much before, not quite that much. But it was his idea in the first place, he started this present bit himself. To get out of seeing me. That was all I wanted when I was a kid, for him to show up at school or camp, just walk in and say, 'Cyn darling, pack your things, you are my darling daughter and I am taking you home to live with me.' Or even just for a visit. If he'd ever just once turned up for one of their lousy Parent's Days, or ever just once invited me for one lousy little weekend … It never happened. He sent me a present instead. I figured if I had to settle for presents, okay, then he could damn well make the presents worth settling for."

"Kid stuff," said Joe curtly. "You're a big girl now. Twenty-one. That's old enough at least to know there's a limit to how much the traffic will bear. I'm not saying there isn't money in the travel agency business, but that kind of money? Unless he had other strings to his bow."

"Don't look at me. Marian's the one that knows about his financial affairs. They ran the agency together. He always seemed to have money to buy me presents before. Why should it be different this time?"

"And if it was, why didn't he say so? That's what doesn't make sense to me. Why didn't he just say he was too broke to buy you a birthday present, you'd simply have to wait?"

"Why not?" Her smile was reminiscent and somehow not very pleasant. "Well, for one thing, I'm no good at waiting. And then it's a special birthday, your twenty-first. I expect he was especially anxious not to disappoint me." She paused, still smiling, and tilting her head at Joe, checking his reaction. "Plus this guilt thing he had about me. That's one more good reason."

"It still doesn't seem like enough to me," Joe began. But outside the taxi hooted; there wasn't time, as he had hoped, to solve the enigma of Fritz Wall, or at least pry out of his daughter what clues were available. If any. She could have been putting on an act, leading him on just for kicks.

"Come on." She jumped up, slung her shoulder strap purse into place, and made for the door, leaving the baggage to him. "Bring the pictures first, let's hope they'll fit in. You can put the other stuff in front. Hurry up, we haven't got all day." Oh, she was a great director of operations. A brat. A real pill.

As they pulled up at the station, they heard the train coming, whistling around the bend. "Perfect timing," said Cynthia, who was no good at waiting. At the last minute, while Joe was wrestling her paraphernalia onto the rack above her train seat, she cried, "Oh Gawd, my bag, my overnight case! It's not here, I must have left it at the Stewarts. It's your fault, you should have—"

"I didn't even know you had a case! There isn't time to get it now. What's your address? I can send it to you."

"No, no, that's no good. I'll have to come back for it, or—Listen, Joe, can I trust you to keep it for me? Till I come back or till you come to New York, or something? I can't think now, but I'll call you, or you call me. Here, here's my number." She scribbled, while the conductor trumpeted "Aboard!" Joe grabbed the slip of paper and leaped off as the train started to move.

"Don't worry, I'll keep it for you!" he yelled from the platform. She probably couldn't hear him; her face, pressed against the window, had an anxious, demanding look.

But of course she could trust him, not only to keep the case for her but to call her, too. Not for the sake of her delightful company, that was for sure, but because of the conversation there hadn't been time to finish today. And because of the idea that had started to work in him when he first found out she was Fritz's daughter. It had a firm hold on him now. He wasn't going to rest until he found the person Fritz had wanted so desperately to help. If it wasn't Cynthia—and he was pretty sure it wasn't—she still might give him the clue he needed.

When he walked back to the Stewarts, he found her bag there, a chunky, pale blue case like an oversized lunch box. Having made sure it was closed securely—as a matter of fact, it was locked, which rather surprised him—he carried it back to his rooming house.

There was nothing to do. He thought about going out for something to eat, but he wasn't hungry. Thought about Ellie, but decided against calling her. He had not seen her today, except for a few minutes early this morning. He remembered her eyes, big and scared-looking, and his feeling that if he were to touch her she would have to steel herself so as not to shrink away from his hands. Right or wrong, that had been his feeling; he would rather not put it to the test.

His head still ached. He stretched out on the bed, with his hands behind his head to get them out of sight, and after a while fell into an uneasy, mustard-yellow doze, in which he searched feverishly for someone whose name and face and even sex were all unknown to him.

Three

Two weeks later Joe packed his own belongings, which were not much more numerous or complicated than Fritz Wall's had been, and caught the train to New York himself. It seemed a good place to go, for several reasons. His sister Tess was away on vacation with her husband and the kids, so he could use their apartment; he had enough money to live on till something else turned up. Besides, New York had been Fritz Wall's home, the place where his family and friends lived. Among them his daughter Cynthia: Joe had a conversation to finish with her. And her bag to return to her. That was how they had settled the matter, after a number of long, involved telephone discussions and several changes of Cynthia's mind. So there the bag squatted, up there on the rack beside Joe's beat-up canvas job.

He picked the early morning train, and took care not to broadcast his plans: the fewer good-byes the better. All he wanted was to get the hell out and never come back. Ellie? It wouldn't have hurt him to call her, he supposed. But what was the point? He had seen her only two or three times in the last couple of weeks—self-conscious little excursions to the movies, and a decorous good-night kiss as the windup, because he still had this feeling … It hadn't been the same; oh no, nothing like the way it used to be.

That left only one good-bye to be said. He said it as the train pulled out and he caught a last glimpse of The Starfish. (He wished to God there had never been a first glimpse.) So long to the Joe Florio that used to be: model bartender; minor, all-purpose genius; too happy-go-lucky to know how happy he was, or how lucky. He had died along with Fritz Wall, and it was never going to be the same without him.

New York simmered in one of its summer steam baths. The first thing he did when he got downtown to Tess's apartment was strip off his sticky clothes and take a shower. It wasn't too bad with the fan going. He poured himself a cold beer and called Tess, up at the lake. She sounded breathless, as usual, and there was the usual background obbligato of yammering kids. "You okay, Joey? Is it all settled?"

"All settled. They called it justifiable homicide." Just as everyone had predicted, especially the boss.

"Thank God, thank God. I knew they would. Listen, Joey, you forget about it now. Just put it out of your mind. Forget it. Okay?"

"Okay." Good old bossy Tess.

"What you ought to do is come on up here with us. Get out of the heat and relax. No kidding, Joe, it's terrific, we're sleeping under blankets. Plenty of room. The boys can double up, or there's the couch …" When he had talked his way out of that one: "Well, it's up to you. If you change your mind, all you have to do is get on the bus, you're always welcome. Down there too, of course. Make yourself at home. There's loads of stuff in the freezer. The sheets are in the chest in our bedroom, bottom drawer, and the towels—wait, the kids want to say hello."

By the time he hung up he was feeling fairly cheerful. Like the rest of his family, Tess was a great comfort, especially when she was at the other end of a long-distance telephone call. It was the thought of the toll mounting up that inhibited her; otherwise she would have gotten off on why didn't he settle down and find a nice steady job, a nice steady girl to marry …

He grinned to himself, thinking of what she would have to say about Cynthia Wall and his—what was the word, involvement?—with her. It couldn't have been less romantic, but try and tell Tess that. He was going to call her up, wasn't he? Going to see her again? Well, then. To Joe's family, no other kind of involvement existed; they had had him married—in most cases against their wishes—to every girl he looked at twice.

"Who?" said Cynthia, when he got her on the phone—finally, after hours of no-answer. "Joe who? Oh yes. That Joe. Did you bring my case?"

"That's why I called." All right, it was one of the reasons. "Do you want me to bring it over?"

"Sure. If you can make it before six. What time is it now?"

"Four. I'll be there in half an hour."

When he saw the apartment house she lived in, he couldn't help wondering if Daddy had been responsible for paying the rent, which must be a tidy sum. It was one of those big, new, glassy places with jutting balconies and rubber rhododendrons and a doorman and geometric sculpture in the lobby. For all Joe knew, of course, Cynthia herself might be footing the bills. She could have a job. This could be her day off. But the possibility seemed remote to him. Very, very remote.

The elevator noiselessly elevated him, the doorbell ping-pinged, chains rattled and locks clicked.

"Hi," she said, above the wailing of the record player.

He would hardly have known her. The bird's nest was gone, and good riddance; left to its own devices, her hair—hooked behind her ears, to be sure, and with a straggling thatch of bangs—swung down below her shoulders, straight, shiny, and pecan-brown. Barefooted, in shorts and shirt, she looked like a real live girl. Smaller than he remembered. Even rather pretty.

But underneath the same spoiled brat. "Can I help you, or are you just looking? Come in, if you want to. There's no charge for admission."

"Sorry," he mumbled. "You look so different—"

"You don't. Not a day older. Or brighter. I'd know you anywhere."

"Thanks. And it was a pleasure lugging your goddam case in. Don't mention it, I enjoyed every minute of it." He handed it to her and turned, half-minded to stalk off and call it quits, in spite of their unfinished conversation and the leads he hoped to get from her.

"Oh, come on in and have a drink. Don't be such a blah. It's all over, isn't it, the business about Daddy? And now all you have to do is find another job. Me too. We have so much in common."

"You're looking for a job?" He let himself be drawn into the room, which was large and predictably L-shaped; the color scheme set his teeth on edge. Orange, cinnamon, and hot pink.

"I'd better if I want a door to keep the wolf away from. This place is mine till October, courtesy of J. Randolph Muggins. My ever-loving stepfather. But after that I'm on my own. Time I was self-supporting, according to J. Randolph. He paid my way here from California—that's where they live—and got me that lousy job with the airline, and I'm supposed to be grateful for the rest of my life. Was it my fault they fired me a couple of months ago?"

"Well," said Joe, "wasn't it?"

"Just because I didn't make it every single morning right on the dot of nine. They want a robot, let them build one. Here, sit down. Gin and tonic all right with you?" On her way to the kitchen she scooped up an armful of clothes from one chair and transferred them to another, which was loaded with records. "What I'd really like is a modeling job. I'm very photogenic." After a minute or so she popped back with the drinks. "Of course if nothing turns up I can always threaten to go back to California. That'll turn him on. After all, I can't scrape along on what my mother slips me out of her housekeeping money—I mean, not indefinitely."

"How about your grandmother?"

"Not a prayer. She's hanging on to what she's got left—which isn't much, I guess, except for the house on Perry Street. They all live there, Gran and Aunt Vera and Uncle Arthur. And Duffy, of course. Vanished glory, you know. Gran went there as a bride, they had the whole house to themselves in those days, a staff of servants, dinner parties for fifty, et cetera et cetera. Now the top floors are rented out as separate apartments. That's what she lives on, the rent." She reached over, and to Joe's relief, turned down the volume on the record player. "Even if she had dough, I probably wouldn't see any of it. She thinks I'm like Daddy. A spendthrift. The fights they used to have about money!"

"All this must have been a shock to her, though. An elderly lady. And with a bad heart."

"You make her sound too too pathetic. Actually, she's tough as nails. I was scared to death of her when I was a kid," she added rather wistfully. "Oh brother, did she crack the whip! You did what she said. Or else. You'll see what I mean when you meet her."

"When I meet her?"

"That's where I have to go at six o'clock. You want to come with me? You don't have to. It's nothing to me, either way."

"I'd like to," said Joe. "Only—well, how will she feel about meeting me? Won't it upset her?"

Cynthia shrugged. "We don't have to tell her who you are. You can be Joe Somebody Else. She never approves of my boyfriends, anyway."

In spite of her casual tone, she was watching him closely. She wanted him to go with her—for what reason Joe could not imagine, except that it was undoubtedly not altruistic. But then neither was his reason for wanting to go. When you got right down to it, part of what he hoped to accomplish with this search of his—for the one person in the world who had mattered to Fritz—was the easing of his own bad conscience. So of course he welcomed the chance to meet Fritz's mother, maybe her whole household. It would further his search, if only by the process of elimination.

"Don't be coy," prodded Cynthia. "You know you're dying to go. You were dying to see me again, too. Weren't you? The traveling case was a good excuse, but you would have called me anyway."

"Sure. Because you're so irresistible."

"I know. I used to worry about not being beautiful. But sexy is even better." She flipped her hair complacently. "That's settled, then. Fix us another drink, will you, while I get dressed. It'll take us half an hour to get down to Gran's."

The kitchen was a worse mess than the living room. Dirty dishes in the sink, the skeleton of a barbecued chicken on the stove, and in the refrigerator a very peculiar smell. When he came back with the drinks, Cynthia had disappeared; her voice, and one arm, emerged from behind a screen outside what must be the bathroom door, at the angle of the L. "Put it down over here. Somewhere where I can reach," she ordered. There wasn't any free space except the floor; he set her glass down there and returned to his chair.

"All right, Irresistible," he said. "The real reason I called you was because you didn't finish telling me about your father and the birthday present. Remember?"

"I did so! Guilt complex, I said, and special birthday. That's why he needed the money. To buy me a special present."

"Yes, but you also said—earlier, before we went to the Stewarts—that there might have been a little more to it. That's what interests me. The little more." He waited, but there was no response. "Cynthia? Cyn?"

"This damn zipper." She made exaggerated huffing noises. "Help me, will you. It's stuck."

It wasn't, really. Poor kid, she had a backbone like a stray dog's. "The little more," Joe repeated. "What did you mean by that?"

She was standing in front of the full-length mirror on the bathroom door, putting glop on her eyes. "It isn't any of your business, you know," she said reasonably. "Just because you've developed this thing about Daddy, that doesn't give you the right to know everything about his private life. On the other hand, it can't possibly make any difference to him anymore." A pause, while she concentrated on a tricky stroke along the edge of her eyelid. "I understand how you feel, Joe. Honestly I do. I'm very sensitive to other people's feelings. Especially when it's somebody I like."

No suitable comment occurred to Joe. He saw what was coming, and waited.

"So I don't see why I shouldn't tell you, especially when I was going to ask you to do me a favor, anyway. Just a small favor. I'm sure you won't mind."

"What is it?" he asked cautiously.

"I'd do it myself, only Otis has these snoopy neighbors. They're always watching who comes and goes, and drawing conclusions. They'd make a federal case out of it, if they knew I had a key."

"Who's Otis?"

"I'm mad for him. Absolutely mad. If he were in town, I wouldn't be here. But that's the point—he got sucked into one of those gruesome family things, driving up to Canada. Five days, nine hours, twenty-two minutes before he gets back. I'm not sure I can bear it."

"The favor," Joe reminded her.

"Well, naturally I have a homecoming present for him. Besides my pure white body, I mean. Don't ask me what it is, because I won't tell you. It's very special. Too, too in for anybody but Otis to appreciate. It has to be there in his apartment, waiting for him when he gets back. If I have to, of course, I'll take it there myself, but I hate to give those nosey neighbors the satisfaction. They're always giving him a hard time, bitching about the noise, et cetera et cetera."

"So the idea is for me to deliver Otis's homecoming present for you," said Joe.

"You don't mind, do you? It's just a little package. And it's not as if his apartment was in Brooklyn or the Bronx or something. It's in the Village, not far from Gran's. You're one of the few people I'd trust with it."

"Uh-huh." Joe thought it over, looking for the catch. Did there have to be one? Why shouldn't Cynthia ask for, and get, a return favor? Typical of her: an opportunist born and bred. She was standing in front of him, looking childish, even fairly innocent, in her straight, sleeveless white dress. Her eyes were fixed on him anxiously. If he had no guarantee that she would tell him the truth about her father, she had no guarantee, either, that he would carry out his half of the bargain. He might lose Otis's homecoming present, keep it for himself, just not bother to deliver it. Give her credit, she really must trust him.

"Well?" she said. "Take it or leave it. What have you got to lose?"

"Nothing much, I guess. Okay, it's a deal."

She gave a jubilant hop and lunged, as if to kiss him; hastily, he held out his hand, and they shook on it instead. Her little paw felt feverish with excitement.

"You're a sweetheart, Joe. Here, I'll give you the key, and the address, oh yes, and the package. Maybe you can leave it tonight, after we leave Gran's. Or tomorrow, if you'd rather ..." She bustled around happily, finding her purse, digging out the key, writing down the address. When she darted to the far end of the room, Joe discovered that he could still watch her in the bathroom door mirror. With a key that hung on a cord around her neck, she unlocked the chunky traveling case he had brought in on the train and took out a small, flat package securely taped with brown sticky paper. It had been in Joe's keeping all the time, then— Otis's homecoming present, bought well in advance. Well, young love was like that.

She was back again. "Here it is. I told you, just a little package, it'll fit in your pocket. Don't don't don't lose it. And if you dare open it, so help me, I'll …" She broke off, grinning. "Now, now, no need to get huffy. I know you're a man of honor, that's why I picked you. We're all set, as soon as I do my hair."

"Aren't you forgetting something?" She gave him a blank look, and Joe elaborated. "How about your end of the bargain? You were going to tell me about your father."

"Oh. That." She began brushing the bejesus out of her hair. "Don't expect anything too earth-shaking. For all I know, he needed money for lots of other things besides just a birthday present for little old me. Daddy liked to live it up, you know. Maybe he'd been embezzling from the travel agency funds and Marian caught him with his hand in the till."

"Nothing like that came out in the investigation. All Stewart said was that he played the horses once in a while."

"Yes, and if Marian happened to hear about it, didn't she give him holy hell! You're right, he couldn't have been embezzling, he was too scared of Marian to try any funny stuff with the business. He could have been gambling with borrowed money, though." She shot a sidelong glance at Joe. "Then if he lost, he'd be on the spot, wouldn't he?"

"Quit stalling," said Joe. "If you know anything, tell me. If you don't, say so and shut up."

"All right, tough guy. I know he had been playing the horses, and I know he lost. Furthermore, I know he was shacked up with a blonde bunny type with expensive tastes and just barely brains enough to come in out of the rain."

"You mean he told you—"

"Ha! I saw them together one night at Lindy's. That's how I know. It shouldn't happen to a dog, but it happened to Daddy. He didn't see me. Too busy feasting his eyes on the goodies beside him. But I saw him, and naturally I was interested." She stopped, once more stricken with one of those crises in her throat. When she had it under control: "So a couple of days later I dropped in at his apartment and had a little chat with the bunny type. She talked her head off, the dear girl. As I say, no brains.

So I expect that's why Daddy was especially anxious not to disappoint me on my birthday, because if Marian happened to get wind of all this, there'd be hell to pay."

There was a longish silence. Then Joe said, "You mean you were blackmailing him. That's what it amounts to. Blackmail."

"I suppose it does," she said brightly, "if you want to be crude about it. I'm ready. Shall we go?"

Four

The house on Perry Street had a brick front, with chipped stone curlicues here and there. There were crisp white curtains at the front door, which badly needed painting; a window box full of purple petunias; and a graceful balcony with a broken railing outside the second-floor windows. The general effect was one of brave respectability: crumbling around the edges, but still proud of itself.

A comfortably plump, brisk little woman opened the door to them. Her cotton print dress was unfashionably long, and the snowiness of her hair suggested that it had originally been red. She looked like somebody's grandmother, Joe thought. Too much so to be Cynthia's.

"Hi, Duffy. This is Joe, he's a friend of mine. He came along."

"So I see," said Duffy. Tart but pleasant. And so I expected, her knowing little nod seemed to imply. "Pleased to meet you, Joe. Come on in. She's waiting for you. Getting fidgety."

"We're not really late. Not more than a couple of minutes." Cynthia paused briefly in front of the hall mirror to smooth her dress and push her sunglasses up above her bangs.

Upstairs a door opened, and a woman's voice called imperiously down the wide curving stairway with its worn, dark red carpeting. "Cynthia? Is that you, Cynthia? I want to see you, so don't try to—"

"I've got a friend with me, Aunt Vera! Come down and meet him!" Cynthia yelled back. Without waiting for a reply, she made for the living room door, sweeping Joe along with her. But he caught a glimpse of Aunt Vera peering down at them over the banister: a narrow, pale, hostile face.

After the glare and heat of the street, the living room with its drawn shades seemed as cool and dark as a cave. It took a moment or two for Joe's eyes to adjust to the dim light. Then he saw that the room, though spacious, was so cluttered with furniture that it looked half its actual size. The last citadel of old Mrs. Wall's shrinking world, crammed with the possessions she had refused to relinquish—the rosewood piano, which must once have graced a special music room; the heavy, gleaming chests of drawers from bedrooms now rented out; the bookcases and desk from a lost library; the pictures and knick-knacks and small Oriental rugs on top of the threadbare basic one.

Mrs. Wall herself sat on a brocade love seat, upright and unsmiling, tapping her fingers impatiently. She looked not in the least like a relic. On the contrary, very chic. Her dress was black, some thin, summery stuff that softened the spareness of her figure. Her hair was dramatically streaked with white, and drawn up into a twist on top that showed off her small, well-shaped head.

But her voice was cracked and husky, a seventy-year-old voice. "Well, there you are. Who's that with you?"

"Sorry if we're late, Gran. I ran into Joe and brought him along." Cynthia deposited a small duty kiss on her grandmother's cheek. Joe—relieved at finding that nobody seemed to bother about last names—shook her hand, which was dry and brittle, like a bundle of sticks.

"How nice." Mrs. Wall smiled ironically. "I heard you and Vera, screaming at each other in the hall. You know I don't like that sort of thing in my house." Having administered this rap over the knuckles, she became the gracious hostess. Sherry was offered, and served by Duffy, who poured herself a bottle of beer and settled down on the other half of the love seat. Small talk was made. Had Cynthia found a position yet? Nothing definite, but a promising lead. Joe was looking for a job too, as a matter of fact …

"Any particular kind of a job?" asked Duffy. There was a good deal of shrewdness in her faded blue eyes; he had the feeling she might be riffling through his career—from paper boy to bartender—as if it were an open book.

"Whatever comes along first," he said. "I'm kind of a jack-of-all-trades."

"Are you, now. I didn't know there were any of those left. It's all specialization these days. One fella to tear up the bathroom tiles, another one to put them back. And try and find anybody to do the little repair jobs. I'm thinking of the stairs," she added in an aside to Mrs. Wall. "Somebody's going to break their neck if we don't get them fixed pretty soon. Not to mention the paint job you promised the top floor last spring. I don't blame them for yammering."

"Duffy," began Mrs. Wall grandly, "I hardly think this is the time or place to discuss our household problems. I don't suppose Mr.—Ummm— would be interested, even as a stopgap, while he's looking for a regular job …" Her voice raveled out. Her eyes, hooded and dark, fastened on Joe, appraising, waiting.

He waited a moment too, aware of a prickle of excitement. What better setup for finding out about Fritz Wall than to work for his mother, right in her house, where he could get to know not only her but the rest of the family? It was almost too good to be true.

"I'm pretty handy at most jobs around the house," he said cautiously. "If you wanted to take a chance on me, I'd be glad to try."

"Painting?" demanded Mrs. Wall.

"I'm not a professional. But I know how to paint, sure. And carpentering. If it's not too complicated."

"Not complicated at all. That's the point, you see, they can't be bothered with the small jobs. Beneath their notice. And the prices they charge. Fantastic. I hope you're not thinking in such terms. You admit you're not a professional."

"No, I'm sure we could work that part of it out. I'd want to look the place over, you know. See what's involved."

"Naturally. If you could come around tomorrow morning at ten? We can discuss the details then."

"Thank the good Lord that's settled," said Duffy. "I was beginning to think I'd never see the day."

"Don't say I never did anything for you, Joe." Cynthia sounded a little tentative, as if she weren't sure how much she liked the way things were shaping up. "Now that you're fixed up with a job, how about me? If my lead doesn't work out, maybe you'll take me on as handyman's apprentice. We'd make a great little team. I'm pretty handy myself."

"Too handy for your own good, if you ask me," said Duffy darkly. "I'd better get out some ice, in case Vera and Arthur come down. They'll want gin." She got up and bustled out to the kitchen. Crashing noises ensued.

"Honestly, Gran, she's getting impossible. Why don't you tell her off?"

"That's enough," snapped Mrs. Wall. Then she turned to Joe with a bland smile. "Duffy's been with me for years. Almost like one of the family. She's inclined to take liberties now and then. Ah, there's Vera at the door. Let her in, will you, dear?"

Like her mother, Vera Henderson was tall, thin, and chic. But without the strong, regular features; Vera's nose was over-long, her chin over-sharp, her whole face over-narrow. She had an air of restless discontent, as if she were itching to be somewhere else, with someone else, doing something else. The martini Duffy brought her had too much vermouth in it. One chair was too straight, another too soft. She wound up perching on a hassock, like a bird poised for flight. The hostility that crackled between her and Cynthia made Joe uneasy; the others seemed to take it for granted.

"You're still in the same apartment? What happens when the lease runs out? … Arthur says they're looking for a secretary in his office, but of course you haven't the skills, have you, dear? … I see you still bite your fingernails. Such a revealing habit. You're getting more like your father all the time. Remember, Mother, how Fritz used to bite his nails? Down to the quick? More like him all the time. In more ways than one …"

"Stop picking on the kid," said Duffy, comfortably. "Where's Arthur? Working overtime?"

"He's picking up the car. I hope. If we can't get out of town for the weekend I'll cut my throat. They're supposed to have it ready tonight. It's never run right since Ned cracked it up before he went away."

"You and Uncle Arthur always blame Ned for everything," said Cynthia. "I'm glad you're not my parents. If I were Ned I'd just stay down there in Mexico or wherever it is and never come home."

"Central America. I'm glad we're not your parents, too. One problem child is enough."

"My grandson Ned is an archaeological student," Mrs. Wall stated, loftily ignoring the bickering of the underlings. "He was one of a small group chosen for this expedition. We're expecting him home this weekend."

Joe didn't know quite what to make of Fritz Wall's family; it was going to take time to sort them out. They didn't seem to go in much for togetherness. As far as Fritz was concerned, Joe had a sneaking suspicion it wouldn't disturb them in the least to know they were socializing with the man responsible for his death. They might even congratulate me, he thought uncomfortably.

A cross-eyed gray Persian cat entered regally from the kitchen, swishing her tail, and, after surveying the scene, vaulted with deliberate grace to the broad window sill. She looked as if she didn't care much for anybody either.

"Hi, Dutch," said Cynthia. "Well, it's time we buzzed off. You wanted to see me about something, Aunt Vera?" It was a definite challenge, made in the certainty that it would not be accepted. Insolently safe, she stood up and looked her aunt in the eye.

"It can wait." Then the doorbell rang, and Vera smiled. "That's Arthur. He forgot his key. You're already up, dear, you don't mind letting him in, do you?"

Cynthia hesitated, stripped of her insolence. The circle of eyes watched her impassively. But as Joe rose, Vera put her hand on his arm. "Wait a minute, please do. Stay and meet my husband." And Mrs. Wall said, "Run along, child, let him in. What's the matter with you?"

"I'm going." She squared her shoulders and went.

At once they all started chattering. Vera held forth on the weather; Duffy offered more sherry; Mrs. Wall launched into a description of her house as it had been in its heyday, before the tenant invasion. Trapped, a captive audience, Joe waited tensely for Cynthia to come back.

What she did instead was to scream. "Joe!" He shot out of his chair. "Joe—" This time it was choked off into a shuddering sob. A man's voice rumbled, ominous and wordless as thunder.

He rushed out into the hall. She was backed up against the newel post; beyond the meaty shoulder of the man she was struggling with Joe caught a glimpse of her face—eyes screwed tight shut; mouth wide open and screeching. "Let go of me, you son of a bitch, don't you dare— Joe! Joe!"

The man heard Joe behind him and turned, but without releasing his grip on her wrists. A heavy, florid face, even redder now with rage, set in an incongruously grin-like snarl. Joe advanced, complete with threatening noises, and hoping to God they would suffice. Socking this guy would be like hitting a brick wall.

In the nick of time Mrs. Wall's voice rang out, cracked but still commanding. "*What* is going on out here? Stop this racket at once. Arthur! Cynthia! I told you before, I will not have this sort of thing in my house."

She was old and frail and she had no doubt whatever in her own authority. No one else had, either. Arthur let go. Cynthia shut up. Joe heaved a sigh of relief.

"A disgraceful performance," said Mrs. Wall. "Vera, take your husband upstairs and keep him there till he's pulled himself together. Shut the door, Dully. As for you, Cynthia—"

"It wasn't my fault, Gran! He started it!"

"I'll expect an apology from you tomorrow. And I'll see you at ten in the morning, Joe. Good evening."

Out on the street the heat smacked them like a wet towel. Joe couldn't tell whether she was crying behind her sunglasses or not. "Don't cry," he said, and she sniffed ostentatiously. "Are you all right? Did he hurt you?"

"Of course he hurt me. Look at my arms, they'll be black and blue tomorrow."

"But why? What was it all about?"

"He's a monster. Can't keep his hands to himself."

"You mean he was making a pass at you?" But Vera had smiled in triumph when she heard the doorbell ring. Had pressured Cynthia into answering it. Could any wife be that perverse? "Come on, now, you don't expect me to believe that."

"I don't care what you believe." She gave another fake sniff. "He's still a monster. They all are. Even Gran."

Even Cynthia herself, when it came to that. Apparently she saw nothing out of the way about blackmailing her father. His tough luck. If that wasn't being a monster … Joe stole a glance at her and saw, to his astonishment, a genuine, human tear sliding down the side of her nose. And she was pretending it wasn't there, ignoring it with a forlorn pride that touched Joe's heart. He heard himself saying, "How about having dinner with me, if you haven't got a date?"

"Good," she said matter-of-factly. "You owe me something for getting you a job. Let's go somewhere expensive. I'm hungry."

Five

When, next morning at ten o'clock sharp, he put in his second appearance at the house on Perry Street, he was still unenlightened as to what went on with its inhabitants and Cynthia. Dinner—an expensive one, as specified—had not made her any more communicative. Quite the opposite, in fact: her concentration on the steak and other groceries had ruled out all but the most primitive form of conversation. And, having wolfed down the last crumb of Nesselrode pie, she had practically fallen asleep over her empty plate. Nothing to do but take her home. The last thing she said to him was, "Don't forget Otis's present, will you?"

It was still in his jacket pocket. He intended to deliver it this morning, after his session with Mrs. Wall. Strictly a business session; just as he expected, she made no reference to last night's scene. There was no sign of either of the Hendersons. Duffy escorted him upstairs to show him the top floor apartment, which certainly needed a paint job, and the spot in the stairs, which certainly needed fixing. "Don't let her beat you down too much on the price," she said behind her hand, on the way down. "She always did drive a hard bargain, even when there was no need."

Joe quibbled a little, just for the sake of appearances, and because he had a feeling the old lady would have been disappointed if he hadn't. In full daylight she looked worn and not very well; there were puffy little pockets under her eyes, and a slight tremor to her head. But there was nothing weak about her will. She was going to be an exacting woman to work for, he could see that already. But then he wasn't in this for pleasure, or for money, either.

Once the matter of Joe's pay was settled, he was sent forth with detailed instructions as to what supplies to buy, where to buy them, and how much to spend on them. The repair job on the stairs was scheduled for this afternoon, the painting for tomorrow.

First of all, though, there was Otis's present to be delivered, and since the address was in the same direction as the hardware store, Joe decided that this little errand need not be mentioned to Cynthia's grandmother. Something told him she wouldn't have liked the idea, if only on the grounds that it encroached on what she considered company time.

The house was middle-sized and ordinary-looking. It had been renovated fairly recently, with a fake-brick front and a self-service elevator on whose walls somebody had scratched the customary obscenities. Joe was the only passenger, and when he got off, the third-floor hall was deserted too. No sign of neighbors, snoopy or otherwise. But they had sounded fishy to him, anyway; whatever Cynthia's reason for not wanting to come here herself, he didn't think it was that.

He approached 3-B, key in hand, and as he opened the door sound erupted from within: the thump of a drum, the plunk of a guitar, voices raised in nasal keening. He had a momentary impression that the outburst was mechanical, somehow triggered by his turning the key in the lock. The fact that it emanated from real live people did not register until he too was inside Otis's apartment.

There were two of them, skinny, long-haired creatures of indeterminate sex, dressed identically in tight tattered dungarees and dirty T-shirts. The gaze they turned on Joe was glazed and impervious; they did not pause in their drumming and strumming.

"Excuse me," he said. "I didn't think anybody would be here. Are you— is either of you Otis?"

He was beginning to think they hadn't heard him when the one with the drum broke into a strange, crooning refrain: "Hey, Otis. Man wants to know are we Otis." The one with the guitar took it up: "Hey, hey, Otis. Please take notice." And then in unison: "Man wants to know, man wants to know, man wants to know are we Otis!" They ran through this several times, with rhythmic variations that apparently enchanted them, while Joe stood beside the door, paralyzed by a through-the-looking-glass sensation.

The room itself contained little besides the two kids—male, Joe had decided by now—and their instruments. They sat on the floor, the drummer crouching, the guitarist propped languidly against the wall. The few pieces of furniture were all crippled. The straight chair had a broken leg; the overstuffed one was partially disemboweled; the couch was swaybacked, and further afflicted with a bedraggled pink chenille spread. Though it was broad day, the overhead light still burned, adding to the desolation and stale heat. A nearly empty gin bottle and a pie tin full of cigarette butts were planted on the floor between the occupants.

They were still embroidering on their Hey, Otis theme.

And might go on for hours, thought Joe. Were they drunk? High on dope? Or simply bemused by the mindless monotony of the sounds they were producing? Who the hell were they, anyway? Friends of Otis's, most likely. Unless Joe had somehow blundered into the wrong apartment … But no, the key worked; this had to be Otis's place. One of them might even be Otis, God forbid. The thought of Cynthia's being "absolutely mad" for either of these types threw Joe into a swivet. He neither liked nor trusted her himself; but he felt obscurely, irritably, responsible for her. More so than ever, now that he had met her family. If in addition she was mixed up, as she must be, with a bunch of kooks, that left Joe holding the baby for sure.

And the package. The homecoming present for Otis. He patted his inside breast pocket. Still there. He could, of course, just leave it here, just put it down somewhere and walk out. Mission accomplished. That is, he could if one of these birds turned out to be Otis. But on second thought, there was no good reason for jumping to such a conclusion. Simply because they were here—as Cynthia had certainly not expected them to be. Joe couldn't see them having any qualms about opening other people's packages and appropriating what was inside if they felt like it. Or destroying it, if they felt like that. No, he had made a bargain with Cynthia, and he wasn't going to go back on it.

Silence had fallen. The two on the floor were peering at him through their sheep-dog coiffures. As he turned to leave, they sprang up with one accord and converged on him. It wasn't exactly menacing, but it was disconcerting, to see them move with such swift precision. They seemed to glide. Again he thought of dope.

"Just a minute," one of them said. "What you want with Otis?"

"It'll keep." The door had some kind of a snap lock, and it was apparently stuck.

"Yeah, but what you doing here if you don't know Otis when you see him? You wanted to know are we Otis. What makes you think we're not?"

"Well, are you?"

Grins. Eye shiftings. "Depends on what you want with him."

"Nuts," said Joe. "I don't want anything with Otis. I didn't expect him or anybody else to be here."

"Sure. Makes sense. That's what I always do, too, drop in on my pals when I don't expect them to be there. I find it makes for a more meaningful relationship. Don't you? Listen, you. What's the idea? What you trying to pull?"

"Nothing." The damn lock was still stuck. "I don't know Otis, but I know a friend of his. Cynthia. Cyn. She asked me to do an errand for her, that's all."

"Yeah, an errand. What kind of an errand?"

"That's her business," said Joe. One last yank, and the door flew open. So, unfortunately, did his jacket; he was aware of the two pairs of eyes, fastened with the unnerving synchronization he had noticed before on the package in his inside pocket. The elevator needle pointed to six, so he made for the stairs.

"Wait!" one of them called. "Hey, you, wait up!"

He was already halfway to the second floor, and he did not look back to see whether they were running after him or ringing for the elevator. Or both, for that matter, if they were capable of tearing themselves away from each other. But when he reached the street floor, the elevator needle had not budged, and he heard no pursuing footsteps. Good. He was rid of them.

Out on the street, he kept taking deep breaths, to clear away the fusty atmosphere of that apartment. What he could not shake off was the echo of their thumping and strumming. It infested his mind, nagging and pointless and chronic as cockroaches. No wonder they looked glazed; they had thumped and strummed themselves into a stupor. Yes, but they had been sharp enough to spot the package, sharp enough to make the connection between it and the errand he was doing for Cynthia. Once or twice, on the way to the hardware store, he imagined that those two pairs of glassy eyes were still fixed on him; at the corner he even glanced back to see if they were watching from the window. It was possible. The apartment was on the front. No sign of them, of course. Pull yourself together, Joe. What's the matter, scared of a couple of kooks? Just because they're kooks, that doesn't make them hopheads.

He got no further with his pep talk. Hopheads. It wasn't a word that made for peace of mind. He couldn't help it; a chill crept over him at the thought of the package that Cynthia didn't want to deliver herself—on account of the snoopy neighbors. The package he mustn't lose or open— but she knew he wouldn't because he was a man of honor. The package, furthermore, that had been in his charge all this time, without his knowing it. If she was capable of blackmailing her own father, and she was, why should she blink at conning a sucker like Joe into doing her simple little errands? And if Thump and Strum were samples of Otis's pals, as they must be, why expect Otis himself to be any more savory?

Having reached this point, the pendulum of Joe's thoughts swung back of its own weight. Wild-eyed theorizing. Guilt by association. Too many tabloid stories about degenerate youth. Suspicion was one thing; proof another. The least he could do for Fritz Wall's daughter was to give her the benefit of the doubt. She had little enough moral support, God knows, without Joe's turning against her for no better reason than he had now.

He tried to call her from the next phone booth he passed—there would be no chance, once he got back to her grandmother's—but nobody answered. Okay, so he was stuck with the package, whatever it contained, for the rest of the day. What were a few more hours, when it was already a matter of weeks? Nothing, really; except that he hadn't known before that he was stuck. Now he did, and it seemed to make a difference.

"It's about time," said Mrs. Wall when he showed up at Perry Street again. "What took you so long?"

"Sorry," said Joe. Brisk and cheery; that was the tone he found himself taking with her. "Too many customers in the store, and not enough clerks. We're all set. They'll deliver the paint this afternoon. I'll get at the stairs now."

One thing about her, she didn't breathe down his neck while he was working—though she probably would have, if she hadn't been forbidden to climb stairs on account of her heart. The bad spot was just above the landing on the second floor, which was occupied by the Hendersons. Still no sign of Vera; Arthur—problem husband, monster, whatever—was presumably at work. Joe slung his jacket over the newel post and got busy. It was one of those tricky little jobs that take longer than anybody expects. He foresaw cutting comments from the old lady.

About one o'clock Duffy came bouncing up with a sandwich and a bottle of beer for him. "Don't tell her. She's having her nap, otherwise I'd have brought it before. You must be starved, poor boy. Ham and cheese, I hope you like it." She plumped herself down on the step and watched him eat, obviously enjoying the sight and the chance for a gossip. "Not that she's stingy about everything, mind you. Wages, yes. I'd be ashamed to tell you the salary she pays me, and after twenty-three years, too. But when I had my gallstones, she footed the bills, every cent of them. Surgeon, private room, special nurse, everything. I've got a place in the country, upstate, she bought it for me. Three different times she's sent me abroad, all expenses paid, nothing but the best accommodations. When she makes up her mind to splurge, she splurges. No, Joe, she's got her little quirks, but add it all up and I can't kick about the way she's treated me. And then, you know, contrary as she is, there's something about her—you've got to hand it to her, she's not a quitter. She hasn't had it so easy, especially these last few years."

"Yeah," said Joe. "I can see she's come down in the world."

"That's not all." Duffy lowered her voice portentously. "Did Cynthia tell you about her father? Fritz?"

"I heard about it, yes." He took a generous bite, thus incapacitating himself for further comment. It wasn't necessary, anyway; Duffy was clearly ready, willing and able to keep the conversational ball rolling unaided.

"Not that they saw much of each other anymore. And they always did have their differences when it came to money. He spent it like it was water. I never saw the beat. Then when it was all gone he'd come to her for help, and if he happened to hit her in the right mood she'd ante up. I'll say this much for him, he always paid her back. Off he'd go to the races and like as not make another killing, and there it was, the same story all over again. You couldn't blame her for getting tired of him and his shenanigans. Still and all, it was a shock to have him wind up the way he did. A miracle it didn't kill her, with her heart condition. I had to tell her, you know, I couldn't let her read it in the papers. Hardest thing I ever did in my life," said Duffy with mournful relish. "But it was up to me. Vera went all to pieces, of course."

"They were close, Fritz and Vera?" She might be the someone he was looking for, Joe was thinking: that nervous, discontented woman with her bully of a husband.

"Not so's you could notice it," said Duffy. "If she'd had her way, Fritz wouldn't have been allowed on the premises. She begrudged him every nickel the old lady ever loaned him. He might not pay it back, see, and she's counting on getting whatever's left when her mother passes on. Or most of it, anyway. No, with Vera it was the disgrace. And then she's high-strung. The least little thing and she blows up. I've often thought, if she'd married a different kind of a fella—but there, she married Arthur, and that's that."

"How did he and Fritz get along?" asked Joe.

"They didn't. Arthur's not the brightest man in town, and Fritz liked to tease him. Lead him on, you know, and then show him up. Oh, I tell you, the fur used to fly when those two got together."

"When Cynthia and he get together too, judging by yesterday. I don't know yet what that was all about."

"Cynthia didn't tell you? No, I bet she didn't." She cocked her head at him quizzically. "Well then, you needn't think I will. You're on your own with Cynthia. And good luck to you. I must say, you don't seem like her type."

"If that's a compliment—"

"It is. Poor kid, I don't know where she finds them. But then what can you expect, with her upbringing? Her grandmother was the only one that ever told her what to do. And she overdid it. It's my opinion she did the same with Fritz. Too strict with him. Oh, she kept him under her thumb, even after he was grown. Nothing would do but he must go into the paper plant when his father died. It was her idea, not his, and she wouldn't admit she was wrong. By the time the war came along and she had to let him go, he'd all but ruined the business. She claimed he did it on purpose, to get even with her for pushing him into doing what he didn't want to. I wouldn't put it past him, but I can't see what difference it makes. Even with the best will in the world, he never would have been a success in business. He just wasn't cut out for it. Too reckless. Couldn't resist taking a chance. What's more I think she knew it too, knew she was in the wrong, and that's why she used to help him out of some of his scrapes."

"But not the last one," said Joe. "Did he ask her for help, I wonder?"

"Not that I know of. He could have called her, or even come to see her, when I wasn't around. But I doubt if he'd try anymore. He hasn't had any luck with her in years now. She claims she's too poor."

"Claims?"

"Well, she hasn't got what she used to have, no two ways about it. Still, if she knew it was a matter of life and death …" Duffy's faded blue eyes looked off into space. "I hope he didn't come to her this time. For her sake. I mean, if it was my son, and I'd turned him down when he was that desperate—I'd never forgive myself."

That opened up another track to Joe. Duffy herself might be the someone Fritz had meant. After all, it didn't have to be a member of his family. And Duffy had the kind of warm, motherly heart that Mrs. Wall apparently lacked. "You must have thought a good deal of Fritz yourself," he ventured. "It sounds like you and he were pretty good friends."

"Oh, I liked Fritz in a way. He could be good company. But that doesn't mean I approved of him. No, when it came to a choice between him and his mother, I'd side with her every time, and he knew it. He didn't trust me. Thought it was my doing, you know, when she got so she'd turn him down. I never opened my head on the subject, one way or the other. She wouldn't have listened if I had. But he held it against me, anyway." She paused. Shook her head. Sighed. "I just don't understand it. How he could do such a thing…."

"According to Cynthia, he needed the money to buy her a birthday present," said Joe.

"Oh well. Cynthia. Always making herself out the center of the universe. Though you wouldn't believe, the money he spent on presents for that child. Scandalous. No wonder she's such a handful. He spoiled her rotten." She stood up, smoothing down her neat print housedress. "It wouldn't surprise me if there were others he was buying presents for," she added primly. "Girls no older than Cynthia, like as not. You'd think he'd be ashamed, at his age. He was past forty-eight. Well. Had enough to eat?"

"Fine. Thanks."

As she started off with the empty plate and bottle, her eye fell on his jacket, slung over the newel post. "Here, I'll take that along and hang it up downstairs. It'll get all out of shape this way."

"Wait!" The package. He didn't dare let it out of his hands; not only because he had promised Cynthia, but because of what it might contain. "Wait, let me get my cigarettes," he said, and fumbled in the pockets. The package was just big enough to be awkward; in spite of his efforts to slip it out unobtrusively, he had a feeling Duffy saw what he was up to. She didn't miss much. Well, he couldn't help it if he had started her wondering. As long as all she did was wonder, he had nothing to worry about from her. When she had bustled off down the stairs, he put the package—he was beginning to think of it as a kind of albatross—in his back pants pocket and got back to work.

And while he worked he mulled over Duffy's offerings. If she was to be believed—and he saw no reason to doubt her—his chances of finding his "missing person" within Fritz's family circle seemed pretty dim. One by one Duffy had crossed them off the list: Fritz's mother, his sister, brother-in-law, Duffy herself. And of course Cynthia; she had never been a likely candidate, anyway, if only because Fritz had spent so much money on her. That left only nephew Ned, the archaeological type who was due home from Central America this weekend. But then it didn't have to be one of the family. There had been plenty of other people in Fritz's life. His business partner, Marian Bishop, for one.

She had been out there for the hearing. Joe remembered her chiefly for her air of impersonal efficiency. The prospect of tackling her—and from here it looked as if he would have to—was definitely nervous-making. She would be a tougher proposition than Duffy, no question about that. He didn't see Marian Bishop chattering away about her own or anybody else's intimate feelings. Didn't see her sympathizing with, or even understanding, this search of his. For there would be no masquerading with her. His face and name were no doubt filed away in their proper place in the card index of her mind, instantly available. As a matter of fact, if she happened to be on friendly terms with Fritz's family; if she were to come calling this afternoon …

She didn't. For the next couple of hours nothing much happened except for tenants stepping over him on their way in or out, and Vera Henderson, who didn't have to step over him on the several trips she made up and down the stairs. The first time she emerged from her apartment she paused on the landing long enough to exchange a perfunctory Good Afternoon with him. After that all he got was a nod. Possibly she was embarrassed over yesterday afternoon's finale. Possibly it was a matter of principle with her not to hobnob with the hired help. She looked the same as yesterday—pale, stylish, and discontented.

Then about four o'clock Mrs. Wall called up to him from the downstairs hall. "Joe! Cynthia's on the phone. She wants to talk to you." Her tone was disapproving; so was her face, he saw when he sprinted down the steps. She made a point of absenting herself, thank God, while he took the call in her living room. And he could hear Duffy banging the hardware around in the kitchen. From the window sill the Persian cat eyed him with cold distaste.

"Joe sweetie, how are you? I won't keep you long on account of Gran, I suppose she's standing over you with a stopwatch."

"No, she isn't, but we'd better make it quick. Listen, I want to see you. How about tonight?"

"Can't. Have to apologize to Gran. She's taking me out to dinner. I just wanted to make sure about, you know, the errand you were going to do for me. Is it all squared away?"

"No, I—"

"Joe, you promised! What did you do with it, you bastard?"

"Take it easy. I've still got it, but that's the trouble, I couldn't leave it because there was somebody there."

"Somebody? Who?"

"I don't know. A couple of kooks with a drum and a guitar." That damn thumping and strumming was still with him, incidentally; just when he thought he was rid of it it would start up again, as maddening as ever. "I couldn't get any sense out of them."

"Drum, guitar … Oh! It must have been The Zowies! Of course. That's who it was, The Zowies. Aren't they terrific?"

"Are they?" said Joe. "Anyway, I didn't like leaving it, with them there."

"I should hope not. Absolutely not. So everything's great, sweetie. Nothing to worry about."

"But what—we can't talk now, Cynthia. Cyn. I've got to see you. I mean it."

"Well, of course. Only not tonight. I won't be late, though, if you want to call me."

"I do. I will," Joe promised grimly.

"Good. Meanwhile, hold everything. Remember our bargain. 'Bye now."

He hung up and sat still a moment, fuming. The cat sprang down and closed in on him for a better view out of her cross eyes. What was the name Cynthia had called her? "Hey there, Dutch," he said absently.

There was a sound behind him. "Her name is Duchess," said Mrs. Wall from the doorway. "I wouldn't advise you to pet her."

Well, it wasn't the only false lead Cynthia had given him, he thought as he went back up the stairs. Nor—unless his suspicions about the package were all a lot of blah—the most serious. So everything was great, was it. Nothing to worry about. That remained to be seen. She wasn't going to find it so easy to brush him off tonight. If she expected him to go on holding everything without knowing what he was holding, she could look for another sucker. Personally, he had had it.

Another half-hour and he was through for the day. Duffy appeared to check the completed job, issue instructions for tomorrow, and bring him his jacket. She had bustled back downstairs, and he was transferring the package from pants to jacket pocket when he heard Vera Henderson's voice from the landing. Chatty as all get-out now; a complete change from her earlier, stand-offish tone. "All finished? And how nice it looks! You can't imagine what a relief it is to have that place fixed."

She must have opened her apartment door very quietly. He was so startled that he dropped the package, and by the time he had retrieved it there she was beside him, still running on about what a great workman he was. And just to make it peppier, Arthur Henderson came pounding up the stairs at that moment, home from the office and even fuller of conversation than his wife. He was as burly as Joe remembered him, one of those red-faced, pseudo-hearty guys with hard little eyes. It was easy to see that, for all his bluster, he took his orders from Vera. Not the brightest man in town, as Duffy had said; and almost embarrassingly hungry for his wife's approval. She kept him on short rations, if Joe was any judge of the little glances—anxious on his part, faintly contemptuous on hers—that flickered between them. Everybody pretended he and Joe had not met before; the friendly chatter continued while Joe fumbled himself—and the package—back into his jacket.

He couldn't very well get out of it when they offered to drive him home. Arthur had the car right outside; they were going out anyway; it was on their way. No bother at all. They insisted.

Well, then, he might as well do what he could toward improving the time. "You must be looking forward to seeing your son again," he said from the back seat, while Arthur maneuvered his way out of the close quarters in which he had parked. "Mrs. Wall said he's due back tomorrow?"

"Tomorrow morning," Vera burbled, still working hard on the

sociability bit. "We've missed him, of course, but it's been wonderful for him. A chance to have his little fling. Get it out of his system. As I told Arthur, now he'll be ready to settle down to something sensible."

"He better be," rumbled Arthur. The car lunged forward in triumph. Inches to spare.

"He's not going on with archaeology, then? I had the idea that was his main interest."

"Well, it's not a very practical career, is it, for a boy in Ned's situation," Vera said over her shoulder. She sat with her thin arm stretched along the back of the seat; tense, proprietary, fingers fidgeting with the plastic cover. "I mean, if he didn't have to think about making a living—I'm sure it's fascinating, digging up all those fossils and things, but there's the future to consider. The financial opportunities. I'm afraid they're extremely limited in a field like archaeology."

"For the birds," said Arthur. "Craziest thing I ever heard of. Kiting off to some jungle in Central America when he could have had a job for the summer right here in my office. I had it all set up for him. A job that would have paid him good money, let alone the experience. You know how much he got for grubbing around down there in the jungle? Not one single solitary nickel. That's how much. Not a goddamn cent."

"Arthur. Please."

"Well, I'm sorry, but it gets me sore every time I think about it." The back of his neck looked sore, all right. Fiery red. "Okay, so now he's had his fling. So now he can quit fooling around and get on the ball. Or else. I'm not putting up with any more of this bull, and he knows it. I let him have it straight. Go ahead, I said, go on down there and dig up the jungle, but just remember, when you go back to college this fall you either switch to something that makes some sense or you can damn well pay your own way. You're not throwing away any more of my dough, I told him, and—"

"You should have turned back there," said Vera. "Now we'll have to go all the way to Sixth." She sent a brilliant, insincere smile in Joe's direction. "Traffic gets worse and worse, doesn't it. Intolerable. I'd leave New York in a minute, if it weren't for Mother. But it's no use talking, she'll never sell the house. We couldn't afford to leave, anyway, with Ned still in college."

"Yeah," said Arthur. "Besides, where would we go?"

"Anywhere!" Her hand clenched in a spasm of frustration; she pointed her long chin outward, past Arthur and New York and all the other intolerables of her life. "I don't know. Just away …"

Six

The day had left him in a vaguely unsettled mood. He felt cleaner and cooler after his shower, but not any more relaxed. The apartment seemed empty without Tess and the kids; he kept prowling around, trying to make up his mind what to do with the evening. A movie? Television? Books, magazines? Nyah to everything. He couldn't even decide about dinner, except that eating out of Tess's freezer definitely did not appeal. All right, that meant going out. Such as where?

Well, there was his cousin Louie's place, down on West Fourth. A little family solidarity, after the Wall's conspicuous lack of same, might be just what he needed. Already cheered—maybe just because he had settled on something positive—he reached for his jacket, and was once more reminded of his personal albatross, the package Cynthia had palmed off on him. But for this one evening at least, he could be rid of it and its dubious contents; not even Cynthia could expect him to tote it around with him everywhere he went. In fact, Tess's apartment was a safer place for it than his pocket, particularly if he tucked it away somewhere out of sight.

He did not know exactly why it should seem so important to hide the package, but he spent quite a little while considering various spots. Finally he thought of the freezer, and stuffed it in behind a frosted carton of mixed vegetables. There. If Otis's homecoming present couldn't stand the cold, it was just too bad.

Louie and his wife, who supervised the cooking in their little restaurant, welcomed him with open arms. He ate a lot of spaghetti and drank a lot of red wine—probably more than he needed, but as Louie pointed out, it had been a long time between reunions, this was a festive occasion. The last customers trickled out, and Joe sat on at the table with its stained white cloth and let the mellow glow spread through him. The wine was only part of it. There were the familiar spicy smells; the easy laughter and warm, quick voices spilling out reminiscences, news, questions, unsolicited advice. Reunion was right: he was back with people he understood. He was himself again.

It was nearly midnight when he left, but the narrow streets still swarmed with humanity. Youthful humanity, for the most part: a profusion of beards and general hairiness, tight pants and pierced ears and thong sandals. Joe strolled along, still pleasantly aglow. He remembered, in a remote way, Mrs. Wall's paint job tomorrow, and decided the walk back to Tess's apartment would do him good. Nothing bothered him, not even the fact that he kept thinking he saw The Zowies. They were such a common type in these parts that his recurrent illusion, impression, whatever, was perfectly natural. Inevitable, in fact.

Even when he turned up the Avenue and the people started to thin out, he still seemed to catch an occasional glimpse of a pair of familiar, slouching figures behind him. Once he actually paused in front of a store window for a surreptitious checkup. Nothing, of course. They might conceivably have trailed him to Mrs. Wall's house this morning, but to spend the whole day doggedly following him around … No. Fantastic. Why should they?

All the same, he was beginning to feel a little jumpy by the time he reached Tess's street. It would be a relief to get inside. The lock on the outer door of the house was out of whack again—kids were always breaking it—but he heard no footsteps behind him as he entered the empty lobby and headed for the stairs. It wasn't worthwhile waiting for the elevator, with only two flights to climb. He took them two steps at a time, with the key ready in his hand.

The last thing he remembered was putting it in the lock. No warning. Not even any pain. Just that second of violent, splitting blackness as he put the key in the lock. Then nothing.

He came to in stages, none of them easy. He had a raging headache, a withering thirst, and in all probability he had gone blind. He couldn't keep his eyes open long enough to be sure; even closed, they throbbed in loyal rhythm with the pain that was rampaging around behind them. He made another try, and got the same black dazzle. Well, maybe not quite so black, and maybe the jabs were not quite so fierce. Partial blindness instead of total. Next time, he was able to make out the shape of his hand, hoisted with great effort from the rug. Rug? That meant he was lying on the floor. Not the hall, though; it was tiled. He began to get interested. Where the hell was he? His hand moved, cautiously exploring, and came up against a smooth wooden object that swung at his touch. After a good deal of research, he figured out what it was: a child's rocking chair, like the one that belonged to Tess's kids.

He was in Tess's living room, then. Just inside the door; dragged there by whoever had clobbered him. He knew he could not have gotten there by himself, as surely as he knew somebody had clobbered him. He stayed where he was—later he might try moving his head; later— laboriously piecing things together and practicing his eye exercises. By now he could distinguish other, comfortingly familiar pieces of furniture, by the light from the street lamp coming in through the window.

Presently he became aware of another light, jumping around in the bedroom across the hall, and of hurried rustling sounds. Somebody was moving around in there with a flashlight. Whoever had clobbered him. Still here, ransacking the bedroom.

The Zowies! Cynthia's package!

Forgetting his infirmities, he reared up. The effect on his head was disastrous; he groaned from the bottom of his heart and toppled against the rocking chair, which contained its usual miscellaneous load and capsized with a rattling of marbles and twanging of pull-toys. In the bedroom the flashlight flicked off and the rustling sounds ceased. What now? Would they come back and smack him again? Well, this time it wasn't going to be in the dark, Joe decided. He forced himself on to his hands and knees. There was a lamp on the table by the couch. A little farther than the wall switch, but lower, more his level. He made for it at a painful, ignominious crawl. The toughest part was the upward reach for the switch, but that too he managed, with the couch for a boost-up.

As the room sprang into light, there was a rush of footsteps in the hall. Here we go, he thought, bracing himself against the couch and turning to face them. But it was too late; already the footsteps had thudded past the living room on their way to the outer door. It slammed open and shut before he could do anything more than let out an indignant, croaking "Hey!"

Gone. Just like that, without his catching so much as a glimpse of them. Was he even sure it was "them"? Yes; there had been two sets of footsteps, one lighter, quicker, than the other. He could forget about trying to follow them. By now they would be down the stairs and out of the house.

The police? Not much point in calling them, unless he was prepared to give them the whole story about The Zowies and Cynthia's package. Which, of course, might have no connection whatever with tonight's episode. It might have been just a routine mugging. If so—

Well, if so, his wallet would be empty, for one thing. He felt for it and discovered, first, that all his pockets had been turned inside out and second, that their contents were strewn on the floor beside the upset rocking chair. He made the journey back on his two feet, groggily, but at least he had graduated from hands and knees. As far as he could tell, nothing was missing. Keys, change, address book, twenty-one bucks in his wallet, along with his driver's license and collection of snapshots. Including one of Ellie; his conscience smote him briefly.

So it wasn't just a routine mugging.

Furthermore, the living room showed signs of having been searched, hastily but thoroughly. Drawers pulled out; the desk lid down; the liquor cabinet open. Nothing was missing from it, either, and the kids' piggy bank was intact.

It was the same story in the two bedrooms. Not that Tess and her husband owned so many valuables, but an ordinary sneak thief wouldn't have passed up the transistor radio or the few pieces of jewelry or the olive bottle nearly full of half-dollars.

No, they hadn't been looking for money or the usual loot; they had been looking for the package, which was still there in the freezer, behind the mixed vegetables. Fortunately or unfortunately; who could tell? All Joe knew was that he was still stuck with it.

He put the chain on the door. Inspected the lump on the back of his head: much less spectacular than he had expected. Took a couple of aspirins. Checked the time. Another surprise; it wasn't quite one o'clock. The whole business couldn't have taken more than half an hour.

All these activities enabled him, for a while at least, to dodge the issue: Was he, or was he not, prepared to give the police the whole story about The Zowies and Cynthia's package?

He took it out of the freezer and peered at it. The police would have no compunction about opening it; they hadn't made any promises. Unlike Joe. Who had promised; and gotten clobbered for it; and who even now—with his thick, honorable head aching—could neither open the package himself nor pass the buck to the police. Certainly not without letting Cynthia know …

That was the thing to do, of course. Call Cynthia and find out why The Zowies or whoever should take such an alarming interest in Otis's homecoming present. She had gotten him into this; the least she could do was tell him what it was all about.

She was a long time answering the phone. Well, if he had wakened her out of a sound sleep, that was just too bad; he wasn't having such a restful night himself. He plunged right in and told his story.

"Oh God," she said. "They know you've got it, you dope. I might have known you'd bitch things up."

"I bitched things up! Did I know they were going to be at Otis's place? Or that they'd spot the package and come after it? An innocent little homecoming present. Ha! People don't go around bopping other people unless they think it's worthwhile. Not even The Zowies." Silence. A lot of silence. He wouldn't put it past her to hang up on him.

But no. "I didn't know it, either," she said at last, in a queer, muffled voice. Then she got back to normal. "Well, anyway, they didn't get it. So what's the problem?"

"No problem. None whatever. Except I'm still stuck with the damn thing, and what's to prevent them from having another go at it? I don't like being bopped. And I don't want them busting in here while I'm gone, either. What's the problem! Excuse me for bothering you. I should have called the police in the first place."

"The police! Joe! You wouldn't!"

"Oh no?" But his heart sank. Here was proof—if any further were needed—of all he feared and suspected about the package. The thought of dope pressed in on him, uglier, closer than ever. "Listen, Cynthia. Cyn. What kind of a mess have you got yourself into? I want to help you, but how can I, when I don't even know what's in the package? I mean, if you're mixed up with a bunch of hopheads—"

"It's my business, who I'm mixed up with," she snapped back, so quickly that his heart gave another dip. "And don't worry about helping me, thanks very much, I can take care of myself. Don't worry about the package, either. I'll come down right now and relieve you of it."

"Now wait a minute." He had an unexpectedly poignant mental image of her stray dog backbone, and of how fragile her skull must be, under the straight, pecan-brown hair. They wouldn't hesitate to clobber her. Might surmise he would call her and be watching, this very moment, in case she showed up. "You can't do that."

"Certainly I can. I wouldn't dream of burdening you with it any longer. What's the address again?"

"I'm not going to tell you."

"It's my package! My present to Otis. You've got no right to keep my property."

"Listen," he yelled. But he didn't have the strength. Whatever he said, she would only turn it upside down. "Stay right where you are. I'll bring it up to you." He hung up quick, before she could get in any of her topsy-turvy licks on that. And before he could change his mind.

The only thing that got him out of the door, complete with package, was a good stiff jolt of Tess's brandy. No one skulked in the hall, waiting to ambush him. The elevator stood ready, safely empty. Downstairs he ran into a middle-aged couple—he recognized them as first floor tenants—who were just coming home, mildly liquored up; he grabbed the cab they had vacated, and that was all there was to it. Duck soup.

No snags at the other end, either. Rather to his surprise, he found that Cynthia had not only stayed where she was, she had alerted the doorman, who ushered him in like an old friend. So did Cynthia herself—a crotchety old friend given to his little quirks and blind spots, but never mind, he was entitled to them.

"Poor Joe," she said. "You didn't have to come all the way up here. Really. And I am sorry about your poor head. Are you suffering?"

"Skip it." He took the package out of his pocket and handed it to her. "Here's your quote present to Otis end quote. All I can say is, he's welcome to it. I hope nobody bops you before you unload it."

"They won't," she said serenely. She was wearing a pale blue robe and no makeup. The effect was quite ethereal, except for the glint in her eye. "I've thought of a way to fix them. You want a drink or anything?"

"No thanks." He did not even sit down; he felt safer on his feet, more in control of the situation. But he couldn't resist the bait. "What do you mean, a way to fix them?"

"You gave me the idea. When you mentioned going to the police. Remember?"

"I remember. That's how I know there's something funny with the package, because the thought of the police sent you into such a tailspin."

"You should worry now. You're not stuck with it anymore."

"Yes, but—"

"Can I help it if The Zowies come up with this crazy notion that there's something in it for them? They're kooks from way back. *Terrific*. But kooks."

"You don't have to tell me. That's what's got me scared."

"I know, dear. Hopheads. Like you're always reading about in the *Daily News*. Whether they are or not … The point is, I'll simply tell them you threatened to go to the police and have them arrested for mugging you, only I managed to talk you out of it. That'll do it. That'll make them lay off."

Joe swallowed hard. "I'm not absolutely certain it was them," he said. "I didn't see them."

"For all they know, you did. So let them think so. Let them stew. From now on they won't dare make a move."

"Now wait a minute. If I saw them, why didn't I call the police myself?" The way I should have, he thought. Would have, if I had a lick of sense.

"Because they didn't take anything," Cynthia explained glibly. "You called me first—luckily for them—and I calmed you down, and we're giving them a break, see, letting them off with a warning. This time. But there better not be a next time. And there won't be. If you call that a tailspin I went into at the thought of the police—well. I mean, they'll really flip." She gave an excited, jubilant laugh.

"What if it was somebody else, not The Zowies at all?"

"Who else could it be?" Her laugh rang out, even more elated. "You thought of them yourself. And of course it makes sense. They're the logical ones."

"Yes, but if it wasn't them, then threatening them with the police won't do any good. I mean, whoever really did it won't be getting the message, and—"

"Oh, you and your ifs! I'll be able to tell, when I talk to them, whether or not they're the ones. From the way they react. If they're not—well, why worry before we have to? Especially when it's one chance in a million. Right?"

"I guess so," he said uneasily. "When are you going to call them? Do you even know where to get hold of them?"

"I'll get hold of them, all right. Leave it to me. They're not getting away with this."

But Joe wasn't so sure. It depended on how seriously they took her warning, which depended on how badly they wanted the package, which depended—home base again—on what it contained. They wanted it badly enough to risk their hit-and-run attack on him, so they must believe that it contained something valuable. Joe himself was inclined to agree with them. Valuable, and illicit.

"How do you know they won't call your bluff?" he asked. "That's what it is. A bluff. You're as anxious to keep the police out of the picture as they are."

"But you're not, and you're the one that's threatening to call the cops. Not me. Remember? I interceded on their behalf."

"On your own, you mean."

"So what?" She stared him down, coolly confident. As well she might be. In spite of herself and his better judgment, he was committed to her. Because she was Fritz Wall's daughter; because she had the family she had; because of those occasional crises in her throat and her stubby little hand trying to hide them … Whatever she was mixed up in, however foolhardy and dangerous, he was still with her. He drew a deep sigh.

"Listen, Cynthia. That damn package. Get rid of it, will you? I'm not asking you what's in it, I don't even want to know, I just don't want you stuck with it."

"I won't be. I'll think of something," she said airily. Then she added, with an exaggeratedly straight face, "That is, until Otis gets back and I can give him his present."

"Oh, sh—" He caught himself in time, and switched it to, "Shut up. Okay, so you're not going to get rid of it. But you can at least let me know what happens. If anything goes wrong, if there's any trouble or anything. You'll call me, Cyn?"

"Nothing's going to happen, you dope. I've got them where I want them. Over the barrel." She ducked her head so he couldn't see her eyes. "I'll call you, though, if it makes you happy. Oh, and by the way, thanks. You know, for everything."

On this effusive note they parted.

Seven

He woke up, not particularly bright, but early—which was fortunate, since he had forgotten to set the alarm. One thing he didn't need today was a chewing-out from Mrs. Wall for being late. The bump on his head still hurt when he touched it. The answer to that being don't touch it. You dope.

The house on Perry Street was even quieter than it had been yesterday. To his relief: painting was just about his speed today; people might have been too much for him. The only person he saw all morning was Duffy, who let him in and reappeared at one o'clock with another ham-and-cheese and beer. The top floor tenants, bless their hearts, were no problem; once they had approved the colors, they fled the premises for the weekend and left him to it. Mrs. Wall was presumably still in bed when he arrived, and she stayed downstairs where she belonged. Probably hadn't climbed to the top floor in a decade. And there was no sign of the Hendersons, which also suited Joe.

"They took off this morning at the crack of dawn," Duffy reported when, as on the day before, she settled down to gossip and watch him eat. "They weren't supposed to leave till tonight, but that's how Vera is. Decided she had to get out of the heat, and off they went. After being out half the night, too. It was at least one-thirty when I heard them come in. I can't remember when they've stayed out like that. And then this morning—they didn't even wait for Ned, he got in about ten. Not that he expected them to meet him or anything, but still. Poor kid, he's beat. They must have worked him like a dog down there in Central America, and from the look of him he hasn't had a square meal since he left home. I said to his grandmother, for pity's sake, I said, let him sleep, he's dead on his feet, plenty of time to talk later. Made her mad. But she'll get over it."

"Ned's her favorite?" asked Joe.

"Ned? Whatever put that into your head? No, if she's got a favorite, I guess it would be Cynthia. Not that they don't get into it every now and then. But the truth is, you know, she kind of likes it, for somebody to fight back. And that's not Ned's way. He's more the quiet type. Not enough ginger to suit her. But I don't know what else you can expect, the way he's been raised. They've always run him down, especially his father. No matter what Ned does, it's wrong. It's a wonder he's got any gimp left at all."

"He must have, though. This summer, for instance—I gather his father was against the Central American trip. But he went, anyway."

"I know. I didn't think he had it in him. But then Ned's one I never could figure out. He keeps himself to himself. Look at the way he acted today. Just sat there like a bump on a log, all the time his grandmother was talking about Fritz …"

"You mean he hadn't heard about it till now?" asked Joe.

"He knew Fritz was dead. I sent him a wire. But he was off somewhere in the jungle and didn't get it till a couple of days ago, just before he started back. So he didn't know any of the details till today. As I say, like a bump on a log. You'd have thought she was talking about the weather. Of course he was dead tired, but even so."

"Yeah," said Joe. He had been counting on Ned—the last hope, as far as Fritz's family circle went—but this didn't make him sound like a red-hot prospect. Surely, if there had been any kind of a bond between him and Fritz, he couldn't have listened to the story of his uncle's death without giving some sign? It didn't seem natural to Joe, bond or no bond.

Duffy stood up and gave him a sharp look. "You don't look any too brisk yourself today. Have a hard night?"

"So-so," said Joe modestly. He checked the lump on the back of his head. Still sore.

"Well, just so long as you don't lay down on the job. I've got to hand it to you, you've pitched right in." She had already inspected the work in progress, no doubt on Mrs. Wall's instructions, and pronounced it satisfactory. "The rate you're going, you might even finish up tomorrow and not have to work Sunday. Stop in and give her a report before you leave tonight, she won't like it if you don't. If I get a chance, I'll sneak you another beer later on this afternoon. You look to me like you could use it."

He could have, but Duffy either forgot or didn't get a chance. He drank water instead, and worked on through the long hot afternoon, in a not unpleasant glaze of suspended mental activity. At six o'clock he called it a day, cleaned up in a sketchy way, exchanged paint-smeared coveralls for slacks and shirt, and started down the stairs. Evidently his brain remained quiescent; there was no other explanation for what happened when he reached the second-floor landing.

A lad in shorts shot out of the Henderson apartment, almost colliding with him, and after muttering a distracted-sounding "Excuse me," asked, "Who are you?"

And Joe—or rather the robot who had taken up residence within him for the time being—promptly answered, "Joe Florio."

"Who did you say? Joe Florio?" The lad wore horn-rimmed, owlish glasses; blinking, he pushed them into place on the bridge of his nose.

Then he reached out and grabbed Joe's wrist. "Wait a minute. Joe Florio. What are you doing here?"

Again the robot spoke his piece promptly: "Painting the top floor." He then abdicated, leaving Joe and all two of his brain cells to deal with the situation. "I mean—listen. Your grandmother doesn't know, that is, doesn't know—you're Ned, I guess? Ned Henderson?"

"Go ahead. What is it my grandmother doesn't know? That you're Joe Florio?"

"No. Yes. She doesn't know. If you'll give me a chance to explain, I mean, somewhere more private—"

"Come on in." An order, not an invitation. Still grasping Joe's wrist, Ned opened the door to the Henderson apartment and hustled him inside. He stood in the foyer, his back to the door, peering at Joe as if he were a specimen under the microscope. A fifth-rate specimen. "Go on," he said. "Explain."

Joe cleared his throat and plunged. "The thing was, I didn't want to upset her. Your grandmother. That's all it was. That's why we didn't tell her my last name."

"We? Who's we?"

"Cynthia. I met her out there, see, she came out there to—when it happened. So after it was settled and I came to New York, I called her, and she asked me to come over here with her, to see her grandmother."

"I see," said Ned. Again there was the business of pushing his glasses back up on his nose. Apparently a habitual gesture. He had his mother's narrow features, but not her pallor—he was both sunburned and fiery with insect bites—and his hair wasn't as dark as hers. He was skinny and long-legged, but he would be okay once he caught up with himself. And his face was rather attractive, in a hyper-sensitive way. Would have been, that is, with a different, less sullen expression. "It figures. Of course Cynthia would be in on it."

"I don't know what you mean by in on it." As if it were a plot, he thought. Well, and hadn't it been? At least a bargain between Cynthia and him, an arrangement to their mutual advantage: he had wanted to meet Fritz Wall's family for his own reasons, and for her own reasons Cynthia had wanted someone with her on that particular visit. The right hand washing the left. "There was no point in upsetting Mrs. Wall. I didn't know I was going to wind up working for her, of course."

"That was all her idea, I suppose?"

"I don't remember now just how the subject came up. Duffy, I think it was Duffy, mentioned that they needed some work done around the house—repairs, painting and so on—and I was looking for something, so I offered, and she hired me. That's all it was. Nobody planned it. It just happened."

"What happened to your bartending job?"

"I quit," said Joe. Damned if he was going to elaborate.

Ned gave a contemptuous laugh. "I see," he said again. He had a slow, cold way of speaking. Too slow; as if he were holding himself back from the edge of hysteria. "And it just happened. Does Duffy know who you are? Or my folks?"

"No. Cynthia. And now you."

"Yes, and now me. I caught you off guard, didn't I? Otherwise you'd have lied to me, too, so as not to upset me. Such delicacy. Such consideration for others. Too bad you're not a little sharper. What's Cynthia going to say when she finds out I'm on to you?"

"Listen," Joe began hotly. Then he got a grip on himself. This was what the kid wanted—to needle him into losing his temper. When he went on it was in as even a tone as Ned's (and he hoped as maddening). "I expect she'll say I'm not very sharp. And I'm not. I have to have things spelled out. If you don't mind. Like what this is all about, what it is you're accusing me of."

"I owe you an explanation? That's a laugh." Shove with the glasses. Didn't know he was doing it. Probably didn't know, either, when he raised one sneakered foot to scratch a bug bite on his shin. "You're the one with explaining to do. If you don't mind. Like what you're really up to, you and dear sweet Cynthia, oiling your way in here under false pretenses. And don't give me any more bull about not wanting to upset Gran or the rest of the family. I know them too well for that. So does Cynthia."

"So do I," said Joe. "Now. But I hadn't met them then."

"You had met Cynthia, though. You must have cozied up to each other, right from the start. Seems a little odd, doesn't it, in view of the circumstances. What was it, love at first sight?"

"No it wasn't. Love's got nothing to do with it. I—well, I felt sorry for her, on account of her father—"

"Why?" Ned cut in harshly. "He pulled a gun on you, didn't he? He had it coming to him. And furthermore, if Cynthia gave you the grief-stricken daughter bit and you swallowed it, you're dumber than you look."

"She didn't," said Joe. "I felt sorry for her, anyway."

Ned gave a single, jeering hoot of laughter. "Sure, sure. Poor pitiful Cynthia, all she ever had to do was ask Daddy and it was hers. Not only that, but whatever she does it's all right with Gran, whatever she says Gran believes her."

Okay, so you hate her, thought Joe. Gloom settled on him. Partly because he had counted more than he realized on Ned's being his missing person, the one Fritz had cared about. It didn't seem likely now, not the way Ned had spoken of Fritz. But the kid would have depressed him in any case, corroded as he was by envy and hostility and suspicion. His overwrought air, too; reminiscent of his mother.

He was pressing on: "Well. This is one caper Cynthia isn't going to get away with. For once Gran's going to—"

The phone rang. He scooped it up from the little occasional table beside him and answered. "Hello … Oh. Just a minute …" He pressed what was apparently an intercom button, his eyes fixed on Joe as on a desperate prisoner who might make a break for it. It was an idea, at that. But not a very good one, Joe decided. Nothing to be gained by making himself look guiltier than he already looked to Ned. And even if he got away—especially if he got away—Mrs. Wall was going to hear the tale of his duplicity. Better for him to be on hand to defend himself as best he could. While he worked this out, a peripheral section of his mind was busy registering the fact that the Hendersons' phone was an extension of Mrs. Wall's. "You there, Duffy?" Ned was saying. "It's for you."

He hung up and turned back to Joe. "For once Gran's going to listen to me. Duffy, too. And let me tell you, you'll have to come up with something pretty good to explain to them how come Cynthia smuggled you in here. You and your paintbrushes and your kind heart. That's a little too much, even for Gran, especially on top of what else has been going on around here lately. Cynthia's overplayed her hand this time."

"I don't know what you're talking about," said Joe. But he felt a premonitory inner chill, like a draft from a subterranean passage. Could Cynthia's package be a family affair, after all? Last night he had convinced himself that it belonged in some other department of her complicated life. But supposing he was wrong. Supposing, supposing … "What do you mean, what else has been going on?"

"Ask your pal Cynthia. She knows. She can tell you. If she hasn't already."

"Well, she hasn't. And it seems to me you might at least give her a chance to tell her side of it, instead of sneaking around behind her back—"

"I'm sure it seems like that to you. And incidentally, look who's talking about sneaking. Sure, you'd rather Cynthia was here. I would too, if I were in your shoes. She's a faster talker than you are. Who knows, she might get you both off the hook. This way you're on your own. Tough, isn't it?"

Joe itched to smack him. Or no, not even smack him. Just take hold of him and shake the sneer off his face and a little sense into his head.

Of all the jerks, of all the smart-alecky, spiteful …

At that moment, when Joe was as close to hating a fellow creature as he had ever been in his life, Ned took off his glasses to wipe them on his shorts; and was instantly transformed. There were his eyes, without frame or protection: his naked, shy, suffering eyes. The young-old look was like Fritz. The unconscious revelation was like Cynthia with her hand at her throat. Then the glasses were back in place, and the moment was past.

Duffy's voice soared up to them from the downstairs hall. "Ned? What on earth's keeping you? Your grandmother's waiting!"

He jumped to open the door and call back to her. "Be right there, I've been talking to Joe!"

She waited, crackling with curiosity, while they came down the stairs together. "Well, I must say, a fine time to be talking to Joe, when you know how she is … What's the matter with you? Faces down to here, the both of you." She crackled even more when she saw Joe follow Ned into Mrs. Wall's living room, where he hadn't been officially invited; and trotted after them, busy as a hound on the scent. Whatever was up, Duffy wasn't going to miss out on it.

Mrs. Wall sat on the love seat, in what looked like the same dress she had worn the first time Joe saw her, and in much the same attitude, impatiently tapping her fingers. She said, as she had said to Cynthia that first time, "Well, there you are." Then she spotted Joe, and stiffened slightly, not in pleasure. "I expected you fifteen minutes ago. Who's that with you? Joe?"

"Good evening," said Joe apologetically.

But she had diminished Ned too; reduced him, with no more than a flick of her wrist, to a naughty child who arrived not only late but unsuitably accompanied.

He started out bravely enough. "Gran, there's something I—" Then he got rattled and lost the thread. Silence, while his grandmother waited, elaborately forbearing. He wound up flailing his arm in Joe's direction and blurting it out. "You don't know who he really is, this guy. He's Joe Florio. Florio. The one that shot Uncle Fritz."

The gasp came from Duffy. Mrs. Wall was not given to melodramatic demonstrations. Her back may have stiffened a trifle more, her hooded eyes may have sharpened. "There's no need to yell," she said icily. "You'd better sit down, both of you. Joe?"

"I'm sorry." Obediently, he perched on the edge of the sofa. He felt his face reddening with schoolboy shame. "It's my fault for not telling you right at the start. I'm very sorry."

Ned stayed on his feet. He had a cause to sustain him, a point he was burning to make. "Cynthia knew it all along. Knew it when she brought him here. It's part of the deal they've cooked up between them, to get him into your house, on the inside. I guess this proves—"

"Keep your voice down, please. And stop scratching." Having nipped her grandson off at the ankles, she turned to Joe and said, in a tone of unnerving neutrality, "I assume you have some explanation? Or at least some comment?"

"Yes. Sure. Sure I have. It's true Cynthia knew who I was from the start. But it's not true about the deal. What the hell does he mean, cooking up a deal? I wasn't trying to pull anything, not telling you my name. It just seemed simpler that way, not to remind you. Okay, maybe I should have told you when the job business came up and you hired me. I'm sorry now I didn't. But at the time it seemed okay to let it ride."

It sounded feeble, hollow. That was how he felt. He forced himself to meet her eyes; after all, he was telling the truth. "Why did you come here?" she asked, as neutral as before.

Before he could answer, Duffy broke in: "Well, because Cynthia talked him into it, of course. Naturally she wasn't going to show up by herself if she could help it. She's been ducking the whole family, ever since—"

"That will do, Duffy. I didn't ask you. I asked Joe."

"It wasn't a question of talking me into it. She just said she was coming to see you, and why didn't I come along. That's all."

This time it was Ned who erupted. "That's all. He wasn't trying to pull anything. Not much he wasn't. Just a little matter of getting the lay of the land for Cynthia's next stunt. Yes, and how do we know he wasn't in on the first one? How do we know when he met her? They could have teamed up any time, long before, and that could be, that might even be why—" He stopped, strangling on his own excitement.

"Are you out of your mind?" inquired his grandmother. He did have a strange look, as if he might be in some kind of a state of ecstasy. They were all staring at him—Joe with his mouth hanging open; Duffy clearly on the verge of boiling over; Mrs. Wall rigid with a kind of social disapproval, as if he were a dinner guest who had just emptied his soup plate over his own head. She went on decisively, "If you can't control yourself, Ned, and you obviously can't, then I'll have to ask you to leave the room. I will not have this sort of thing in my house. I simply will not have it."

"All right, you won't have it. It's your house. Your granddaughter." He leaned toward her in one last spasm of frustrated spite. "And your necklace. Don't forget that. And don't think I'm through with your precious Cynthia and her pals, either. I'll prove it to you yet."

The door slammed behind him. Mrs. Wall leaned back, her face alarmingly pale. At once Duffy set up an anxious bustle: "I declare, that boy, what's he thinking of, stirring up such a rumpus. Here, put your feet up while I get your pills, I won't be a minute …"

Joe stood up, ready to go, but at once the hooded eyes flipped open, and the quavery voice gave him his orders. "Stay. I want to talk to you." He sat down again.

After a pause, during which Duffy came back with the pills and remained to hover, the old lady removed her feet from the hassock and straightened up. "All right, Duffy. Fine. I'm all right now." Her voice was much stronger, and the color was back in her face. "Stop fussing and go cook dinner or something. I think I'd like a glass of sherry, please, Joe. Will you join me?"

Duffy tightened her lips and looked mulish. But she went. And Joe poured the sherry.

"I must apologize for my grandson's ridiculous performance," said Mrs. Wall with finality.

As if that disposed of the subject, thought Joe, and he felt himself bristling in resistance. This talk of theirs was her idea, at her request. Okay, then, let her talk. She needn't think she could sweep everything Ned had said under the rug with one cavalier stroke. There were too many odds and ends. "Your necklace," for instance. What had Ned meant by that?

"I'd rather you'd explain than apologize," he said bluntly. "I've got a right to know what he's accusing me of. Me and Cynthia. What's it all about?"

"You're sure you don't know?" She gave him a straight, appraising look. He met it squarely, and after a moment her hand lifted in a half-salute, as if she were giving him credit, not only for telling the truth himself but for pressuring her into doing the same. "All right, then. I'd rather tell you myself than have you hear it from the rest of the family. Or Duffy," she added, with a glance toward the kitchen door, behind which Duffy was undoubtedly listening. "I hardly know where to start."

"The necklace?" Joe found it necessary to clear his throat.

"Yes. The necklace. I haven't much left in the way of jewelry. No occasion to wear it anymore, either. Years ago, of course, before my husband died, we went out a great deal. It was different in those days. Why, I thought nothing of inviting twenty-five people for dinner. We had the whole house to ourselves, plenty of servants … That's the time for diamonds, when you're young. I've got no use for them anymore. As I say, I haven't much left, except for the necklace, and the last time I revised my will I decided against leaving it to Cynthia. So it seems only fair that she should wear it once in a while now. She won't have the chance after I'm gone. That's why I'd lend it to her, you see, whenever she had a special party."

She took a sip of sherry. So did Joe, but it did not dispel the subterranean chill.

"Unfortunately, the last time she borrowed it, it was stolen."

"Stolen?"

"The usual sort of mugging. Again unfortunately, she had quarreled with her escort at the party, so she came home by herself. Somebody attacked her in the hall of her apartment house and made off with the necklace." She spoke tersely, and kept her eyes fixed not on Joe but on the cat Duchess, who as usual was ensconced on the window sill, with one front paw dangling languidly over the edge. It was hard to say which looked more disdainful, cat or mistress. "That was Cynthia's version of what happened. I chose to accept it."

"How about the Hendersons?" Joe had to clear his throat again. "Do they think Cynthia—"

"It's their privilege to think what they please. They have produced nothing to prove their theory. Until and unless they do, Cynthia's version stands. After all, the necklace was mine, not theirs."

But the Hendersons would take a longer view, especially if they knew the old lady had decided not to will the necklace to Cynthia. Surely that must mean it would one day—very likely quite soon—be Vera's. Provided it was recovered, that is. Provided they could prove that Cynthia had stolen it. Oh yes, the Hendersons would take an intensely personal interest in getting their hands on that necklace. Cynthia and her package would have special implications for them. And they had known about it. Vera had seen Joe with it, they could have … His battered mind shied away from them and the package (later, later) and headed for safer ground.

"Well, but surely the insurance people," he began.

"I have never believed in that sort of insurance," Mrs. Wall stated. "The police have a description of the necklace. Cynthia called them the first thing. Naturally. Not that it's done any good so far. They weren't very optimistic about being able to trace the necklace. It could easily be broken up and sold or pawned, stone by stone. And even if it weren't, it's not all that distinctive, they still might miss it. They can't be expected to check every pawn shop in the country. They must have hundreds of such thefts to investigate every day." She leaned back wearily. "So there's your explanation. Now you know."

He did indeed. All explained now: the current of hostility between Vera and Cynthia; her fight with Arthur; her reason for bringing Joe along, that first time—as an outsider, he would be a restraining influence on the Hendersons, a safeguard against another barrage of accusations from them—Duffy's knowing air when she opened the door, and the cryptic little remarks she had dropped from time to time.

He even went all the way back to his first meeting with Cynthia, when she was telling him how she had asked her father for a Jaguar or a mink coat. "No diamond necklace?"

Joe had said, or something like that, and had wondered why she snapped back at him so sharply. Well, now he had the answer to that one, too. His problem was too many answers, more than he felt able to cope with at the moment. Eventually, of course, he was going to have to face up to the package, but not now, not yet, not with Cynthia's grandmother watching him out of her inscrutable old eyes.

"I'm still not sure," he said carefully, "exactly where I'm supposed to come into the picture. Ned must think I'm some kind of an accomplice of Cynthia's. But why would she need help from me or anybody else? To dispose of the necklace for her? In that case there'd be no point in 'oiling me into your house.' Just the opposite, in fact."

"It would seem so," said Mrs. Wall. "Besides, if Cynthia stole my necklace it would be because she wanted to keep it for herself. She wouldn't be interested in disposing of it. Utter nonsense, all of it. As I said at the start, a ridiculous performance. Simply because you're a friend of Cynthia's, that makes you suspect to Ned. He's always resented her. The more trouble he can make for her, the better. Not that I approve of everything Cynthia does, you understand."

"I know. Like striking up a friendship with me. I don't blame you. To tell you the truth, Mrs. Wall, it shocked me when I found out who she was. I mean, if it had been the other way round, my father that had been killed, no matter what the circumstances—"

"Or your son. I suppose that shocks you too, that I should be sitting here drinking sherry with Joe Florio instead of ordering him off the premises." She sounded amused. And hopeful; it came to him that they weren't too different, Cynthia and her grandmother. "Not very motherly of me, is it? But it's been some time since I've felt very motherly toward Fritz. And I'm afraid the circumstances do matter to me. Not only the circumstances of his death, but the circumstances of his whole life. It wasn't out of character for him to wind up trying to hold up a bar and getting himself killed in the process."

"To me it was," said Joe stiffly. "I didn't know him well, but still.... In the first place, he didn't seem like the type that would care that much about money."

"He didn't, except to spend it. When I think of the money he wasted, simply threw it away on anything, nothing ... Hopeless, an absolutely hopeless spendthrift." Her voice hardened with the accumulated bitterness of years. Nothing forgotten. Nothing forgiven. "It's thanks to Fritz that I'm reduced to living as I am now, forced to rent out my own home to strangers. His inefficiency. His irresponsibility. His mismanagement of my husband's business. He was above such things. Only money, he used to say. But in the end it was a matter of life and death to him. Only money."

"If I knew what he wanted it for, who he wanted it for—"

"Does it matter?"

"It does to me!" He struggled to his feet, clumsy with the strength of his feelings. "I might be able to make it up, somehow or other. It matters to me!"

"So that's what you're after," she said after a moment. She sounded thoughtful, rather gentle. "That's why you wanted to meet Fritz's family. Well, Joe, if I could help you I would. But I don't know who Fritz wanted the money for. Except that it wasn't for me." She smiled wryly. "It may take me a little while to convince Ned of this, you know. He won't give up his plots and skullduggery without a fight. But I'll see that there's no repetition of today's nonsense."

"Look, Mrs. Wall, it seems to me it might be best for all concerned if I didn't come back. Just go away and stay away, before I stir up any more trouble."

"What? And leave the top floor half painted?" She finished her sherry and stood up. She was as tall as he. Frail. Indomitable. "I'll expect you in the morning," she said. "See that you're here by eight."

Eight

He walked back to Tess's apartment. There he sat down in peaceful solitude and faced what he had shied away from till now: Cynthia and her package in the light of the Hendersons' theory. Himself, too. If Cynthia showed up in that unkindly light as a thief, he showed up as a fool. He had bumbled along with his kind heart and his guilty conscience, not only letting her dupe him but duping himself. The Zowies, for instance, were his own contribution; he, not Cynthia, had translated a pair of kooky kids into the menacing figures responsible for last night's clobbering and ransacking operation.

But it was the Hendersons who knew the address of Tess's apartment. It was they who had a solid reason for trying to snatch the package. Which Vera could have heard about, thanks to the phone arrangement in Mrs. Wall's house, and which she had certainly seen in Joe's hands.

The footsteps alone should have told him—the two sets of footsteps he had heard, one light and quick. Like a woman's. Then there was Duffy's report on how late the Hendersons had been out last night, how unusually late.

Naturally, Cynthia had leapt on The Zowies when he held them out to her. The wonder was that she had been able to suppress her cries of joy over such a windfall. Even without them, would he have spotted the Hendersons as the culprits? Probably not, he thought glumly; Cynthia would have scraped up some kind of dust to throw in his eyes. Now, of course, it was absurdly obvious, like a jigsaw puzzle with all the pieces fitted into place.

Here was Vera, picking up the phone in her apartment and listening in on his conversation with Cynthia yesterday. (Whether or not they had mentioned the package outright, it had not been a discreet conversation—for Cynthia must be aware of the intercom system. But she had been in a flap over the package, and anyway, discretion was not Cynthia's long suit.) Vera wouldn't need much. At the merest hint of a mission assigned to Joe by Cynthia, she would be hot on the trail. Besides, she had seen the package with her own eyes, there on the landing when she popped out on Joe and he dropped it. He was still trying to fumble it into his jacket pocket when Arthur came galloping in—summoned, no doubt, by Vera—and insisted on driving him home. Arthur too had seen it. So had Duffy, when it came to that. But Duffy, even if she subscribed to the Hendersons' theory, presumably had little to gain by proving it. Mrs. Wall would be far more likely to leave her diamond necklace to Vera than to Duffy, now that she had decided against Cynthia. And then Duffy was too short to clobber him; she'd have to stand on a stool. Whereas Arthur …

So here were the Hendersons, electrified at the prospect of proving their theory, finding out where he lived through the simple expedient of driving him there, lying in wait for him—with his head full of red wine and Zowies he would never notice—and then failing to get their hands on the package, after all. And it would all be Arthur's fault, thought Joe; poor bastard, he would never hear the last of it from Vera. Especially after Cynthia called them and threatened them with the police.

For of course it was the Hendersons she had called, not The Zowies. Let Joe keep his convenient little delusions. Cynthia knew who her enemies were, and furthermore knew when she had them by the short hairs. They were stymied for sure: to press their theory on Mrs. Wall now would be to invite disaster for themselves. They couldn't afford a police investigation of Cynthia for fear of exposing their own excursion into crime. And it would be exposed, all right. Trust Cynthia for that.

They were hard luck kids, the Hendersons. Last night couldn't be the first near miss for them. They must have been nipping pretty close to Cynthia's heels at the time of Fritz's death, close enough so that she hadn't risked leaving the package in her apartment in case they searched it while she was gone. Once out there, she had snatched at the first chance to get rid of it—for a while, till the heat was off—and she was still playing it safe when Joe turned up in town. She obviously didn't trust her grandmother to hold out against the Hendersons' arguments. Joe had observed no signs of any such weakening, but then Mrs. Wall was not the sort to pour her heart out indiscriminately. It had cost her plenty, just to tell him the little she had to.

All the pieces fit, right up to and including the Hendersons' taking off ahead of time, at the crack of dawn this morning. Joe didn't blame them for preferring to avoid him, believing as they did—thanks to Cynthia— that he had recognized them last night. Just their luck, to miss out on the unmasking of Joe Florio. He couldn't help wondering what their reaction would be when they learned his true identity. Would they see it for what it was, an irrelevancy? Or would they side with Ned, for once in their lives?

Irrelevancy. The word lingered in Joe's mind. He sighed. In a way his identity, far from being irrelevant, was the key piece in the whole puzzle. Because he was who he was, he had met Cynthia in the first place; had let himself be drawn into her dubious doings; had not pulled free, though he knew she was a liar and a blackmailer.

And now a thief. (Not Fritz's kind of thief, either, Joe reminded himself; Cynthia had stolen out of simple, selfish greed, and from her own grandmother.) But because he was who he was, Joe had listened to the tale of Mrs. Wall's diamond necklace and never opened his head about the package. He could have settled the matter then and there. Instead, he had pressured a proud old lady into exposing her family's unsavory problems while he sat dumb, hugging his secrets, refusing to admit their implications, even to himself, until he was safely alone.

It was not too late. He could still tell Mrs. Wall what she had every right to know. Let her take it from there. It was her diamond necklace. Her granddaughter.

Why not? Basically, he neither liked nor trusted Cynthia. She, not he, had done the trusting—out of necessity, and warily, expecting at any moment that he would turn out like everybody else. Maybe that was his reason for sticking with her, in spite of his doubts and her perverseness. Anyway, he had done it. And even now …

He would be turning not just her grandmother loose on her, but the Hendersons too; and he was damned if he was going to side with the

Hendersons, no matter how much Cynthia might deserve it. On the other hand, he wasn't going to let her think she was still pulling the wool over his eyes. There was a limit to how much he would take, even from Fritz Wall's daughter.

He picked up the phone and called her, and when—rather to his surprise—she answered, he wasted no time on preliminaries. "Listen," he said, "I know what's in that famous package of yours. Your grandmother told me all about her diamond necklace, and I just—"

"Gran?" It was a despairing little croak. "Gran told you?"

"Right. It's about time somebody told me, isn't it? Considering how long I was stuck with it. But of course if I'd known what you were up to I wouldn't have been in such a hurry to help you out. Good old fall guy Joe."

"Good old double-crosser Joe, you mean. I might have known better than to count on you. A fine pal you are, ready to believe any load of blah you hear about me. Well, it's nothing to me if you want to take Aunt Vera's and Uncle Arthur's word against mine. I could snitch on them too, if I wanted to, and it wouldn't be blah."

"I know it. But you didn't want to for the very good reason that you'd have to tell me why they were after the package. The Zowies! Ha! As for whose word I'm taking, I don't need to take anybody's. Now and then I can figure something out for myself. As a matter of fact, Vera and Arthur scrammed out of town this morning. They weren't even there. Ned's the one that started it."

"I bet he did," said Cynthia. "And you're the one that finished it."

"Me? All I did was—"

"Don't tell me. Let me guess. I know what you did, all right. And now that you've spilled the whole story to them, you call me. Because you're not just a plain rat, you're a fancy rat with a conscience. I've heard about you and your conscience before. Kicking up again, no doubt. So you think maybe it'll help if you call me and confess. I'm supposed to absolve you? Or thank you for warning me? Okay. Thanks. Thanks a lot for everything, Pal Joey!"

He heard the crash of the receiver, but he went ahead and explained anyway; passionately: "Cynthia! Cyn! Wait. You've got it wrong, I didn't tell them about the package. I'm not going to tell them. So help me, Cyn …" The words bounced back at him from the dead phone. He hung up.

There was no answer when he tried to call her back. He kept trying, on and off, for the next hour. Then he decided the hell with it, let her think he was a rat, he couldn't care less.

All the same, he woke up several times during the night, in a sweat of frustration because he kept trying to get across this dream street, only the light never changed and the traffic never stopped, and there he was, stranded, unable to reach whoever it was on the other side.

He gave her another ring before he left for Perry Street. Still no answer.

"Morning, Mr. Florio," said Duffy, poker-faced, when she opened the door to him. And that was the one human contact of the morning. Which was all right with Joe; Ned in particular was one he would just as soon skip. Apparently Mrs. Wall had clamped the lid down on her "ridiculous" grandson, whether or not she had convinced him of the error of his ways.

Somehow Joe thought not. The kid might be temporarily silenced, but just let him start comparing notes with his parents, and he would be back in there fighting. And Vera and Arthur right along with him: a family united at last, solidly lined up against Cynthia.

She had no one left now. Or so it must seem to her, with not only Joe defecting, but her grandmother wavering enough to divulge the necklace story. He remembered with a pang of uneasiness the despair in her voice: "Gran? Gran told you?" No telling what she might take it into her head to do if he didn't get hold of her and set her straight. He paused, paintbrush in hand, eyeing the top floor tenants' telephone, which was presumably not an extension of Mrs. Wall's. Though he wouldn't put it past her; with her view of tenants as intruders in her house, she might figure they were not entitled to privacy.

Actually, what stopped him was the possibility that Duffy or Ned might walk in on him and catch him, if not in the middle of a complicated explanation to Cynthia, at least making free with other people's property. Much better to nip out to a phone booth, he decided— at lunch time, if, as seemed likely, Duffy had struck him off her sandwich list.

But at twelve-thirty here she was, with the regulation provisions. And without the poker face she had put on when she greeted him this morning. "Pulled one over on us, didn't you?" she began in her usual cheerful, gossipy style. "Well, as I told Mrs. Wall last night, I said, if by any chance Ned's right and there is something fishy going on, then one thing sure, we've seen the last of Joe. He'll make himself scarce, I said, tomorrow morning will tell the tale. Mind you, I never for a moment doubted but what you'd turn up."

"I'm glad to hear you testify," said Joe.

"Ned and his foolishness. Though I must admit, you could have knocked me over with a feather when he came out with it about you being Joe Florio. The fella that shot Fritz," she added, in a marveling, superfluous footnote. "That's why Cynthia took up with you, of course. Typical. Whatever most people would do, she's got to do the opposite."

Joe hesitated a moment, chewing. Then he came out with it. "Do you believe she stole that necklace?"

"Do you?" Whatever she saw in his face, it made her chuckle. "I wouldn't put it past her. But give Vera a chance, and I wouldn't put it past her, either. The pot calling the kettle black, if you ask me. No, I'm not taking sides. It's up to Mrs. Wall to decide, and she's decided, and that's that."

"Fair enough. I don't suppose you've heard from Cynthia lately, like this morning? I couldn't get her on the phone when I tried."

"Oh, she's gone off to Connecticut. Mrs. Wall had a note in the mail this morning. She's got friends up there that she visits. Left last night, she didn't say for how long."

"I see," said Joe. "It must have been kind of spur-of-the-moment. She didn't mention anything about going away to me."

"Well, that's how Cynthia is. Spur-of-the-moment." She shot him an oblique, probing glance. "I hope you're not taking her too seriously, Joe. I wouldn't like to see you getting in beyond your depth or anything. A nice boy like you."

"I don't think you need to worry," said Joe stiffly. "In the first place, I'm twenty-six. Not exactly a boy. And not about to get in beyond my depth with anybody, let alone a kid like Cynthia. I feel more sorry for her than anything else."

"Pardon me," said Duffy. "How about Ned? You feel sorry for him too?"

"I can choke back the tears." But even while he was coaxing a grin out of Duffy, the image of Ned's face without glasses darted past his mind's eye, as unexpectedly touching in memory as in reality. Maybe that's my trouble, he thought. I can feel sorry for practically everybody. "What did Mrs. Wall do, lock him in the closet for being a bad boy? I haven't heard a peep out of him this morning."

"He slept late. And when he did get up he didn't eat any breakfast. Claimed he was going to see Marian Bishop, but it may have been just talk. You know. Fritz's business partner."

"I know. She was out there for the hearing." She had put Joe off, with her aggressive self-assurance and efficiency. Not a bad-looking woman—certainly not the dog Cynthia had described—but she had seemed less like a human being than a business machine, accurately and concisely disposing of each question as it was put to her and then waiting for the next, reducing Fritz Wall to a set of neatly punched cards. "Is she a pal of Ned's?"

"I wouldn't put it that strong," said Duffy. "They've always gotten along, as far as I know. Which is more than you can say for her and Cynthia. Even so, I don't see Marian going all the way with Ned and this folderol he's cooked up about you and Cynthia. It's just too far-fetched. And she's the one to tell him so. If anybody can set him straight, it's Marian. She's got no use for Cynthia, true enough, but that doesn't mean she's going to let herself get carried away."

"It sure doesn't, judging from what I saw of her. Maybe it was just a front, but the way she clicked out the answers, like a damn computer … As if she hardly knew Fritz, let alone liked him."

"Well, she did at one time," said Duffy bluntly. "Liked him too much for her own good, if you ask me. A smart girl like Marian, no wonder she got tired of him and his shenanigans. It would have served him right if she'd sent him packing long ago. That's what I would have done. But she hung on for business reasons."

She would, thought Joe. "How do you mean? Doesn't she run the business pretty much on her own?"

"The office details, yes. The financial end of it. But Fritz was better with people. He had a likable way about him, you know, I can see how he'd go over big at conducting tours and so forth. That's how he met Marian. She took this tour that he was conducting, must be ten years or more ago, and they wound up starting a travel bureau of their own. It was her idea, she had some money to invest, and I suppose he hit it lucky at the races for his share. They were a good combination. Made a go of it right from the start. You'd think that would have been enough for him, wouldn't you? A nice little business, and a girl like Marian. But not Fritz. Never satisfied."

"Cynthia made her sound like a fishwife. Claimed he was scared of her." Again he thought, could Marian Bishop be the one Fritz did it for? And again the prospect of tackling her, making up some excuse to see her, produced a sinking feeling in the pit of his stomach. "Does Mrs. Wall like her?"

Duffy made a *comme ci comme ça* gesture. "They leave each other alone. Always have. It's just as well, too. They both want to be the boss." She stood up, with all the usual fussy accompaniments: the twitch to her skirt, the settling of her belt, the hairpin reanchored in her bun of snowy white hair. "Well, time I was getting back. Don't worry about Ned. If he's got anything to say to you, you can bet he's not going to say it here, on account of his grandmother. Anyway, I guess you can handle him."

"I can," said Joe. "Don't worry."

By mid-afternoon his hopes of finishing before tomorrow faded. The plaster in the kitchen needed more patching than he had realized, and the casement windows in the bedroom slowed him down. He went down at five-thirty to consult with Mrs. Wall. It was a question of staying till God knew when to finish tonight or coming back tomorrow; he didn't know which alternative appealed to him less.

"Tomorrow, by all means," said Mrs. Wall decisively. "If you try to finish tonight you'll be too tired to do a good job. Besides, there's all the cleaning up to do afterwards. I don't want the tenants complaining about the mess when they get back Monday."

So that settled that. Well, it was okay with Joe. He had put in a long enough day as it was. And he could use an early evening, he thought as he let himself out and started down the steps to the street. A quiet evening, for a change. He might not even go out for dinner; might just fix himself a snack at Tess's place and settle down with a book or TV.

"There you are. I've been waiting for you," said a thick voice, and a figure emerged from behind the bushes in the miniature front yard. It was a moment before Joe recognized either voice or figure as Ned's. Could the kid be drunk? He seemed none too steady on his feet, and he sounded a little blurred.

"What's on your mind?" asked Joe.

"Plenty. I've got it figured out. I know what the score is now." He moved forward to the little iron gate, swung it open, and made a sweeping gesture at Joe. "Come on. Let's go somewhere where we can talk. Mustn't disturb Gran, you know. That's why I waited out here."

Joe walked through the gate. He had no choice, and only one hope—that it wouldn't take long. He wasn't in the mood for a whole evening of listening to whatever Ned had figured out. "Okay," he said. "I'm heading for home. Come along, if you want to. We can talk on the way."

Ned fell into step beside him, more or less—again he noticed the slight tendency to lurch—but in brooding silence. Not a word out of him till they reached the corner, and then he seemed to be talking to himself more than to Joe. "Lies. All lies. I see it now. I've got it figured out."

"What do you mean, all lies? If you're talking about Marian Bishop—Duffy told me you were going to see her. You think she lied to you?"

"You." There was a fanatic gleam in his eye, the same strange look Joe remembered from yesterday. "You've been lying in your teeth ever since it happened. You and Cynthia too. You're not going to get away with it, you know. I'm on to you. I'll find a way to prove it. Who's got it now, you or Cynthia?"

Joe couldn't help it, he gave what Ned no doubt interpreted as a guilty start. "Who's got what? If you're talking about the necklace—"

"If I'm talking about the necklace! Who do you think you're kidding? Listen. I know you had it. That's what Cynthia meant by the package." He stopped and faced Joe, jabbing an accusing finger at him. "Isn't it? Isn't it?"

"Cynthia?" croaked Joe.

"Yeah. Cynthia. I went to see her last night. She wouldn't let me in, but we exchanged a few pleasantries through her apartment door. Among them her crack about the package. I gather she thinks you ratted on her, and who am I to disillusion her? 'So I gave him the package,' she said, 'so what? It still doesn't prove anything.' End of quote."

"I see." Joe started walking again, fast; and Ned stayed with him, right there at his elbow. The authentic Cynthia ring, he thought; it was like her to jump the gun and force him into ratting on her in spite of himself. Because what was the use, now that she had let it out … Wait. What had she let out, after all? The existence of the package, a package she had given to him. But he still didn't have to admit, to anybody except Cynthia, that he knew damn well what was in the package. Didn't have to. And wouldn't—not yet, not until and unless the Hendersons told Ned about that middle-of-the-night clobbering. Call it token resistance, a hopeless stop-gap gesture, whatever you liked, but it was the best he could do, the only way of salvaging anything at all out of the situation.

"A classic case of thieves falling out," Ned was saying, with galling assurance. "You can't very well deny that there was a package, can you?"

"Sure there was a package," said Joe. "It was a present for Cynthia's boyfriend. He's away on a trip, and she asked me to leave it at his apartment for him. She didn't want his snoopy neighbors to know she had a key. But I didn't leave it because there were a couple of kooky kids there, and I didn't like their looks."

"Oh, come on now. This is too much." Ned stopped again, for effect, and Joe spoiled it for him by plodding steadily on. He had to hurry to catch up. "You expect me to believe you were just an innocent bystander, an unwitting tool?"

"I don't give a damn what you believe," said Joe coldly. "You've got no proof that Cynthia stole the necklace. Package or no package. It's going to take more than that to convince your grandmother, or Marian Bishop either." Two blocks to go before they reached Tess's apartment. God help him if he didn't shake Ned by then. "Because it's easy enough to see what's eating on you. Marian didn't buy the story you're peddling, so now you're taking it out on me. What beats me is why you expected her to buy it in the first place."

"I don't care whether anybody believes it or not. I'll prove it. I'll find a way … Lies. All lies." Ned's voice soared, reedy with tension. Joe could feel him trembling.

"This is where I came in," he said wearily. "Lies. Everybody's lying to you, and you've got something figured out, you know what the score is— Well, *I* sure as hell don't. You can either give it to me straight, whatever it is you've got on your mind, or you can—"

"I'll tell you, all right. I'll give it to you straight." Only a block to go now. Less than a block, once they got across the Avenue. Ned kept his eyes fixed on the traffic light, waiting for it to turn green; he no longer sounded excited. On the contrary, chillingly detached. "You're not fooling me with the fake holdup bit. I know why you killed Uncle Fritz."

The light turned green. Like two mechanical toys they marched across, side by side, eyes straight ahead. Then, with a whir like an alarm clock, Joe's brain caught hold again. "Fake holdup, you said? But it wasn't a fake. He pulled a gun on me. He meant business."

"Sure he did. But it wasn't the money he was after. It was the necklace. I know, I know." Ned's hands made impatient, slapping gestures, as if to drive away a swarm of gnats. "You claim you didn't meet Cynthia until afterwards. Never even heard of the necklace until yesterday. Well, you're lying. I told you I've got it figured out now, and I have. I see how it all fits in, you and Cynthia and Uncle Fritz. I see it all."

There he stood—Joe had stopped in front of Tess's house, and so had he—oblivious to the heat and grit and noise of the street, with that unearthly light in his eyes, as if he actually were seeing a vision. Drunk? Or crazy? Or just (excuse the expression) disturbed?

In any case, Joe was stuck with him; out of curiosity, if nothing else, he had to hear the rest. "You'd better come up with me," he said, and guided Ned inside to the elevator.

Neither of them spoke until they reached the privacy of Tess's living room. Ned perched on the edge of the sofa, hands pressed between his knees, a trancelike set to his face, his body swaying back and forth in rocking chair rhythm while he talked. "You and Cynthia either pulled the necklace job together, or she stole it on her own and then passed it on to you to keep. The fuss my folks were kicking up, she didn't dare keep it herself. They might get into her apartment and catch her with it. Gran would have to believe them then. Anyway, you've known each other longer than you say, and you were holding the necklace for her till things quieted down and the heat was off. Because you're her current boyfriend, or one of them ..."

"No," said Joe. "But go on. Go ahead."

"Real neat. Cynthia thought she had it made. Only Uncle Fritz got on to you, somehow or other. That's why he went out there, because he knew you had the necklace and he'd made up his mind to get it back. He wasn't a thief, he wouldn't ever do a thing like that, hold up a bar. Sure, he took his gun. He knew you weren't going to hand the necklace over just because he asked you for it. You'd have to be persuaded."

"How about the nylon stocking over his head? More persuasion, I suppose?"

"Could be. Or you could have planted that, to back up your holdup story, after you killed him. And you got by with it, you got by with murder, because Uncle Fritz was the only one that knew about you and Cynthia and the necklace. It wouldn't bother her that you killed her own father. What's a little thing like murder, as long as she gets what she wants? I didn't see it myself, at first. But I do now. Yes. It all fits. It all falls into place." Back and forth he rocked, back and forth, hypnotizing himself with the power of his own vision. For a weird moment Joe seemed to see it too, everything fitting, everything falling into place, and the two of them swaying in unison …

"You're crazy," he said sharply. "Of all the cockeyed, screwy … For God's sake, if you really believe I'm a murderer, what are you doing here, tipping your hand to me like this? Why shouldn't I kill you too, now that I know you've got my number?"

"It would be one way of proving my point," said Ned. "You wouldn't get away with it. I told Marian Bishop I was going to see you."

"In that case I'd better not risk it." Silence. The kid just sat there, not rocking anymore, but still in that cramped, tense attitude, as if he had to hold himself together. Joe added, "And the same goes for you. You'd better not risk killing me, either."

"Oh, I don't know. Maybe I don't care whether I get away with it or not." Suddenly he was on his feet and across the room, bending down to thrust his face—drawn-looking, in spite of the sunburn, and shiny with sweat—close to Joe's. Again Joe could feel him trembling. "All I want from you is the truth. Admit it. Admit I'm right. That's all you have to do."

"What are you trying to do, threaten me?" With a shove, Joe got himself out of his chair. He grabbed a handful of Ned's shirt front and gave him a little shake. "I can tell you right now, it won't work. You must think I'm as crazy as you are."

"No," said Ned. "I think you're a fool. Still trying to cover up for Cynthia. What's the point? What have you got to lose? As far as she's concerned, you've already ratted on her. The way she would on you. Don't kid yourself. The way she will, at the first opportunity."

Joe shook him again; his arms dangled like a rag doll's. Miserable, spiteful little bastard … That was what it boiled down to, and that was all: pure, simple spite, with Cynthia as the target. Well, Joe wanted no part of it. In a burst of angry contempt, he loosened his grip, casting Ned and his visions aside. The abruptness of the gesture sent Ned staggering backward against the end table.

So far he had shown no inclination to fight back, or even defend himself. But now his face changed; his hands, no longer limply dangling, groped for and grasped the first weapon they found—a heavy, sharp-cornered glass ashtray. While Joe stood, shocked into immobility, he raised it, balancing it like a spear, taking his aim before he hurled it. He meant to, all right; belatedly Joe's nerves shrieked the alarm, alerting him to the menace of that glittering, weighty missile.

And then, at the very moment he was braced to duck, Ned's arm slumped and the ashtray bounced harmlessly to the floor. He peered down at it in what seemed to be bewilderment. His hand wavered upward toward his glasses, but instead of giving them the automatic little shove Joe expected he suddenly snatched them off and knuckled his eyes like a child trying to hold back the tears.

Unsuccessfully: he made for the door at a stumbling run, determined to get out before he broke down completely. But determined to say something else. It came out in a gulp of bitterness and despair: "You don't need to worry ... If I kill anybody, it won't be you ..."

Then the door slammed shut behind him. Joe was alone with his so-called thoughts.

Nine

An hour later—scrubbed, slicked down, presentable in drip-dry suit, white shirt and one of his more understated ties—he was ringing Marian Bishop's doorbell.

She greeted him with just about as much enthusiasm as he expected, which was very little. She hadn't been enthusiastic over the phone, either, and he couldn't honestly blame her. On the other hand, he couldn't shake off his conviction that Ned's precarious state of mind was somehow traceable to her. (The part, that is, that wasn't traceable to Joe himself.) That was why he had insisted on seeing her. He could only speculate as to why she had agreed. Having done so, she was apparently prepared to make the best of it. He got no handshake, but she ushered him in politely enough. She even offered him a drink, and he was so overcome by this token of cordiality that he accepted. While she mixed them each a Scotch and soda, he took a look around from the easy chair where she had parked him.

Her living room did not surprise him. Forbiddingly tidy—he hesitated to sully an ashtray—tasteful, all the colors coordinated, all the furniture chosen with an eye to texture, line, even a certain amount of comfort. And Marian Bishop herself was much as he remembered her: a reasonably attractive, well-groomed woman, expensively dressed in a style that Joe had never found very interesting, but that was neither here nor there; hair expertly rinsed to bring out the copper-brown highlights; squarish face, expertly made up; hazel eyes, not brown as he had thought.

"Now then," she began, in the brisk tone of a chairman calling the board meeting to order, "what's all this about? I know part of it, of course, because Ned was up here first, carrying on about you and Cynthia and Mrs. Wall's necklace. As if it mattered to me, whether Cynthia stole it or not. Or whether you helped her, just in case you've got the same idea Ned had, to enlist me on your side. If that's what's on your mind, forget it. As far as the Walls are concerned, I'm strictly neutral, from here on in."

"No, it's not that. I told you over the phone, it's Ned I'm worried about. I don't know what set him off, but—"

"It's fairly obvious, isn't it? He was counting on me, I suppose because I've got no use for Cynthia, and never have had. So he thought I'd believe all this nonsense of his, and when I wouldn't he blew his top."

"You don't believe any of it, then?"

She hesitated briefly, long enough to take a sip of her drink. "Oh, I think he's probably right about Cynthia and the necklace. And she's perfectly capable of conning you into holding the baby for her. I don't see how he's going to prove it, though, as long as Mrs. Wall refuses to do anything about it. She's the bottleneck."

"That's not all he's accusing me of," said Joe cautiously. "He may not have told you, but he did me."

"I suppose you mean about Fritz." Her voice sharpened with impatience. "Utter nonsense, and I told him so. In the first place, Fritz couldn't have known about the necklace when he went out to the Stewarts' cottage. It wasn't even stolen till after he left. So that's not why he took his gun. Yet he did take it—something I've never known him to do before, it was a war souvenir, he kept it in the office—so the idea of a holdup must have been in his mind. Probably nothing definite. Fritz wasn't the type to plan ahead. That's one reason he was always getting in these financial binds."

"This time he must have been really desperate."

"Obviously," she said, and got back on her own track. "In the second place, I was in on the investigation, remember, and I know it was thorough. If it hadn't been, believe me, they'd have heard from me. They checked you up and down for a previous connection with Fritz or any of his family, and they didn't find any. Nobody in his right mind is going to take Ned's theory seriously. He must see how ridiculous it is."

"He didn't sound to me exactly in his right mind," said Joe. "That's what has me worried. I mean, it doesn't seem normal for him to get so worked up just because you told him he was talking nonsense."

"He's always been high-strung, a little on the unstable side. Too much repression, if you ask me, not only from his parents but from his grandmother too. Her idea of child-rearing is to keep the lid on tight, and maybe it's not such a bad idea in some cases. In other cases— anyway, Ned's the kind that holds everything back up to a point, but when he does let go he does it with a bang. The more he's been holding back, and the longer, the bigger the explosion. You see?"

Joe nodded. He was beginning to see a good deal.

On she went: "I wouldn't make too much of the business with the ashtray if I were you. He was just blowing off steam. He's been under quite a strain for some time now, what with his parents pressuring him to switch from archaeology to business. Arthur was furious with him for going off on this trip, you know, and he's not going to foot any more college bills unless Ned gives in and switches. So it's been a rough summer, even if Fritz hadn't …" Her voice, ordinarily so crisp and assured, faltered.

"Yes, I can see how it would upset him, especially if he was fond of Fritz."

"Fond of him," she echoed. "Didn't you realize? They were devoted to each other."

"Ned didn't let on to me," said Joe. But then he wouldn't; he was the kind that holds everything back.

"It started before my time, way back when Ned was a little bit of a kid. He was sickly, bronchitis, asthma, all that sort of thing, and this particular winter Fritz was staying at his mother's because he was broke. Not only broke but at loose ends, between deals. He spent a good deal of time with Ned—partly out of boredom, I suppose, nothing much else to do—playing games with him, reading to him, teaching him to paint. Well, of course Ned thought he was wonderful. The funny part of it is that it was mutual, Fritz got just as attached to him."

"Seems natural enough to me."

"You didn't know Fritz the way I did. Another drink?" He nodded, and as he watched her cross to the bar, waggling her well-girdled tail behind her, he found himself revising his original impression of her. A human computer? Maybe, but with a hell of a lot more accent on the human than he had figured.

"He was a strange man," she said when she was settled again in her chair. "A strange, unhappy man. His own worst enemy. It seems so ironic for him to die like that, trying to steal something he had no respect for. Money. It didn't mean anything to him. It honestly didn't. He used to drive me crazy." She smiled rather sadly. "I'm money-minded myself.

Very much so. Oh, the times I've lit into him for gambling!"

"I know," said Joe. "Cynthia told me."

"Well, and why shouldn't I, I'd like to know! He didn't know when to stop. Give him half a chance, and he'd have been dipping into the company funds, gambling them away too. I wasn't going to let him bankrupt us. Not after all the time and effort I'd put into the business. All the money." Her voice rang out, passionate, metallic. Fritz must have been all too familiar with that ring. "I can't help it, it *hurt* me to see him throwing money away on things he didn't want, for people he didn't care about. But that was the point, that was the only use Fritz had for money. To keep people out of his hair. Pacify them. Toss them an expensive present instead of—instead of—" Her eyes filled with tears, to Joe's embarrassment. Not to hers; she was too intent on what she was saying to care. "He was too scared, too cagey—anyway, not willing to commit himself. Except for Ned. In all his life, Ned was the one person who ever really got to him."

Only one reason I wish I had money, Fritz had said, that night in The Starfish. Only one person I'd like to do something for.

Not Cynthia, who had grabbed at the expensive presents because they were all he ever tossed her way. Not Marian, who must once have been in love with him and who had wound up sticking with him for the sake of the business they had built up together. Not his mother or Duffy or anybody in all his life except Ned.

Joe's search was over. Success. Eureka. Whee.

"So that's why he did it. For Ned. Because Arthur was going to cut him off if he didn't drop the archaeology."

"Of course."

"But for God's sake, a holdup," Joe burst out. "Did he have to go that far? I mean, if he'd come to you and told you he wanted a loan from the business for Ned's education—"

"I wouldn't have believed him," said Marian bleakly. "I'd have thought it was just another of his floozie episodes. No, he used up all his credit with me years ago. And with everybody else. He'd been to too many wells too many times. Anyway, to get back to the facts—" The phrase seemed to comfort her; once more she spoke with clipped confidence—"I knew, of course, that he was worried about Ned, afraid he'd have to give in to his parents, the way Fritz had done with his mother. It was her doing, you know, that he went into his father's business instead of studying art. He never forgave her, or himself, either, for knuckling under. So to him it was history repeating itself. Every once in a while he'd get off on what a crime it would be if Ned got stuck the way he had, how every human being deserved the right to do what he wanted to with his own life, and so on. The money pitch, too. All the money he'd made and spent on people that didn't matter, but never a penny on Ned. But I'd heard him talk like that before, I didn't realize …"

There was nothing for Joe to say. He stared into his glass; she stared into hers.

After a moment she went on: "I should have guessed, from the mood he was in when he went out there to the Stewarts' cottage. All keyed up. Excited. He may not have known exactly what he was going to do, but he'd made up his mind to do something for Ned. It's as clear as crystal now. Why couldn't I have seen it then?"

"You weren't the only one," said Joe. "I wonder if his family sees it even now. You're the first person to mention how Fritz and Ned felt about each other. Didn't the rest of them ever notice?"

"Of course they did, when it first began. Maybe they think Ned's outgrown it by now. I told you, he's not the kind to show his feelings, certainly not to his parents or grandmother. Neither was Fritz, when it comes to that, and anyway, he hardly ever saw them anymore. Just Ned. And Cynthia, when he couldn't get out of it. She knows, all right. That's the reason she and Ned can't stand each other. She knows perfectly well why Fritz did what he did. Though I don't suppose she'll admit it. Any more than Ned will."

"Ned?" Why should it hit Joe with such a sick little jolt? Of course Ned must know; he couldn't have helped knowing, even without Marian to spell it out for him. As she had undoubtedly done—with more than her usual bluntness, to judge by the defensive tack she was taking.

"I suppose you think I shouldn't have told him," she said accusingly. "Well, as far as I'm concerned, facts are facts and they have to be faced sooner or later. That's all I did, was give him the simple, plain facts. How did I know it was going to set him off the way it did?"

Her conscience was already giving her enough trouble; there was no need for Joe to answer. For unlike Joe, she had known how Ned felt about Fritz, and should have had the perception to go easy with her simple, plain facts. No wonder Ned refused to accept them: they made him responsible, in his own eyes, for Fritz's death. No wonder he was so frantically determined to find another explanation. And what Marian had started Joe had finished. Between them they had sent the kid halfway around the bend. With a chill of alarm, Joe remembered his final words: "If I kill anybody, it won't be you …"

"What's the matter?" Marian asked sharply. "Why are you looking like that?"

"I'm scared," said Joe. The simple, plain fact. "The state he was in, he might— I'm scared of what he might do." He stood up. So did Marian;

she looked a bit pale herself.

Give her credit: she might not be the most perceptive woman in town, but she was practical. "We could call Duffy," she said. "Check on whether or not he's home yet. Better still, call him. If he's not there—"

"If he's not there, Duffy will answer." With the phone in his hand, Joe paused to cast an inquiring glance at Marian, who reeled off the Hendersons' number without a moment's hesitation. The computer mind, never at a loss.

Joe, on the other hand, was quite unprepared for what he got: Ned's voice on the second ring. "Hello?" And after a moment's wait, while Joe tried to pull his startled wits together, a second, more irritable "Hello?"

"Is that you, Ned? I just wanted to make sure—I mean, the reason I called—"

"Who is this?" asked Ned. It didn't surprise Joe; he hardly recognized his own voice, it sounded so husky and overwrought, damn near as distraught as Ned's voice of a couple of hours ago.

"Joe. Joe Florio. Listen, Ned, I'm sorry about what happened. I didn't get the pitch, I didn't know—believe me, I'm sorry."

"So you're sorry. You mean you've decided to admit I was right about you and Cynthia and all the rest of it?"

"No, of course not. I don't mean that at all. I mean—"

"Then do me a favor. Drop dead," said Ned, and he hung up.

So did Joe, eventually.

"Well," said Marian, "does that set your mind at rest? He's there, all right. I could hear him, and he didn't sound exactly suicidal to me."

Joe didn't argue with her. Ned hadn't sounded suicidal to him, either; and what did it signify, that he was still clinging to his shaky theory? Marian would call it a face-saving device, nothing more. Ned was a high-strung, unstable adolescent, and Joe was an alarmist; she had labeled them neatly and filed them away in their proper compartments, and as far as she was concerned there they would stay.

All the same, she had given him the pitch on Ned and Fritz. And there had been the tears in her eyes when she spoke of Fritz, and her glimmering, belated awareness of Ned's feelings.

Joe thanked her and left her—he suspected—to empty the ashtray, wash his glass, and plump up the cushions where he had sat, congratulating herself, as she did so, on her own noninvolvement with the Walls. Strict neutrality, from here on in. That was her vow; she intended to keep it; and who could blame her?

Not Joe, and he ought to know, God help him, he was involved enough with the Walls. Getting more so by the minute. If this kept up, he might even see the day when he would envy Marian Bishop and her neutrality.

Ten

Sunday was gray and soupy. Joe's mood was likewise. He had spent a restless, unprofitable night, as incapable of putting the Walls out of his mind as he was of untangling his involvements with them. The end of his self-appointed quest had resolved nothing. On the contrary. In addition to the prickly problem of Cynthia, he now had Ned to contend with. How did you go about atoning to someone who asked of you only that you drop dead?

Meanwhile, on with the paint job. If he was temporarily defeated by the human element, he could at least finish the top floor kitchen and get off the premises before any more hell broke loose. With luck, he ought to be through and out of here by noon. One o'clock at the latest.

And so he would have been, except for the doors on the cabinets in Mrs. Wall's kitchen. He heard about them while he was trundling the ladder and other paraphernalia down to the cellar, and incidentally savoring the prospect of escape. It seemed they didn't close properly, these doors; never had, hung wrong in the first place. Would Joe mind, as long as he was here ..." And there was no sense letting the leftover paint go to waste; it would do very nicely for the shelves above the sink.

With a sinking heart, he looked from Duffy's face to Mrs. Wall's. Trapped. If he fabricated another job for himself, starting tomorrow morning, they would say, All the better if you finish up for us this afternoon. And if he pleaded a Sunday afternoon date, they would say No hurry, come back another day.

He opted for this afternoon, on the assumption that it gave him a better chance of avoiding the Hendersons, who weren't back yet but who would be tomorrow.

"Good boy," said Duffy. Pleased as Punch. "I knew we could count on you."

Mrs. Wall also expressed appreciation. Got so carried away, in fact, that she instructed Duffy to provide him with lunch. On the house. The previous sandwiches, it was clear, had been dispensed without her knowledge; Duffy slipped him a wink and inquired, with a great show of innocence, how he felt about ham and cheese.

She was in some sort of happy flap, anyway. The reason now came out: Duffy was being granted one of her rare afternoons off to attend the wedding of a niece. In honor of this occasion she was wearing her double strand of pearls and a touch of lipstick. Her print dress—though it looked to Joe just about like the others he had seen her in—was of silk, not cotton; and her front hair was festively frizzed.

Even so, she had time to settle down on the kitchen step stool and watch Joe eat his sandwich. "What's new?" she asked, and something in the cock of her head made him suspect that she had at least an inkling of what was new. Had she listened in on his phone conversation with Ned last night? Or—equally possible—had she glanced out of the front window at the right moment yesterday and seen Ned and Joe walking down the street together?

He shrugged. "Where's Ned today? Sharpening his claws for another go at me and Cynthia?"

"A lot of good it would do him. And I think he knows it. I told you Marian Bishop would straighten him out." She paused, giving Joe a chance to comment. He did not take it. "Anyway," she went on, "there hasn't been one word out of him on the subject, either last night or this morning. Quiet as a lamb. Not only that, but he offered to stay with his grandmother while I'm away this afternoon. I don't like to leave her alone, she hasn't been doing so well lately. Don't worry, he won't give you any trouble as long as she's around. When his folks get back, of course, it may be a different story. Like as not they'll get him all stirred up again and—"

She jumped up as the swinging door was pushed open and Ned peered in. At sight of Joe, his face went stony with hostility, and stayed that way, while Duffy rattled bravely on: "There you are, Ned. Your Gran's in her bedroom, having a lie-down. Want some lunch?"

No answer from Ned. No change in the baleful glare he fixed on Joe. After a moment he backed out, and the door swung shut.

"Oh dear," whispered Duffy.

"Yeah. Oh dear. Just don't think up any more jobs for me, Duffy. Please? This afternoon, and then we call it quits?"

Her head bobbed up and down remorsefully. "I had no idea," she began, fumbling at her belt. Then her eye fell on the kitchen clock, and she gave a little yelp. "Look at the time! If I don't get a move on I'll be late!"

She whisked through the door. Joe could hear her flurried, last-minute instructions to Ned, and the bustling search for her umbrella. Silence at last. He finished his sandwich and got to work.

Duffy had been right on one score: Ned didn't give him any trouble that afternoon. But Mrs. Wall kept popping in on him, presumably to make sure she was getting her money's worth. She would have done better to leave him alone: even without her questions, which took time and patience to answer, she made him nervous, standing there watching him.

On one of these visits, she disconcerted him further by saying abruptly, "I suppose you know Cynthia's gone to Connecticut. I've never met her friends up there. Have you?"

"Who, me?" He turned, hammer in hand, to blink at her.

"I thought you might have. After all, you're a friend of hers. In a way. Why shouldn't you meet some of her other friends? She certainly doesn't go out of her way to introduce many of them to me. I sometimes wonder what sort of people make up her social circle."

As well she might. "You've got me," said Joe. "I haven't met any of them, unless you want to count The Zowies."

"The Zowies? What an unusual name."

"Well, it's sort of— That's what Cynthia called them. Apparently they're friends of a friend of hers. A fellow named Otis?" But Mrs. Wall had obviously never heard of Otis, either. "They're sort of musicians. That is, a drum and a guitar. And they sort of sing."

"A guitar," said Mrs. Wall. "I understand it's quite a popular instrument nowadays. I've never cared much for it myself. The Zowies. What was your impression of them, if you don't mind my asking?" When Joe hesitated, she added curtly, "I worry about Cynthia, you know."

"I just barely met them." Joe cleared his throat. "They're all right, I guess. Otis is the friend she's mentioned oftenest to me. I don't know what he's like. Never met him. He's off on a trip with his parents." That touch ought to reassure her, he thought; it made Otis sound proper, acceptable, a young man of family. Whether he was or not.

"I see. It would be so easy for a girl like Cynthia to fall into the wrong company. She's so—" Her brittle, heavily veined hand spread stiffly, in an old woman's gesture. The slight tremor of her head became more noticeable. "I was headstrong, too, as a girl. But I had some judgment about things. Some respect for authority. And of course I wasn't permitted to run wild, the way Cynthia does. An apartment of her own, if you please, and picking up with any kind of riffraff that comes along."

"Like me, for instance?" He tried to grin.

"At least you don't play the guitar," she said, and retired to the living room and the company of her other grandchild, the one she hadn't mentioned. The one she didn't worry about? Maybe that was the story of Ned's life, thought Joe; nobody to worry about him except Fritz, who was dead, and Joe, who—as far as Ned was concerned—ought to be.

He worked on without further interruptions. Outside the kitchen window rain began to drip down; sad, dogged rain that kept the ailanthus tree in a constant state of shudders. The light faded by slow degrees; the afternoon waned; from the living room came the occasional quiet murmur of voices and soft music from the record player.

Then, suddenly, came a jarring thud; Ned's voice, shrill with alarm; utter silence for a moment, while Joe crouched, paintbrush in hand, too startled to move. Finally, after a rush of footsteps, the kitchen door swung open, and there was Ned's face, white and stricken. "Quick, help me! Gran, something's happened to Gran …"

She lay in a heap, like a castaway on the Oriental rug island, somber and all askew against the glowing colors. One long, out-flung arm seemed to point accusingly; the other was buckled beneath her. Her face was bluish-gray, her half-open eyes milky. Her breathing made a fitful, scraping sound, like dry leaves skittering before the wind.

From the window sill the cross-eyed cat watched impassively while they fumbled one of her capsules into her mouth—but Joe didn't think she swallowed it, and the thin scraping sound had stopped—called the doctor, undid her collar, decided to move her, not to move her, searched frantically for her pulse … All the futile fuss that was nevertheless essential, to them if not to her.

Ned was no longer sending out his appeals to her: "Gran, Gran!" When he talked now it was to Joe, in a jumpy whisper: "She was just going to draw the shade, I was pouring us a sherry, and all at once—oh God, if only the doctor would come, he said right away, lucky I caught him in. There, I felt her pulse, I'm almost sure—"

But Joe had thought of another essential nonessential, a wet towel for her forehead, and was already off to the bathroom. He was still in there when the doorbell rang. The doctor. He paused, undecided and feeling suddenly superfluous. The doctor would order a wet towel if it was needed, he wouldn't want an outsider like Joe bumbling around underfoot, getting in his way. To say nothing of Ned, who had forgotten his hostility toward Joe, but only momentarily, only under the pressure of desperate anxiety. He wrung the towel out again. A ridiculous idea in the first place; though he had not admitted it until now he knew that she was beyond the reach of such homely remedies. Or any others. She was gone. Dead. Through with all her worries, her fierce pride and resentments, even through with her possessions. Headstrong as she was, woman and girl, she had let go of them at last.

By now Ned must know it too. Out there in the living room the doctor must be telling him. Sorry, Ned. (He was a friend of the family.) Nothing I can do.

But what Joe heard when at last he emerged from the bathroom was not the gentle, regretful tones of a family doctor, but what seemed to him a hullabaloo of voices. First of all, Duffy, home from the wedding, and erupting: "What's going on here? What's the matter? Oh dear God, Mrs. Wall! Get out of my way, let me … I'm here, I'm back, it's Duffy … What have you done to her?" And while she was still spouting there was a further commotion in the hall and Arthur Henderson sang out, "Hi! We're back! Anybody home?" The next moment he came charging in, trailed by Vera; the scene in the living room brought them both up short.

Mrs. Wall lay straight out now, less like a human castaway than a spar. Beside her knelt the doctor, stethoscope dangling, solemn bald head uplifted, a friar surprised at his devotions.

"I should never have left her," Duffy was bursting forth again. She turned on Ned, her silk print front heaving, her face under the flowered hat red with outrage and grief. "I might have known it would be like this, you'd have to kick up another rumpus with Joe when you knew good and well she couldn't stand it—how could you! Oh, how could you!"

"Now, now," said the doctor soothingly. He stood up, fumbling with his equipment. "Remember, Duffy, she was a very ill woman. Any moment. The least excitement."

"Exactly! That's what I'm saying! The least excitement. But he had to start in all over again—"

"But he didn't," Joe began, because Ned just stood there, dazed and speechless.

That was as far as he got. Arthur Henderson bore down on his son, full of bluster and authority. "Now then, Ned, you've stood there like a dummy long enough. What does she mean, you kicked up another rumpus? This guy, he's supposed to be a friend of Cynthia's, what's he doing here in the first place?" A look of sudden alarm crossed his face, as if he were belatedly aware of what a touchy subject he had brought up. Of course, thought Joe, the clobbering episode: Arthur was under the impression (thanks to Cynthia) that Joe had recognized him. Still, out of habit or desperation, he blustered on. "What's going on around here, anyway? Well, speak up. Did you forget how to talk, down there in Central America?"

Ned flared up at that. "If you want to know what he's doing here, why don't you ask him? And while you're at it, ask him who he is. A friend of Cynthia's. That's not all he is. He's the guy that killed Fritz!"

There was a moment of quivering silence. Duffy, though her face was red and screwed up like a crying child's, still found the breath for words. "You see what I mean! As if that had anything to do with anything! And to think I didn't have better sense than to leave her here with Ned, and Joe working in the kitchen—"

"Now listen, Duffy," Joe broke in, in a loud, clear voice. For further emphasis he brandished the wet towel, which was somehow still there in his hand. "Pipe down and listen to me. I was here and you weren't, so I know what I'm talking about. There wasn't any rumpus of any kind.

Ned and I didn't even see each other, and he didn't get into an argument with his grandmother, either. I would have heard if he had because—it's the one thing you're right about—I was working right next door in the kitchen. They had a nice, quiet afternoon listening to music and visiting. You can take my word for it." He saw that Duffy was wavering, and produced his clincher. "Why should I lie about it? We're not exactly buddies, Ned and I."

Ned turned a startled glance toward him. Then he said stiffly, "I don't care what anybody thinks. Let her say what she wants to about me."

Duffy went off into another fit of the weeps. A double-header, so to speak; by now she was blaming herself for having blamed Ned, poor boy, of course Joe wouldn't lie, she had been too upset to know what she was saying … The doctor patted her shoulder and made comforting sounds.

Meanwhile, Arthur had apparently been groping for a mental grasp of the situation. "I still don't get it," he announced belligerently. "This guy, this friend of Cynthia's, you say he's the one that shot Fritz? Well, all I can say is, there's something funny going on here, and I intend to get to the bottom of it or know the reason why. And I mean everything, including your grandmother's—"

"Please, Arthur, not now," said his wife in a bereaved voice. Up to this point she had stayed in the background, her long face longer still with shock; now she stepped forward, reminding Arthur, maybe warning him. If so, she was too late.

"I suppose you mean the necklace," Ned said flatly. "Well, you can forget it. Gran told me this afternoon, she willed it to me, and now that it's been stolen—"

"To you! She willed it to you!" Vera drew in her breath with a hissing sound. Like a snake, thought Joe; the narrow head, the out-thrust neck, the cold, malevolent eyes.

"Now that it's been stolen," Ned continued, "she was planning to change her will and leave me something else instead. She told me that, too. It's why I promised not to go to the police about Cynthia. So it's all over as far as you're concerned. None of your business anymore." He stood like a soldier at attention, enduring the withering regard of his parents.

"You promised," Arthur said at last. "I always knew you were a damn fool."

"Right," said Ned, and marched out of the room.

"How can you?" sobbed Duffy. "Squabbling like this, with Mrs. Wall not even …"

Joe couldn't have put it better himself. A family, they called themselves. A family! Somehow the crowning touch, to him, was the recollection that, after a summer of separation, the Hendersons had not dredged up so much as a word, a gesture of greeting for their son, nor he for them.

He slipped back to the kitchen, put away his tools, and left Mrs. Wall's house—for the last time, he hoped—without saying goodbye to her daughter and son-in-law.

He had never been much for solitary drinking, but that evening he got rather drunk, sitting there in Tess's apartment all by himself. He didn't realize it until the phone rang and he found himself stumbling over his own feet on the way to answer it. A fine how-do-you-do, he thought, and there he was, saying it out loud, "This is a fine how-do-you-do," in a thick, surprised voice. "Just a minute," he added to the phone, which naturally kept on ringing.

The easy way out, and probably the path of wisdom, would be not to answer. But it might be somebody he wanted to talk to, like—well, say somebody like Ellie, not that he really expected it to be her, or Tess. Yeah. It was probably Tess. She wouldn't care if he was a little bit squiffed. Good old Tess. And if it turned out to be one of the Hendersons, or Cynthia, he could always say "Wrong number" and hang up.

It was no one he had thought of, but Duffy, sounding so anxious that he barely recognized her voice. "Joe? Is that you, Joe? Listen, have you heard from Cynthia? Do you know where she is?"

"Connecticut," said Joe, with a little difficulty. "Visiting friends in Connecticut."

"But that's just it, she isn't! I finally got hold of them, and she's not there, they haven't seen her or even heard from her in weeks."

"But you told me—"

"I know what I told you! That's where she said she was going, in her note to her grandmother. Only she didn't go, and as far as they know, never planned to. I've been calling everybody else I can think of, and it's the same story, nobody knows where she is. As if I didn't have enough, without her to worry about … Well, why don't you say something?"

"I'm thinking," said Joe.

"Thinking, is it! You sound to me like you're drunk. Are you?"

"Certainly not." It was suddenly true: Duffy had jolted him into stark sobriety with her news. It was also true that he was thinking, in his alarmist way, about Friday, the night of Cynthia's disappearance. Ned had gone to see her that night—or rather, according to him, had talked to her through her apartment door—so his was the last available report on her. For what it was worth; even then, Ned's state of mind hadn't been the stablest. And who knew where the Hendersons were that night? They hadn't hesitated to clobber Joe. Having failed to find the package in his possession, why shouldn't they decide it must be back in Cynthia's hands, and pull the same stunt on her?

"We could check with the doorman at her apartment," he said. "He might remember seeing her leave Friday night, if she really did go somewhere—"

"You mean she might still be there, not answering her phone? Now I know you're drunk!"

"Well, she'd let him know, wouldn't she, if she was going to be away for any length of time. At least he might remember if she took any luggage with her."

"That's so," Duffy conceded. "It might give us something to go on."

"I'll go over there and check with him, if you want me to."

"Would you? And listen, Joe, while you're at it—I think Mrs. Wall had a key to her apartment. Maybe you could pick it up and just make sure. Not that I really believe she's holed up there, or anything. Still, with a crazy kid like Cynthia—I suppose it wouldn't hurt. If you could come right away, you won't have to worry about running into the Hendersons. They're at the funeral parlor."

"Right away," said Joe. The key was an unexpected stroke of luck. Without it, he would have had to resort to a bribe or even lock-picking. For he was determined to get into Cynthia's apartment; there was no other way to wipe out the lurid picture of that pecan-brown hair matted with blood, the frail neck, the skimpy, feverish little body.

Besides, it had occurred to him—in the light of his own telephone conversation with her on Friday night—that Cynthia had a perfectly good reason for disappearing on her own, without any assistance from her enemies. Convinced, as she was, that he had ratted on her, spilled the whole story of the package to her grandmother, she might well decide that her best bet was to make herself scarce. Maybe Duffy couldn't see her holed up, as she put it, but Joe could—still hanging on to the necklace that was now Ned's by right.

And that of course was the other reason why he was determined to get into her apartment. He hadn't ratted on her, and didn't intend to, but he was going to do his damnedest to see that the necklace wound up in the hands of the only person Fritz Wall had cared about. Whether Ned liked it or not, he was stuck with Joe as an ally.

Eleven

An hour later, armed with the key which he had picked up from Duffy, Joe stood in front of the door to Cynthia's apartment. It was a solid, smug-looking door, painted a light olive-green, with a gleaming brass doorknob and, below the peephole, a button that chimed when it was pressed. Sweating slightly, Joe pressed it again; again there was no response.

He had arrived at a moment when the doorman was not at his post but on the corner whistling at cabs for an old lady who waited in front of the building. Joe had walked in without answering or asking any questions.

Now he stood in front of Cynthia's door with the key in his hand, steeling himself to use it. There was nothing else to do. Open the door and find out. If he waited much longer, someone would come along and wonder what he was up to.

In the end that was what forced him into action: the sound, from around the corner, of the elevator stopping, and approaching voices. Convulsively he thrust the key into the lock; the door clicked open; in he charged, braced for disaster and fumbling for the light switch.

The shock of no disaster—no pool of blood, no battered body in the middle of the living room rug or anywhere else—was almost too much for him. He collapsed on the couch, trembling and sweating in earnest. Disaster could have struck Cynthia somewhere else, of course; but he would think about that later. Meanwhile, she was not here, and maybe the necklace wasn't either, but he intended to find out.

He made a systematic, thorough search of the apartment, beginning in the kitchen (in case the freezer seemed as good an idea to her as it had to him), working his way through the L-shaped living room, and winding up in the bathroom. He didn't bother much about trying to hide the traces of his search; it was justified, in his opinion, and he would have no hesitancy in telling her so. Besides, the place was in its normal state of disorder. She probably wouldn't notice the difference. He hesitated briefly over one item he found in the chest of drawers. Fritz's gun. The war souvenir he used to keep in the office but had taken with him on that last, fatal trip. At least Cynthia hadn't taken it with her, wherever she was. It was comfort of a sort.

He did not find the necklace. Either she had taken it with her, wherever she was, or she was a better hider than he was a seeker. Then there was the third possibility, that someone else had been here before him. The Hendersons, or Ned, might have slipped away from the funeral parlor, talked the doorman into giving them the key to Cynthia's apartment, and made off with the necklace an hour ago. It was Ned's property; he was entitled to it, if he had been telling the truth about his grandmother's will. And why should he tell such a pointless, easily disproved lie? He had sounded remarkably calm about his lost inheritance. Maybe because it wasn't lost? After all, he needn't have waited to snatch the necklace till he knew he had a right to it. Again Joe's thoughts turned to disaster. He saw Ned—or his parents, for that matter—luring Cynthia away from her apartment Friday night, forcing her to hand over the necklace and write the note to her grandmother, and then …

And then she had disappeared. Except for her grandmother's death, it might well have been another week before anyone missed her. Even now, Duffy was as much irritated as she was concerned, and Joe himself—with less excuse than Duffy, because he knew more than she did—had wasted time hunting for a damn string of diamonds instead of for Cynthia. It was all very well to say she had a good reason for dropping out of sight. She also had enemies, and nobody but Joe to look out for her. If she had disappeared voluntarily, it was because she thought he had turned against her: in that case he was all the more responsible.

He turned off the light and headed for the door. Then, with his hand on the doorknob, he stopped, aware of footsteps outside. Voices, too, and a jangling of keys. Holy Mother, whoever it was, they were coming in here! There was just time for him to nip into the front closet before the door opened and the light was switched on.

"Thanks very much," Ned was saying. "Now if I can just find the name and address of her Connecticut friends we'll be able to get in touch with her."

The doorman was more than cooperative; Ned must have slipped him a nice piece of change. Plus a very convincing story. "Sure. Okay. Sorry to hear about Miss Wall's grandmother. Just be sure to shut the door after you when you leave. It locks automatically."

Off he went, leaving Ned to search for names, addresses, and anything else that might interest him. All Joe hoped was that he wouldn't start in the closet. He held his breath and waited, expecting at any moment to be discovered, ignominiously huddled between Cynthia's raincoat and another anonymous garment that felt like a teddy bear.

Whatever Ned was doing, wherever he was starting, he was being abnormally quiet about it. The silence grew more unnerving by the second. Cautiously Joe shifted his position so he was facing the door, which was not shut tight; the crack was wide enough to give him a limited view of the living room and of Ned's back. What the hell was he doing, just standing there like that? Not moving a muscle, with his head thrust forward in an attitude of rapt attention, peering at something on the chest of drawers. He gave a sudden, soft laugh. The sound startled Joe so that he all but toppled out of his hiding place. Now, through the widened crack, he could see what it was that Ned found so fascinating— Fritz's collage, propped up there on the chest of drawers. He bent closer and his hand reached out, not quite touching, tracing in mid-air the outline of that strange collection of objects.

Strange to Joe; to Ned obviously entrancing. Again he laughed, in complete, unselfconscious delight. Absorbed as he was, would he even notice if Joe were to step forth and out of the apartment? Joe rather thought not.

He didn't dare put it to the test, though. Instead he stayed where he was, while for another minute or two Ned gave himself over to the pleasures of the collage. At last he remembered what he had come for and began pulling out the drawers of the chest, as Joe had done before him. He too hesitated over the gun, and in the end left it where it was. His search was neither so methodical nor so concentrated as Joe's; he kept coming back to the collage, pausing for another look, oblivious of the urgent thought waves Joe was sending out from his cramped, stifling station: Hurry up, get on with it, no, not this way, the other arm of the L, you dope, give me a chance to get out of here …

Once Ned headed straight for the closet, and he was sure all was lost. He closed his eyes and prayed. But when he opened them again, Ned had apparently changed his mind in midstream, and was now headed, just as purposefully, for the other arm of the L. At last. Joe waited a moment or two, in case of another mental switch; then he eased his way out of the closet, keeping a wary eye on the crook of the L and at the same time reaching for the knob to the outer door. If his luck held, if Ned stayed put for just a minute more, he could whip out and away, with no one the wiser.

He wasn't quite that lucky. He got the door open, all right, and himself through it. But then—through nervousness, or maybe an access of self-congratulation—he let the knob slip out of his hand. There was an appalling click as the door shut behind him.

"Hey!" yelled Ned from inside. The next instant—or so it seemed—he was yelling it from outside, while he sprinted down the hall after Joe. "Hey! Hey!" Joe had a head start, and he wasted no energy on words, or on looking back; he made it to the elevators first. One of them was thank God sitting there waiting for him. Just before the doors slid shut he caught a glimpse of Ned's outraged face.

Downstairs, he forced himself to walk, not run, past the doorman, and on to the corner. There he risked a backward glance. All was still quiet: no blowing of whistles, no excited raising of voices. Was Ned still hung up waiting for an elevator? (It wasn't very likely that he had gone back to finish his search; the door to Cynthia's apartment must have slammed, automatically locking behind him, when he took off after Joe.)

Or had he decided not to sound the alarm at all? Having Joe arrested as a housebreaker—much as he would relish the idea—might lead to some pretty embarrassing questions about his own activities, and his parents' as well, assuming he was aware of their little excursion into mugging and allied crimes. Even if he wasn't aware of that, once he started making noises about Joe, the fact that he himself had gotten into Cynthia's apartment on false pretenses was bound to come out. Not to mention Cynthia's disappearance, which he might or might not know more about than he cared to tell. Obviously, whatever else he had done Friday night, he had not forced her to hand over the necklace or he wouldn't have been there searching for it tonight. But that didn't mean he hadn't tried. He could still have lured her away and struck her down in a rage when she refused to give it to him.

No, the more Joe thought about it, the more it seemed to him that Ned would prefer to stay away from the police. But that didn't mean Joe was getting off scot-free. Far from it. For Ned had certainly figured out that he too was looking for the necklace, and—for all Ned knew—might have it in his pocket at this very moment. Probably had, to judge by his behavior. Why else would he hide in the closet and then hare off like that?

Well, why had he? He didn't know exactly, except that it had seemed like the only thing to do at the time. A sort of reflex action that, in retrospect, made very little sense. Because, if he had found the necklace, he would have turned it over to Ned. They were allies, he and Ned, both working toward the same end. The trouble was that Ned didn't know it, and Joe, who did know it, had acted as if he didn't. With the result that, in Ned's eyes, he was even more of an enemy than he had been before: a crafty thief to be tracked down and brought to justice, on a strictly private basis.

All right, so Ned was probably following him. Good. Fine. The sooner he let himself be caught, the better his chances of convincing Ned that they were allies. Let Ned see for himself that the necklace was not in Joe's pocket, and let him see it quick, before there was any opportunity to dispose of it.

He had been walking briskly uptown, toward Grand Central. Now, with cooperation in mind, he slowed down. He stopped looking for a cab; it was still raining lightly, so finding an empty one would have been a problem, anyway. He dawdled in front of store windows, he waited conscientiously for traffic lights; he bought a pack of cigarettes. To make it even easier, he took to looking back, in the hope of catching a glimpse of his pursuer. But there was no sign of him, though the Avenue was not overpopulated with pedestrians at this hour on a rainy Sunday evening. Either the kid was an expert tailer, or Joe's theory was wrong in the first place. In which case he might as well forget Ned and concentrate on Cynthia.

It was while he was having a hamburger—he had suddenly remembered all those drinks and no dinner—that inspiration came to him. Otis. How could he have overlooked Otis? Of course that was where Cynthia would go if this vanishing act was her own idea.

He couldn't call, because he had no idea what Otis's last name was, or indeed whether that dismal apartment contained a telephone. Anyway, he had a better chance of catching her—or them, if Otis was back from his trip—without the advance notice of a phone call. By this time he was next door to Grand Central, handy to the subway, so he shuttled across, took a downtown train, and walked the rest of the way. It had stopped raining, but the air remained thick and hazy. The pavements glistened with damp; lights glimmered as through steam. He hurried along, mentally rehearsing what he would say to Cynthia and how he would say it.

Her grandmother's death, first of all; no use trying to break it gently, he would just have to tell her straight out (who could predict Cynthia's reaction to anything?) and go on to the next point. Which was that he had not "ratted" on her to her family, and that even now—in spite of the way she had lied to him, tricked him, used him—he was not ready to check her off entirely. The necklace must be turned over to Ned; that was all he asked. If she could think up some kind of a tale to save her own face, fine and dandy. He didn't care, as long as Ned got what was his by rights. Because he was Ned's ally now as well as Cynthia's, and if anybody thought it was easy …

He would tell her that, too. If and when he found her.

Otis's apartment was on the third floor, he remembered; scanning the row of bells, he made the interesting discovery that the name was Otis, first and last. Otis B. Otis, Esquire: 3-B. No kidding. Esquire. He pushed the bell and waited, poised for the buzz that would let him in. It did not come, though he rang time after time. He gave up at last. Either the apartment of Otis B. Otis was empty or whoever was there was not answering the doorbell. Well, at least he had been spared another turn with The Zowies. And now that he knew Otis's last name he could check the phone book and, if he found a listing, try that approach.

It was all he could do—or was it? Why not leave a note? His hopes of catching them without advance notice were pretty well shot now, anyway, so what did he have to lose? "Otis," he wrote with his ballpoint pen on a leaf torn from his address book, "please call me about Cynthia Wall." His name. Telephone number. It didn't seem very persuasive. He thought a moment and added, "Urgent. For her own good."

There. It was the best he could do. He folded the note and was on the point of slipping it into Otis's mailbox when the outer door flew open, a hand closed over his, and a rather breathless voice said, "Just a minute, if you don't mind. If you don't mind, I'd like to see that message."

It was Ned, his elusive pursuer, out in the open at last—and rattled at being there, to judge by the shakiness of his voice and the clamminess of his hand.

Joe was startled enough to say the first thing that came into his head: "Where the hell have you been? I'd about given you up."

"Okay, wise guy. The note. Just hand it over. I knew if I followed you long enough you'd lead me to Cynthia."

"Oh, you did, did you? Well, for your information—"

"The note," Ned repeated. He narrowed his eyes at Joe. Tight-lipped, ominous, absurd. Apparently it surprised him when Joe handed over the slip of paper without putting up a fight. Through his glasses, which had slipped as usual, he peered suspiciously, first at Joe, then at the note. "Otis," he said, when he got around to reading it. "What's this Otis bit?"

"Code," said Joe flippantly. "Try and crack it. It's baffled the experts of seven separate and distinct nations. And three indistinct. My lips are sealed. Torture will get you no place … Look, Ned. I don't know where Cynthia is, either. I'm trying to find her too, and the reason I came here is that Otis is her boyfriend. He lives here. See his name? Otis B. Otis. Esquire."

Ned leaned forward for a better look, giving his glasses the customary shove with his free hand; his right remained clamped on Joe's arm. "Okay, her boyfriend. That's what you say. What about 'for her own good'? What's that supposed to mean?"

"Well, to reassure her. According to you, she thinks I've turned against her, and I just wanted to—"

"Uh-huh. You just wanted to let her know the coast is clear, nobody's going to call the police, and you can split the loot from Gran's necklace the way you planned in the first place. Or did you just want to let her know you're in the driver's seat now because you've got the necklace? That's what you were after in her apartment, you can't kid me."

"That's what I was after," said Joe evenly. He wrenched his hand free and started pulling out his pockets. "Go ahead. Search me. I didn't find the damn thing. I haven't got it. And you've been following me, you know I didn't have a chance to ditch it."

"Then she's still got it. No wonder you're in such a sweat to find her. Reassure her, ha! What you're doing is warning her. She's skipped out on you, I could have told you, she's a double-crosser from way back, and this is your way of telling her she's not going to get away with it. Right?"

"Why ask me? You're the guy with the answers." In this case, an answer that wasn't so screwed up, after all: Joe didn't intend to let her get away with the necklace. But for a reason quite different from the one Ned ascribed to him; was there any way to get that across? He looked up into the hostile face of his ally and tried. "Listen, Ned, I know what you think of me, and I don't blame you. But so help me God, I'm on your side in this. If I had the necklace you wouldn't have to follow me, I'd follow you to give it to you. That's what I'll do if I ever get hold of it. Hand it over to you. Will you take my word for it? Will you—"

"No," said Ned. "You can peddle your deals elsewhere. I'm not interested."

"Deal? Who's talking about a deal? Damn it, I'm trying to help you!"

"Then God help me. With you for a friend I don't need an enemy." He turned; with his hand on the outer door he paused for a parting shot. "Go ahead. Leave your billet-doux. Don't forget, I'll be watching to see where it gets you. You can take my word for that."

Twelve

The following morning, at a quarter past eight, Joe was back at the old stand, pushing the bell of apartment 3-B, Otis B. Otis, Esquire. The session with Ned, and the restless night afterward—waiting for a phone call that never came—had left him feeling battered beyond recognition. But looking much as usual: this fact had struck him with a dull thud of astonishment when he inspected his face in the bathroom mirror. The same crooked nose and spiky hair, the same cheerful expression. Cheerful! He gave the bell another hopeless jab. The note was gone from the mailbox, but what did that signify? Ned might have come back and fished it out, for some screwed-up reason of his own. Cynthia might have found it, if she was actually holed up in Otis's place, and lit out for parts unknown, under the impression that it was a warning. The Zowies might be using it as a springboard for one of their plunges into rhythm: "Man says it's urgent. Urgent detergent …"

He was so completely unprepared for the buzzer that he all but jumped out of his skin when it came; in the nick of time he lunged for the door and got in. Still in a state of mild shock, he emerged from the elevator on the third floor just as the door of 3-B opened. A young man stepped briskly toward him, a very proper young man in a gray suit and neatly shined shoes; briefcase in hand; furled umbrella hooked over the other arm.

"Did you ring?" he asked. He looked quite a bit like a butler, come to think of it. Otis B. Otis, Esquire, in the scrubbed, well-fed flesh. His jowls were firm and pink; the part in his hair (another couple of years and the recession would be definite) was as sharp and straight as a knife edge; the gray suit was artfully draped to conceal incipient portliness.

Joe found his voice and mumbled, "I'm a friend of Cynthia's. Did you get my—"

"Joe!" And out popped Cynthia, very bright-eyed and full of chatter. She had been meaning to call Joe, how nice to see him, this was Joe, Otis, she had told him about Joe …

She probably had, in a judiciously abridged form. Otis's expression remained blankly affable. He gave Joe a sincere handshake, his eyes meanwhile straying toward the elevator. Precedent-breaking cases no doubt awaited him in his office, documents to be drawn up in quintuplicate, hairs to be split, nits to be picked.

"Otis darling, don't let us hold you up. I'll see you tonight. Call me if you get stuck." All very wifely. Otis responded with a last, resounding kiss, bustled off and left them eyeing each other, two jolly old hearty old pals.

"You bastard," said Cynthia. "Barging in like this. Leaving that note for Otis. Lucky I found it before he did. It's not enough that you've turned Gran against me. No. You've got to try the same thing with Otis, blabbing all that stuff—"

"I didn't. Wait. Listen." He grabbed her and shoved his way in before she could slam the door in his face. "Listen to me. The reason I came, the reason I had to find you—your grandmother's dead."

"You're lying. It's a trick," she said loudly. But she bit her lip to keep it from trembling; her eyes got bigger and bigger. "It's not true? Joe? Gran's not dead?"

And there it was again: the logical feelings he had toward her—the distrust, exasperation and anger—seemed only to sharpen the illogical, aching pity. She looked such an orphan child, in shorts and that incongruous pinafore thing, with her hair hitched up in an Alice-in-Wonderland effect. Gulping back the tears. Clinging to him with both her feverish little paws. It was a good thing he had rehearsed his speech in advance; otherwise he might not have had the heart.

It came reeling out like a recorded tape. All of it, working back from the circumstances of her grandmother's death, through his scenes with Ned and Marian Bishop and his inescapable conclusions about the necklace. Conclusions which he had nevertheless kept to himself; he had to set her straight on that point, if no other.

"Cyn, look at me." But she would not. She kept her head stubbornly bent. "Cyn, you can't believe I turned your Gran against you. If I had, she'd have called the police Friday night. Or at least tracked you down herself. Yes, and I would have been right there egging her on, steering her to Otis long before this. Don't you see? That proves it, I never told her or anybody else about the package. And I wasn't going to tell Otis. The only reason I came here, the only reason I thought of him, was because I was worried—"

"Worried?" came the quavering, muffled echo from the back of her head.

"Nobody knew where you were. Of course I was worried about you. How did I know the Hendersons hadn't clobbered you the way they did me?"

"Why should you care, if you think I'm a thief?"

"Well, because—"

She waited a moment, shivering; then she pulled free and rushed over to the window. She kept her back to him, but when she spoke the old ring of challenge and contempt was back in her voice. "You're not denying it, are you? Not honest Joe Florio. You think that's what was in the package. Gran's necklace. Ned's necklace now, if I understood you correctly. You think I stole it."

"All right. I know damn well you stole it," he said despondently. She had turned, hard-eyed and smiling, her armor once more intact. The chink—if it had really been there—was closed now; he would probably never find it again. "Are *you* denying it?"

"Not much point. I know a closed mind when I see one."

"A closed mind! My God, I covered up for you! I won't give you away even now, if you'll just—it's no use lying to me anymore. I don't care what you tell the others. Tell them I stole it. Anything. But you've got to hand the necklace over to Ned. That's all."

"Can't," said Cynthia. She patted her hair. "I haven't got it."

"Don't give me that stuff. You wouldn't dare sell it or pawn it, not with the police on the lookout. It's the necklace you want, anyway, not the money. Stop lying and—"

The doorbell rang. She stood rooted, fear and suspicion flaring in her eyes. "Maybe Otis forgot his whereas," said Joe, and pushed the buzzer.

She found the breath to say, "Aren't you funny." And enough locomotive power to cross the room. He had opened the door; they stood side by side, waiting to see who would get out of the elevator. When it turned out to be Ned, she whispered, "Now we'll see how much you covered up for me."

So he hadn't convinced her, after all. It figured: she was too unreliable herself to trust anyone else. It also explained why the doorbell had given her such a jolt. The police, she must have thought; Joe realized that the jaunty mockery of her greeting to Ned sprang as much from relief as nervous tension. "Well, well. Look who's here. Quite the early bird, aren't you?"

"Not early enough," said Ned, with a withering glance at Joe. "I see my friend here beat me to it."

"Everybody's friend," said Cynthia, patting his sleeve. "He was just telling me how worried he was about me. Weren't you, Joe sweetie?"

"Actually, I was just telling you—"

"Oh well, other things too, of course. Gran. Poor Gran …" She quivered her lip, her voice, her eyelashes, mocking herself along with everybody else, making a parody of what had been—Joe was sure of it—genuine grief.

"And poor Gran's necklace," said Ned, "Surely he mentioned how worried he was about that. Almost as worried as he was about you. I can't say that I blame him. After all, he's entitled to it; he did the dirty work."

"Oh Gawd." Cynthia rolled her eyes heavenward. "Still off on that pitch, are you? Yes, he gave me the rundown on you and your theory. Come on in, as long as you're here. You might as well get it straight, once and for all." When Ned was inside, and the door closed behind him, she went on in a reasoning tone that was no doubt calculated to infuriate. "Look, Ned, you're the one with the high I.Q. You must see how ridiculous you're being. I don't mean because you think I'm a thief. That figures. You've been brainwashed by your folks. And you never liked me, anyway. What beats me is this bit about Joe and me being accomplices in crime. You can't possibly believe it yourself. Why, we never even heard of each other till after Daddy—"

"Leave Fritz out of it. I don't care to discuss him with you. The necklace. That's all I'm interested in. I have not, by the way, been brainwashed by my folks. They couldn't care less, now that it turns out to be my necklace instead of Mother's."

"Yes," said Cynthia contentedly, "that must have given Aunt Vera a turn. She always took it for granted Gran would leave it to her. Well, so did I. I never dreamed you'd be the lucky kid."

"So lucky it hurts," said Ned.

"Sorry. I always seem to say the wrong thing to you, don't I?"

They could have kept this up indefinitely. No doubt would have, if Joe had not intervened before Ned could get in the next lick. "Cut it out, both of you." He thought they looked rather startled, as if they had forgotten he was even there. "It's a waste of time, this sniping at each other. I haven't got the necklace, Ned. If you want to search me, okay. I'm perfectly willing."

"Well, so am I!" The glitter in her eye, Joe decided, was elation at the risk she was taking; she doted on danger. "You took the words right out of my mouth, Joe. Here. Here's my purse, and my case—" She hauled it out from under the couch, the familiar, chunky, oversized lunch box. Her purse was a capacious, shoulder-strap affair; with a prodigal gesture, she turned it upside down and dumped its contents on the couch. The result was a miniature avalanche. Edibles, cosmetics, reading material, even smaller items of wearing apparel—why, the kid could have lived out of it for a week. "Go to it. I want you to, Ned. I insist. Search the whole place, the way you did my apartment, you and Joe … It's the only way to prove I haven't got Gran's necklace. Let's settle it, here and now. What's the matter? Why are you hanging back?"

"I'm not." He straightened his glasses; behind them his eyes looked out, appraising and skeptical. "I'll search, all right. Since you insist. Or should I say even though you insist? I'll call your bluff, if that's what it is. After all, what have I got to lose?"

Cynthia watched, with a fixed, bright smile, while he poked through the contents of her purse. She kept up a more or less running commentary on what came to light: "There's my gold earring, I thought I'd lost it … And my other sunglasses … Good Lord, look at all the keys. Those are for my place. And an extra set, just in case. Otis's. Gran's house. Daddy's. I'd forgotten I had them, they can go out. This one, God knows … Peanuts, anyone? They're probably stale …"

When it came to the oversized lunch box, she plucked out a pair of bell-bottom pants and a blouse, shook them to demonstrate their innocence, and said, "If you'll excuse me, I'll nip into the bathroom and change into these. Or no, wait, you'd better search the bathroom first, hadn't you? While you do that maybe I ought to call Duffy."

Somebody certainly ought to set Duffy's mind at rest; Joe hadn't been able to offer much in the way of reassurance last night. Now he could hear her squawking away at a great rate into the phone, which Cynthia held at a precautionary distance from her ear, brandishing it in an offhand way while she lit a cigarette. But though she batted her eyes and made imitative mouthing gestures for Joe's benefit, her responses to Duffy were properly respectful and subdued. "Joe's here now. I'm at a friend's. No, not Connecticut, I changed my mind, I'll explain it all when I see you. Joe's going to take me up to my place first, and I'll be over as soon as I get organized. I know, Duffy, I know …" She stopped making faces at Joe and shut her eyes tight, overtaken by another genuine fit of gulps.

He pretended to be busy in the kitchenette; when he looked around again Ned was back and she had disappeared into the bathroom. On with the search. It didn't take long. The one, scantily furnished room provided precious few hiding places. Now that he had time to notice, Joe realized that it looked different, much better than he remembered it. No Zowies, for one thing. That helped. And then, though there was no more furniture than before, and it was basically in as bad shape, it was—wonder of wonders—clean. Even the bedspread had been washed, even the windows. Cynthia must have scoured the place from stem to stern, in honor of Otis's homecoming. There was a pleasant, homely smell of soap and floor wax and breakfast coffee, and a red geranium on the window sill. He was touched and impressed. Give the old Esquire credit, he must have something if he could domesticate Cynthia.

She popped out, looking remarkably undomesticated: the bell-bottom pants exposed her navel. "No luck?" she asked brightly. Ned had given up and was slumped in the healthier of the two chairs; Joe stood beside the chest of drawers, which held a neat stack of books, a set of military brushes, and a gold-plated wristwatch band in an open-faced box. "That's my homecoming present to Otis," Cynthia explained. The unholy gleam was back in her eye. "Isn't it beautiful?"

"Very nice," said Joe. It was about the right size and shape; it could have been the package.

"Never mind, Ned." She tucked shorts and pinafore into the case, clicked it shut, and began stuffing her belongings back into her purse. "We all make mistakes. I don't resent it that you called me a thief. I'm sure Joe doesn't either. Don't bother to apologize."

"Apologize!" Ned slammed himself up onto his feet with such violence that the chair went into convulsions. But he went on in a tone almost as silky as Cynthia's. "Apologize? On the contrary, I congratulate you. That's what the situation calls for. Congratulations. I take my hat off to you, both of you. A winning combination, if I ever saw one. My mistake was in thinking I could pin anything on a pair of sharpies like you. It can't be done. Fritz tried it, and look what happened to him."

"So you won't admit you're wrong, even now. You always were a poor loser. As for what happened to Daddy, you didn't want to discuss him. Remember? I'm not worthy to mention his name, or something."

"Right." They faced each other, in a transport of hate. But Ned was no such seasoned hater as Cynthia; he was the one Fritz had loved, and therefore vulnerable. "I don't want to discuss him. I just want to—" He fought to keep his voice under control. Failed. Made a rush for the door.

Cynthia was after him, jeering like a blue jay. "You just want to go on pretending. Ostrich. Head in the sand. You can't bear to face what he was. Or what you are, either." By now he was in full flight, halfway down the hall; she stood in the doorway, mercilessly bombarding. "Because if anybody's to blame for what happened to him, it's you. You know that, don't you? He did it for you! It's your fault, you're to blame ..."

Joe yanked her inside and slapped her. The shock took her breath away. For a moment only. "Well, it's the truth. I knew all along it wasn't for me. Oh, I wasn't making it up, about the bunny girl and all that. But it didn't matter that much to him, nothing mattered that much to him except Ned. I knew all along it was for Ned."

"So does he. You weren't telling him anything he hadn't already heard from Marian Bishop. That's what's eating on him." And on Cynthia, he might have added, but didn't. "Come on. Get your stuff. Let's get out of here."

"You don't have to come with me."

No, he didn't have to; and maybe, if she hadn't stopped at the last minute to water the geranium, he wouldn't have. For some reason that settled it.

It also turned his thoughts toward Otis. (He preferred to skip the slap; besides, she had deserved it. Skip it for now, along with Ned and the whole painful scene.) Good old stuffy safe Otis; what a comfort he was. Not to mention what a surprise.

"Did you say The Zowies are friends of Otis's?"

She was sitting as far away from him as the cab permitted. Eyes straight ahead. "Don't be silly. Where did you get that idea?"

"Well, they must have a key to the place ..."

"It's a sublet. They're friends of the guy Otis got it from. They knew he was away, or they wouldn't have been there."

"I see. I just wondered. They didn't seem like his type."

No comment. Not another word out of her till they were upstairs in her apartment. Then, as soon as the door was shut behind them: "You hate me too, don't you?" She stood in the middle of the room, slumped, stomach sticking out, breastworks—hardly worth mentioning, anyway—caved in. "And why not? I hate myself. Hateful, hateful."

"I'm not arguing with you," said Joe.

"You didn't have to slap me, though." The orphan child voice. Very subdued. Quavery.

He hardened his heart and said, "You didn't have to do what you did to Ned, either. At least now you know I didn't rat on you about the package."

"That's just it. That's why I—" Without warning, tears filled her eyes, brimmed over, streaked down her cheeks in mascara-stained trickles. Her mouth spread out and lifted into a clown's ludicrous grimace; her nose ran; her face grew red and stiff with misery. She flung herself on the couch. "Joe!" she wailed. "Oh, Joe!"

He was a coward when it came to crying fits; his impulse was to turn tail and run. He staved it off by shifting from one foot to the other and making sympathetic noises. Finally, in a gingerly way, he patted her hair. It was silky-soft, like cashmere.

"Don't touch me! Leave me alone!" She clutched him, wound her arms around him as if she were drowning. Caught off balance, he went sprawling down beside her. In a paralysis of astonishment, he felt her tighten her stranglehold on him and plaster herself against him. One part of him seemed to stand aside, observing this grotesque embrace, struggle, whatever the hell it was; at the same time the ancient, mindless excitement set up its thrumming in his blood. Her kisses were tear-salty, feverish and—the observer in him noted dispassionately— extremely skillful. She was no novice, she knew what she was doing, if this was what she wanted …

Fritz Wall's daughter, he thought, and that did it. The excitement died an instant death. Shame, shame, shriveling shame. He peeled himself loose from her and the couch.

"Good God," he whispered; if he had had the strength he would have crossed himself.

Cynthia, Fritz Wall's daughter, stayed where she was, unappalled, blinking up at him like a cat. "So what struck you?" she asked. "What's wrong?"

"What's wrong! Everything! I never meant—"

"No?" She propped herself up on an elbow and reached for a cigarette. "Sorry. My mistake. After all, I owe you something for not ratting on me. So naturally, when you started moving in on me … Oh well, no harm done. I just got the wrong message."

Moving in on her. It had been such an ordinary, human gesture, the little pat he had given her hair. To comfort her because she was crying. Well, and to appease his own conscience because his first, cowardly impulse had been to flee. But the compassionate impulse had been there too. Comfort, sympathy, a flicker of affection. Could these be such rare commodities, so unfamiliar to her that she had failed to recognize them? Yes. The answer was there in her sad, hard child's face. For once in her life she was not lying: she had not recognized, still did not understand.

"In the first place," he said, "what about Otis?"

She shrugged. "No reason why he should hear about it, is there? Go on. In the second place?"

"Well …"

"Okay. In the second place, you hate me. The way Otis will, I suppose, sooner or later. Someday, when the novelty wears off. He'll change his mind about wanting to marry me. He'll start hating me, too. The story of my life."

"But I don't hate you. Neither will Otis, if you—"

"That reminds me, I've got to call him." She waited pointedly, her hand on the telephone. "As soon as you leave, I mean. Not that I'm rushing you off or anything."

He went quietly. There was no point in bringing up the necklace again; she would only lie some more. He was fed up with her and her lies. And yet. And yet. Liar though she certainly was, thief almost certainly, she had a special pathos that made it impossible for him to check her off entirely. Everybody's friend, she had called him derisively; and that was it, that was his trouble. He was caught in the crossfire between Ned— who needed no enemy et cetera—and Cynthia, who did not know how to be a friend, or how to have one. She had him, anyway, and so did Ned. He could not help it: he felt responsible for them, both of them. God help them every one.

Thirteen

Thus it was that he wound up at Mrs. Wall's funeral the next afternoon. He had not planned to attend. "No?" murmured Cynthia when she phoned him around noon. "Oh. It doesn't matter, really, except that Otis is tied up, and I thought if you were going anyway … But I don't mind going by myself. Really. It doesn't matter."

He saw her running the gauntlet of her enemies, the Hendersons: three pairs of eyes trained on her like guns, three mouths tight with animosity. Four, in case Marian Bishop put in an appearance. Even Duffy could not be counted an unqualified friend.

There was no one but Joe. She was his responsibility. The least he could do was divert some of the hostility to himself.

The hostility was there, all right, plenty for both of them. The impact of the first withering glare from the Hendersons rocked him back on his heels; Cynthia stood it better than he did. After all, it was old stuff to her. But the first moment was the worst. Throughout the service—which was mercifully brief—Vera made a point of ignoring them. Her narrow, pallid profile was interposed, like a statue, between her son and her husband. Ned had a glazed look. Arthur's face stayed red with outrage; now and then he leaned forward slightly for another vindictive glance— past Duffy, who served as the buffer state—into enemy territory.

Marian Bishop, true to her vow of strict neutrality, did not show up. There was a handful of elderly ladies, even an old boy or two, remnants no doubt of the days when Mrs. Wall had worn her diamonds and had thought nothing of inviting twenty-five people for dinner. Another handful who might be friends of Vera and Arthur, or the dutiful sons and daughters of the old guard. It was all very correct and restrained. Poor Duffy—who would have liked a rousing good wake, but it wasn't her funeral, it was Mrs. Wall's—confined herself to sniffling unobtrusively into her handkerchief. She rode to the cemetery in the same car with Joe and Cynthia; even there she behaved as Mrs. Wall would have wished. But the strain showed in her face, which came as near to looking gaunt as was possible with such chubby basic ingredients. And on the return trip she burst out tearfully, "I just don't see how I can face it. That's the hard part, the going back and her not being there, and all my things to pack … Twenty-three years, it's like I'm losing my own home …"

"You're not going to stay, then?" asked Joe. He would have patted her hand, only Cynthia was sitting between them, expressionless in her sunglasses.

"Stay? And watch what they do with it? Oh, they can't wait to get rid of it, lock stock and barrel, every last thing they can get a nickel for. Well, I can't stop them, but I'm not staying around while they do it. No thank you, I said to Vera, thank you very much but you'll just have to manage without me. I've got my own place to go to, my own house in the country that she bought for me, and the sooner I get up there the better I'll like it." She blew her nose and added, "I don't care what anybody says, she may have been stingy in some ways, but in the long run you could depend on her to do the right thing. It's thanks to her that I've got a place to go to. She knew how it would be when she was gone. She made her provisions."

"I never thought she was stingy," said Cynthia unexpectedly. "Of course I was her favorite. Even though she did leave her necklace to Ned."

Duffy blinked, momentarily at a loss. Was this an endorsement of her own views? A form of bravado? Or an oblique attack? "Well, it was her property," she pointed out. "If she wanted to leave it to Ned—she meant to do the right thing by him too. It was her way of making it up to Fritz."

"To Daddy?"

"Of course. Oh, she'd never admit it, not in so many words, but she knew she was wrong, all those years ago, pushing him into the business the way she did. She was trying to do for Ned what she didn't do for Fritz. It's so strange, when you think about it, that she couldn't quite manage it this time, either …" Again Duffy dissolved, overcome by what she obviously saw as the hand of God, sternly denying his creatures a second chance.

Cynthia's face remained as expressionless as ever. But she surprised Joe again when they got back to town. "Is it all right if we come in with you, Duffy?" she asked. "Just for a couple of minutes. One last time. I like Gran's house too, you know."

It set Duffy off into a forlorn kind of bustle—embarrassment, pleasure, apprehension in equal parts. "I was just about to ask you … I didn't know if you'd want to … A cup of coffee or a drink. Yes, of course. The very thing …"

"You don't mind, do you, Joe?" The sunglasses were trained on him.

"Not if you don't." Maybe the Hendersons weren't back yet. Maybe they still restricted themselves to their second-floor apartment. He clung to the thought.

And yet when he walked into Mrs. Wall's empty living room he could almost have wished for anyone, even the Hendersons, to take the edge off that oppressive vacancy. Mrs. Wall's absence was as dominating, in its way, as her presence had been. For a moment they stood huddled together, the three of them, peering into the shadows, listening to the hush. Then the Persian cat descended, with her usual stately air, from the window sill; Cynthia gave a nervous little laugh and said, "What happens to Dutch?"

"I'll take her. She's never cared for Vera. Unless you want her?"

"No. She's used to you." Her voice was abstracted. Her manner, too: while Duffy clattered around in the kitchen, making coffee, she wandered the length of the room, pausing now and then to touch a vase, a lamp, the clock on the mantel. "I broke it," she murmured. "It's never run right since. Gran blew her top and smacked my hands with the ruler …" She turned on Joe irritably. "Sit down, why don't you! Stop jittering and sit down!"

"Excuse me for living," said Joe, and stalked out into the hall.

His mistake again: there was Ned, just coming in the front door. "Well," he said. That was all. Well. He closed the door behind him and leaned against it, staring dully at Joe. He seemed to exude inertia; a leisurely, thick, heavy fog of inertia that threatened to immobilize Joe too.

Anything to fend it off. "Did your folks come back with you?"

"No," said Ned eventually, when the message had permeated. "They went off with some people. Friends." They slogged their way through another pause. Then: "Where's Cynthia?"

"In the living room. Communing with her memories or something. Duffy's making coffee."

"I thought she'd be here. There's something I want to ask her."

"Who, Cynthia? Listen, if it's about the necklace—"

"Don't worry," said Ned. The inertia took on a tinge of weary scorn. "I know when I'm licked. She can keep it. You can keep it. Whoever's got it. What's the difference?"

"What's the difference?" echoed Joe. "You mean your folks have changed their mind? They're going to help you, even if you don't switch your college course?"

"Ha." It was not a laugh. "I mean I give up. They're probably right, anyway, I'd flunk out or something … The hell with it. Who needs it, archaeology? My father's immortal words, and he's the guy that knows. I don't know, that's for sure. I don't even care anymore."

"Well, but—" Joe felt his face go hot with indignation; it was as if Ned had betrayed him personally. "No! You can't do that, just give up like that. You do care, Ned. You've got to care! You can't let Fritz down like that!"

The name jolted Ned out of his inertia. He stiffened as if Joe had hit him. And as if he were about to hit back: his fists clenched; he moved forward blindly. "You've got the nerve. You." Then he stopped in mid-step, and it was like their other, first encounter. He snatched off his glasses, exposing the suffering, young-old look of Fritz himself. Joe saw the total defeat in his face. Why cling to his hopes, and Fritz's, when they had led to nothing but Fritz's death? For Ned knew that they had; along with his hopes he was giving up the rickety explanation of Fritz's death that he had fabricated out of desperate need. He had admitted to himself that it was false, might even be on the brink of admitting it to Joe.

This was the moment Duffy chose to come barreling out looking for Joe. "Coffee's ready. What are you doing out—Ned! I didn't know you were back." Flustered but game, she carried on. "I made plenty. Come along too, if you'd like some."

Ned put his glasses back on and got his voice more or less under control. "Thanks, I would," he said, contrary to Duffy's expectations. Joe's too, until he remembered that there was something Ned wanted to ask Cynthia.

But whatever it was he kept it to himself while they had their strained, decorous little kaffeeklatsch. Duffy and Joe made laborious conversation. Cynthia perched on the hassock, munched cookies, and now and then curled her lip at Ned. Who retreated into the self-protective glaze that had served him at the funeral parlor.

It was a relief when the last cookie was gone and Cynthia rose from her perch. "Coming, Joe? I'd better fade away before the rest of my charming relatives get here." She took a last look around. "So long, Duffy. Send me a postcard from the wilderness."

"I'll drive you home," said Ned, who had sprung up the instant she opened her mouth. "The car's right around the corner. My father didn't take it."

"No thanks, don't bother. You've probably got a bomb rigged up under the seat."

"What's the matter? Chicken?" To this he added a contemptuous smile. All that was needed to clinch the deal.

"Oh well, since you insist." She flipped her hair and headed for the door. There she paused. "What about you, Joe? Joe? It's nothing to me, one way or the other."

"Or to me," said Ned.

Joe said goodbye to Duffy and followed them around the corner to the car.

He sat in the back seat beside Cynthia and waited for Ned to come out with what was on his mind. But nothing of the sort happened. During the drive to East 39th Street the conversation, such as it was, went like this:

Cynthia, pretending she couldn't care less: "I assume there's something more to this ride home than just your heart of gold. Not that you haven't got one. I've always sensed it, beating away there, under the dank exterior. All the same, there must be something a little more to it than that."

Ned, intent on traffic: "Right. Something I want to ask you."

Cynthia, long-suffering but gracious: "It seemed to me we covered everything yesterday morning, but if you don't think so—by all means. Certainly. All you have to do is ask."

Ned, with finality: "It'll keep."

And it did keep, throughout the search for a parking place, the short walk to Cynthia's address, and the noiseless ascent to her floor. By then dusk was gathering; even before Cynthia switched on the lights Ned was making straight for his goal.

But of course, thought Joe. Fritz's collage.

It was where it had been before, propped at a careless angle on the chest of drawers, and as before it sent Ned off into a transport. His eyes lit up, as at sight of an old friend; his face, so often guarded and somber, took on an expression of uninhibited gaiety. That baffling, meaningless mishmash, thought Joe; was it just because Fritz had concocted it that Ned found it so irresistible? Whatever the reason, it obviously made him feel good. It made him happy.

Cynthia could not see his face; she was at the window, adjusting the blinds. But she noticed what he was looking at. "That piece of junk," she said, over her shoulder. "Daddy's."

"I knew it must be his. I saw it when I was here before."

"Oh. Oh yes." She sounded odd to Joe. Wary, somehow. After a moment she crossed to Ned's side and gave him a long, hard look. He went on enjoying the collage. Finally her patience snapped. "Well! I can't hang around here all night. I've got a dinner date with Otis. He's expecting me. If that's all you came for, just to stand there and—"

"I'd like to have it. That's what I wanted to ask you. Will you sell it to me?"

"Sell it to you? You mean you want to buy it?"

"You catch on quick, don't you? I'd hardly expect you to give it to me. Even though you don't like it yourself."

"Who says I don't like it?"

"You called it a piece of junk." After a brief, cold glance at her he turned back to the collage.

"Well, but that doesn't mean I want to get rid of it. After all, it's the only one of Daddy's pictures I've got."

"Stop," said Ned. "You're breaking my heart. And if you're too bitchy to let me have it, you might at least stop jittering and let me look at it in peace."

"I'm not jittering." But she was. Twitching at her hair. Picking at her fingernails. Chewing her lip. The longer Ned looked, the more nervous she grew. "I didn't say I wasn't going to let you have it. I mean, it's not something you decide just like that. If you could tear yourself away for a minute, so we could sit down and talk about it …"

Typical of her, Joe supposed. Just the kind of dog-in-the-manger trick she might be expected to pull, especially with Ned. His mistake had been to let her know how much he wanted the collage; now that she did know, he was going to have to pay for it through the nose. The puzzling part was her nervousness. She ought to be purring over the situation. Instead, here she was, in a sweat of anxiety.

"Didn't you even hear me? I said, if you could tear yourself away for a minute—"

"All right." Ned gave a sigh and took a backward step, his eyes still fixed on the collage. Suddenly he froze. "Hey. What's that? What's that doing there?"

"What?" whispered Cynthia. She closed her eyes.

"It doesn't belong. It wasn't there before." He pointed accusingly. "I thought there was something different. Not quite right. I don't know what you thought you were doing, sticking that on."

"What are you talking about? I didn't—"

"Well, who did, then? It wasn't there before. It doesn't belong, anybody can see that. It's not even glued on. Look at that. Scotch tape."

He plucked it off, whatever the hell it was that offended his aesthetic sensibilities; and before Joe could get across the room to find out, Cynthia made a snatch for it, missed, and set up a shrill yammer: "Give it to me! You've got no right, it's not yours, you give it to me!"

Ned had no trouble holding it out of her reach, but he couldn't shake her loose—she hung on to his arm, feisty as a terrier—and whatever else she failed to accomplish, she jolted him out of his preoccupation with aesthetic sensibilities. Joe saw the change in his face: the startled, dawning look, the flash of comprehension. He also lost his gentlemanly inhibitions and clipped her a good one.

She went down screeching for Joe, who was already closing in on Ned; the curiosity that had brought him this far was now reinforced by a purely automatic impulse to spring to Cynthia's defense simply because she was a girl and somebody had hit her.

Ned was braced for him, and taller, but he didn't know as many tricks. Even so, there was a good deal of grappling before Joe managed to give his arm the backward twist that was needed. With painful slowness Ned's hand unclenched and dropped what it had been clutching; one last shove and he went sprawling. Joe himself landed on his hands and knees. And there it was beside him. As he grabbed it Cynthia began again: "Joe … He's got no right … Give it to me …" She was sitting up groggily, her hair in her eyes, her face pale and pinched.

He did not give it to her. He surged to his feet, peering at the key and feeling his own face fall into Ned's expression of growing awareness. It was a chunky key of a type not unfamiliar yet not exactly ordinary, either. A door, a desk, a suitcase? Not ordinary enough for any of those, though the idea of a suitcase produced a peripheral kind of twang. Not a suitcase, but something connected with …

"A public locker!" he said in a low, breathless-sounding voice. "That's it. A key to a public locker."

His thoughts raced off in all directions, like a splash of quicksilver. He was suddenly conscious of the quick, hard beating of his heart, and of Cynthia watching him.

She was on her feet, hanging onto the chest of drawers, shaking the hair out of her eyes, watching him.

She didn't look groggy anymore.

Fourteen

"All right," she said. "A public locker key. What about it?"

He did not answer. He was busy chasing his quicksilver thoughts. So that was where the package was, the necklace. Since Friday night, probably, when, thanks to Joe and what she took to be his defection, she got the wind up and decided to clear out of her apartment. They would have to catch her first, she must have figured, and if they did, she wouldn't have the necklace on her. Even now, nobody had caught her with it. No. But the key was enough.

No wonder Ned's fascination with the collage had sent her into such a state of jitters. No wonder she had been so cooperative down at Otis's apartment, urging them to search, dumping the contents of her purse out on the couch. The key must have been right there in plain sight, if only they hadn't been too package-minded to see it—as she had gambled on their being; it was the kind of risk she loved. And if only she had been willing to let well enough alone and leave it in her purse …

That had been her downfall, switching it to the collage. Yet it was easy to see what an inspired hiding place it must have seemed to her. Too intriguing to resist, and so safe, besides. Who would ever notice one more item in such a jumble of irrelevancies?

Ned would. That was who.

He had picked himself up, too, by now. "Listen," he began, "if you think you're kidding anybody, with this 'what about it' business—"

"Shut up. I didn't ask you. I asked Joe."

Joe cleared his throat and said, "Grand Central, I suppose. That's the nearest."

"Nearest and dearest. Never mind the details. It's my key. Are you going to give it to me?"

"Your key but Ned's necklace. I'm going to see that he gets it."

"Oh no, you're not," said Cynthia. She lifted her hand so he could see what was in it: Fritz's gun.

He had started toward Ned; he stopped with one foot in mid-air. Ned drew a quick, harsh breath. After a moment Joe lowered his foot, with great care, to the rug. Far down below, in the other, real world, a fire siren shrieked. Up here there was the hum of the air conditioner, and Cynthia's pinched face, her bright, bright eyes.

"I'll tell you what you're going to do," she said. "You're going to put the key down on the table, Joe, and then you and Ned are going to march into the closet, like good boys, and I'm going to lock you in. It may be a bit crowded in there, but it shouldn't take you too long to break down the door. Long enough, though. Just about as long as I need."

"But you—Cynthia. You can't get away with this."

"I'll take a chance on it." She moved forward, in no hurry, but purposeful.

"You think we won't call the police?" Ned produced a laugh. Of sorts.

"Of course you will, dear. Even though you promised Gran you wouldn't."

"Well, but that was when there wasn't any proof! It was different then."

It sure was, thought Joe. Not only no proof. No gun.

"Trust you to rationalize it," said Cynthia. "Nobody can beat you at that. With Joe here, I expect it's a matter of conscience. He'll see it as his civic duty to call the police. Besides, it's for my own good. He'll be doing me a favor. He's my friend, Joe. My trusty, faithful friend."

Well. She had always had a way with the needle.

"Call the police and see where it gets you. They won't find the necklace, that I can promise you. If I can't have it for myself, and it seems I can't, I can at least keep Ned from getting it. And I will. Believe me. I will. This time it's going where nobody will find it. Including me. Nobody's going to see it again, ever."

There was another sharply drawn breath from Ned. Joe hadn't seen it coming, either. But they both should have. Of course she would not hesitate to jettison the necklace, now that she could no longer hope either to keep it for herself or stay out of jail if she was caught with it. And she wouldn't be caught with it. That closet door—metal, if memory served, and Joe was afraid it did—would give her the few minutes' head start she needed. Another gloomy recollection: Manhattan is an island, surrounded by bodies of water …

"You really would, wouldn't you," Ned said in a hushed voice. "You'd throw it away before you'd let me have it."

"I really would. I really will. With pleasure."

She smiled. There was more than vindictive triumph in that smile, there was a lifetime of rankling resentment. At last, at last, she was getting even with the one Fritz had loved instead of her. That was the unforgivable thing, even more unforgivable than what Gran had tried to do. Throw away the necklace, and with one soul-satisfying stroke she would be paying them all back—Fritz and Ned and Gran. Not to mention Joe. Oh yes, he was in on it too; this was what he had accomplished with his bumbling, meddling efforts at atonement. He stared at Fritz's daughter with the gun in her hand, and felt again the weight of Fritz's death—unnecessary, meaningless—settle like a lump of lead in his chest.

"The key, Joe. Put it on the table," she said, still smiling. "I don't want any trouble with you. My friend."

She was going to make with the needle once too often. In fact, she had already done it once too often; anger flashed through him like an electric shock. She must have seen it, and jabbed again. "Everybody's friend," she amended. "Put the key on the table."

"No," he said. "I won't. You'll have to shoot me."

Out of the corner of his eye he saw Ned's jaw drop. He was pretty astonished himself. Not so much at his own words, completely unpremeditated though they were, as at the instant, soaring release he felt. The fact that he was also scared seemed only to heighten the sensation. He took a backward step toward the door. He was literally, physically giddy.

"Do you think I won't?" she whispered.

"You'll have to," he repeated.

It seemed all too likely that she would, if only out of sheer funk. That pinched face; those wild, bright eyes. And Ned—she would shoot Ned out of uncomplicated hatred. Hastily Joe stepped between them, and shoved Ned toward the door. He did not turn his back to Cynthia; if she did shoot him it was going to be while she was looking him in the face. In case that made any difference.

He heard Ned click the door open and backed toward it fast. Her eyes were wide open, blind-looking; she was holding the gun with both hands and her whole slight body was strained forward, as if poised to propel itself along with the bullet she would let fly when she squeezed the trigger. This instant, or the next, or the next …

He couldn't believe he had made it through the door. The slam of it behind him rang in his ears like the shot he had been braced for. It took a yank from Ned to get him back on the beam. After that neither of them lingered; they sprinted, neck and neck, for the elevator, and neither of them wasted any breath on words till they were inside it, staring at each other as the door slid shut.

Ned's voice matched his expression: thick and dazed. "She didn't shoot," he mumbled. "Why didn't she … She didn't shoot."

"Yeah. I noticed." Joe was in no condition to figure it out. The elevator wall was all that kept him upright; he sagged against it, heart thudding, sweat trickling down the backs of his legs. He still had a death grip on the key, though there was no longer any real need. In fact, no real reason why he shouldn't just hand it over to Ned and bow out. Except that he couldn't. No, it was impossible. He had been through too much. He had risked his life for that damn key. He was going to see it used on the locker it was intended for. With his own eyes he was going to see Ned with the package in his hands. Then and then only would he be through with Fritz Wall and his family.

"If she follows us," Ned began. "She's crazy enough. She might."

"Maybe." And while it might take them awhile to spot the right locker, she would know exactly where to go; they might find her there waiting for them, crazily determined to keep them from winning even if she couldn't hope to win herself. "I'm going anyway. You can suit yourself."

"I didn't mean that," said Ned stiffly. "Let's not waste any time, is all. What's the number on the key?"

Joe unclamped his hand long enough to look—it was 3069—and they stepped out into the lobby with its glass doors, its polished brass, the doorman smiling his automatic smile. It seemed dreamlike to Joe, but no more so than the cab that stopped for them the moment they hit the street—at not quite a run—or the ride itself, or the steely ranks of public lockers inside Grand Central. They had picked the Lexington Avenue entrance because it was handiest to Cynthia's apartment, presumably the spot she would be most likely to pick herself. And they had guessed right; the search for 3069 could hardly be called a search at all, it was so brief, so dreamlike.

She had not followed them. Or at least she had not gotten there first.

So there was no one to notice, much less interfere, when Joe turned the key in the lock. Certainly the stream of belated commuters hurrying past, intent on their own destinations, paid no attention. Why should they? A guy opening a locker, that was all. An ordinary guy with a broken nose that made him look tougher than he was, taking a package out of a locker and handing it to the kid beside him, a studious-looking type with glasses.

"There," said Joe. "It's all yours."

So much for the presentation speech. His big moment; and all he felt was a kind of nervous constraint, something like embarrassment. He shifted from one foot to the other. He noticed that the package was getting a little worn around the edges. (As well it might; it had been through a good deal too, it too had narrowly missed destruction. His old pal, his albatross, the familiar package.) He remembered wistfully the elation that had leaped up in him so unexpectedly back there in Cynthia's apartment. Not a trace of it now, when it would have made some sense.

Naturally, Ned wasn't adding much to the gala occasion. Still in a fog. Maybe—who knew?—still dedicated to the proposition that Joe and Cynthia had been partners in crime and that what he had just witnessed was the final falling out of thieves. He was peering down at the package as if he expected it to explode.

You better be a good archaeologist, thought Joe. Aloud he said, "Go ahead. Open it if you don't believe me. Make sure it's the real McCoy."

Ned's head jerked up; already ashamed of himself, Joe watched him swallow convulsively, struggling to get the words out. In the end he managed. "No. I believe you. I just can't—"

Well, neither could Joe. Fritz stood between them, an impassable barrier, an unbreakable bond. "Skip it," he said. He turned and headed for the street. Halfway there he had an impulse to look back. As if at a signal Ned, who had set off in the opposite direction, swiveled, and for a moment Joe had a clear view of his face, sparking miraculously into life. Then other faces intervened. He would remember it, though; he would remember how Ned had looked to Fritz.

He plodded on, again aware of the lack of elation. Somehow he had thought it would be different, once he accomplished his mission ...

"Joe! Joe!" He heard her before he saw her. The breathless, urgent cry cut through the hum of other voices, the shuffle and echoing tap of footsteps. He stopped, and she darted toward him, the skinny, straggle-haired girl who for some reason hadn't shot him. And wasn't going to now. No gun, no wild-eyed look; as she pulled up in front of him her stubby little hand jumped to her throat in that unforgettable gesture. "I ran all the way," she panted. "I had to tell you—" Her eyes got big and luminous; he could see the tear tracks on her cheeks. "I couldn't kill you, Joe. I wanted to, I meant to ... And then afterwards I couldn't kill myself, either."

"Congratulations," he said. "On both counts."

The effect was the opposite of what he had hoped for; here came the tears. "Joe!" she wailed as her head collided with his collarbone. "Don't hate me, Joe, don't hate me. I can't stand it!"

"All right," he admitted after a moment's thought. "I don't hate you." He had been irritated, shocked, infuriated, touched by her. Not to mention scared of her. But it was true: he had never hated her.

"You ought to. You ought to have me arrested."

"For not killing me? After all, you didn't. For stealing the necklace? It's where it belongs. Ned has it. Of course, if they put people in jail for lying—"

"I hate myself! I can't stand it! What'll I do, Joe? What'll I do?"

He patted her heaving shoulder, nervously aware that a few passersby were beginning to cast curious glances in their direction. Did it look like a lovers' quarrel? The thought made him even more nervous. He drew her into a doorway. "First of all, you pull yourself together. Blow your nose. Mop up."

"I didn't bring my purse, I haven't got a—"

"Here." He gave her his handkerchief, and she used it. Very obedient. Very subdued. The sobs slacked off into occasional, subterranean hiccoughs. "Now then," he said. "Now then."

There she stood, quietly waiting for him to tell her what to do next. She had meant it literally: "What'll I do? What'll I do?" Wherever he steered her, she would go. Unaccustomed as she was to trusting anybody, she trusted him—single-mindedly and recklessly, in true Cynthia fashion. He had asked for it. Well, now he had it. The question was, the unanswerable question …

Right or wrong, he put her in a cab and gave the driver Otis's address. "He's expecting you," he told her authoritatively. "You've got a dinner date with him. Give the geranium my regards."

"I will," she said seriously. The orphan-child look lasted for another moment, while he continued to peer in at her, with the door still open. Then with a haughty flip of her hair she snapped back. "Well, make up your mind. If you're going to kiss me goodbye, let's get it over with."

"Amen," said the cab driver.

They got it over with in record time. He closed the door and watched as the cab zoomed off. The last he saw of her she was looking out the rear window with both hands doubled up against her throat.

Right or wrong, he thought. Would she lie to Otis? Undoubtedly. Steal from him? Possibly. And if some day she might want to kill him, would she find she couldn't? Maybe he was a fool, but Joe was gambling on it.

His heart suddenly lifted, buoyant as a bird. He looked up at the hazy, rose-flushed strip of sky: what an evening it was, what a balmy summer evening. Somewhere behind him a girl laughed softly, secretly. Not like Ellie, but a little like her.

If he were to call her—a telephone booth had sprung up out of the pavement—she probably wouldn't be there. Wouldn't be interested, even if she were there.

But the telephone booth, the burden lightened, the joyful soaring in his chest …

She was there.

She sounded very glad to hear him.

THE END

Jean Potts Bibliography
(1910-1999)

Mystery Novels:
Go, Lovely Rose (1954; winner Best First Novel Edgar Award)
Death of a Stray Cat (1955; reprinted in omnibus as *Dark Destination*, 1955)
The Diehard (1956)
The Man With the Cane (1957)
Lightning Strikes Twice (1958; reprinted in the UK as *Blood Will Tell*, 1959)
Home Is the Prisoner (1960)
The Evil Wish (1962; finalist Best Novel Edgar Award)
The Only Good Secretary (1965)
The Footsteps on the Stairs (1966)
The Trash Stealer (1968)
The Little Lie (1968)
An Affair of the Heart (1970)
The Troublemaker (1972)
My Brother's Killer (1975)

Mainstream Novel:
Someone to Remember (1943)

Short Stories:
The Lady Afraid (*Woman's Home Companion*, Feb 1942)
You're All I've Got (*Woman's Day*, March 1942)
The Other Woman (*Collier's*, Aug 24, 1946)
Restless Redhead (*Liberty*, Feb 1948)
The Box of Apples (*McCall's*, March 1949)
A Family Affair (*McCall's*, Nov 1949)
The Bracelet (*McCall's*, Dec 1951)
The Heart Must See (*McCall's*, Apr 1952)
The Engagement Ring (*Thrilling Love*, Oct 1952)
Let's Start All Over Again (*American Magazine*, Apr 1953)

The Girl He Didn't Marry (*Woman's Day*, Jan 1954)
A Long Day's Journey (*Cosmopolitan*, July 1954)
The Ideal Gift (*Family Circle*, Oct 1956)
The Withered Heart (*Ellery Queen's Mystery Magazine*, Feb 1957)
Murderer # 2 (*Alfred Hitchcock's Mystery Magazine*, Jan 1961)
Just Like Jessica (*Redbook*, Feb 1963)
The Only Good Secretary (*Cosmopolitan*, July 1965; condensed version of novel)
The Inner Voices (*Ellery Queen's Mystery Magazine*, Apr 1966)
In the Absence of Proof (*Ellery Queen's Mystery Magazine*, July 1985)
Two on the Isle (*Ellery Queen's Mystery Magazine*, Jan 1987)
The Lady Macbeth Case (*Ellery Queen's Mystery Magazine*, Nov 1990)
Family Circle "Family in Trouble" series (commentary by John L. Schimel, M.D.):
Families in Trouble (April 1969)
Families in Trouble - Alone Again! The Agonizing Problem of A Lonely Wife (June 1969)
Families in Trouble - "My Youngster Is Taking Drugs" (Oct 1969)
Families in Trouble - "My Job Made A New Woman Out Of Me!" (Feb 1970)
Families in Trouble - The Credit Card Nightmare (March 1970)

Unpublished Short Story:
Lady Bountiful

www.ingramcontent.com/pod-product-compliance
Lightning Source LLC
Chambersburg PA
CBHW061229210726
48293CB00003B/706